TITANS

THE RISE OF LEGENDS

C.J LLOYD

Titans: The Rise of Legends by C.J Lloyd

ISBN: 978-1-7348764-0-6

Cover design by Paganus at 99designs
Edited by Sarah Fox

ALSO COMING BY
C.J LLOYD

Titans: Dark Catalyst

Titans: Cold-Blooded Orphans

Titans: Revelation

To My Wife Stephanie and Son Isaiah

Contents

Chapter 1

Dark Legacy

Under the dim streetlights, a couple dashed from one alley to the next. Against the slick cobblestones, their shoes slapped with the beat of their thrashing hearts. Cole's lungs stabbed as he inhaled the frigid evening air, cursing himself amid the white puffs that escaped his thin chapped lips.

How the hell did they find us? he thought, wiping the sweat from his forehead. Car tires squealed against the backdrop of blaring sirens that weren't too far behind. Cole Moore was sure they lost *them* back in Florida. They hadn't been in Mass two weeks when the curfews hit. Then the news went crazy. Their faces plastered over every news network from here to Maine.

Now the streets have long since been evacuated. Not an easy thing to do for a city like Boston. But Colonel Cloud had his ways. Only Cole and Selene's ghostly silhouettes danced amongst the brick walls, forced to run through the rain-soaked streets.

As they raced in the darkness, Selene's soft cold hands slipped from Cole's fingers as she stumbled. From the shadows, a dark hand whipped around her waist, gripping her and the bundle she held tightly to her chest. To the naked eye, the apparition of a large clawed hand was nothing more than a shadow, but Cole knew better. That *shadow* could crush a car like a soda can or turn a platoon of soldiers into mincemeat. A nasty thing that darkness.

He stopped, digging his heels into the cobblestone, and snapped back, expecting Selene to fall into his arms. The darkness kept her balanced. The one good thing *it* had ever done. Cole gently clasped her hand as the shadow faded.

"You both ok?" he asked with messy black strands stuck to his forehead. Selene looked down at the bundle softly. "We're both fine. Keep going," she whispered with pleading eyes.

No, there was nothing like *it* before. That darkness. That sinister presence that made his belly swell with a hatred for humanity. The entity showed him the sins of the world, and why the world so rightfully deserved to be destroyed. But it was Selene that kept the everlasting darkness from devouring him in turmoil. He owed everything to her. Especially redemption.

His only focus now was sanctuary—refuge—from something far worse than even the beast that once dwelled within him.

They rounded a corner into an alley. Cole's bones seized as a police cruiser wailed by, the flashing blue and reds set Selene's horrified gaze ablaze. He wrapped his arms around her and the bundle, pressing their cold damp bodies against a brick wall. He eyed his love, and the jolts of life coming from the ball of blankets she clutched firmly. He hated this world now more than ever.

The instinct to kill was equal to the love Cole had for his family. His only family. Colonel Cloud would be proud. Tickled pink, actually. The man was insane, thirsting for power, and Cloud undoubtedly believed Cole's power would quench that thirst. Even if it meant tearing that power out of Cole's infant son.

Selene's fingers cracked around his, holding desperately to the sweaty palms of the one she trusted most in this world. In her left

2

hand, she held the reason why the most powerful government in the world hunted them so ruthlessly.

The last two weeks were bittersweet with one of the few consolations being able to see his son's eyes. *"Dark chocolate like his father's,"* Selene said proudly. They ate comfortably at a South Boston burger joint; the smell of greasy fries and grilled onions saturated the air. Cole radiated with joy holding the small warm body close to his face. The boy's eyes gently opened, and Selene couldn't have been more wrong. Those eyes were brilliant and dazzling, overflowing with limitless potential and hope. Cole's eyes were the exact opposite. Years of running and death all around him left him hopeless until that moment.

The thought of Cloud taking his son made Cole wish he had the darkness within him again. He'd end it all right then and there. Even if it meant stepping back into hell with that beast. Even it meant losing his humanity.

Tears welled up in Cole's eyes. Once out of Selene's sight, he rubbed them away. *Got to keep moving, Dad.*

Cole hugged the wall waiting for their next dash, breathing in the salty poignant breeze from the Fort Point Channel. With a deep breath, he gave a gentle squeeze to Selene's hand. They bolted across to the next alley. She was close to his back. At the same time, two soldiers came down the eastern side. With his focus stolen, he stepped into a giant pothole masked by water, and rolled his ankle. A deep groan escaped his lips, muffled by his hands. He thrust Selene into the alley as they made for a dumpster a few feet away.

Draped in a clear tarp with metal beams and wooden slabs leaning up against the sides, he nestled Selene in and crouched in front, pulling the tarp over them.

Cole's breath stuttered in his lungs as he squinted through a torn flap in the covering. *Control your breathing*, he thought. One of the very few things he remembered his father teaching him while hunting deer in Vermont. Only ten at the time. Twenty years later and the reaction crawled back in. Absolute silence, unwavering patience, and opportunity.

The soldiers stopped in front of the alley, scanning the area with flashlights, faces still dripping from the heavy rain that subsided earlier in the evening.

Cole slowed his breathing—He'd stop his racing heart if possible. Five years of outwitting Colonel Cloud's forces, skirmishes, and fighting for their lives had made them both professional escape artists. But this whole situation wasn't like the others. They were up against a mad man desperate for power and fearful of what was coming to this world, and he saw their first-born child as the answer.

The bundle in Selene's arms jolted with a gurgle. She dug her fingers into Cole's shoulder.

"Sorry," she whispered.

Anxiety rolled down his throat like a barbed stone. It wasn't her fault, and it damn sure wasn't the baby's. It was *theirs*.

A flashlight shined in their direction.

"What the hell was that?" a lanky figure in fatigues asked, inching over. Fear gripped Cole like a vice. He tightened his fist, watching as the lead man's flashlight crept closer. The soldiers rifle raised towards the dumpster.

The misshapen figure shuffled closer to the plastic covering. Selene gripped Cole's hand; his joints cracked from the tension. He glared into the bright light, feeling the wet, gritty sides of the dumpster. His fingers closed around a thick piece of metal, gripping it until his knuckles snapped and turned white.

The boots thudded with a heaviness that supported the fully armored soldier. Cole's dark brown eyes burned through the plastic, orchestrating in his mind every move he'd have to make. Smash this piece of metal across the face of the first soldier. Grab the next by the throat and hit him beneath the chin. He'd stack their unconscious body's behind the plastic. *Then keep it moving*, he thought.

That's how it always was. Every step calculated. It was all he had to go on. Without the darkness at his fingertips, he was vulnerable. They all were. When the beast was within him, it was the closest thing to being immortal. Inhuman regeneration, able to turn dark energy into protective shields and structures. It was bad ass. Well, until the darkness got ahold of him and then he would go berserk. Losing his mind and becoming a monster. But none of that mattered now.

A loud screech of static broke the tension in the shadows as Cole raised the piece of metal. "Let's go! Alpha says they got something on West Street."

"Roger," another voice replied. "Could have sworn I heard a baby. Man, screw this place."

The heavy footsteps trotted away into the darkness as the glint from their flashlights vanished. A sigh of relief escaped Cole's lips and then a raspy chuckle.

He turned to the long exhausted narrow face of Selene who rocked the lump of wrapped cloth. He rose to his feet and searched the side of the building finding a grey metal door. He turned the rusted knob. Locked. Wrapping his fingers around the icy knob, he focused. His pupils flickered red.

Darkness slithered from his sleeves into the keyhole in a slithering stream. Cole could hear the metal corroding and bending followed by a loud *thump* from the other side. The knob disintegrated into springs and flakes of rusted metal, the pieces chiming as they fell to the floor. Cole eased the door open, greeted by the scent of saw dust and fresh cut lumber. He scanned the room as he shuffled in.

He rushed back out, guiding Selene by the hand. She wrapped her arm around his neck, legs trembling from exhaustion. She found an old chair and sat with a quivering moan. He slipped off her soaked sneakers and socks and massaged her feet. Her toes were ice cold and blistering from the wetness. Hating himself for putting her through this, Cole fought back his bitter tears.

A playful *coo* caught his attention. He looked up at the wrapped cloth wriggling with joy. Stripping off his jacket he covered the dry portion around her feet and stood with admiration.

Watching their infant son, a warmth overwhelmed the bitter cold hatred that gripped his chest. The baby's tiny hands clenched in a fist as if ready to fight. Selene's long, gentle fingers combed through the soft tangled mess of black curls.

"You did good," Cole said caressing her wet cheek. Redness from crying and exhaustion filled her eyes, fighting the pain. She'd never show him her tears, not in a situation like this. Too stubborn that girl, and a little bit of crazy too.

Doused with rain, Cole tousled his messy curls, pressing his fingers down his face. He paced back and forth thinking of their next escape. Even with the size of the city, his pursuers had the entire block overrun with soldiers and Boston's finest. And being labeled as America's most wanted domestic terrorists meant trusting no one. Who would help anyway? All of this for the power Cole passed onto the cherub face boy in Selene's arms.

"You're a feisty one. Aren't you, Elric Blake?" Selene rubbed her narrow-reddened nose across the baby's forehead.

Cole smiled down at them, holding back tears that came from knowing his son would never have a normal life. His power would make him a target by the government and others. And though Elric wasn't alone, it was a rarity to meet another Titan. Only six in the world, including his son.

He kissed Selene on the forehead and rubbed Elric's head, stepping out the door. The light pitter-patter returned as puddles sprung to life, and gutters spewed small streams. The dark symphony beat against his heart and battered his will to press on. They couldn't keep this up, not like this, not with Elric. He looked up into the blackened sky. The symphony shattered by a loud gregarious boom of thunder. Then the heavens opened over him, the rain heavy like a waterfall. The salty streams that race down the corner of his eyes brought him to his knees. Defeated. Tired. Broken.

If they kept Elric with them while on the run, it would ruin Elric's chances of having a childhood. At the same time, it would mold him to hate humanity. Cole feared that the most.

He thought of his own childhood. The one without a mother. The childhood where his father left him in the woods when he was thirteen, never to be seen again. *Is this the destiny you talked about, old man?* He thought of his father and their last conversation as he looked up at the darkened skies above.

A helicopter roared overhead with lights searching above the city. He hid as tears raced down his narrow chin, thinned by hunger and exhaustion. His fist tightened as he made up his mind on what their next steps were. Selene would hate him, and he prayed Elric would somehow forgive him in the future for his decision.

Cole wiped the tears of bitterness away, swallowing hard. He mustered a hardened face and stepped back into the building.

Selene was in the middle of rocking Elric back to sleep when he eased in. He closed the heavy door behind him. She looked up with quivering lips reaching for his hand.

She looked deep into his eyes, her nose grazing his chin, searching for a glimmer of hope. There was no more to give. She rubbed her moist hands through his scruffy face. He kissed her hand then reached for his son.

Elric was fast asleep. His tiny hands still moving as the chubby digits maneuvered around the tight blanket. Cole's lips curved upwards, admiring the innocence of his legacy. His son was a fighter.

Without warning the words left his lips. "We leave him."

Selene scoffed as her brows bunched together. It was as if Cole told her that everything in the last five years was a joke. "What did you say?"

"Elric." He swallowed hard releasing a tear that raced down his chin. "If he stays with us, his life is at risk. At least if we leave him, he'll stand a chance. The darkness won't let any harm come to him."

"His life is at risk no matter what we do!" Her eyes became madness, wild like a mother grizzly.

Cole closed his own eyes. Holding her close.

"No!" She sobbed. "No, I won't do it! I won't leave my only son in some abandoned building in downtown crossing." She beat her hands into his chest tears soaking Cole's shirt.

He guided her back into himself. "If we leave him here and make a run for it. They'll be focused on us. We'll lure them out of the city." His tone was cold and matter of fact.

She shook her head using her damp clothes to try and dry her eyes. "They've taken everything from us," She sobbed. Face red like fire. "We don't deserve this." Her cry a sorrowful moan like a coyote howling into the moon.

He swallowed hard. It didn't matter how innocent they were or how good they strived to be. From the day Cole was born, he was cursed. Though others saw power and strength, they wanted to exploit him. He had been running for so long it that became all he knew until he met Selene; now she inherited his demise.

"Selene." He forced his lips to move, forced his throat to make a sound. "I'm sorry . . . for everything I've put you through. You had everything, even your family—"

"No!" She wiped her eyes, forcing a smile. "You and Elric. You're my family."

"You don't have to—"

8

"Cole!" She looked up with intensity. The blue and green hues of her eyes were fierce. "I'm sorry. That's not like me. I'm just tired."

Anguish. Hatred. Anger. She hid them behind rising cheeks as her lips rose. Selene was the one that kept them moving forward when he fell apart. She feared nothing. With the world against them, she barred her teeth and tightened her knuckles. Cole prayed Elric would get that fighting spirit, or at the least find someone like her.

He coursed his rough fingers through Elric's soft delicate hair. The tears came easy now. He hunched over, resting his head on Selene's shoulders.

They walked into a side room where wood and tools were organized in a corner. He stacked the wood in a box frame and placed the child inside. *Please stay quiet for a bit, Elric. Give us some time, ok?*

Selene fed him one last time. Smiling and rocking him like the first day he was born. She whispered sweet things to the boy who slept and nursed. She built the frame up with blankets and her hoodie, so he'd be warm.

"Will that damned *thing* protect him?"

Cole nodded. "Yes, fortunately."

They both stepped back, watching their sleeping child. Selene dug in her back-denim jean pocket and pulled out a moist sheet of paper. She searched around the empty halls and rooms of the lot hoping to find what she was looking for. She eased over with a black permanent marker.

She wrote in large letters:

Whoever finds our baby boy, please take great care of him. Keep him safe and out of the rain. He doesn't like being alone, and he doesn't like the dark. Please take care of our darling baby boy, Elric Blake.

She tucked the note underneath Elric. He shivered and then smiled, never opening his eyes. Tear drops fell on his forehead. Selene placed her hands to her mouth and turned, burying her face into Cole's chest.

He wrapped his arms around her keeping her close. "Did you have any last words for our son?"

She nodded crouching down beside the wooden frame.

"Elric." Her voice crackled with trembling words. "Make sure you take care of yourself, stay away from drugs, alcohol, and find yourself a nice girl." Her tone softened to a whisper. "I know it'll be hard growing up alone without us, but your father and I will always be with you. Never stop fighting and always be the best person you can be. I love you so much."

She stood up as Cole took her place. Selene's brittle whimper and tears were enough to release the breath Cole didn't know he was holding. He arched over his son.

"Elric, Son." His brown eyes softened. "I'm sorry I won't be there to help you understand a lot of things. I guess the last person I wanted to be like, was my father. Yet here I am abandoning you. Like he did me." Cole cleared the sadness from his throat. "Don't let the darkness inside ruin your life. You own *it*. Not the other way around. Never use the darkness for your own personal gain, but only to protect the people you love most. There's going to be a lot of pain in your life. Overcome it and become something better than even I was. Keep your powers hidden, or you'll end up like me being chased by the world for the rest of your life. The last thing . . . is, I love you more than life itself."

The bundle stirred with little kicks. Cole took off his over hoodie and draped it over Selene's shoulders. He covered his face with a scarf, allowing just enough opening for his eyes. Selene nodded, wiping away a tear as she sat down. Cole dried her feet and put her socks and shoes back on.

They stepped into the alley and kissed. It was long and warm like the first time and came with an embrace that melted the cruel moment of their reality. It fed them hope. And quenched the despair in their hearts. Not a single word left the warmth of their lips. Their foreheads touched as they exhaled in the canvas of the rainy darkness. They turned their backs to the door. And stepped into their sacrifice.

They hid next to a subway station. Selene tore down a laminated poster of their faces which was taped to the station door entrance. *Wanted for multiple murders and planning terrorist attacks.*

They pressed on, fighting the hunger, exhaustion, and sadness of it all. The motivation behind it was Elric's glowing cherub like face back at the empty lot.

A bright light flashed from the side as a car door slammed from behind. Ice shot down Cole's spine; cautious scuffling boots creeped behind.

"Don't take another step!" A deep voice yelled. "Slowly! Put your hands behind your heads!"

Cole clenched his fist, feeling the last bit of darkness surge through him. He jerked around. A flash of orange lit the darkness from the officer's pistol, just as a dark mass escaped Cole's hand, smashing into the officer's chest. The blast flipped the officer over the hood of his cruiser.

Cole grabbed Selene's hand and they took off, running through the alley. It wasn't long before the sirens began to roar down every street corner from where the incident took place. The flashes of red and blue beat against the darkness.

"Cole," Selene cried as she slowed, gripping the sides of a wall. "I can't—"

She fell, splashing into a puddle.

Cole turned to help her stand, but fear seized him as his eyes meet the crimson flow. His jaw chattered. *She's alright, just a graze,* He thought. "Selene. It's alright." He grabbed and helped her into another alley. She stumbled across until they made it behind a box truck.

Her eyes searched him beneath the streetlights. Her lips broke apart. Each breath was shallow, quick. Then a gurgling.

He ripped off her hoodie and lifted her t-shirt revealing a gunshot wound to the upper right of her chest. Streams of dark blood pulsed from the wound, seeping through the back of her clothes. The yellow T-shirt changed into a macabre of scarlet patches.

He laid her on the cold damp ground, tore off a sleeve of his hoodie and dressed the wound, applying as much weight as she could take. *I can't, I can't stop it.*

Her lips and jaws moved. No words. Her eyes rolled around the alley.

His voice was like a frightened child alone in the dark. "Selene, I can't stop it."

Her breathing slowed. "It's ok," she whispered. "It's ok."

"No. Selene . . . please? I can't do this alone. I can't lose you too." Their eyes locked as he cradled her, her breathing became a deep rattle.

Selene's face relaxed with a smile, like the one she gave the morning they found out she was pregnant. Her lively cheeks faded into a ghostly pale, like wax, and a trembling hand reached for Cole's face. Elene's fingertips grazed his chin as her hand drifted away. Her chest fell in the rain, those beautiful blue eyes fixed on him, but empty.

Standing up as the blood continued to seep down her abdomen, Cole noticed the exit wound coming out of the back of her upper shoulder.

His tears mingled with the rain as a gasping wail echoed in the darkness. A battle cry he hoped everyone across the globe could hear.

He smashed a hole clean through a brick wall. The pulverized stone left a gaping hole into a kitchen of a restaurant. Pots and pans clang and rattle across the tile floor.

He pulled back, overwhelmed by the aching pain of his knuckles. Bright red. Already swelling. A searing pain he had never felt before when he had the darkness. But nothing compared to watching the mother of his son fade away. The rain washing her blood into the babbling street gutters.

Cole rubbed her forehead with swelling fingers. Swallowing his pain, he lifted Selene up, leaning her against a brick wall. He pulled her long black hair over her shoulders. She loved wearing it that way, like the first day they met. He folded her hands on her lap and closed her eyes.

What, no last words ole man? She died because of you, he thought. What could he say? No one would reply. He thought about what would happen if he had the darkness in him. He'd probably destroy this entire city. No one would stop him. Millions of lives lost, devoured by the blackness, their blood washed into the sewers. Like Selene's. Like sweet, innocent Selene.

He took a deep breath, collecting his thoughts. Then took off running. He ran through the streets. The cooing of his newborn son, and the lifeless eyes of Selene pushing him forward.

Sirens screamed on the opposite ends as helicopters raced above. He leaned up against another building, hiding in its entrance. Only a matter of time now.

He took one step out of the entrance and fell, scraping his face across the tar. Blood trickled from face and a strange irony taste soaked his tongue. A helicopter roared above, dumping a bright light over him.

He jumped to his feet, stumbling forward, the helicopter following. The floodlights were a cryptic tether as he dipped through alleyways and streets. He wouldn't be able to outrun the terror above. But that was fine. Just perfect.

C'mon, just a little more. he raced forward down an alley. *Give them both just a couple more steps!* The thought of his shattered family filling him with grief.

The streetlights at the end of the alley were like a beacon of hope. He didn't know why. Maybe it was a way to ignore the jagged pain of his shin splints. The clicking of his swollen ankle that screamed with each footfall.

He broke into the light, stumbling face to face with a large army. To his left were a dozen men. To his right were just as many. He turned to go back, but the gap behind him was filled by soldiers, weapons raised high.

He turned to face them. Warriors strapped with armor, Kevlar helmets, and weapons that could turn him into a pile of meat. They wanted revenge just as much as he did. He lost count of how many soldiers he had killed. Soldiers that sought to do him and Selene harm, were dismembered or worse. Not that it made a difference, but he didn't want to kill anyone. That ships long since sailed, and Selene was on it.

The massive group began parting, creating a lane as a man came down the middle. He wore black boots and a woodland camo uniform.

His left hand wrapped in bandages. A desert eagle holstered on his thigh. From the right side of a fresh shaved face, rolled in the man's teeth a thick cigar. Smoke bellowed from his mouth like a chimney. His eyebrows thick and bushy, but through the thickets Cole could still see the glistening cold blue eyes.

"So, it's been almost three months, but here we are," said Colonel Cloud. "You and the Miss have cost me a lot of time, and really good men." He searched around. "And where's Selene?"

"She's gone." He sighed thinking of her alone in the alley. "We split up hours ago."

"Smart plan by a smart man." He smirked. "I guess the body we got zipped up in the chopper isn't hers then huh?" He bit down on the cigar.

Cole gritted his teeth. "You bastard!"

The man pulled a drag from the cigar and blew the smoke forward as he placed it back in his mouth. Cole's face cracked with anger as he tightened his fist by his side. The men raised their rifles.

Cole yelled, throwing his hands forward to release a mass of blackness. The old man covered his face as the entire army did the same. They knew the price that would come at the edge of Cole's fingertips. But nothing happened. A wisp of blackness went up around him but produced nothing.

The man chuckled to himself and threw his cigar to the ground, crushing it beneath heavy black leather boots. He strolled forward chest out, and chin high with confidence. "Looks like you're out of juice kid. Such a shame. You were a worthy adversary."

A soldier snuck up from his left smashing the buttstock of a rifle across Cole's face. He crumbled to the ground as two more soldiers grabbed him, hoisting him to his feet.

"You won't get what you want, Cloud!" Cole spat blood on to the tar streets.

Colonel Cloud laughed. "Cole, after doing this for so long, it's like you've become like a close friend of mine. Look, all I want is the boy, and it'll all be over. I have no use for you anymore."

"I'll never give him up; you'll have to kill me!"

The downpour hissed as the drops became heavier. The lightning flashed brighter than the burning streetlights.

"That can be arranged," he said with a low raspy voice, thick with the musky aroma of his cigar.

"You'll never find him," Cole said out of breath.

Cloud grabbed him by the chin. "Look I get it, I do. I have an eighteen-year-old at home, the apple of my eye, full of piss and vinegar like his old man used to be. But he's my boy." He glared into Cole's eyes and sneered. "But you know, and I know, I'll find your boy. With power like that? Nobody can keep that under wraps for long."

Cole tried to raise his arms to break free. He couldn't get it passed his waist. The burning of his muscles, the pain of his legs. This is what it felt like to be human?

"Amazing, you must feel like garbage now without your powers. Nothing to protect you. No power to make you feel like a *god*!" He smashed Cole in the stomach.

Cole hunched over, spitting blood, gasping for air. Coughing as his lungs tried to replace what was lost. The man walked away with the crack of a smile etching across his lips.

"You have no idea what that power feels like and you never will!"

Cloud turned and winked. "We'll see." He turned to the soldiers. "Bring him back to the AO, we'll get what we can out of him there." He looked back at Cole. "But right now, search every building. Every damn nook and cranny for my weapon. I don't care if you have to tear this city apart to find it!"

Cole was thrown into a helicopter. Both hands and feet bound with zip ties. His eyes met a dark-skinned man with long braided grey hair. And his blood boiled.

"You!" Cole gurgled from his blood-filled mouth. "This is all your fault, you son—"

A heavy boot came across his face knocking a couple of teeth from his lips. Another smack of a rifle followed just behind.

"Shut your damn mouth!" a soldier yelled.

The man looked down at Cole, lips quivering. "You know this has to be done. It didn't have to be this way!"

"Sir, you don't have to waste your time with this garbage. He's killed too many of our own!" a soldier replied from the front of the helicopter.

Right eye swollen shut, the taste of salty iron drowned Cole's tongue. He pushed the blood from his lips as he looked up at the man. "We trusted you! Selene trusted you!"

"You know and I know, Cole, that there's a war coming. One that'll change this world forever! Billions of lives will be at risk. You could've changed all that. You could've changed everything! Why didn't you try?" The man's tone fell as if his heart was breaking.

Cole spat out another tooth. "Because *it* doesn't want peace. If you think for a second that having that power will stop a war from spilling into our world, then you're dumber than I thought, Neil! Evil can't bring peace, especially with the kind of greed that ravages this world."

The man sat draped in a long black leather trench coat. His fingers resting on pressed lips, eyes covered with shades so black Cole could see himself in them. But even beneath the shades, Cole noticed the tear that rolled down the right side of his face. Even in the darkness. "Well then, it's a sad day indeed."

Cole turned his face away from Neil, the cold steel floor of the helicopter a balm to his swelling cheek. He hoped and prayed that Elric was well hidden, safe from the grasps of a madman willing to kill an infant. Tears soaked the right side of his face as his eyes caught sight of the long black body bag just across from him and he thought about Selene. He wished he could reach for her, touch her soft skin one last time.

Neil's plea echoed over his throbbing skull. Cole didn't care about Ermak, the parallel world to Earth. He couldn't care less that it was ravaged by a horrible uprising. Word on the streets was that it wouldn't be long before it spilled out into this world, anyway. It couldn't be stopped. Once that happened, everything this world knew would be shattered.

He wondered if Cloud would find Elric. He thought of the last words he and Selene left for their son. His bloody lips cracked high. Whatever happened. Whatever path Elric chose, Cole would always be connected to his son just like he would be connected to the Titans before him.

Unlike the others in his bloodline that gave into the corruption, pain, and darkness of the beast. Cole knew his father was one of the few to fight the temptation within, and with that strength flowing through his father down to him, Elric would also have that strength.

"My kids going to flip this world on its head." His eyes narrowed on a soldier. "I just wish I lived long enough to see him do it."

"Shut up!" a soldier smashed the butt of his rifle down on the back of Cole's neck, his body went limp. Fading into the blackness.

The helicopter rose to the air hovering away into the darkness of the calming storm. The silence of Selene and Cole's sacrifice for love lost in the deluge.

In the darkness of the lot, Elric searched above him, into the blackness. But instead of crying in fear of the darkness, a joyful giggle escaped his toothless gums. He kicked his feet in excitement. He had no idea that his parents were gone. No longer there to cherish him. To play with him. And speak sweet words to him. The only two beings he'd ever received love from, were no longer with him.

The now orphaned boy had no idea of his worth and true power or of the legacy crawling through his veins, and what the future held for him. His fingers closed into a tight fist but in his searching dark brown eyes, he smiled.

"It's alright little one." Out of the darkness crept a figure. Pale skinned hands reached for the child and lifted him up. Elric could barely open his eyes as he looked on. "Such innocence in a child. No one would ever suspect that deep down inside, trapped, is a creature that's only aspiration is to destroy." The shadowy being picked up the letter, which was the only fragment left of the couple and faded into the darkness with Elric in its grasp.

Soldiers kicked in the door to the building, searching it from top to bottom. A soldier found the boxed in area and the empty damp cloths that the child had been wrapped in.

"Sergeant, they were here!" The soldier looked up.

Another uniformed man scanned the area. "Then where the hell's the weapon?"

Chapter 2

Elric Blake

Sunlight poured in through the windows of the classroom, gleaming across freshly waxed vomit-green tiles. Outside echoed with the laughter of fourth periods P.E class as the students played lacrosse. Excited to eat rotting leftovers from the dumpster just behind the school, a flock of seagulls cried, covering the skies. Silence swept the inside classroom. The light snaps and pattering of pencils meeting paper could be made out. But just barely.

Tensing against the shaking of his limbs and fingers, Elric's eyes raced over the math test spread before him, drinking in the silence. Anything to counteract the consuming anxiety that forced streams of sweat from his armpits. *Math sucks. This test sucks. Mrs. Guttridge, sucks!* The internal thoughts scratched the inside of his skull.

Algebra, Geometry—all of it was insanity. *How could Jen love math?* Understanding that was like trying to understand the argument of how Batman could beat Superman. During their "study dates" that he secretly cherished, she'd go on and on about numbers, like poetry. Jen loved numbers with a passion; Elric hated it with just as much agony.

Elric snatched his thigh to stop the tapping of his feet, but the symptoms of math test jitters prevailed. Coursing his wafer-thin digits through tangled black hair, his eyes gaped over the mishmash of formulas and shapes.

A desk rattled on his right as Dan Philips, Lexington High's starting right tackle, put two hundred pounds behind erasing one of his mistakes. Elric could almost see himself snatching the pencil out of Dan's brawny hands and sending it across the classroom. Almost.

Last weekend had been a mistake. He should have studied instead of treating it like a two-day vacation. Maybe then these equations might have made some sense. Procrastinating in Mrs. Lee's garden, reading comic books, seemed like a good idea. The sun had been shining, the days stretching out ahead. Now, in the gloom of this abysmal classroom with geometry like a foreign language, and an hour to get some answers, regret dug its claws into his back.

His knee twitched below the table. He pressed one hand into it setting it quiet, picked up his pencil and began to write. He was going to fail . . . again.

The last bell of the day rung like a gong of humiliation. Mocking his futile attempt to battle the math gods.

He sat back with a deep sigh. "Here we go."

He caught the gaze of the girl on his left who rolled her eyes in disgust. She tossed her dirty blonde curls over her shoulders and left with celerity. Elric snatched the exam from his desk and was permeated with sweat as he dragged himself to the front of the class. Mrs. Guttridge eyes burrowed into him.

"What are the results today, Mr. Blake? Passing, I hope?" Her voice patronizing.

His eyes fell to the floor. "Just the first test, right?" Elric shrugged, forcing a grin.

Her nose wrinkled as if catching a whiff of something revolting. "Let's not make this a repeat of last year, Mr. Blake! I would hate to see you a third time!" she bellowed so everyone could hear.

His eyes rose to meet hers. Smoldering with resentment and a with a face that was beet red, Elric dug his teeth into his bottom lip. *Always respect your elders, no matter what.* Mrs. Lee's words sweetly flowed into his brain. He jerked around and darted out the classroom.

Screw her! He cursed Mrs. Guttridge for calling him out like that. *And screw Geometry!* He maneuvered through the sea of students, keeping his face grounded. He was an expert at utilizing his peripherals to get him from point A to point B. Surviving at Lexington High required him to develop a particular set of skills, but he was no Liam Neeson.

He walked down the stairs, passing the football players who hung out at the end of the hall. *Alright, particular set of skills on.* Elric stuffed his hands in his pocket and kept his head low. Fading into the crowd. So he hoped.

"Blake, please tell me you passed Mrs. Guttridge Geometry test today?" A kid with a blue and gold letterman's jacket asked with sarcasm.

A deep exhale escaped Elric's dry lips, his shoulders dropping in defeat.

The kid continued and asked, "I think they only give you two strikes before they boot you out of high school, right?"

Elric lurched around to face the boy with a dirty-blond comb-over and shaved sides—Dillon Kursh, Lexington High's star quarterback. Next to him were two of the starting offensive linemen, built like bulls, and Dan Phillips. Dan looked to be crafted out of a brick house blueprint.

Dillon's boxed chin; crooked smile; and a beak of a nose always entertained Elric from a distance. But this was too close for comfort.

I'm not in the mood for this, Elric thought looking at the three beasts that towered over Dillon. Not that Elric ever had a frame of mind to be bullied, he just couldn't hold his tongue anymore.

"Blake, maybe if you repeat the tenth grade a third time, you'll get all As and somehow get double promoted?" Dan taunted.

Elric scoffed at Dan's half-assed verbal bullying attempt. It was bad enough they terrorized him on the daily. He at least deserved award-winning bullying.

"Or, you could just drop out and come back for your GED in your forties." One of the giants laughed with a flopping gut.

Screw it! Elric snapped back. "I guess paying off the smart kids all these years with Daddy's money came in handy after all, huh, Dillon?" Elric's rant rolled off his tongue, guns blazing. "Otherwise you'd be the first sixteen-year-old to graduate from middle school!"

Dillon's entourage cracked with cackles that ruffled him out of his letterman. He slung it to the side and rushed Elric, pinning him against the lockers. The three behemoths hovered over for extra intimidation. It worked. In comparison, the four rugged brutes were full grown, unneutered, purebred German Rottweilers, Elric was a Chihuahua. His feet dangled as his toes fought to touch the ground.

Dillon snickered. "It's a shame Blake. Thing is that when you have Division I colleges scouting you, pounding scrubs like you into the ground isn't worth losing a scholarship, is it?"

"Yeah, makes sense." Elric choked, focusing on the faded green tile floors of the hallway.

"Great." Dillon lowered Elric to the ground. "Now it's homecoming week. I really don't have time to have you running around Lexington naked playing 'I Spy' for your clothes. I'll pencil you in sometime next week?" he said sarcastically.

"Right." Elric's face reddened as he avoided Dillon's eyes. With his hoodie scarcely clinging to his shoulders and hair tussled wildly, they sent him on his way. The dissolving hackling of the goon squad faded into the dimly lit hallways of Lexington High which was near empty.

He slammed a clutched hand into a locker. "Damn it!"

He grabbed his hand, fighting back tears. The daily harassments from the jocks and other students became the norm especially after Mr. Lee passed.

The death of his only father figure was a crippling blow that sullied the crumbling puzzle that was Elric's childhood. If it wasn't for Jen, he would've bolted himself in his bedroom with a pile of comic books for the rest of his life. Mrs. Lee, on the other hand, found solace in getting a third party involved to assist with the grieving process.

"Males tend to show emotions less and compartmentalize more." Elric remembered the last conversation with his therapist. She was a tall pale woman with cropped brunette hair and olive-green eyes. For someone who made a living off depressed stricken teens, Dr. Trevino herself looked like she needed to take her own advice. The dark rings around her reddened eyes and poor blush application couldn't hide her own pain and suffering. "Elric, you must learn to accept and process grief. If grieving goes on for too long, it'll evolve into something far worse. This can put you down a road of self-blame, perpetual depression, even hatred." Her brittle voice rained pity on Elric just before she wrote a prescription for Lexapro.

Remembering, he shuffled down the hallway. His hands were stuffed in his pockets and he had drooped eyelids that could only be seen through a few strands of his messy hair. His eyes glinted with excitement and new life as he stared a few lockers down. Jennifer Reeves was tugging away at her locker. She threw a punch. A knee. And a swift kick that slightly dented its metal frame. Four years of kick boxing at its finest.

The corners of Elric's mouth turned up. "Need some help?"

Her eyebrow cropped up as a sliver of teeth greeted him. "Oh, and those skinny arms are gonna do what?" She laughed as the locker squeaked open. "Look at that. And all by myself without the help of those *guns* you have for arms." Sarcasm seeped from her plush lips.

Her feet came out of her flats as she stretched into her locker. Her shirt lifted, revealing her bronze, slim torso. He turned away quickly. The soft sensual scent of her Roja Parfum was inviting and exotic.

She stuffed a few books in her bag, giving one more stretch for the last one. Most of her long, dark brown hair cascaded over her shoulders as a few strands flowed down the right side of her face. He yearned to gently move the strands behind her ear for a better view of her dimpled plumb cheeks.

"Good day so far?" He swallowed hard.

She sighed. "No pretty boring actually. I heard that geometry test blew though. Please tell me you passed?"

What is it with everyone and this geometry test? He tilted his head. "Geometry was created to spite me. I don't get it; it's not like I'm trying to get into MIT or something...."

She stopped and slowly turned from her locker. "Does that mean you passed?"

"It's not completely out of the realm of truth?" Elric thought about his answers. If he passed, it would be because Mrs. Guttridge had sympathy for him. She had none.

Jen slammed the locker closed as screws rattled in the inside. "Are you kidding me, Elric?" She clinched her jaws shut. "Mrs. Lee's going to ground you!"

"Yeah. I know. I know." Elric pressed his lips together, racing his fingers through the dampened strands of his hair. Her puckered forehead was right at his nose. Even through the deathly glare of her hazel eyes, joy consumed the torment he endured. The Lexapro would remain tucked in the medicine cabinet draw tonight.

They sauntered across the darkened main hallway as the golden rays of the sun gleamed through dusty windows. The light cascaded off the panes and danced throughout the room. The bright yellow and faded blue cinderblock walls screamed 'Lexington Pride.'

"So, how was the party Saturday? I'm surprised you didn't text me." Elric nearly bit his tongue off. He didn't have nearly enough units to have a full-blown conversation on his Tracfone.

Jen sucked her teeth. "You know I hate those things; I get that my dad has to go to charity events to save face, but it's just a bunch of stuck-up pricks if you ask me. Not to mention it was on a yacht!" Her mouth twisted as if tasting something sour. "I don't care how smooth the ride is; my stomach was up in arms all day Saturday."

"But come on, a yacht party? That's pretty cool?" Elric gleamed a smile from the corner of his lips.

Her eyelids thinned. "I should have brought you then. You probably would've loved it. It's been a few years since you've come to a party with me," Her tone softened. "I mean, since—"

"Yeah, I know." Elric shrugged remembering the last charity party he attended with the Reeve's.

Held at the Portland Harbor hotel, July of 2017. They had a ball. He and Jennifer found jubilation, leaning against a wall, idly people watching, scoffing at the philanthropy of the deep wrinkled tycoons. The tycoons strutted in thousand-dollar suits that were perfectly tailored to hide the guts. Young supermodels were attached to the men's arms, draped elegantly in cocktail dresses. Back then it puzzled Elric. But as a second-year sophomore at Lexington High, he was more than aware that money talked. Those supermodels must have been serenaded. He and Jen laughed for hours at the materialism of it all.

"Maybe next time?" A couple strands of her brown hair fell over her light hazel eyes.

Elric was captivated by her gaze. "Yeah, I would love to—" He cleared his throat. "Like to!"

A smile slipped from her pressed lips.

They pushed through the double doors that emptied into the school yard. The sweet air tangled in the salty breeze that wrapped around their shoulders. Colorful sets of school cliques waited for buses or individual rides home; one group circled in an acrobatic game of hacky sack. Another draped in black clothing, fingernail polish, and lipstick were tucked in a corner by the edge of the school, covered in a cloud of vapor smoke. Buses were pulling away as another line of vehicles took their place. Fortunately for Elric and Jen, they didn't live too far; their neighborhood was only a couple of blocks away.

With the excitement of the day falling away, the self-judging critic within Elric began to lay into him as the geometry test cut into his Jen time. *I can't repeat the tenth grade for a third time.* He slouched as his confident walk next to her became a lurch like the undead.

She turned looking up at him. "Geometry test still beating you up, huh?"

Elric's head waggled as he tightened his grip around his book bag. "If I can pass with at least a D, I'll be satisfied."

Jen nudged him with enough force to make him stumble. "You can do better than a D, Elric! Stop spending your time reading comics and watching T.V. I get it, everything with Mr. Lee, it sucks. But he wouldn't want you living like this."

He swallowed hard, knowing she was right. The old man would have drilled into him hard. *Put everything you are into everything that you do. That's all you can do!* Elric remembered Mr. Lee's words when Elric brought home his first C.

"You're right." His voice was low.

She nodded, giving him a nudge. "Of course, I'm right. For the last ten years, I've never been wrong!"

"Something about those New York girls I guess?"

She raised her eyebrows. "Something!" She laughed.

Elric learned to hide his feelings around Jen. After ten years he mastered the art. But deep down, it was always the same when he was around her. His stomach sunk to his knees. His heart pounded up his throat, threatening to break through his teeth. And a chill would strike the back of his neck. He felt the same way since he first looked into her eyes.

Then a five-year-old Elric, watched from the comforts of the park, legs dangling from a swing as the Reeveses moved into what Elric thought was a castle. He remembered watching the little girl with curly dark brown hair struggle to drag her pink suitcase into the house. He leaped off the swing and ran out the park. Mrs. Lee shrieking at the top of her lungs just behind him as a minivan nearly clipped him. Something guarded him, but something more powerful drew him to her. His lips spread wide, revealing a gap of missing teeth, and together they brought the bag in.

Once inside, she looked up, revealing the same smile, both front teeth gone. Her stunning eyes glowed like gold, taking his breath away. He was so lost in her gaze; he hadn't even noticed Mrs. Lee ripping him out of the house and screaming about nearly giving her heart attack. That was the day he received his first whipping. It was also the day something sparked deep within him, and that something now roared like a fire whenever he was around Jen.

"Hey, let's take the shortcut home. I want to get started on this new book I'm reading," she said, picking at a scab on her arm.

"Are you serious?" He tightened his grip on his book bag straps. "I'm not going down that tick-infested trail. It's bad enough I'm math illiterate. Now I got to get Lyme disease too?"

"C'mon. This is the last day I'll have off before soccer gets serious. Once that happens, I won't have time for anything. Plus, you want me to tutor you, right? You kinda owe me?" She looked up with a face of desperation. "What could possibly happen?"

"You could get Lyme disease, attacked by a black bear. Have you heard of fisher cats?" He thought about all the wildlife Maine had to offer. Thank God for the Discovery Channel.

She rolled her eyes. "Elric, don't be a wuss."

Elric sighed and nodded. "This book better be worth it."

"It is!" Her lips broke away.

They walked behind the school to a thin footpath that was intertwined with thick tree roots. The path was winding endlessly, tucked away deep within the shades of the forest canvas. He stopped at the entrance, dreading his decision.

Exhaling deeply, Jen smiled and walked past him, shaking her head. "Elric, don't punk out now. We're already here."

Sulking and with a bitter taste in his mouth, Elric followed behind her, keeping his eyes on his shoes and pant legs for ticks. Jen was one of the most stubborn girls he had ever met. His protests fell on deaf ears. He saw it as one of her greatest strengths and weaknesses as if that were possible.

The dirt path was riddled with large, thick, tree roots that seemed to reach and grab for his feet. He tripped and stumbled constantly as he tried to keep up with her. Jen, on the other hand, was relaxed and serene, enjoying the dark green backdrop of the forest. Purple, yellow, and orange wildflowers blanketed both sides of the trail, swaying with the sweet scent of dandelions.

"Elric, this isn't bad at all. You were crying about nothing." She leaned forward, pushing through the brush.

"Crying? You got to be kidding me." He shook his head. "Trying not to get eaten alive by ticks and mauled by a black bear is crying?" She stopped. And raised her hand to silence him. Jen's eyes sharpened into a squint. Elric tried to catch what she was looking at. The trees became silhouettes as he focused. Jen's walk became a careful tiptoe. She pressed Elric to get down as they hid in the bushes. The sound of people talking further down the road echoed as they froze.

He whispered softly. "Who is it?"

Jen shook her head. "You don't want to know."

With trembling hands, he peeked through the bushes.

"This day just keeps getting better and better," he whispered, shaking his head in disappointment.

Sitting with a group of his friends was Simon Cressy, the bane of Elric's existence. With teeth stained yellow from cigarettes, and a haircut most likely styled by his mother, Simon was *Webster's* definition of a school bully. Sure, Dillon was bigger, but he didn't make it his job to make life a living hell for Elric.

When Simon wasn't skipping school or suspended, he made it his routine to bully Elric. The kid was a wolf and Elric was a sheep separated from the herd. Most kids found it funny to watch Simon trip Elric with a tray of food in his hands. One year, Simon went through a phase of cutting holes in the bottom of Elric's book bags. The moment Elric picked up the bag, all his papers and folders would cover the hallway floors. He went through four bags that year.

"I have a plan. Let's stay off the trail, and we'll walk on the other side. They won't see us," she whispered.

Elric swallowed. "Alright. Let's do it."

Simon sat on a rotted log surrounded by a few others. They were engulfed in cigarette smoke, laughing and talking about who knows what. Elric carefully stepped through the brush, thinking of the consequences if Simon caught them. They were deep enough to keep an eye on Simon and the others, while the foliage was too heavy for them to be seen.

Snap!

A branch snapped beneath Elric's foot, cutting clean through the conversation coming from Simon and the others. He bit his bottom lip. *You've got to be kidding me.* He cursed himself. *He's going to tie me down and leave me in the woods like he did in the fifth grade.*

He looked down in fear at the tree branch that snapped beneath his whopping weight of a hundred and twenty-five pounds. The sound echoed through the woods, catching not only Jen's attention, but the small group's attention.

"What was that?" A head jerked up.

"Looks like it came from over there!" another said, looking in Jen and Elric's direction.

They froze, not moving an inch. Jen bent over and wrapped her fingers around a large stone.

"What are you going to do? Knock one of them out?" Elric whispered.

"No, are you crazy? Just watch." She drew her arm back, and with all her might, heaved the rock in the direction behind him.

The loud crash made Elric dive to the ground. He dug his fingernails into the dirt, wishing to become one with it. His eyes screwed shut.

"What was that? You think it was a deer?"

Elric heard Simon's voice on his right side. "I don't know. Let's check it out."

Footsteps raced over to the other direction. Elric's face was now smudged with dirt and sweat. He prayed they wouldn't be found. His eyes slowly rose from the ground to meet Jen's. She wiped the dirt from her hands and began to step forward.

"Well, hey, guys!" Simon said, coming through the woods. "You must think we're stupid, huh?"

Simon stood tall but lanky. Narrow chin, high cheekbones, and thin eyebrows made up his facial features. His eyes seemed to sink in as his dark brown pupils looked down on Elric in pity. He wore ripped black jeans with a faded Metallica shirt, which reeked of cigarette smoke.

Jen sighed as Elric kept his eyes closed, wishing it were just a nightmare.

"Look, all we're trying to do is go home, Simon. Unlike you, we didn't skip school,"

"Nobody was talking to you, Reeves."

He turned and focused his attention on Elric who had decided to stand strong and take his bullying like a champ. He missed Dan right about now.

"Besides, what's a hot girl like you doing hanging out with deadweight like Blake?"

She balled her fist. "The only deadweight I see here are you and these idiots."

Simon grinned. "You're weird for a rich kid. You tools belong together. No wonder neither one of ya have real parents." He chuckled, shaking his head.

Simon loved making fun of Elric, and the fact he was part of the foster care program. Elric never understood what was so funny about it. And who the heck would make fun of a kid who didn't know his real parents? Wait. He knew. Simon freaking Cressy.

Jen smacked Simon across the face with a left hook. He stumbled back, tripping over a root and hitting the ground with a thud. Everyone took a step back in surprise and the boys behind him started laughing. "Holy smoke! She split your lip, Simon!"

They laughed and hollered as he rose to his feet and spit saliva filled blood at Jen's feet. He looked back with a deathly glare that silenced even the largest of the group.

"Well, since you want to hit like a boy, you can get knocked down like one too!" With all his might, Simon shoved her.

Jen fell back, and with a heavy crack, hit the back of her head on an oak tree. Her body went limp, sliding down to the roots of the tree.

"Jen!" Elric crouched over to see if she were all right. "Jen, wake up!" He shook her shoulders anxiously.

She was lifeless.

Chapter 3

The Awakening

"Simon, we should beat it!"

He pushed the kid out of his way to get to Elric. "Now it's your turn, Blake!"

A fist slammed into the side of Elric's face. The force knocked him forward. He hit the dirt face-first. A horrible pain followed on the right side of his ribs as Simon gave him a swift kick to the body, knocking the wind out of him.

He tried to stand but was ruthlessly punched down. His left eye throbbed from the punishment it was taking. Even through the beating, he couldn't take his eyes off Jen; her motionless body lay at the base of the tree.

His chest burned with anger; his blood boiled. A strange chill came over his body as his heart raced with excitement. Something inside him was giving way to a desire he'd never felt before. Every kick Simon delivered was nothing more but an empty thud. The pain numbed.

The group of boys stepped back, startled. Simon stopped kicking and stepped back as Elric rose to his feet.

"Think you're tough, huh?" Simon went to swing.

Elric slipped to the side and grabbed Simon's wrist, catching him off guard. They both looked down as Elric squeezed. He felt the bones in Simon's wrists give way and it was like crushing an egg with his bare hands. The boy's bloodcurdling scream made Elric let go.

Simon fell to the ground, clenching his wrist, screaming an agony. A kid immediately took off running into the woods while the other two stood frozen with wide eyes and slack jaws. Simon's breathing quickened as he looked up.

"I'll kill you!" Simon struggled to stand and then charged.

Elric grabbed him by the throat. His palm pressed against Simon's Adam's apple, and he slammed him to the ground. Elric gaped. Shocked by his actions, Simon returned the expression as he looked up. Elric let him go.

Simon grabbed his wrist, scurrying back against a tree. The rest of his entourage helped him up as they all looked impatiently, waiting for Elric to make another move.

Elric's heart raced out of control; he didn't mean to hurt Simon. Not like that. But this excitement and rush. It was strangely fun. His adrenaline was at its peak, and the high made him feel invincible.

Darkness clouded over him as he everything began to spin. His knees knocked and then buckled beneath him as he hit the ground. He tried to keep his eyes open, but everything went black.

In the darkness. His heartbeat was heavy. Like the bass of a drummer. His eyes searching for light. *How dare you...*a voice rumbled in the darkness all around him.

Large, red ovals pierced through the blackness high above him. Glistening like rubies, reflecting light. But there was no light to reflect. A burning sensation crept over him trickling down his arms, chest, and legs. And he realized the glistening stones were pupils. A heavy quake shook his body as the eyes grew closer. This feeling was no longer excitement. But horror.

"Elric? Elric? Are you okay?" Jen's voice pierced through the blackness.

He snapped out of the darkness, opening his eyes. "What's going on?"

She sat back, sighing in relief. "Don't scare me like that, dummy!"

He gasped for air. His heart beating against his ribcage. He could still see those terrible eyes. A cold shiver consumed him.

"Relax, E. What did he do to you?"

"What?" He looked up, confused, and then began searching around him as he rose to his feet. "Simon, where . . . where did they go?"

She looked confused. "I don't know. When I came to, they were gone?"

He felt his face, searching for the warm trickle of blood or the dull ache of a bruise. "I don't remember a lot. I remember Simon hitting me across the face and kicking me in the ribs. I think I broke his wrist. Then I don't know. This strange feeling . . . " He looked over at Jen. "Forget about me. What about you?"

She rubbed the back of her head. "I've had better days, but I'm alright."

He looked down at his hands. Remembering the crunching of Simon's wrist. *Did that really happen? No couldn't have.* Simon must have really knocked him out. That had to be it. He was knocked unconscious.

Jen picked up both their book bags, shaking her head in disbelief as she handed him his. "Simon! That asshole!"

Elric coursed his fingers through his messy, tangled hair, expecting sharp pain or the dampness of blood. Nothing. Not even a lump or scrape.

"What is it?" Jen walked over. She pushed her finger through a torn hole in his shirt. Touching his chest.

A chill raced down his back. His heart nearly leaped up his throat.

"You said he punched you across the face, right?"

He nodded, eyes darting away from hers, saving himself the embarrassment of his failed attempt to save her.

She laughed turning his face. "Elric, you don't have a scratch. I don't think he laid a finger on you." She caressed his chin. "Did you pass out or did you play dead?"

"What? No! I remember getting nailed in the back of the head, and my eye." He felt his face, trying to remember. "He punched me in the face."

She shook her head, smiling. "Not a thing. Maybe his bark's worse than his bite?"

His fingers raced over his cheek. "Yeah...maybe?"

They made their way out of the woods and back to civilization. Jen complained of a splitting headache that was driving her crazy. But for the most part, they made it out ok. That's saying a lot after an encounter like that with Simon.

"You should get that checked out. What if you have a concussion or something?"

"Elric, please. That's the last thing I need with soccer season starting out. Coach would kill me if I had to miss a game."

She fixed her flowing, dark brown hair into a ponytail. "I'm going to go home and see if I can get some aspirin. You sure you're okay?"

"Yeah." The fear he felt was just starting to loosen its grip around his chest. "I'll be alright. See you tomorrow?"

She nodded with a smile and began to walk away.

"Hey, Jen." Elric looked up, took a deep breath, and exhaled. "Why did you stick up for me like that? I mean, they weren't after you."

Her lips turned up. "Don't worry about it. You owe me. I'll see you tomorrow." She trotted around the corner to the street that led to her house.

Elric continued, still confused about what happened. Everything played back in his head. Fighting Simon. Possibly breaking his arm. Then the thrill of it. Like he was enjoying it?

It was surreal. He would never enjoy causing someone else pain like that. He looked down at his torn jeans and tattered shirt, which were the only evidence of what happened. There was stained blood as if he had a scrape. But his skin was smooth, not even a scar.

He came to an old, tan, colonial. The wood siding was starting to crack and fade, and even the screen door hung by a hinge. Holes riddled the screen door from when he used to poke pen's through it as a kid. The crabgrass ran rampant and even began to take over the cement path to the house.

Mrs. Lee, his adoptive mother, would kill him if he didn't get it done this weekend. She already rode him for his grades in geometry. And with the test he bombed today, coupled with his incomplete chores, he would never see day light again.

He could usually hear her inside preparing dinner. The kitchen had a dark eeriness to it. She was probably over at the neighbors.

The door creaked open as he tossed his book bag to the side. The empty house groaned as a strong wind blew from outside. It nearly pulled the screen door out of his hand. He closed it and flipped the hook latch in.

He sighed, looking down at his clothing. The dirt and deeply engrained grass stains would never come out. If Mrs. Lee saw his clothes, she'd lose it. It would maybe be even worse than the she did when he and Jen got back home from playing by the shore in their Easter clothes. They were seven.

He trotted up the stairs, tossed his sneakers on the top step, and opened the door to his room. His bedroom walls were covered in a massive collage of comic book covers and clippings. His Fortress of Solitude.

He dug through a large pile of comic books and pulled out a thin booklet with wrinkled edges and a bent spine. He could get lost for hours in his comics; the lives of the heroes he read about were fascinating and tangible. They always came out on top against all odds, even when there was nothing else left to give.

He yearned to live their lives. But those were comic books. In the real world, he had no heroic abilities. He didn't have million-dollar gadgets like the Dark Knight. Or alien blood to make him the Man of Steel. He was simple, ordinary, Elric Blake. A repeater of the tenth grade who absolutely sucked at geometry, struggled to learn French, and was often swirlied in the boy's locker room.

As if laying a sleeping newborn back in its crib, he gently laid the comic book down with great care. He rummaged through his draws for fresh clothes. The bottle of Lexapro rattled, catching his attention. *I'm fine,* he thought as he shoved the bottle deeper into his dresser.

He took a refreshing, warm shower and got dressed, not skipping a beat. He threw the tattered clothing in a garbage bag and stashed it beneath his bed. He'd take care of them tomorrow morning.

As the steam cleared in the bathroom, he stared at his face and searched it in disbelief. Still nothing. He firmly pressed his hand around his face, expecting pain.

He exhaled in frustration. He should have been happy. Mrs. Lee would drive him crazy if she found a scratch on him; it was bad enough his clothes were trashed. Deep down something strange happened today. It was more than the sinister feeling that chilled him to the bone. It was that voice. Those eyes. Eyes that sought to kill and destroy anything they encountered.

Chapter 4

Homecoming

Crudely drawn posters of Lenny the Lynx mauling a Viking were posted down every hall of Lexington high. Swaying with each passing body, vivacious blue and gold streamers draped from all the entrances. A sixteen-foot long banner read *GO LEXINGTON! BEAT OXFORD!* Students flooded the staircases. Everyone was decked out in glamorous blue and gold socks, letterman jackets, and custom-made sneakers. People dazzled T-shirts with gold lettering that said, *Go Lynx's!*

Yeah. Smells like school spirit alright, Elric thought, closing his locker.

He was swept away by the sea of students that flowed down to the gymnasium for the pep rally. Unchecked body odor was tied in with the stale smell of cigarettes. But once you walked by the cheerleaders, the smell was mingled with pomegranate, coconut, and a hint of lavender. Elric smirked. *School spirit.*

Though the hallways roared of the big homecoming game against rival school, Oxford Hills. Elric was just excited to see no sign of Simon. Three days had passed since the fight in the woods. Not a second went by that he wasn't looking over his shoulder.

41

The chants and screams of praise shook the wooden floors of the basketball court as the students walked in. Drums bellowed, and trumpets flared over the howls of pride from the schools marching band.

"Elric, over here!" a voice yelled from behind.

Jen's small hands waved frantically as she jumped up and down amongst the river of students. Elric fought his way through traffic, apologizing with each brush of an elbow, and grunt he received.

"Hey," she said with risen cheeks. "Better get a good seat, huh?"

The chill came quickly this time. Even Jen was wrapped up in the homecoming spirit. Her dark brown hair spilled over the blue and gold lettermen's jacket, her knee-high blue and gold socks racing to the edges of her soccer shorts.

Elric swallowed. "Yeah. Let's go."

The gymnasium was packed full of students and teachers alike. The only free space was near the top of the bleachers—right in front of the school banner that had a drawing of a lynx jumping with its mouth ajar.

As they went up the row to the empty seats, a group of the girls' soccer team screamed and begged Jen to sit next to them. She ignored them. In frustration, their deadly scowls focused on Elric. He focused on the bleachers. "Everything ok with the team?"

"Everything's fine." Her tone said otherwise.

They took seats at the top of the bleachers, getting a view of hundreds of people that filled the gymnasium. The school colors of blue and gold swam in the crowd of students who wore ridiculous shirts and hats.

The crowd roared as the school band began to play. The cheerleaders came out in a triangular formation, getting the crowd excited. With each beat of the drum, their formation changed.

Separating into four groups. Each group launched a girl into the air who twirled freely with a bleached-white smile, fitting of a toothpaste commercial. As the bases received the flier below, they pushed the fliers back up. The fliers stretched their legs high into arabesques and scales, cheering loudly. Screams and yells of pride echoed over the gymnasium.

In the excitement, Jen grabbed Elric's hand tightly. He looked down, confused by the gesture, praying that his palms didn't start to sweat. She jumped to her feet clapping and yelling to the cheerleaders.

Excitement reached across his face. He was captivated by the girl he longed for all these years. Sadly, Elric didn't have the courage to tell her how he truly felt. How could he? How could he tell her that in kindergarten, he was the one that left wild dandelions at her desk every Friday? Or that in the fifth grade, he was the one that slipped that poem in her locker. She talked about it for months. When they had class together, he'd gaze at the way her hair spilled over her shoulders. Her caramel complexion was radiant under the classroom lights. But most of all he loved her because she understood him.

Polar opposites. But one in the same. Elric couldn't understand it himself, but he was drawn to her. Connected. It was like some invisible chain locked their hearts and souls together.

His fantasizing was taken away by the call of manhood. "Hey, I'm going to go use the bathroom. I'll be right back."

She nodded. "Hurry, okay?"

His cheeks rose, still thinking about how she grabbed his hand. He rushed down the bleachers, nearly tripping. Even the steps were crowded with students.

The hallway was silent; only the echoes from the gymnasium trailed the halls. The sound of all the fall sports teams being called to the center of the gym caught his ear. Jen would be the first one down screaming with pride; she loved being an athlete.

Maybe if he was a jock like Dillon, he might appeal to her. Sports weren't his thing, though. He'd rather spend his time reading comics than getting bruised or beat up just for kicks. It just wasn't him.

Jolted from his musings, Elric was grabbed from behind, twirled, and slammed into a group of lockers. Frantically, his eyes searched his attackers. Simon came into view with pressed lips. Bandaging was wrapped around his right arm. The flicker of that memory haunted Elric now. Simon's scream, that awful sound his wrist made. Elric wanted to throw up.

"Hey, Elric. I hope I wasn't keeping you from anything?" He nodded at the boy who pinned Elric to the lockers.

Elric cowered. "Hey, Simon. About Tuesday . . . That was a mistake, man. I mean. Things just got carried away, right?"

"You know what? You're right!" He slugged Elric in the stomach.

Elric hunched over, gasping for air. They let him flop to the ground. He did all he could to keep his lunch from spilling onto the floor. They yanked him to his feet, smashing him back against the lockers.

"The only reason I haven't broken your arms and legs is because of that stupid mall cop! But tonight, at the game …" Simon's eyes were fierce. "You better believe, I'm going to make you pay for what you did to me." A dark grin stretched from ear to ear.

The boys let Elric drop to the ground. He coughed, trying to catch his breath.

"Oh, and by the way, Blake, you better show, or Reeves will need more than just an ice pack after I'm done with her. I'm not about hitting girls, but she thinks she's a guy anyway, so …" Simon shrugged.

Elric's nemesis and his friends walked away, laughing. Simon was laughing the loudest. Elric wobbled to his feet. He took a deep breath, adjusted his posture, and shuffled to the bathroom. He slammed his fist into a locker in frustration. The metal bent. He was too pissed to care.

When he made it back to the entrance of the gymnasium, he stopped, listening to the roars of excitement and joy: emotions that were stolen from him. He took another deep breath. Swallowing hard, he put on a fake smile and opened the doors. He made his way back to the bleachers where Jen awaited.

Jen raised a brow. "You're sweating. Is everything okay?"

"Yeah." His eyes shifted away from hers.

"You missed it. They called all the sports teams down for the fall."

He forced excitement into his tone. "Yeah, I heard."

Everyone was excited for tonight. Too bad he would be going home on a stretcher. It would have been one thing if Simon wanted to beat him up; he just wouldn't show. But Simon had threatened Jen, too. If Elric told her anything, she'd flip and go off the deep end. He had to suck it up and go with it. Anything to protect her.

The pep rally ended.

Everyone filed out of the school. High fives and fist bumps were shared around for the big game tonight. He tasted the sour sting of vomit coming up.

"Hey, what time did you want to head up to the game?" Jen nudged him.

He gulped it down. "Umm, I ..." He thought about Simon's words. "How about six-thirty?"

She tilted her head. "Cool. That should work. See you then."

She headed to the girl's locker room to get ready for soccer practice. He shook his head, wishing he could tell her.

He left and took the long way home. A dead man walking. That's exactly what he was. No one would protect him this time. Jen had fought his battles long enough; it was time for him to do the fighting for once and make his comic-book fantasy somewhat of a reality.

He made it home. He dropped his backpack at the door and slunk his way through the kitchen. The living room was quiet. The sweet scent of vanilla and coconut faintly hovered. *Mrs. Lee must be in her room relaxing.* He crept to his own room and gently closed the door. He dug up a comic from his newly bought pile and plopped on his bed. Distress left his lips in the form of a disgruntled sigh.

He fidgeted through the pages, hands shaking, wondering what life would be like with superpowers. Elric imagined being loved and praised by some and feared by the villainous. He wouldn't have to worry about douchebags like Simon and Dillon hassling him.

If he had superpowers, he'd show *them* a thing or two. He'd show all of them; that's for sure. He tossed the comic across the room.

Tonight was going to be a massacre, Texas-chainsaw style. Simon and his crew only treated him like this because Elric couldn't beat them.

He slammed his fists against the bed and planks of wood splintered and shattered.

What the hell? He looked down at his hands. The bed post looked to be smashed by a sledgehammer.

Elric looked down at his hands and fingers. Not even a bruise.

"Elric Blake, you up there?" the low crackle of Mrs. Lee's voice called.

His heart seized. "Ah, yes ma'am! I'll be right down!"

He tossed the broken piece of wood under his bed. Brushed the splinters onto the floor and kicked the shattered remnants under his carpet. *What's going on with me?* His stomach twisted with anxiety. He pressed his fingers against his face.

"Everything ok?" She called again.

"Just fine, coming!"

He shook his head. Sucked in a deep breath and raced down the staircase. The door slamming closed behind him.

"Home early? Hopefully not a bad thing, right?" A thin, fair skinned woman sat down at the couch. She smelt of coconut and vanilla. Like the candy bars she used to bring home from her job as an RN.

Mrs. Lee's face was softly rounded. Slight wrinkles pressed down her soft blue eyes. The creases of her pointed nose outlined rosy warm cheeks that bubbled passionately as her lips turned up. He loved seeing her happy.

He sat down beside her. "We had the pep rally today, remember? Tonight's the big homecoming game," he said with a phlegmatic tone.

She combed her fingers through his short black strands. Placing a round chin on his shoulder. "Oh, that's right!" Her eyes dazzled with excitement.

Elric shook his head, annoyed by her overzealousness, but a quick glance at a picture of the late Mr. Lee advised otherwise.

Mrs. Lee and her husband had raised him for almost twelve years before Mr. Lee passed away. Elric started off as their fifth foster child and after a couple of years, they adopted him, making him their final foster, but very first child.

When she was younger, Mrs. Lee had been in a terrible car accident that took away her ability to have children. So instead, they started taking in kids, giving their hearts and souls to each child that stayed with them.

She provided the warmth, love, and motherly affection while Mr. Lee provided the strict, straightforward guidance that gave Elric courage. He loved them both dearly especially Mr. Lee.

He'd been a tall, stout man who in his earlier days was probably a brawler. He had a strong chin with a dimple that he always kept raised above Elric's head. Elric still remembered as a kid how Mr. Lee would come home from a double shift and even as exhausted as he was, he would pick Elric up and hoist him over his shoulders. Parading Elric around the house like a boxer who just won the world heavy weight title. That's how Elric felt anyway. Back then nothing could touch Elric. He was unbreakable. Unshakeable. But things change when a loved one dies.

It probably would have been different if Mr. Lee had died of a stroke or something that took him quickly, but cancer has a way of bringing the most powerful people to their knees. It started with severe headaches. Mr. Lee's hands would shake like crazy. Then there were the seizures. It took brain cancer three months to bring down the most powerful man Elric had ever known. It felt like eternity, watching the man he loved and respected as a father, go from a proud parent of strength and joy, to an emaciated shell of his former self.

There were times where Elric could hear Mrs. Lee crying in the darkness of her bedroom. He would stand frozen in front of her bedroom door, pale fingers clutching the doorknob. What could a twelve-year-old boy say to a woman who had lost the other half of herself? How could he comfort her? He'd continue up to his room and drown himself in his comics to numb the pain.

Those days he'd kept to himself, hating the outside world, loathing it more and more each day. He wondered, why him? Why did he have to lose his father? Wasn't it enough to know his parents abandoned him? He hated Mr. Lee for leaving them. Abandoning them. Abandoning him.

In those days, Elric wondered what else the world would take from him. He'd lost a lot of friends that year; the only one who stayed by his side and helped him through it was Jen.

Through it all, Mrs. Lee treated Elric like her very own. Every now and then he would slip up and call her mom. She would blush and hug him close. Caressing his black curls and digging her nose into his forehead. He made a promise to himself then, that he'd never let anything happen to her. His mom.

She caught Elric gazing at the picture.

"When the doorbell rung that awful stormy night, Reginald and I would've never thought waiting for us, right on our front steps, was an absolute blessing." Her voice was hoarse, cracking. The water works were coming. Mrs. Lee always cried when she told the story. "When we lifted that bundle of blankets and cloth and found you smiling up at us, your dark brown eyes gazing up in awe? We knew then, God had given us our boy. The son that Reginald always wanted, and the child I'd always dreamt of."

Elric cleared his throat, fighting back the flood of emotions that came with this story. "If I was such a blessing, why did my real parents abandon me in the rain?"

She rubbed Elric's cheeks. "Sometimes people don't know what they have until it's gone. All I know is that for fifteen years, I bathed you. I fed you. I cleaned up your messes. And through it all, you've made me into a person that I never thought possible, Elric. You *made* me a mother." Tears rolled down those bubbling cheeks.

Elric couldn't help but smile. "Can I ask you something mom?"

Her cheeks rose. "Anything."

"Why didn't you and Mr. Lee give me your last name?"

She sighed and reached for Elric's hands. "We wanted to leave the doors open for you, and for your parents if they decided to come back for you."

Elric lowered his gaze to the floor. It's been fifteen years. If they hadn't come back by now, then they found a better life for themselves. A life without him.

Mrs. Lee squeezed his hand, pulling him out of his thoughts. "So, do you want something to eat before you—"

He wrapped his arms around her tightly. Something forced him to embrace her. Maybe it was the spirit of Mr. Lee nagging him, but an overwhelming joy swelled in his chest. He fought back tears. "Nah, I'm not all that hungry. I think I'm gonna have my fill later this evening."

"So, where's Jennifer?" Mrs. Lee's tone was almost taunting.

"Oh, come on. Don't say it that way."

"Like what?"

"Like we're together. You know she's my friend?"

"You two have been friends since the Reeveses moved to Lexington. Besides, I know how you feel about her. You just don't want to admit it. I bet she already knows too. Women can sense these things you know. It took Reginald two years to finally ask me out."

Elric turned to the picture of the gruff man. Mr. Lee's eyebrows arched in a you're-damn-right expression. Elric sighed again.

"Why don't you just tell her how you feel? Who knows? She may feel the same way."

"Absolutely not! Don't even start this again. And please don't say anything next time you see her." Elric shook his head frantically. "Jen and I are just friends. I think that's as far as we'll go."

Her blushing bubbly cheeks bounced. "Look, I know you haven't had a male figure to talk to you about women but – "

"No! No! That's fine. I'm heading out anyways. I'll see you later tonight." He quickly rose from the couch.

Her cheeks bubbled again. "Thanks for giving the television back. Have a great night!"

He shook his head, avoiding any further embarrassment as he headed out the door.

Chapter 5

Attack on Lexington

Elric strolled through town. Streets were filled with people getting ready for the game. Posters and fliers hung everywhere. Stores were closing early. Most of the shops set up small stands outside the stadium, selling their goods out of trailers.

The cackling and gossiping of multiple voices echoed from around the corner. Elric ducked into a hidden entrance of a shop. He peered out as the small chuckling group walked by. They wore blue and yellow soccer jerseys. Jen was in the middle, talking about how much fun she had at the pep rally.

"I don't get it Jen. You can have any guy you want, but you're always hanging out with Elric Blake. Do you just feel sorry for him?" A girl with dirt blonde cropped hair asked distastefully.

Jen bristled. "No, he's my best friend. We've always been best friends. Why should I feel sorry for him?"

"Well ..." The girl crinkled her nose.

"Well what? I think he's cute." Jen's glare sliced through the very soul of the girl who looked away nervously.

"It's nothing. To each their own, I guess." She chuckled to herself.

The girls vanished around the corner, continuing to talk about that pep-rally.

Elric's heart leaped out of his chest. *She thinks I'm cute.* Jen's words filled him with new life. His face must have been red. *Why don't you just tell her how you feel? Who knows? She may feel the same way,* Mrs. Lee's words echoed in his head. Maybe she was right? Maybe he should see how Jen feels. Maybe she feels the same way?

Elric crossed the street to the local gas station. He needed something to cure his dry mouth from anxiety. An older man with a thick, heavy beard came out and held the door open for him. The burly man tipped a cap that read, *Go Lexington Lynx's!*

Elric stepped in as a couple of people stood watching the television. He passed by and went to the back to grab a drink. When he came back, the clerk was glued to the television. Elric recognized him from gym class. Elric peeked over to the television screen. A news reporter talked about strange heavy storm clouds sweeping the nation.

The clerk turned around. "Sorry about that, dude." He grabbed the change Elric left on the counter.

"No worries."

Elric took his time walking to the stadium. In a half hour, trumpets and drums would bring in the warm night air and a crowd of hundreds would be cheering right along. At the same time, Simon would be shoving a fist down his throat.

Elric sluggishly walked through the empty streets, trying to buy more time and build up courage. He replayed multiple plans back in his head. None worked out in his favor. He looked up to the night sky. Blackness canvased everything. There wasn't a glimmer of a single star or the illumination of the moon. The sound of people chanting and talking snapped him out his stargazing. A crowd made their way to the field as a school bus, filled with the traveling team, parked in the next lot over.

"Elric, wait!" He turned to see Jen in her soccer jersey. "This is the biggest game of the year. It always is with Oxford Hills!" She smiled expectantly. "You excited?"

Elric nodded unctuously. The thought of her words were still fresh.

They made their way to the metal bleachers of the football stadium. He looked around nervously. *He's around here somewhere, waiting.* It drove Elric insane not to know when it was coming.

Jen pulled him up the steel bleachers. The metal framing screeched with each step. There were two seats at the top. On the way up, two of Jen's classmates asked her to join them. They were the same girls who questioned her about Elric earlier.

She turned to Elric, ignoring them. "Let's go. I see two good seats at the top."

He looked at one of the girls who had a face of sour regret. "You should sit with your teammates. I can find somewhere else to sit." Jen grabbed his hand and pulling him to the open seats.

He asked, "Why didn't you sit with them? They're going to be pissed."

"Trust me. If they were going to be that upset, they would come right over and sit with us."

He thought about the conversation that he eavesdropped on when they walked past the store. "Why do you always stick up for me? I mean. You're easily one of the most popular kids at school."

"Because good friends are hard to find these days." She raised a single brow. "What about you? Why do you hang out with me, Elric Blake?"

This was it. The perfect chance. *Tell her!* he thought. *Tell her you've loved her since you first laid eyes on her. That whenever she gives that half smile, you want it to be for you! Tell her when you look into her eye in that moment, in that one second, you're in bliss. Tell her you're madly in love with her!* His lips quivered. "Because we've been best friends for as long as I can remember." Like a man sneaking into a private masquerade ball, he wore that fake smile shamefully.

"True." She shrugged playfully eyes returning to the field.

With dark brown eyes slinking away from hers, he looked down at the first set of bleachers and noticed one of Simon's goons looking up at him. As soon as they made eye contact, he waved Elric down. Jen hadn't noticed; she continued to watch the football field. Good. It was better that she hadn't noticed.

Elric tightened his fist. "Hey."

She looked up. "Yeah?"

"I-I have to go to the bathroom. I'll be right back."

"Oh, ok." She nodded and looked away.

He trotted down the steel bleachers to his death.

He followed the kid down behind the bleachers and across the track and field stadium. It was completely empty. The sound of the band and cheers from the crowd echoed from the opposite side. The football team must have entered the field.

"Hurry up, Blake!" The kid pushed him up front.

Elric's eyes darted all around. He wondered when the attack would start. He followed the boy behind a group of shacks used as concession stands during track season. A cloud of cigarette smoke bloomed from the shacks as four boys came out from the side. Simon stepped out. The smoke flushed from his nostrils.

"You really showed up, huh?" Simon exhaled, blowing smoke in Elric's face. "Man, you're really crushing hard for Reeves, huh?"

Elric ignored him, shoving his hands in his pockets.

"You know what I don't get? What Reeves sees in you." Simon dug a thin, pale finger deep into Elric's chest. "I mean, I know what you see in her. She's hot. Rich. That's obvious, but what is it about you?"

He slugged Elric in the stomach and Elric dropped to his knees, groaning. The pain was sharp. At least he remembered not to eat anything, or his dinner would have covered Simon's sneakers. More fuel for the fire. A deep wheezing came from chest. His lungs sucking back air.

"What gets me is nobody likes you, Blake. Honestly, I would hate to be you." Two of the boys picked him up. Elric winced; the air completely knocked out of his lungs. "Listen up, Blake. I'm gonna break both your arms and legs. At least that way when you get your casts, you might get a little more attention. Heck, I might even sign it."

They all laughed.

Fear enveloped Elric as he awaited a rib-cracking punch. He held his breath and closed his eyes.

Amid a bone chilling explosion, Elric was swept away by a horrifying sensation. His body thrown into the concession shacks. Glass, and shards of wood tore through his flesh. The stinging and burning didn't last long. He could feel warmth running down his arms and legs. His eyes locked tight. His heart pounding against his chest. Through the ringing in his ear. The terror of a new reality set in.

No longer did he hear trumpets and drums beating of

Lexington pride. No cheers and chants of *Go Lynx's beat those Vikings!* Just horrific screams. Blood curdling screams that Elric could only relate to hearing in horror movies. Wails of grown men in agony. Then a swirling wind whipped him halfway across the field like a rag doll. The roaring wind was hot. Dry. Tearing away at his flesh like a butcher filleting meat. He hit the cool grassy field with a thud.

Elric struggled to stand. His knees wobbled as he staggered, trying to catch his balance. He looked down at his bloodstained, tattered clothes, his sight blurry. Eyes slowly beginning to focus. The ringing was like the high-pitched sound of a television that had gone off-line.

The salty air of the harbor was replaced with a thick blackness of burning rubber, wafting all around. The powerful wind eased. Elric stepped forward. His legs were heavy like lead. The howling faded. The shrieks of pain and anguish spread like wildfire. His skin crawled as goosebumps swept over his skin.

People were running, covered in blood. Some had their cell phones out, recording what was happening. It was like something you would see on the news, after a horrible bombing or attack.

Jen! he thought, racing toward where the bleachers once were.

"Jen!" he screamed.

His yell was nothing compared to the bone-chilling shrieks of pain by the people around him. His fear was overpowered by the rise in adrenaline. *Is this a terrorist attack? Are we being bombed by another country?* The thoughts didn't stop.

"Elric!" Jen screamed.

He looked over to where the bleachers were. They had been blown over. The stand where the announcers were had been splintered into nothing but thin planks and shredded wood. Only blood stains remained. The football stadium. Non-existent. The explosion turned the athletic field into a barren land of tangled metal and chaos. Particles of clothing, shoes, and hats littered the bloodstained grass.

Jen limped over quickly, holding her ribs. "We have to get out of here!" Her face covered in dirt and sweat.

"What was it? What happened?" Elric scanned the mayhem.

Her voice cracked in a sorrowful tone. "Didn't you see it? Look!" She pointed with a trembling, dirt-caked finger over the football field.

An Ominous black mass covered the remnants of the field, whirling in a strange funnel speckled with blue dots of light. It hissed as it stretched across the width of the field; its outer edges blurring anything behind or around it. Heat spewed from the strange blackness, like an oven had been left open on high.

"Elric, what's going on?" She gripped his arm.

"I don't know. But we have to get out of here!"

A mighty roar tore through the swirling mass, rattling Elric's bones. The air quivered from its crackle. The ground shook from heavy thuds and clanking metal. Elric stepped back. Bracing himself. A chill raced down his arms as a large, beastly foot came through the swirling vortex.

Chainmail like armor draped from the thighs as the full body came through. The beast had the head of a lion; its black mane was braided with beads and shells. Large amber eyes flickered in the light as they looked down on Elric and Jen.

Its large beastly hands clutched a massive battle axe. Its five clawed digits were covered in desert sand colored fur. Formed to the beast chest was a glimmering dense metal that was strapped on tightly. Fiercely wild eyes gaped over the broken crowd of confused and frightened people. Black lips peeled back, revealing large canines.

Elric froze in shock.

"Is . . . is that a lion?" Jen's voice cracked in fear.

The beast scanned the area with savage eyes.

"Wraths, forward!" it roared.

Dozens of creatures marched through the darkness in unison. Wolves with jet-black fur, crept out, walking upright. They sniffed the air, holding thick sharp spears. They were also draped in metal. Large, beastly tigers stomped forth with bellowing roars, beating their metal-plated chests with clubs. Dragging heavier limbs that made the ground quake, large rhinoceros creatures moved forward. They had fists the size of truck wheels.

Overpowering and nauseating, the heavy musk, and fur caked with death drowned out even the choking black smog. The smell made the hair on Elric's neck stand on end. It was the same feeling he got when he smelled a dead animal but couldn't see it. The tingling of your fight or flight receptors igniting.

"Humans!" the lion-like beast roared as an army formed just behind him. "This is the day of reckoning. The day that we, the Wrath, take back what's rightfully ours and destroy everything you are!"

The other creatures roared and howled with clawed fists in the air.

Like a deer caught in the headlights, Elric froze. He didn't notice Jen screaming. Trying to pull him away, but he couldn't move. How was this possible? This wasn't real. It couldn't be!

Chapter 6

———— ）（《〇》）（ ————

The Wrath

"We claim this world for Blight!" The beast roared and pointed the massive axe of steel and bone towards the crowd. "Wraths, crush them all to dust!"

"Elric!" Jen smacked his left cheek and jerked his face around. "We have to get out of here. Now!"

He nodded as they both took off running. The earth shook as if just behind them were a stampede of elephants. Well, some of them were elephants. They rushed past people struggling to stand or trying to help others; they were swept away by the mass of creatures raging behind them. Their roars and snarls bellowing in the night sky.

"Run, everyone! Run!" Jen screamed.

"What are they?" A man looked behind them.

Beastly feet dug into the earth and crushed the tar with their weight. The fear was suffocating and heavy. Elric turned to watch a man get crushed by a large club. Women and children were slung in the air.

"Kill the men," the beastly lion roared as it rushed through the streets with its army. "Chain the women and children!"

Everyone screamed in fear as panic swept the crowd. People were getting battered and crushed by large legs and torn to shreds by claws and weapons.

Elric struggled to keep up with Jen as she fought through the crowd. *This is just a horrible nightmare. It's not real,* he thought. Some of the creatures dropped to all fours, tackling those trying to escape.

Jen yelled. "Elric, you got to keep up. Run!"

A man just beside him was tackled to the ground by one of the large wolves. "Easy for you to say. You're faster than everyone else!"

The fight or flight instinct kicked in as adrenaline flooded his blood vessels. No way on God's green earth was he fighting. He stumbled through the crowd, cursing his lack of athleticism. The crowd spread vigorously out of the way with screams.

The army of beasts flooded Main Street, crushing cars and hurling them through buildings. They ripped down streetlights, telephone poles, and traffic lights.

Car alarms blared in the distance. Sirens echoed and the flashes of police lights flickered in the blackening streets. A subtle relief came over Elric. *The police would take care of this.* He trailed Jen as she dodged behind one of the restaurants.

An old rusted green dumpster reeking of old salmon and cabbage became sanctuary. Guttering flames from the fires that consumed Lexington gave enough light to see. Jen and Elric watched from the dumpster. Shadows of the beasts danced on the brick walls as the beastly warriors purged Main Street.

"What the hell just happened out there? What did we just see?" Jen whispered, bewildered. Her hands didn't stop shaking. Her fingers dug into Elric's as she squeezed around his palm.

"I don't know?" Elric looked down at his fingers twitching. "This…this can't be real. It can't be."

The smell of death overpowered the rancid salmon and cabbage as fear weighed over Elric's shoulders.

The sound of claws dragging across the tar and the rattling of a metal gate, silenced them. Jen gripped Elric's hand like a vice. He held his breath. Heart beating like a drum. Snarls and heavy snorts crept just behind the dumpster.

"Humans," a deep, raspy voice snarled as if its master were playing hide and seek. "I can smell your sweat and fear in the air."

The shadow took form in the light. Tall, wide, muscular. Claws dragged across the ground. Elric gulped as they pushed themselves deeper into the crevice of the dumpster. It growled, sniffing the air. Its eyes glowed in the flickering light. The creature, a giant wolf strapped with armor and with a hatchet at its side, was heading toward a tin shed just in front of them; it hadn't found them yet.

"One male and one female." It growled, its long jaws gnashing. Globs of drool plopped at its feet. "I wonder what you taste like!" It smashed open the door to the shed.

They both jumped, gripping each other. Elric watched the beast. The only thing coming close to mind were the stories of werewolves. But this thing looked to be like a werewolf on steroids and dressed for war.

The shed rocked back and forth, creaking from the wolf's weight as shreds of cloth, and metal pour out the shredded door.

"Where are you?" It snarled. The creature stepped out of the shed. Black fur wildly blowing in the wind. A pungent smell came from the wind, it smelled like death and a hundred wet dogs.

Its perked ears were going crazy, flickering like a satellite trying to pick up reception. Long, sharpened canines gnashed in anger. The light caught something long and silver peaking from its shoulder.

A sheath of metal strapped to its back as it stood upright. Its large, clawed feet kept its wolfish appearance, digging deep into the gravel.

A bellowing horn rattled the metal of a lock that dangled from the dumpster's cover. The large wolf howled in tune with it. Dropping down on all fours, it raced away towards Main Street.

Elric swallowed tamping down a wave of panic.

Worry spilled across Jen's face. "You think it's safe?"

Elric cautiously peeked around the corner. It was too dark to see down the opposite end. From the little light he got from the fires, it looked clear. That awful horn kept blowing, rattled his bones. They covered their ears.

"Damn that horn sucks." Elric sat back, resting up against the dumpster. "It looks clear, but I'm not going out there."

"We just can't sit here. They'll find us eventually."

"Jen, where can we go?" he whispered. "You saw those things – those *animals*. How can they walk upright? That wolf was talking."

"I don't know what's going on either." She peeked around the corner. "Look, if we climb that fence, it'll bring us on the opposite side of Sam's variety store. We can cut through the back and take North Street to get us back home."

"You mean if North Street isn't crawling with the zoo animals from hell?"

"Do you have any better ideas?"

He shook his head. Those beasts were the things of nightmares. Something out of a Stephen King novel for sure. They were merciless, tearing through people like knives went through cloth. The crimson stained grass back at the football field was etched into his mind. He didn't think twice about Simon and the others.

His mind told his body to get up and move, but his arms and legs said *screw you*. His legs were starting to cramp up and his arms were doing the same; he wouldn't be able to keep up with Jen. The slowest person was bound to get caught regardless, and Elric knew that would be him.

"Let's go." She ran and jumped the metal fence with a single bound.

Elric hesitated. The fence rattled and clanged like dinner bells. He cautiously began crawling over and jumped down only to get his shoelace caught in the fence. He hit the ground with a thud.

"Are you kidding me?" Jen came rushing back over and pulled his shoelace through. Elric struggled to his feet and looked around in fear.

They kept to the shadows, creeping their way to the store. Sirens bellowed down the road as dozens of police cruisers swarmed the street; they lined their vehicles the width of the road. The deep flames that consumed vehicles were the only light in the night sky, the black smoke of burning fuel and tires was unbearable.

Jen's eyes widened with excitement. "Elric, let's go!"

They rushed towards the police cruisers. The men quickly looked over and drew weapons.

"Whoa, don't shoot!" Elric yelled, covering his face with his shirt as they broke through the columns of smoke.

"You kids need to get out of the streets! It's not safe!" The sheriff lowered his revolver as they came out of the shadows.

One of the officers scanned the mayhem. "What the hell's going on out here?"

Jen shook her head. "I don't know, but there's an army of monsters out there!"

"Monsters?" The sheriff looked Jen and Elric up and down, noticing their tattered clothing and eyes wild from fear. "Are you kids okay?"

"I know it sounds crazy, but you got to believe us." Jen looked on. "People are dying!"

"Look. Help's on the way, okay? You kids relax and sit." One of the officers came and helped them sit down on the curb next to a cruiser. "Tell me everything."

The horn bellowing in the night sky forced everyone to cover their ears. A thunderous crash and men yelling in fear came from further down the street. The officers drew their guns, getting behind their vehicles as they watched the road.

The sirens of a fire truck blared down the opposite end. The motor wailing from the driver slamming his foot against the gas. The ground shook with rhythmic thuds.

The large red truck whipped around the corner screeching towards the cruisers. Men clung to the sides for dear life. Another fire truck rolled into a building just behind the first.

An officer stepped in front, gesturing the driver to slow down. The driver laid on the horn. His eyes were as big as saucer plates. All the officers began to clear out as they jumped from their vehicles. Elric and Jen leaped to their feet and raced to the side of a brick building.

The fire truck plowed through the wall of police cruisers. One of the firemen was thrown from the vehicle as it kept plowing through. The officers scrambled to their feet to assist the man as he skipped across the tar like a rock on water.

Elric and Jen watched from the corner of the building.

The ground shook as Elric's eyes perused the street. A massive rhino-like creature, cracking its tire-sized knuckles, was strutting

65

down the street from the direction where the firetruck came. Elric's eyes gaped, as a deep gulp surged down his throat.

"Hey!" Elric yelled, his voice trembling. "If you want to point guns at somebody, how about at that thing?" He aimed a finger at the massive creature. Coming right for them, its horns were large enough to rip right through a fire truck.

Shock fell on all the officers, now standing witness to what leveled the fire truck.

"Well, that explains why that driver kept it moving," an officer replied.

The creature's massive shoulders and its chest like the grill of a sixteen-wheeler rippled with muscles spoke with a booming voice.

"Such a feeble and weak species." It grunted as it began stomping forward. "It's time we take back what's ours!"

Its skin was thick and grey. Even though armor covered its body, the skin looked strong and rough enough to take on any kind of attack. Two massive horns protruded from the bridge of its nose to the tip of its narrow snout. A large metal helmet glimmered from the light of the flames as a pair of stubby ears stuck out from the sides.

"Is that a damn rhino?" One of the officers looked up, raising a pistol.

Elric thought about the comparison of the beast. Those bullets would be like BB gun pellets.

The creature snarled, making its way closer. Stocky, muscular legs splayed into larger, circular pads. Three rigid toes smashed into the ground. With each step, the cruisers leaped off their suspensions.

Its beady eyes focused on them. "You will be my first trophies to Blight!"

Chapter 7

The Darkness

The officers fired upon the beast. Their bullets snapped and pinged off the metal armor.

"For years, we studied you," it said, yawping with laughter. "This is it? Nothing else? Nothing more?"

"Sheriff, the …the rounds did nothing," One of the officers said backing away in fear. "It didn't even graze him?"

More creatures poured in from behind the rhino. Creatures standing upright easily seven feet tall or more. Much more. They were the spitting image of wolves, tigers, bears, cheetahs, and panthers. The ground quaked from their marching.

The lion-like creature stepped forward with its large axe hanging over its shoulder. The same creature that stepped through the black mass first. It paced back and forth, keeping its eyes on them. Sizing up everyone who wasn't of *them*.

"They're animals, right? How . . . how's this possible?" the sheriff asked, his face surging with perplexity.

"Elric," Jen whispered, pulling his arm. "We need to leave. Now!"

They stepped back quietly. Elric's knees knocked, barely able to control them.

"I'm Kaimus, captain of the first scouting unit of the Wrath," the lion-like beast barked, scanning the streets and the eight police officers that stood in their way. "Is there a warrior in this good-for nothing town or not?" It roared in anger.

Elric couldn't tell if it was fear or amazement that kept the officers from making a move. Sweat beaded from one of them while another stumbled to the ground. The sheriff turned with a hard-set face, swallowing hard as streams of sweat soaked his thick moustache. "Kid, listen to your friend. Get out of here. We'll hold them off as long as we can."

Jen yanked Elric one last time, as he went forward. In the eyes of each man was fear glistening with trapped tears. These were men with families, who had dreams. And yet, they would lose everything tonight.

Jen grabbed Elric's hand. "We have to go now!"

The sheriff nodded with a strange ease of his hardened expression as they bolted.

They raced down the block as the sound of a man yelling, "Fire!" His command echoed behind them. Gunfire broke out in the hellish background, crackling in the blackness. From some unknown reason, Elric ducked, keeping his head low. The crackles faded, devoured by the howls and snarls of the beastly army. Elric swallowed hard, his beating heart heavy with what those men sacrificed.

The acrid smell of gun powder carried easily in the dry night air—a hint of sulfur burned his nostrils as he wiped away stinging tears. They hid behind a large van and checked the streets. The coldness started to set in as they came out of the roaring heat of burning buildings and vehicles.

"Just . . . just a few more bl-blocks," Jen sobbed. Tears racing down her cheeks as quick breaths escaped her lungs. She sunk to her knees. "What the hell is going on?"

Elric crouched and wrapped his arms as tightly as he could around her, struggling to keep his own tears silent. All the blood, the horror. Was this it? Was fifteen going to be the age he tapped out? If so, what a piss poor life it had been. Abandoned by his parents, losing his stepfather, bullied. But he did have Mrs. Lee. He just had to find her.

"I don't know what's going on, we just have to keep moving before those things catch up," He looked back from where they left the officers. "They sacrificed themselves for us. The least we can do is get home, right?" He swallowed hard, surprised by his words.

"Yeah." She wiped her face and nose and rose to her feet. "Let's keep going."

They ventured out again, scanning the glow of fires that lined the streets. A strange sound made them duck as they searched blackened skies. It was like a zipping, something cutting through the air.

"What was that?" Elric asked.

The sound of light flaps in the distance became heavier as they came closer in the darkness. Bulging eyes glinted, catching the glare from the streetlights. Four bat-like creatures slowly descended, boxing them in.

Elric shook his head mutely. He froze again. His blood became like ice. *Move damn it, do something!* He thought of those officers. He thought of his comics and even of Jen and her bravery to stand up to Simon. Why couldn't he do something, anything? He cowered, looking up at them.

They were towering creatures; something Dracula would turn into to make you piss yourself. Large pointed ears made up their face, stretching toward the back of their heads, angled at the evening sky. U-shaped nostrils flared against their flat bunched faces, giving them a permanent grimace.

Bats are like hamsters with wings, he remembered his biology teacher saying once. *They eat bug, and their feces make great fertilizer. What's not to love?* He wondered what Ms. Banks would say at a time like this. She was probably dead . . . like so many others.

Jennifer whispered, "Bat's?"

Elric swallowed hard and bit down on his lip until he broke the skin. *Move!* he thought, tasting the salty fluid. He stepped in front of Jen, body trembling uncontrollably and beads of sweat budding over his forehead. They were trapped, but maybe if he tried fighting them off, at least Jen would get away.

The creatures were tall and lanky. Arms reached down to the ground. If it wasn't for the grey tangled fur that covered their feet, and meat-hook like claws, their feet would almost look human. They were built to pluck people out of the air and tear them apart at the same time. Messy grey fur covered them in greasy curls, barely able to cover old scars and battle wounds.

Elric's eyes watered from the heavy skunk like musk that permeated from them. It smelled like a sack of dead skunks.

The lead creature's arms were folded across its narrow chest. Its gray fur faded into teal over its abdomen. The other two patiently waited just behind.

"Yes, bats," the lead creature spoke with a snobbish tone, golden armor wrapped over its shoulders. Lips moving over its sharpened canines. "Unlike our distant relatives of what you consider bats, we're highly evolved and much more than a simple animal," the creature said tersely.

"A smart-ass bat ..." Elric whispered hoping they didn't hear.

Jen gripped his hand tightly and eased closer to his back. Unlike the three creatures behind it, this one spoke with confidence and a strange elegance while the other three seemed ravenous and bloodthirsty.

A horn bellowed like the one they heard earlier. The large bat's ears perked up as they looked to the sky. Elric stepped back as the towering creature looked down on them in an intimidating manner.

"Pity." The creature flapped its mighty wings as it rose to the sky. "I really appreciated our small conversation; it was actually the first I've ever had with a human. Capture the female. I feel she could be a great addition to a project I'm working on. The male you can do with him whatever you like. Just make it hasty; we have to cleanse this area before general Carnage arrives!" The creature flapped once, and zipped through the sky, vanishing into the blackness.

Elric's hands trembled as he gripped Jen's. He wished he had something to fight them off with, he knew he wouldn't be able to outrun them.

"Elric, we have to split up," Jen said nudging him.

He didn't take his eyes off the creatures. "That's stupid." He shivered. "We're trapped anyways Jen...I...I don't know if we can make it."

"If we split up, we can confuse them and head to the closest house. This is the block where they're setting up all those modular homes, remember?"

"Yeah, but—"

"We'll meet at 112 Norfolk Drive. That apartment is the only one that's finished. Ready?" Jen asked, ready to take off.

The creatures watched with vigilance, ready for either of them to make a move.

"No."

"Run!" Jen raced towards one of the creatures, its claws stretched towards her. She slid just beneath its grasp, beneath its legs and rolled to her feet, taking off down the road in a full sprint. Two creatures took off after her while the other one remained, glaring at Elric.

Jen was a star athlete; she had a chance of outrunning them. Elric on the other hand failed to pass the president's physical fitness challenge. He could already feel the shooting pain racing up his legs.

He took a step back and tripped over the curb, a costly mistake. The creature leaped in for the kill. Its jaws showed teeth that would cut through his flesh like butter. He rolled out of the way as it smashed into the concrete. He scrambled to his feet and bolted. The creature took flight as shrieks of anger echoed overhead.

"I'll tear you to shreds!" The creature lunged forward in the air as its powerful wings flapped just behind.

Sharpened talons just missed Elric's shoulders as he dove to the ground. He rolled onto his back as the creature circled. The only way to escape was up, and as he looked to the sky; he could see the glowing eyes glaring down on him.

It shrieked as it moved in for the kill. Long claws lashing in the air. Elric screamed, throwing his hands up in defense. What good would they do against sharpened meat hooks for talons? He was better off shoving his hands into a meat grinder.

A loud shriek came over him as the hot, awful breath of the creature exhaled over him. Drool splattered over him, oozing down his fingers. He wiped his face in a panic as he slowly looked up.

Chapter 8

Look No Hands

Black tendrils tore through the creature's body, piercing its wings, legs, and chest. Elric frantically looked himself over. He was shrouded in a black mass.

"What's going on? What is this?" He looked down at his hands, watching the dark energy surge from his body.

"What is this?" The creature stepped back and covered a gaping wound as blood seeped through its fur.

Four more black tendrils sprouted from the mass, ripping through the thigh and arms of the creature. It shrieked in pain as its wings tried to flap away.

"What's going on?" Elric yelled, watching the blackness envelop him.

"You." The creature looked over to Elric. "How are you doing this?"

"I-I don't know." He studied the aura that flowed around him.

"I'm the first injury in the battle." The creature slashed away at the tendrils, which faded. It fell on all fours as it dropped to the ground. "I'll kill you for this embarrassment!"

Without warning, another tendril sprouted from the dark mass, smashing through the creature's chest. Its eyes bulged as blood squeezed through its teeth. Elric could feel the strange thuds of its heartbeat.

Its jaws slacked. "What . . . what are you?" The thuds slowed to a halt as its body went limp.

The black mass faded as Elric looked down at the dead beast that lay in front of him. He looked down at his sweatshirt, which was stained red. He eagerly tried to wipe it off. His hands and fingers stained with blood. Elric ripped off his sweatshirt, wiping the scarlet fluid from his hands, and tossed it away. He was afraid to wipe the sweat from his face as he looked down at the creature, which lay with its mouth open and tongue hanging out. It reminded him of roadkill.

He had never killed anything before in his life. He remembered gouging and stabbing a fishhook through an earthworm when Mr. Lee took him fishing in the late spring, but that was it. The fish did most of the work.

He stepped back, trying to pull himself together. His eyes searched the darkness to find what caused this to happen. Shrieks of the large bats that chased Jen snapped him out of his confusion.

"Jen." He remembered. "112 Norfolk Drive,"

He rushed through the streets, hoping Jennifer made it somewhere safe. He ran, trying to convince himself that she was too fast to get caught.

Elric's heartbeat vigorously in his chest. Sweat dripped down the sides of his face and back as he tried to calm himself down.

Another terrifying horn bellowed in the night sky. He paused for a moment as he heard the heavy flapping and looked to the sky as two large creatures zipped through the air with ease.

Jen, he thought. He was not stopping for anything.

He made it to the address, not taking his eyes off the roof of the house, which was partially caved in. Desperation took over as he rushed to the house, throwing debris out of the way. A huge tree barricaded the front door. It was too large to move. He went around the back, but the backdoor was blocked from the inside.

He searched for something, anything, to break in. A large stone lay next to the steps. He smashed one of the back windows in and began climbing through.

As he made it inside, he pulled his hand back in pain, revealing a deep gash in his palm. The long, deep gash bled down his forearm. It was not red oxygenated blood, but the dark, frightening blood that made you one to pass out. He fell to the floor in pain, holding his hand tightly.

Before he could go into shock, the flesh began to reconnect itself. He looked away. When he looked back, it had already healed. Not even a scar remained. The dark red blood still dripped down his forearm, but there was nothing else.

"Wicked," he whispered.

"Who's there? Is anyone there?" Jennifer cried out. He walked into what was left of the living room. She was hiding in a corner. "Elric, is that you?" She shouted, "You made it!" Tears ran down her face.

"I'm fine, I think," he said, thinking of how he killed the large bat and the deep wound that healed on its own. "Are you okay?

Did you get hurt?"

"They smashed down the ceiling. I thought the house would cave in on me." She rushed over and held him tightly. "I'm fine though. How did you get away from them?"

"I'll explain later. Come on. We have to get out of here!" He grabbed her hand and pulled her out of the house.

"Those things chased me all the way here." She wiped her eyes and looked up at the roof, which had been demolished. "Then I heard that horn. Then everything went quiet."

Elric was beyond terrified and confused, and Jen's eyes were filled with that same terror. What was happening?

Burning houses and cars filled the streets, giving them enough light to see. Elric was horrified by the people fleeing beasts of all shapes and sizes. The sounds of sirens, howls, and gunshots filled the air, and in the distance, emergency lights flickered. Lexington was in complete turmoil.

"This can't be happening." He slowed down, searching the dark, empty stores that were littered with large glass shards, splintered wood, and crushed brick.

"We have to get out of here. Let's go where the sirens are. That's where the help is!" she yelled.

He nodded, trying to be as strong as she was.

It wasn't long before they could see Jen's house. The siding was ripped off, and shingles from what was left of the roof covered the street. All the windows were knocked in, and the front door dangled by a single hinge.

They rushed inside. Jen looked around the house as if it were her first time being there. She picked up a shattered picture frame that once held her family picture. Elric looked over her shoulder as a tear drop fell on the remains.

"Mom? Dad?" she screamed, holding the picture frame close to her chest.

She ran frantically through the house, yelling at the top of her lungs, calling up to the second floor. It was impossible to get to her room with half the staircase gone. The roof had collapsed, removing all hope of going upstairs.

Elric could only watch as she ran from room to room. He prayed they were all right. They burst into the guest room, which was filled with debris. They ran to the room next door, but there was no sign of anyone. She raced to the opposite side of the house, leaving him behind.

"Maybe they found some place safe," she said with a reassuring tone. "We should do the same."

They followed the sound of sirens to the outskirts of town, where a huge crowd of people had gathered. Humanitarian organizations set up a large tent for the hundreds of people that begged for help and assistance.

Jen and Elric rushed through the field, searching for familiar faces and hoping they could find her parents.

A woman's voice screamed loudly, "Jennifer! Oh my god! My baby! Are you alright?" It was her mother.

She quickly ran over, grabbed Jen, and held her tightly. Jen returned the embrace.

"Yeah, I'm alright. Where's Dad? How did you guys get out?"

"We heard the explosion, and the wind burst through the windows. We thought it was a tornado, so we ran down to the cellar and waited. I was so frightened you might have been hurt, but your father was sure you were okay," She said, crying trying to comfort

Jen. "How about you, Elric? You alright?"

He sucked in his lips. The taste of blood still on his tongue. He tried to stay confident, and not look too frightened. He loved Jen's parents. They always treated him like family. Maybe that was because he was the first friend Jen had ever had.

"Mom, Elric saved me. I was trapped in a house. If it weren't for him, I would still be in there."

Her mother grabbed him close. Her tall, slim stature and light caramel-colored skin gave her the appearance of a model. Her perfume was strong and calming, the faint smell was welcoming in comparison to the smell of death, musk, and blood.

"I'll be alright," he said, pulling away. "I just need to find Mrs. Lee. She's probably worried sick about me. I'll come find you later?"

"Alright." Jen rushed over and kissed Elric on the cheek. "Thank you," she whispered in his ear, "for everything."

Elric nodded, rushing into the crowd in search of his mother. He was more nervous about the lecture he would get than the monsters that chased him and Jen all night.

Chapter 9

She's Gone

Huge trucks draped with desert camouflage shook the ground as they entered town. Each truck was stacked with men and women on the back. They were holding rifles and standing on mounted weaponry. The smell of exhaust and the roar of their engines blended in with bloodcurdling screams of pain and anguish. There were twelve vehicles waiting idly as the engines hissed and rumbled.

A tall man in camouflage stepped out of the third vehicle in line and began talking through a radio. The soldiers dispersed from their vehicles and set up equipment around the medical site. They flooded the area, angling their vehicles all around the site. Large guns faced out into the darkness.

The man that was on the radio made his way through the crowd and a handful of soldiers followed behind. It was the Maine Army National Guard and for once, his spirit and hope picked up; Lexington had a chance.

Elric stayed on track to go find Mrs. Lee; he had to let her know he was okay. He traveled deep into the scene of bandaged faces and badly wounded people. The screams of women and children in pain were enough to make his skin crawl. The wounded were begging for relief from their pain while children cried for parents that would never be found.

Elric heard some screaming about the creatures that talked and walked upright like humans, people laughed at them, said they were crazy. It was only a matter of time before the ravenous stampede swept them away too.

"Elric, over here. Hurry!" a voice yelled loudly as a neighbor—one of Mrs. Lee's closest friends, rushed over in a panic. Her hair was wet with sweat and tears streamed down her cheeks.

She yanked Elric's hand with such force that it nearly pulled his shoulder out of socket. She was a plump woman with a very round face. Her cheeks reminded Elric of a chipmunk, especially when she ate. She waddled through the crowd, pulling Elric with each step.

She dragged him to a small opening where dozens of people lay on stretchers; some of them were unconscious, others were worse off. Elric hesitated. The eyes of the dead were dark and empty.

"What is it? What's wrong?" he asked, pulling his hand away.

Then he saw Mrs. Lee lying on a stretcher. There was an IV hooked to her left arm with a bag of blood hanging from a pole. Her eyes were heavy with exhaustion.

"What . . . what happened?" he asked, lower lip quivering. He moved people out of the way to get next to her.

"She must have been in the kitchen when the explosion happened; the glass cut right through her."

He crouched next to her and gently held her hand. Mrs. Lee's eyes searched above, and the moment they saw Elric, they overflowed with tears of joy. She was cold to the touch. Her skin was losing its vibrancy. She was bandaged with thick cloths, but the blood still seeped through. Indecently red, he'd never seen her bleed before. Not in fifteen years.

"Elric, they say she can go at any moment . . . " The woman began crying.

Elric's chest tightened. He couldn't breathe. *No. No. No. Not . . . again*, he thought. Why was this happening? Why was he losing her? Mrs. Lee didn't deserve this. All she did was show love and kindness to everyone she met.

Her eyes barely had the strength to remain open. As she tried to breathe, the sound of fluids gurgled in her mouth.

"Mrs. Lee," he spoke with tear-filled eyes "You're okay, right?"

She turned her head and squinted. Her lips quivered, reaching for his hand. "I'm so glad that you're okay. I was so worried, my son." Her eyes softened with relief. Tears fell down her face, mixing with the drying scarlet stains.

"You don't have to talk, Mrs. Lee. It's okay." He struggled to fight back his own tears as the crimson streams fell from her face. "Look, you're going to be okay. They're going to help you." He looked up at their neighbor who looked on nervously.

Mrs. Lee grabbed his hand. "I know it's been so hard for you, Elric." She coughed, trying to breathe and clear her lungs. "Not knowing your real parents. And then when we lost Mr. Lee . . . I'm sorry you had to carry so much. I wanted to give you more."

He tightened his hand around her cold, limp fingers. "No, you did. I just…" He didn't know what to say. "Please, please stay with me," he begged.

"Elric." Her lips tugged into a smile. "My husband and I were so happy that you were our son," She choked. "You were the best thing that ever happened to us."

He nodded, wiping the red tears and dried blood from her face. She exhaled deeply as her body relaxed.

"Sorry," he whispered, watching the life fade from her eyes. "I'm sorry I wasn't there to keep you safe."

Her hand became heavy and fell by her side as he let it go. His right arm twitched as he began to shiver from the realization that the only mother figure he had ever known was gone.

He searched to find the life that was once in her eyes, hoping to find that tiny sliver of hope and light that kept him happy all these years. The love she showered him with and the light that always pulled him out of the darkness was gone.

Elric's tears burned as they trickled from the corner of his eyes. He shook his head as he looked over Mrs. Lee's body. It was as if the body in front of him wasn't her own but someone else's.

They covered Mrs. Lee with a white sheet.

His fist tightened to the point that his fingernails begin to pierce his skin. They grew longer, sharpening when he felt emotional pain. Blood dripped to the ground from the sharp nails.

He shoved his blood-soaked hands in his pockets and went running through the crowd, leaving her body and the woman crying next to her. He broke through the group of people searching for a way to escape this nightmare.

He ran, and ran, knocking people down, and jumping over equipment, but before he could get a good stride, he fell.

"Elric, where are you going?" Jen screamed. "What's going on?"

"Mrs. Lee," he whispered, staring in shock at his bloodstained hands. The skin had already healed, and the nails weren't long anymore "She's gone. She died right in front of me."

Jen cupped her mouth in horror. "What?" She knelt next to him. "What happened?"

She began to sob.

"She was in the kitchen. The blast that nearly killed us must have hit this town harder than we thought." He slammed his fist into the ground. He couldn't repeat the story or think about the fact that she was gone.

She wiped the tears from her face. "Elric, I'm so sorry."

Mrs. Lee had treated her like family too. She was always going to Jen's games and supporting her, even when Jen's parents couldn't go.

"I know you want to run away from all this, but you have to stay." Tears flowed down her chin. "I need you."

She helped him to his feet and kissed him. Her warm lips pressed gently against his. She buried her face into his chest and gripped his shoulders. "I'm sorry..."

"Yeah, me too," he said, looking on with a blank expression. He finally got to kiss the girl he was in love with, but he felt nothing. The pain was too much. His limbs were heavy like lead, chest pounding. Even while gazing into Jen's eyes, he wanted to drop and curl up into the fetal position . . . and die. He was truly alone in the world.

A voice on a loudspeaker took him by surprise.

"Okay, everybody. Listen up. We know you're frightened and confused. We have security around the perimeter, but we need to get everyone to safety immediately. We have transportation vehicles ready to bring all of you up north to Clemson. There we have a relief center set up. Please stay calm and listen to anyone in uniform. This will be an easy and fast process." As he finished, men in uniform begin to lead people onto the back of the large trucks.

"Come with me and my parents, Elric," She looked up and held her hand out. "We can do this, right?"

He gritted his teeth, looking toward the burning town. He wanted to go after every single one of those creatures, anyone responsible for Mrs. Lee's death. He wanted to make them pay. "Come on, you two. We got to get you loaded up. Where are your families?" a man in uniform asked.

"My mom and dad are over there." Jen pointed to a group of people way in the back.

"Well, let's get you over there. How about you? Where's your family, kid?" he asked looking at Elric.

"I don't have one." Elric glared at the dried blood in the palm of his hands.

"He's coming with me. He'll be alright." She grabbed his hand, pulling him toward where her parents awaited.

The crowd was growing anxious. Fights broke out and punches were thrown as people fought for spots on the trucks. Families were separated due to the increasing desperation as trucks were hitting their carrying capacity.

"We know you're scared, but to make this a smooth process, we have to calm down and relax. This fighting and arguing will only halt the process and get us nowhere," the man yelled from the loudspeaker.

Elric looked at the dozens of bandaged faces. Their bodies were battered. They moaned and cried about their injuries. But they were lucky enough to live.

"Elric?" Jen called out.

He hesitated, thinking about going back to the woman to mourn over Mrs. Lee, but he was better off with Jen. With no one else, the only person left was her. He followed her until they caught up to her parents.

Chapter 10

The Darkness before the Dawn

Jen rushed over to hug a slim, dark-skinned man with tears in her eyes.

"Your mother told me you were safe. Where were you?" Jen's father greeted her with a loving embrace. He looked to be in fair condition compared to everybody else. He had a gash over his right eye, which was stitched and bandaged.

"Jennifer, what's wrong?" he asked, then he looked over to Elric.

He couldn't answer Mr. Reeves.

Jen's lips moved slightly as she stepped back. She held Elric's hand. "Mrs. Lee, Dad. She didn't make it."

Mr. Reeves swallowed hard as the lines on his face deepened. His shoulder slump, as he laid a gentle hand on Elric's shoulder. "Elric, I'm so – so sorry to hear that. Is there anywhere else you can go? Any other family?"

Elric shook his head. No one would claim him now, maybe he'd be put in the foster care program again if the world didn't end anyways.

Mr. Reeves took a deep breath. "Well then, you're coming with us."

Elric's brows bunched as he looked at Jen then at her father. "What's that, sir?"

"We're not leaving out here on your own Elric. That's insane. You'll come with us until we're able to get things straighten out, ok?"

He nodded. "Thank you, Mr. Reeves."

The man hugged Elric and pulled Jen in as well.

Shots echoing in the darkness shattered the union; people began screaming. Everyone looked up in fear, facing the direction where chaos ensued. The night air rung with gun fire, nothing like the pistol crackles. These were rhythmic *thumps* of a machine gun, blazing the air, and filling it with the sweet smell of gunpowder.

The energy of the crowd changed from agitation to fear and panic. People began pushing and shoving, crushing each other to jump on the back of the large trucks. Elric heard the screams of a woman begging for them to stop as they were crushing her.

Her arm flailed from the back of a crowded truck. Jen's father pulled him away as they raced to a truck with Jen and her mother; there was still plenty of room.

Elric's heart raced knowing that the army of beasts had finally reached them. Jen's father pushed his wife up and then he helped Jen and Elric on. He pulled himself up and began helping others.

Once the vehicle filled, the truck began to move forward, following the lead vehicle, which was making a U-turn into the exit road.

"Mom, there's not enough trucks for all those people," Jen whispered.

Her mother looked out.

"They've got to have more vehicles coming, honey. Don't worry," she replied.

As the vehicles turned, they could see what people were screaming about. The army of creatures began to pour into the field of people. The roars and screams drowned out the gunfire as the collision of two forces took place. The flipped one of the vehicles over, hurling it into the crowd.

People climbed on the back of trucks as the crowd scattered throughout the town as gunfire turned the area into a warzone. The pings of copper hitting metal sparked as the beast's armor absorbed the bullets.

"Get these people out of here. Now!" the man screamed through the loudspeaker.

In the sky, shadowy figures glided toward them in the distance. Even in the darkness of the night, Elric knew it was the large bats from before.

"Oh, my word. What are they?" a woman asked as she noticed the winged creatures darting through the air.

The creatures shrieked loudly as they descended onto the crowd. One landed next to the truck and began its vicious assault on a small group just beside them. They watched in horror.

Jen's father sheltered Jen from seeing the sight as they all sat quietly without making a move.

The large bat shrieked, showing sharpened fangs that dripped with fresh blood. It slashed through the crowd with claws like steak knives, cutting a bloody path through the frightened crowd like a scythe through a cornfield.

"We have to get out of here," a man yelled to the driver. "Hey, people are being torn apart out here!"

The trucks peeled out through the dirt road, several others just behind.

The monstrosities forced themselves on the innocent people of Lexington, slaughtering them like cattle. Elric tightened his fists, but what could he do?

"I can't believe this is happening. This is just . . . I don't know." Mrs. Reeves gripped her husband's hand.

Smoke rose high above Lexington and beyond it were the orange glow of flames. Gunshots rung in the air over the roaring engine as the town shrunk in the distance, nothing more than an orange glow. Black columns spewing from its center. Elric put his head into shaking hands. His hair damp with sweat; he reeked of burnt wood and vinyl.

A heavy thump shook the vehicle and made everyone alert.

"Just potholes in the road?" a woman asked.

The thumping became louder, heavier, and much more frequent than potholes in the road. Screams of terror rose from behind as the blaring sound of someone laying on a truck horn made everyone jump; they all looked out the back.

Six other trucks made it out of Lexington. One of the trucks was sent flying off the road. Passengers thrown from the vehicle.

"What's going on back there?" A truck blew past.

"You have to step on it. Now!" the driver in the vehicle behind them yelled up to their driver.

The truck's speed greatly increased as a monstrous roar bellowed from behind them.

The thumps became quakes as the roof of the truck behind them was ripped right off its support beams. The vehicle swerved violently and lost control as it slammed into a ditch. That's when Elric noticed the rampaging beast galloping with increasing speed.

A large rhino-like beast, the size of one of the cargo trucks, came stomping through. It gave another bellow as it rammed into one of the trucks, which swerved to keep its balance and speed. Nothing stopped it as it thrashed through the convoy.

"Elric, it's just like the one that tossed that fire truck!" Jen yelled.

They watched as it plowed into the fifth vehicle in the convoy, sending it rolling into the large field of trees. The loud crash and the sounds of screams frightened everyone in the back of the truck.

Elric could feel each crushing force as it bulldozed its way closer and closer to their vehicle. He could see the thick, gray skin of the beast showing through its battered, metal armor.

Don't you want to help them? A rumbling voice spoke from deep within him, rolling through his chest like thunder. *Don't you want to save them?*

A sharp tingling rolled over his shoulders and gripped his chest. Elric dropped to his knees, trying to fight the strange sensation. He closed his eyes, trying to catch his breath.

When he opened his eyes, he was in a strange black cavern. Everyone was gone. No longer was he surrounded by the screams of fear or the grunts of a monster. Just the strange thud of a heartbeat, and humidity that made his skin sticky.

It was just like when he fought Simon on the trail, but this time he could see clearer. The cave was like a dungeon of some sort; humid and wet. Chains rustled in the darkness as he looked up in awe and fear.

Massive red eyes gaped over him; glowing like burning coals. The pupils large and intense; fierce with rage that wanted to devour him. The silhouette of massive beast. A dragon hovered over him the size of a building.

Don't you? the voice growled as the eyes widened.

Elric stopped. He couldn't breathe. His throat tightened. His heart was racing, and everything in him screamed to run! Darkness slithered up his legs, wrapping around him like black tendrils, binding him tightly. He struggled to break free.

What are you? What do you want? he screamed.

The eyes were enticing as they glowed. *To help you destroy everything in your path.*

Elric opened his eyes the cold air, and the roaring of the truck greeting him. He was gripped tightly by Jen and her father who helped him onto his feet. *Did I imagine that whole thing?*

No, I'm right here in you, the deepened voice grumbled from his belly.

Elric searched the back of the truck, but everyone was focused on the beast. *In me?*

Yes.

He looked up as the beast knocked another vehicle into a field. The truck screeched off the road, smashing into the trees and crashed. The horn blared as it faded into the distance.

Nothing stood between the large beast galloping toward them.

"You won't escape either!" it roared.

The metal armor chimed with each stride against its dry, gray skin. A large, muscular arm with thick, chubby fingers reached for the truck. If the beast got a hold of them, it would easily send it flying like all the rest; they wouldn't survive.

Elric glared into the beast's eyes, which were sunk deep into its rigid skull. The mouth formed into a beak as horns protruded from the bridge of its nostrils. It roared in anger, trying to catch up. Its fists crushing the tar as it stumbled forward to keep its balance and speed.

You're what helped me kill that bat earlier, right? he asked.

You were facing death, so I stepped in. The inner voice was like thunder.

Elric thought about Jen. She was all he had left now. He wouldn't let it end this way. Whatever power allowed him to kill that large bat earlier, he had to use it again. He stood up, glaring into the black beady eyes of the creature as it thrashed its way forward. *Alright, help me, please.*

Gladly, the voice grumbled.

A sensation came from within, like a cluster of fireworks going off in his gut. Fear and sorrow vanished. They were thrown out by rage and vengeance. He thought of Mrs. Lee and the people of Lexington—these monsters were responsible for every death; they were responsible for destroying his world and everyone in it.

"Elric, sit down. Have you totally lost it?" Jen screamed as she reached for him.

He pulled his arm away, glaring at the beast.

The voice came again egging him on. *Yes, save them. Let me help.*

Yes, he answered back. *Give me the power to protect them, please!*

The spewing of darkness coursed through his body with a sinister sting that tangled the nape of his neck. Hatred took over as blackness consumed his heart. His pupils burned with a red glow as an impish grin spilled across his face. He stepped toward the beast, which held its large, thick digits out towards the vehicle. He could see the darkness consuming him, but no one else could in the blackness.

"Kid, you got to get back!" A man from the opposite side of the bench came over and tried to pull him to the back of the vehicle. An invisible force shoved the man away.

The darkness shrouded Elric, taking on a life of its own. His insides burned with agony as he fell to his knees. He hunched over, gripping his ribs.

It'll hurt the first time, but once you get used to it, you'll learn to rely on me. The invisible darkness was trying to possess him. *Give me all that you are ...*

Frightened by what was happening, he began to fight the darkness. "No, I won't let you. Not now, not ever." He blurted, catching everyone's attention.

Elric pounded his fist against the floor as he faded in and out of consciousness. He had to keep whatever this thing was from taking over his body.

A loud, thumping echoed from overhead as the glowing flashes of red shells rained down on the beast, catching Elric's attention. A helicopter poured gunfire into the face of the rhino, sending it howling into the woods. Elric clanged to reality watching the beast depart.

You need me, Elric Blake. I'm an inescapable fate that you can't run from. The time will come, and you will give in to me! the voice growled, fading deep within him.

His body began to jerk as he seized, doing all he could to not lose consciousness. To not let that *thing* come back.

Jen rushed to his side rolling Elric over to his back. "Elric! Elric!" He was groggy; barely able to focus on the faces above.

He took a deep breath as the rage and awful energy of the darkness began to dissolve and crumble.

"You alright? I thought you were going to throw yourself off the truck," Jen said, helping him up to his feet.

"You completely lost it, kid. You were talking to yourself and everything. You sure you're alright?" Jen's father asked.

"Yeah, I'll be alright." His vision cleared as he regained his balance. He wiped the sweat with a trembling hand. Elric relaxed, lying his head on the back of the truck. Every time he blinked; he could see those large, glowing eyes. Whatever *it* was, it was trying to consume him.

The helicopter faded into the shimmering glow where Lexington burned to the ground, dark columns trailing overhead. He left all he knew there, including the boy he used to be.

A gentle hand grasped his fingers as he looked over to see Jen. Her eyes were heavy and red like cherries. Her head bounced off the chest of her mother as the rough road rocked her back and forth. He sighed and gripped her hand as he focused on the glow of Lexington.

The vehicle swerved onto I-95 north. The slightest bump put everyone on edge, expecting another monster.

Elric looked out the back and noticed the change in scenery. It was nothing like living near the harbor. The smell of sea salt was replaced by the smell of freshly cut grass entangled with the stench of manure. Buildings were replaced by countryside and farmland.

He lay back and focused on the back of the truck and the signs of I-95. He peeked over to watch whose eyes softened on him. He glanced down at their clenched hands and wondered where he'd go now with no home or family.

Chapter 11

Sanctuary

The changing gears of the trucks woke Elric from his deep sleep. His eyes burned from the lack of rest, but he fought sleep to the very end.

A couple of the adults were already wide awake. Elric could tell by the worry lines on foreheads and deep bags beneath reddened eyes that they didn't sleep at all.

The truck slowed until it came to an abrupt stop. Anyone who wasn't awake was jolted forward. Thank goodness for Mr. Reeves's reflexes as he gently tightened his hold around Jennifer and her mother.

"We actually made it," a woman in the back said, slowly sitting up.

The driver and passenger doors squeaked open and slammed closed, rattling the back of the truck.

"Is everyone okay?" a soldier asked, poking his head from the back of the truck.

A couple of the adults nodded, stretching and yawning as the rising sun peered through the covering on the vehicle.

"If you call almost getting killed by a talking rhinoceros okay? Well, yes, never better," an older man replied with harsh sarcasm.

"Well, you're alive." The soldier pulled a ladder out from under the vehicle. "My name's Sergeant Ray. I hope you enjoyed the rough ride and didn't wet and crap yourselves."

He lowered the hatch of the truck and helped everyone out.

"Never thought I'd see the sun again," Jen's father said, watching the pink canvas of the orange ball that crawled up from behind the mountains. Mr. Reeves grabbed the hands of one of the soldiers and shook it vigorously. "My name's Johnny Reeves, but you can call me John. If it wasn't for you two, I don't think my family would've made it out alive."

"It was at the cost of a lot of lives, but we got a couple out, so the mission wasn't a complete shit show," the man said, looking around. "Half our platoon was left back in Lexington, and we lost a few vehicles with passengers. As soon as we hit north on I-95, we lost communications with them."

Mr. Reeves said, "I know it's not much, but we're grateful. I speak for my family and probably everyone here when I say thank you."

Before Sergeant Ray could get another word out, he was called over by another guy in uniform.

"Hey, you get any sleep?" Jen asked, stepping beside Elric and looking out into the town.

"I'll be alright." He shrugged her off and jumped out the truck.

"Hey, everyone from the twenty-ton cargos, please set up a horseshoe formation around me," Sergeant Ray yelled out.

Everyone huddled up and did as he asked.

"Welcome to Clemson for those of you who don't know. You'll be safe here. From what we've gathered, portals don't show up too close in the same vicinity,"

"Portals? What the hell . . . What is this sci-fi garbage?" the older man continued with his sarcasm.

Sergeant Ray smirked. "It's been a long night, and I guess *some* of you didn't get a chance to watch the news. The entire world was attacked last night. These *portals* or black holes acted as doorways releasing monsters that attacked millions of people. So yes, some serious sci-fi garbage indeed."

"From what they've gathered," Jen whispered, "these things just showed up. How did they figure that out so quickly?"

Elric nodded. "Probably just something to tell everyone so nobody loses their mind like in Lexington."

Jen swallowed hard. "Seems a little too late for that. Look around."

The group was small, nothing in comparison to the field full of people getting help from humanitarian services. Elric wondered if anyone else made it. Soldiers patrolled through the town of Clemson. Armored to the nine with assault rifles. *At least we'll be ok if anything happens, I guess.*

"We have an entire security perimeter set up for your safety and guards all around. Medical supplies are for anyone who needs them. One of the hotels has opened its doors. They are trying to make things as comfortable as possible for you. You get a nice hot meal, and you guessed it: showers. The people of Clemson were also kind enough to donate clothing, too. You'll find a bin in the hotel lobby." A sigh of relief came over the group and whispers broke out.

"If you walk right this way and follow Private Kelly, you'll be all set with rooms and food."

They followed a tall, gangly, pale boy. He looked nervous. His Adam's apple stuck out, reminding Elric of a turkey. His lips quivered as everyone followed.

"Out of twelve twenty-ton cargo trucks, only eight made it to Clemson?" a soldier whispered as they walked through.

Elric trailed Jen as she walked behind her parents, making sure not to get separated. The town was a lot larger than what they were used to. Clemson was a maze of narrow winding streets, lined with shops, and restaurants. Houses and apartments all piled up on top of each other. In comparison Lexington was more of a town that evolved from a village that had no city planning.

"Lexington has nothing on this huh, Elric?" Jen asked, looking around.

"You mean *had,*" he whispered.

"Right." She wrapped her fingers around his hand. "There's nothing anyone can say or do to make you feel better, Elric. But at least we're both here together, right?"

He searched her eyes, wanting to find solace in the fact that he was there with her. He would have wanted nothing more, but there was so much blood spilled, and lives lost. Then there was the fear of losing himself to this thing. He gripped his chest when he thought about it.

They walked through Clemson. There were large strips of stores, and a nice-sized hospital on its own street. On the opposite side was a diner, a post office, library, and a grocery store.

Clemson filled with commotion as a crowd formed around them. People were asking about Lexington. Out of the group that survived the horrors of last night, no one said a word. Elric wondered if it was exhaustion or fear of reliving the traumatic experience again.

They followed the crowd of people over to the hotel, which was the size of a small mall.

"Wow, this looks great. I bet the rooms must be nice and cozy," Mrs. Reeves said.

The soldier brought them all inside to get room keys. The interior of the hotel was classy. The wooden floors were made of redwood and large abstract paintings decorated the walls. There was a nice resting area, which had a large carpet laid out among couches and love seats. It was nothing like the small motel in Lexington, which everyone made fun of because of the bedbug situation.

They dug through the clothing bin, claiming anything that was close to fitting. Once they received room keys, they were guided to rooms. Elric, because he was by himself, was given his own room next to the Reeves family.

"Hey everyone, with everything that's happened, I think we all should take some hot showers and get some sleep. That'll give us some time to process everything." Mr. Reeves said, struggling to find the words. They all agreed, Jen giving Elric a gentle nod and a soft expression of sympathy.

In his room, Elric struggled to accept what happened. He couldn't believe Mrs. Lee was gone nor could he believe he was on his own. He failed. He failed to be there for her, and now she was gone. He thought about Mr. Lee suffering in the hospital, withering away. Now he had the image of Mrs. Lee being covered with a white sheet. Body covered with lacerations and stained red. Tears streamed as he tried not to relive it. The smell of gunpowder and burning tires still stained his nose, and clothes. His shirt stained with the now, brown, aged blood.

The silence was broken by a knock at the door. Elric took a deep breath, wiped his face, and rose to his feet. He cracked the door open to see Jen's worried face.

"Hey. You mind if I come in?"

He nodded, stepping away and leaving the door open.

He fell on the king-sized bed, which was way too big for a person of his stature. He exhaled, gazing at the ceiling.

"My parents went and picked up some Chinese food. You should come eat. We set up the table for four?"

He remained silent. Jen's voice had the kind of gentle concern Mrs. Lee use to have when he got sick.

She came around to the side of the bed. "Losing Mrs. Lee hurts, I know, but—"

"How can you possibly know?" he asked, looking up with bloodshot eyes.

She looked down upon him confused.

"Jen, be real for a second. You've had everything from the start. You were adopted by a wealthy family; you were popular in school; every girl wanted to be you . . . every boy wanted you. I was a nobody from the start. No matter how hard I tried, things always got worse. Now I have nothing ...." He sat up and looked down at his hands. "I shouldn't be surprised."

"You can't mean that." Streaming tears made her caramel cheeks glisten in the dim rom light.

He looked up catching the pain in her eyes. His voice softened. "Look, I just need to be alone, okay? I'm not hungry."

She nodded wiping the tears away. "Okay. Whatever."

She walked to the door and hesitated for a moment. Elric thought she was going to say something else, but she sighed, closing the door behind her.

Throughout the day, he stared at the ceiling until exhaustion took him, drowning him in what he feared the most. Nightmares of last night's events ravaged his imagination. Behind closed eyelids, the darkness filled him with fear of monsters that came out of the black mass. The screams, roars, and gunshots became a twisted lullaby that locked him into his nightmares as he fought to escape them.

The shrieks of those bats and the pounding echoes of machinegun fire pierced through the empty silence of the room. His body jerked and rolled from side to side. He could still smell the burning, thick, black smoke, and the smell of gunpowder. And the strange metallic smell of blood.

Elric woke up, screaming into the night, pillow soaked in sweat and tears. All those people in Lexington, slaughtered like cattle, rattled him. His pain manifested into a newfound rage. Was it possible for any of this to get better?

Chapter 12

Destiny is Calling Me

Elric awoke, escaping the screams and roars of his horrific nightmares. He almost forgot where he was. He sat up, wiping the sweat from his face. His sheets were cold and soaked.

He threw on his jeans and shoes and slipped into the dim lit hallway. He headed out the back, gripped by the bitter cold breeze that blew through his sweater. He stuffed his hands in his pockets and walked around the perimeters of the parking lot. Lights kept the parking lot lit and the moon gave the town an eerie glow. The air was brisk, a sign of the coming fall and blistering cold winter.

He made two laps around the perimeter before deciding it was time to go back in. As he came to the door, he noticed a girl with her back turned. She was looking up at the moon. He shrugged it off and began to head inside.

"You're a strange one, Elric Blake," she said as white puffs escaped her lips.

He stopped; fingertips still wrapped around the icy handle of the door. He wanted to continue pulling; he knew he should. But he let go. He couldn't grasp why he let go.

"What did you say?" He looked over at her.

Her back was still turned. She continued to go up and down on her tiptoes with her arms crossed. Her breath rolled off her right shoulder in a damp mist.

"You said my name," He said edging by her. "Are you from Lexington? How do you know me?"

"I know a lot of things," she said, crinkling her nose.

He stepped back searching her eyes. Body shivering from the site. Her eyes shimmered with color. Like spilled oil on a wet street, swirling with the colors of the rainbow. She moved towards him.

The hair on the back of his neck bristled. "You're one of those things, like back in Lexington, aren't you?" He gulped.

She chuckled. She was young, tall with a slender physique. Maybe in her mid-twenties, and beautiful.

He stepped back taking his hands out his pockets. As the images of last night came rushing back, his heart pounded against his chest. Everything in his body screamed run. His legs were all for it. *I-I won't leave Jen and her parents.*

She stopped and tilted her head to the side. "I'm surprised you haven't taken off into the woods yet."

"If you plan on killing me, I'm not making it easy." His knees knocked, but he meant every word. If he bit the dust now, at least he'd be with Mr. and Mrs. Lee.

"That's a good sign, Elric," she said with a tone of approval.

She walked past him and took a seat on the curb. His eyebrows bunched. "What are you doing? Aren't you going to kill me?"

She pulled a few black strands from her face. "Elric, if I wanted to do that, I would have done it years ago. I'm not one of them."

He looked on with bunched eyebrows. "Who are you then?"

"Someone who wants to help. Especially with everything that's happening." A faint curve to her lips revealed pearly whites.

He shook his head. "Well, if you're not one of those things, then who and what are you?"

"A friend of your father." She beamed with a shiver.

"Mr. Lee?"

"No, Elric, your *real* father…"

Elric's eyes widened. He couldn't grasp it; she must have been messing with him. No, this whole thing, her insane colorful eyes, it was a nightmare, a hallucination.

"Elric, I know what you're searching for." She stood up and stepped closer to him.

He struggled to believe stepping back. "Who . . . who are you?" Her eyes swirled with the colors of the rainbow. "You said you knew my father, my real father!"

She placed her hand on his chest. Even through the sweater, he could feel how cold she was. She nodded looking into his bloodshot eyes. "I figured as much. That beast inside has become a nuisance already." She sighed and walked away from him.

As she did, he placed his hand on his chest. "Beast?"

"The world is changing. Everything you thought you knew is gone. The gears of your destiny have been put into motion," she crooned.

"What are you talking about? None of this makes sense!" His voice was raised with frustration

"I imagine it doesn't right now, but you have a gift." Her vibrant eyes rested on his. "You lost someone close to you last night. A lot of people lost their lives not just here, but all over the world."

He was silent. He couldn't deny the horrors of last night. Death swept through the town he once called home, claiming anyone it pleased. It was hard to believe that last night's events were repeated all around the world, changing history.

"I know you don't know me, and I may frighten you, but if I told you that you have the power to save the world, wouldn't you use it?" Her eyes narrowed.

His efface hardened. "You're kidding me. This thing wants to kill me. How can I use it to save the world?"

She stared into the sky, watching the brightness of the moon. He thought about Jen and her parents. They were all he had now. He had to keep them safe if he had the power to do so.

"If you trust me, stand with me and you'll learn to control your powers. If you don't, just tell me," she said, reverently. "I'll leave right now, and you'll ever see me again."

A chilled breeze blew through his hair and sent goosebumps down his spine. He thought about his comics and how he dreamt of having the power to save the world. Whatever it was inside him wanted nothing to do with saving the world. He got that from those blood red eyes.

"I guess you've made your choice." She began walking out of the parking lot, sneakers scuffing the cracked surface.

He swallowed hard. "What do I have to do?"

She turned. "What was that?"

"What do I do? How can I control whatever this is inside me? I mean, I better learn now. Eventually I'll need to, right?"

She nodded. "Go to Boston and find a man named Zaroule. You'll find the answers you're looking for with him."

He chuckled, taken aback. "What? Are you serious? You make it sound like Boston isn't this massive place. I mean, sure there's not a lot of people named Zaroule out there. But seriously, I think I need a little bit more direction."

"Look, I'll help you find him. You have questions, and Zaroule can answer them. I just need you to do the leg work." She leaned forward. "Can you do that?"

Elric swallowed hard, but he nodded. Whether this was a dream or reality, it didn't matter. This girl knew something about the thing inside him, and if she were right, he could control it.

"Tomorrow night, leave." She began to walk away.

"I can't just leave like that. What about..." He thought about Jen and her parents. "I have people here who need me."

She turned. "Controlling those powers may not only save this world, but they can keep Jen safe as well, Elric. Do as I say."

He looked up, surprised that this girl knew about Jen. If it meant keeping her safe from harm's way, he would do it.

"You look so much like him," Her voice echoed in the parking lot as she vanished into the darkness. "Like Cole ..."

"Wait! Who are you? Where do I meet you in two days?"

She was gone. The scraping of colorful fallen leaves scraped across the parking lot. As much as he wanted to believe it was a dream, the cold air tingling on his neck told him otherwise.

He slid his key into the slot and pulled the door open. He was welcomed by the warm air of the hallway. The corridor was bright but silent. Everyone was still asleep.

He walked into his room and fell on the bed before taking a deep breath. The moonlight pierced through the heavy drapes of the hotel room, filling it with light.

"Boston? Zaroule?" he said to himself, remembering the last words from the strange girl.

Everyone around you safe? a heavy voice came from within. *Why do you want to protect everyone else? They treated you like garbage. This isn't a comic book.*

Elric tried to ignore it, but he could feel the voice in his chest. He could even feel it in his bones. It was like a speaker was embedded in him.

You think you can control me. The voice crackled in laughter. *Many of your ancestors have tried and they all failed. You'll be driven insane if you try.*

Elric swallowed. *Kind of too late for that.*

You will fail, Elric Blake. Like your father, and his father….

You knew my father too, huh? Elric asked.

The voice growled and became silent.

A chill came over his body that made him regret talking to the beast. Maybe speaking to it and realizing its existence made it stronger. He didn't know, but it never spoke again. What did it all mean? He couldn't sleep; he didn't dare to close his eyes.

The dark corners of the room that the moon light couldn't touch, danced with shadows, reminding him of the attack on Lexington. Screams echoed in the silence, creating goosebumps all over his body. In every corner of the room, he could see the shimmering crimson eyes of the thing inside him, searching.

Chapter 13

My Secret

Elric jerked awake from the slamming of a door outside his room. The sunlight creeped in, the curtains adding a golden glow to the morning light. It reminded Elric of the Saturday mornings when Mr. Lee would wake him to go fishing. For a moment his mind conjured the soft voices and giggles of the Lees talking outside his room. Maybe …it was all a nightmare.

A knock pounded against the door. Elric rubbed his eyes and tossed the covers off him. He shuffled over and opened the door to see Jen—whose eyes narrowed, and lips twisted with bitterness. She was pissed.

Her folded arms and stance read: "Kiss my ass." She wore her high school basketball shorts and a white tank top. "

You must have slept good," she said crossly, pushing the door open and brushing by him. "You know its noon, right?"

"Are you kidding me?" He looked at the clock that rested on the nightstand that read twelve-fifteen. "I didn't notice." She shook her head.

"You haven't noticed a lot lately . . . " she answered with a smug attitude.

He nodded, thinking about how he treated her yesterday. He was more than a jerk, and all she did was stay by his side. "Jen, I'm sorry about yesterday. After everything that happened, I honestly didn't know where my head was. I still don't."

"Look, I know you think losing Mrs. Lee only hurt you, but I loved her too, you know." Her voice was strong and sharp, no punches held. "She was family to me, too! She was like my second mom! You can't act like her death only hurt you!" Tears rolled down her face.

He hugged her as she fell into his embrace, crying with tears that he wished to share. He cried so much at this point that his eyes burned.

"Elric, I've always been there for you. I always have and always will no matter what!" She shook her head. "But if you act like an asshole again, I'll give you a beating worse than Simon ever could."

He was lost in the tears of her hazel eyes. "I won't do it again. I promise."

She cupped his chin, racing a finger over his cheek. "I'm going to take a shower. I'll come back in about twenty minutes, then we'll find something to do, okay?"

Elric nodded as she ran out the room. He couldn't stop smiling, thinking about her, the girl of his dreams. He had loved Jen since they were kids. Now he knew the answer to the question that always made him nervous around her: *Does she feel the same?*

He fell on his bed, torn between the love of his life or learning to control a power that could save her and the world.

"Be careful what you wish for," he mumbled, thinking about all the times he wished for superpowers.

He took a nice hot shower washing away the grime and blood of the other night. He threw on some donated clothes from the hotel bin and headed to the lobby. There were a couple of computers opened to guests. Lucky enough, they weren't packed with people.

Elric thought about the strange woman from last night. She called herself a friend of his father. If he were going to be serious about what she advised, then he would have to leave. He thought about Jen and how she would react. He'd have to leave late in the evening without anyone knowing. It was the only way.

He searched the internet, hoping to find an available bus schedule to Boston. Instead, the internet was flooded with news about the attacks and the destruction across the world. Images of beasts were posted all over the internet, videos, and tweets trending *#apocalypse*.

Hundreds of towns and cities across the world were devastated. No government could explain what was happening or where the attacks came from. He snapped out of the chaos and regained his focus for bus schedules, but all transportation was cancelled. Hitchhiking through the Maine woods, especially during the *#apocalypse* was hard to swallow.

"Hey, I thought you were going to stay in your room?" Jen said, leaning over.

He clicked out of the browser. "Yeah, sorry. I ugh . . . got kind of bored and wanted to check out the hotel a little."

She shook her head. "Don't worry about it. Let's just get out of here."

They rushed out of the hotel. Elric could tell Jen needed to get out from being cooped up with her parents. She was flustered and made sure her exasperated sighs were heard.

"Everything okay?" Elric reluctantly asked; he hoped she wasn't still too upset with him.

"My parents have been fighting about where to go from here. My mom wants to go back to New York, and my dad wants to head to the mountains."

"So, your dad wants to stay in Maine then?"

Jen looked up with narrowed eyes. "I just don't think it's going to matter. The TV said these attacks hit everywhere. Maybe this *is* the end of the world."

He thought about her words and the fear behind her eyes. He gripped his chest, thinking about the thing inside him.

"Elric, what if we don't make it out of this?"

He looked into her eyes and saw something he had never seen in her before. Hopelessness. "I've never known Jen Reeves to be afraid of anything. You're talking like me right now."

She shook her head. "Elric, I'm serious!"

"So am I." He put on the best smile he could. "Someone's gonna come along and figure all this out, the army or whoever. Right now, we can't give up. *You* can't give up."

Jen shrugged, crossing her arms as she walked. Elric was surprised by his own words. He wondered where they came from.

They walked through Clemson, which was as empty as the hotel. A few people were seen stuffing their vehicles with bags of groceries and other belongings, but it was cleared out. There were lines of vehicles leaving the town. Fear must have gotten the best of them.

They continued through, checking out the local shops and restaurants. Because of all the destruction that happened just three towns over, nobody would expect a cloudless day with a warm breeze blowing. The leaves were pink and orange as they changed to a pale-yellow tint.

They came to a couple who were packing up a large SUV. Jen stopped to watch as the two frantically moved around the vehicle. Elric wanted to pull her along, but her eyes hungered for answers.

"Where are you going?" She looked around the town. "Why is everyone leaving?"

The women looked up at Jen as if she were crazy.

"You kids don't look familiar. Survivors of Lexington, right?" the man replied, closing the trunk of the large SUV.

Elric already hated the title. "Yeah."

"I'm sorry about what happened. I heard a lot of people didn't make it out alive." His eyes were red with worry and exhaustion. "News says there can be more attacks at any time." The man looked in the back seat placing his hand on the window.

A tiny hand with chubby fingers reached for his hand. Elric understood now. They were all leaving Clemson, abandoning their town. Even with the soldiers patrolling the streets, it wasn't enough.

Jen bit her bottom lip. "If that's the case where are you going to go? It sounds like anywhere is going to be dangerous?"

The women pulled her husband. "That's enough. Let's go. We can't stay here any longer." She looked over at Jen and Elric. "I'm sorry."

They both nodded, watching the couple jump in the truck and peel off down the road. Elric wondered where they were heading; maybe they had some fortified sanctuary or doomsday bomb shelter.

Jen walked away in shock. She sat on a stoop in front of a shop that was locked and boarded up. She was hunched over, gripping her knees close to her chest. Tears fell between her legs, smacking the stone steps of the shop.

He licked his lips and swallowed hard. "Jen, are you ok?" He thought about how dumb the question was, but it was too late.

She clenched her fist as she rocked back and forth. "I don't know what else to do, Elric. Where are we going to go?"

He sat next to her, wrapping his arms around her. "Jen," he said, as she looked up. "I promise on my life that I'm not going to allow anything to happen to you. I know it's hard to believe, and it doesn't seem like I'm capable . . . but I'll protect you."

She shook her head. "Elric, this isn't one of your comic books. We watched people die. They were people we knew. People we loved."

His heart sunk as he thought about Mrs. Lee's words. He thought about the thing inside him and the words of the women last night, and his decision became clearer. He swallowed hard, making another decision. He hoped it wouldn't freak her out.

"Hey." He picked her chin up. "Do you trust me?"

"Of course." She wiped her face and sniffled.

He took her hand, luring her back to the hotel room. He didn't say a word, fighting with his conscience the entire time. He was firm on his decision. He was going try and show her his powers.

He brought her into his room, and before closing the door, he checked the hallway. This was worse than an exam in geometry class. He took a deep breath before looking at her.

"Elric, what's going on with you?"

"Jen, back in Lexington when we split up to get away from those monsters . . . I didn't just escape." He took a seat on the corner of his bed, focusing on the blank TV screen he didn't dare turn on. His reflection looking back.

"What?" She sat beside him. "Then what happened?"

He swallowed hard looking down at his hands. "I killed the one that came after me."

Her face bent in anger "Elric, you don't have to lie to me. We were all scared."

"No." He shook his head, took a deep breath, and closed his eyes. Focusing, knowing he would have to come face to face with that thing. Burning fumes stung his nostrils as he returned to the darkness of the cave. *So, it worked,* Elric said.

The heavy thump of enormous footsteps made the ground shake.

Interesting, the beastly voice replied. Elric looked up into its gaping red eyes. *You've figured out how to come here at will?*

Elric looked down at his hands. He could feel the darkness coursing through him. That was all he needed, just a little to show Jen. He ignored the creature.

The beast laughed. *As I intertwine with you, Elric Blake, know that your emotions will become my emotions, and mine yours. So, keep using my powers as you want. To your heart's content. I will have my way.*

Elric turned to watch the silhouette of the beast stomp away.

What's that supposed to mean?

Only silence echoed in the darkness.

Whatever, Elric mumbled to himself.

He opened his eyes, looking down at Jen, who looked on still confused. "Are you going to continue to ignore me and zone out?"

He shook his head. "I'll show you,"

His eyes flickered to a crimson red as he caught the glow on the TV screen, and a dark aura formed around him. An ominous wind filled the room, blowing his covers and clothes all around the place. Jen's eyes widened. She tucked her head down and clasped her hands over her head.

He saw the distress she was in and stopped allowing the darkness to come through him. Everything halted, and his eyes became dark brown again. He took a deep breath as she gazed into his eyes.

She shook her head in disbelief and ran past him out the room. The door to the other room where her parents were slammed shut, rattling his own door.

He stood frozen. "What the hell did I just do?" His breathing quickened as anxiety took over.

He wondered if he should rush over and grab Jen before she said anything, or maybe it was too late. Maybe they were already calling the police or the Army. He sat on his bed, feeling the world close in all around him. Did he just lose the one person he loved in this world?

Chapter 14

———)(●)(———

How to Say Goodbye

A few hours went by. The shuffling of footsteps came and went in front of his door. Each time they did forced a rock up Elric's throat, and as they trailed away, he swallowed hard. Maybe the police were in front of his door right now, waiting.

The regret of telling Jen was consuming him, but he had to. Jen was losing hope. The fear of the attacks and what happened in Lexington were breaking her down. All he wanted to do was give her hope again.

There was a subtle knock on the door, pulling Elric out of his panic. He took a deep breath and rose from the bed, hesitating as he reached for the doorknob. How would he react if the army was behind the door? Elric prayed he didn't hurt anyone that came to arrest him. He opened the door.

"We need to talk," Jen said tersely barging in. She pushed him out of the way, pacing with hands tight to her hip.

Elric gave a long exhale of relief. "I agree." He closed the bedroom door.

She looked at him nervously. "Elric, what the hell is going on? Please don't tell me you're one of those things?"

"No." He sat down on the bed, thinking about the thing inside of him. "I don't think so. I haven't transformed into a monster or anything like so we can rule that out."

She nodded. "Your eyes were red like . . . like blood." She sat on the edge of the bed.

"Yeah, I think that's what happens when I use my powers. Jen, I brought you back here to show you because I didn't want you to feel hopeless. I really did kill that thing."

"So, you have powers. Why have you been hiding them all this time and for all these years?"

He shook his head. "I just found out myself." He looked down at his hands.

"There's a lot going on that I don't understand. Some of it scares the crap out of me," she said, worry spreading over her face.

"I'm sorry if I scared you."

"Elric." She shook her head. "It's not you. I could never be afraid of you."

He looked up, confused. "You're not going to tell anyone?"

"Why would I tell anyone?" She stood up wiping the sweat from her forehead. "Besides, I think it's pretty cool, in a frightening sci-fi sort of way."

She walked over to the window and raised the shades, allowing the bright sunlight to pierce through and almost blind him.

"Actually, this whole thing seems like something out of an awful movie, or even better, one of your comic books,"

"Yeah, you're right!" Elric jumped up with excitement as it hit him.

"What? Seriously?"

"What if these monsters are from a different dimension? I mean, if they were aliens or something, they would use space crafts of some sort, right? But they're not! Maybe these portals are the only way to get through. It reminds me of one of my comics. The villain came from another world to rule over the humans, but to get his army through, he tore a hole in the space-time continuum."

Jen nodded, willing to accept any explanation. "Well, what happened?"

"Well, a group of superheroes stopped the villain, but this is reality. If what I'm thinking is anywhere close to what happened in that comic book, we won't stand a chance. We'll be outnumbered and overpowered by a force of monsters. If this is the beginning."

"That means things are just getting started." She bit her bottom lip, looking back out the window.

He thought about those awful powers. A tingling raced down his back as he thought about the creature he killed back in Lexington. The satisfaction of the kill took him to a place he refused to go back to.

Jen turned to him biting her bottom lip. "Look, sitting here depressed all day isn't going to solve anything. Besides, I highly doubt Elric Blake is a monster from another dimension," she said.

Happiness flowed over him, blanketing his skin in warmth. He thought about the summers in Lexington. The July cookouts, the fireworks. All of it a memory now, but a good one.

"I'm there with you, Elric. I know we'll find out what's going on together, okay?" She kissed him on the cheek and walked out, closing the door behind her.

He stared at the door, thinking of her words. As much as he wanted her help, he wouldn't take Jennifer away from her parents.

117

Night came quickly.

Now a blackened canvas, the sky was speckled with stars, the moon a beacon. Everyone had fallen asleep hours ago, but his love for Jen kept him locked in his hotel room. The thought of what dwelled within him crept into his heart. He cringed at the thought of losing control and hurting Jen, or anyone else for that matter.

He stacked enough food to hopefully last him four days without spoiling in his book bag. There were also four bottles of water, a rain jacket, and warm clothes.

The bag was ready to burst, but it did its job. He threw on the clothes he had worn the night of the attacks. They reeked of smoke and gunpowder, homage to the event he had to prevent from happening again.

The moon was large and bright tonight. Leaves blew in the wind as it whistled outside the window. He tossed the bag over his shoulder and cracked the window open, inviting an icy breeze that rushed into the small hotel room. He checked the hallway for any signs of life. Nothing.

He climbed out the window and crept to the back of the hotel, the moonlight glinted off his face. He was heading to a trail not too far down the road. From there, he would make his way to the highway and hitchhike.

The trail was dark and eerie. He was just a few yards away from the hotel when he heard someone behind him.

"Hey, where are you going?" Jen's voice danced in the icy breeze.

He turned with an awful sinking feeling in his gut. *Didn't even make it out of the parking lot. Now what?* Jen raced behind him, out of breath, still in her pajamas. Her expression grew to concern the moment their eyes met, and he looked away.

"I'm going for a walk." He looked down the road, avoiding eye contact. Liar.

"Oh, must be a long walk." She bit her bottom lip, glancing at the bag on his shoulders. Elric watched the tightening of her fist, fighting the truth.

A ball of tangled yarn, useless and knotted; that was Elric's emotions right now. Ten years to finally have her, and now, he was leaving her. Beautiful and sweet Jennifer Reeves "There's so much going on right now, Jen. I-I can't explain it. I'm sorry."

Her eyes rolled around the trees and the sky. "What's that even mean?"

"I'm leaving," he said, quick and to the point. He ran his fingers through his hair, shocked that the words came out. Her eyebrows bunched together. She knew his secret, but only a small portion of it. He didn't tell her there was something inside him, something evil. "I need answers about what I am."

"What you are?" she asked. "You're Elric Blake, my closest friend, my only friend . . . " Her words choked by sadness.

A black mass of energy rose from his feet enveloping his body. Like swirling black smoke, the darkness rose to the sky in a flurry, kicking up gravel and debris around them from the flow of energy.

She pushed her hair back out of her face in shock. The growing mass whistled, with a force strong enough to make Jen stumble back. Her eyes widened. The look said it all. The terror. The evil. She felt it.

"I don't care, Elric. All I care about is you. If you can't stay here, please . . . take me with you," she screamed, eyes watering. "We can do it together. You don't have to be alone, not with the world the way it is!"

"Jen, you have to stay and take care of your parents." He stepped away from her. "I have to go alone. This is my burden, not yours."

Tears caressed her cheek. Her hazel eyes gleamed in the moonlight as she wiped her face. Something changed in them.

She began forcing her way through the wind, fighting through the darkness.

"Wait, Jen. I don't know—"

She grabbed his hand and pulled him close, stepping into the black aura. Untouched, wrapping her arms tightly around him, she buried her head into his chest. Tousled by the wild wind, her long strands danced in the moonlight like waves of onyx swaying to a symphony.

"Elric, I love you,"

He looked down at her trembling shoulders, lost for words. Sorrow and joy flooded his insides, he didn't know which emotions to hold on to. If he ever had a wish, that would be the first on the list, to here Jen say those words.

"I know you feel the same. You don't have to say anything. I've always known." She swallowed, wiping the tears away. "People spend their entire lives lost, waiting for someone to find them. Even with everything you're going through, I'll find you, Elric, even in the darkness. I promise."

Jen's lips pressed against his. The fury of the darkness subsided as joy and happiness won the battle, calming the storm. His heart throbbed with ecstasy. A feeling he didn't want to end.

She lowered her head.

He sucked in his bottom lip, savoring the kiss. Who knows if he'll ever have the chance again?

"I know you won't stay, so just make sure you come back in one piece, okay?"

He nodded. "I will."

She turned, walking back toward the hotel in the light of the moon.

Elric turned too, walking toward the darkened trail. The trees were tall and their leaves still clinging to life suffocated the moon light. Both he and Jen were choosing their own paths. He took his love and joy for her and buried it deep within. He had to or he'd never leave. Where he was going and what he had to face required sacrifice; just like those officers did back in Lexington. He just hoped it would all be worth it.

Elric looked back at the shadowy figure that was his bond to this world. Jen disappeared inside the hotel.

The wind hissed, twirling around the large trees. Branches reaching for the dirt trail like claws. He pulled out a flashlight, hesitating to step into the darkness. But the wind pushed him into his new destiny.

Chapter 15

——⧉((◉))⧉——

The Tour of a Fallen Memory

The sun's rays reached across Elric's face, forcing him to open burning, itchy eyes. The cool morning air chilled him to the bone as dew dripped from the leaves above.

After hours of walking the previous night, shooting pains of exhaustion throbbed through his calves as he took refuge behind a tree. Exhaustion swept through him; he tried ignoring it for as long as he could. His motivation: Lexington.

Elric had already made up his mind. Before he left Maine, he'd make one last stop at his hometown. He had to pay his respects to Mrs. Lee and leave behind the life he once had. Otherwise he'd feel unfinished.

He ignored the chills that trickled down his arms and neck and pulled some bread and water from his backpack. He tore into the bread and downed half a bottle of water. Determined. Nothing could slow him down and nothing would throw him off course. If he could control the thing inside him, he'd have power and maybe the ability to protect the ones closest to him. Maybe he'd even save the world.

He threw the backpack over his shoulders, and he once again started walking through the woods. The scenery came to life as the sun's rays pierced through some of the darkened areas of the pines. After a couple of hours, it warmed up.

In the greenery of the forest, there was a strange peace of mind. A salvation. Trees gnarled by the years swayed in the wind, limbs dancing and cracking with each breeze. The ground was soft and easy on his knees. And the earthy smell of soil and pines settled his spirits.

The birds chirped as they fluttered from branch to branch. He tightened the backpack to distribute the weight, giving it a couple of pulls so it sat higher on his shoulders. Then he dropped to his knees, sweat pooling from his face.

His heart began pounding against his chest, stomach lurching as adrenaline flushed through his veins. He was hyperventilating; his anxiety had never been like this before. He threw the backpack off his shoulder and sat back, hands shaking.

"Damn it. Get a grip." He exhaled a shaky breath.

He wrapped his arms around himself, trying to fight the fear that still consumed him. Like a horror movie the events of Lexington came rolling back.

He closed his eyes, cursing himself. That entire night, Jen was the only brave one, leading them to safety. She was confident, brave, everything he wasn't. If it weren't for her, he'd be dead.

He took a deep breath and stood up, snatching his bag, and slinging it over his shoulders. He pushed through the cool air of the countryside, forcing the lingering images to the back of his head.

"I can't be afraid," he said to himself, walking through the vegetation.

In anger, he slammed his fist into a tree that cracked and flaked. He didn't feel a thing. His fist had no bruises or gashes. It was the power within him. Though the darkness would've replaced fear with something much more malefic.

It wasn't long before he came over the horizon, cresting the green hills. The ocean breeze whispered with a poignant salty breath. But it was tainted. The ocean sore was blanketed in a black smog. The black haze was heavy over the remnants of Lexington.

Lexington, he thought to himself. *Already?* He couldn't see the town yet, but it was close. The smoke trails were his guide.

He took the path that brought him to the shoreline and kept south until he saw buildings. Or what was left anyways. Sweat permeated his fingers, and his heart sunk into his stomach as fear breathed down his back.

Trails of smoke still rose as an ominous gray cloud hung over Lexington. The ocean waves crashed against the shoreline. The low rumbles brought back memories of lying back on the docks, listening to the cries of seagulls. Today, there wasn't a single bird in the sky.

A helicopter glided overhead, darting from the field where they had everyone gathered to get on the trucks. Soldiers were everywhere setting up sharp wire and signs that read: "Keep out! Military investigation at work."

Lexington was wired off by barbed wire. The blades enticing, daring Elric to climb between them to get through. For all the trouble it was worth, he could've gone around town, but he had to say goodbye.

Elric hiked around the barbed wire, searching for a break or fracture in the defense. A tall man with glasses pounded steel stakes into the ground. Elric hid behind a tree, watching the soldier wearing a dirty tattered uniform cursing with each heave. The soldier wiped the sweat from his glasses dragging his feet as he went down the lane.

Elric waited for him to get far enough and darted through the outskirts of Lexington. The faint smell of gunpowder and the acrid smell of rotten eggs would never be forgotten.

Bloodstained sidewalks and articles of clothing hung from tree branches, blowing in the wind.

Voices echoed from the opposite side of a house he passed by. He ducked behind a truck that had been turned on its side. Deep claw lacerations tore through its roof. He looked around the vehicle as tan boots clomped from the lawn.

"Still can't believe we got people out of here." A soldier spat a glob of brown spit on the concrete. Cigarette smoke overflowed from the sides of the vehicle, as two soldiers leaned against it.

"Yeah, three convoys made it out, but that first convoy to Clemson got hit hard. Lost twelve out of twenty cargo trucks, only eight made it. Damn *shifters*, man."

Elric's eyes widened, and his heart felt light as he heard them talk about others who had made it out of Lexington alive. At least there was something to be hopeful for.

"Once you call in the 172nd, it doesn't matter if we're fighting the devil himself; we shoot first and ask questions later. That's why we have a dozen of them shifters laid out, and the white jackets are studying them."

"I hear you on that, brotha. You coming to Maine, you better believe we bringin' the pain!"

"What the hell are you guys doing out here, pussyfooting around?" another voice barked. Deeper, harsher.

Elric sunk deeper behind the vehicle.

"Ugh, nothing, sergeant. Just taking a smoke break," a soldier replied.

"Get back on guard duty till you're relieved. If I find you out here again, I'll tear your insides out myself!"

"Roger, sergeant."

The heavy boots rushed back to the side of the house.

Elric checked around the truck to see if the man who was giving orders was gone. There was no one there. Elric ran, darting between homes and hiding every couple of yards.

He swallowed hard as he darted by the high school. The reinforced brick building stood strong, the only noticeable difference was that the windows were smashed in.

Elric watched from the front porch of a house that had half its roof torn off and the front portion caved in. The soldiers must have been using the high school as a base. The yellow school buses were replaced with tan armored trucks mounted with serious fire power.

A blood-stained toddler's sneaker leaned against a curb waiting for an owner that would never return. Elric looked down the road to where the football field was. He hadn't noticed until now, but all the buildings close to the field had been shredded. *We were lucky?* He thought.

He fought his sadness and anger pushing on. It wasn't long before he came to what he searched for. The house he once called home.

The front door was gone, blocked off by caution tape. He stepped onto the front porch glass crunching beneath his feet as he entered. Light poured through the shattered windows, gleaming over the fallen shards strewed over the tiled floor. Mr. Lee spent an entire summer working on this kitchen; it was an anniversary present for Mrs. Lee.

The paint was peeling and flaking off the walls. Rotting food littered the floors of the kitchen, and even plates remained from a dinner that was never eaten. Pork chops, and pale green beans were scattered all over the place. One of Elric's favorite meals Mrs. Lee loved to make for him.

Elric bit his bottom lip, pushing forward.

The living room furniture was destroyed and mangled from the force of the wind. He looked down at the couch, remembering the last conversation he had with Mrs. Lee. He wished he could go back. He wanted to hold her one last time. The shattered plasma screen lay on its back ripped off the wall. He set his bag next to the shredded couch and walked over to the staircase.

The wooden steps creaked and snapped. He made it to the top, entering what was left of his room.

His room took the lesser hit from the destruction. His bed was still a mess, just as he had left it. He fell on it, hoping to suck in the remaining memories that were left there. He looked over at his collection of comic books and began digging through them for insight.

The realization that they were only comics hit hard. There wasn't a hidden message or instructions on how to defeat living, breathing, monsters because it was all fictional. He fell on the floor and leaned against his bed. With all his might, he kicked the pile of comic books over.

"Why?" he yelled as tears raced down his face. "Why! Why! Why!" He tightened his fist, thinking about the overwhelming force that was led by a large, humanoid lion.

He went over to his drawer and packed some boxers and socks. The rattling bottle of Lexapro rolled to his fingertips. He scoffed at the irony. *Gonna need more than that to make it through all this crap,* he thought.

The wind blew through the house as it creaked. Wood twisting and cracking echoed through the walls and ceiling. He gave the room one more glance over, remembering what he once had, and left.

He was halfway down the stairs when one of the steps gave in. Wood ripped through his jeans, tearing through his leg with large splinters

"Ahh!" He pulled himself up.

A warm sensation ran down his leg. He pulled up the pants leg just in time to see the broken tissue reconnecting itself. The large planks were pushed from his calf muscle. Damp blood stained his pants and socks, but the pain and wound were gone.

He looked down, no longer shocked or frightened by the ability that was granted from the darkness within. He made his way into the kitchen and edged over to the sank. The brown stains of dried blood were sprinkled over the countertops; footprints and a dried puddle collected in front of the cabinets.

That's where she laid . . . probably waiting for me, Elric thought hating himself. "I'm sorry I couldn't protect you. I'm sorry I wasn't there for you when you needed me. I promise, on my life, I won't let this happen again! I don't care what it takes!" He wiped his face.

He grabbed his bag and left the house, saying his final goodbyes. Outside the house, a truck roared down the road breaking the silence of the ghost town. He hid back in the house, watching as a camouflaged vehicle—like the one that brought the survivors to Clemson—shook down the street. It halted a couple of yards down.

The vehicle sat idly giving out a loud hiss as a couple soldiers in uniform stepped out looking around, rifles aimed and ready to kill anything that moved.

"Man, ain't no more survivors here. They either in Clemson or shipped over to Brunswick," A soldier said, looking around. He lowered a machine gun almost have his size.

"Yeah, you're right. Even with those portals gone, this place still gives me the creeps," another soldier said, holding his rifle.

"They just vanished without a trace. You think they'll be back?" another said from the driver's seat.

Static blared over a walkie-talkie, the soldier in the driver's seat answered and smacked the door of the truck.

"We're out of here boys. Looks like this place is cleaned out. We got that mission to help out in Portland!"

The two men nodded and hopped into the vehicle as it peeled down the road, roaring past the empty buildings of the small town.

Elric peeked out, listening for more voices. He took a deep breath and pulled his bag tight to his back and dashed across the street to another house.

He walked by a park, which was the final place he wanted to visit. It was where he first saw Jen. She had just moved from New York.

Even until this day, Jen knew nothing about her real parents—she was just like Elric that way—abandoned as a baby. He examined the remnants of his childhood. The swing set torn from the cement foundation, and the twisted metal that was once the slide lay mangled on the ground.

"Beautiful, isn't it?" a voice said from behind.

Elric was startled to see a tall man staring at what was left of the park, thin and very pale.

"Hey, wait! I'm sorry. I know I shouldn't be here but . . . " Elric glanced at the strange man who wore causal clothes, not a uniform like the soldiers. "Are you a survivor?" Elric asked, shocked to see anyone else.

"Not at all. I'm more of an observer really," the bald head man replied with a composed tone. "Just evaluating the fruits of my labor." He wore black shades with a black collared shirt, jeans, and a pair of worn sneakers. "Admiring the beauty of it all."

Elric noticed a smile slip across the man's face. Must have been his imagination. The man stepped next him and exhaled. Elric froze, something wasn't right.

"I've always wondered why humans grip to life. No matter how much pain and suffering they go through, they'll fight to the end. Quite stupid if you ask me." He chuckled.

"Why the hell would you say something like that," Elric asked, his voice hoarse and dry, almost a growl. "About people who died. They were murdered by monsters."

The man turned with a grin; his shades kept his eyes hidden. "Humans are nothing more than apes with the ability to calculate. Nothing more. They waste their world and its potential, so we've come to claim it for our own."

We? With all his might, Elric swung, landing a jaw breaking right hook, shattering the man's glasses, and sending hi first class into a battered sedan.

Elric looked down at his hands in shock. *That's new!* He looked up at the man who was embedded in the car, legs hanging lifelessly. Without a second thought, he killed a man.

He swallowed hard, starting to panic. "No. What have I done?"

The car rattled as the man freed himself from his steel prison. The passenger door fell off the hinges as he dusted himself off. The shirt torn down the abdomen, and sleeves ripped from the seams.

Elric's legs knocked together. No wounds, no bruises. In fact, he kept the snobbish expression, revealing all his teeth. "Y-you should be dead."

Chapter 16

The General

"No, unfortunately for you, I'm not." With blurring speed, the man's hands wrapped around Elric's throat. "I'm guessing with strength like that you're not human either, which is going to make this very amusing."

He stared down at the man who lifted him high into the air. The man's grip tightening like a noose. Elric's heart was blasting against his chest. The saliva thickening in his mouth with the metallic taste of iron.

The man slung Elric through a car. The darkness covered his body, protecting him in a hissing cloak that flowed from his feet and high above his head. He stumbled out of the back seat, gasping for air.

The man smiled, his pale blue eyes glistening with excitement as if he had found something, he'd lost a long time ago.

Two black tendrils rose from the black cloak around Elric's body. The darkness grew wild, he couldn't control it. The black tendrils whipped forward toward the man.

Like an acrobat, the man used his lanky physique to dodge the attacks. Leaning and ducking. The two tendrils split into four separate appendages that whipped forward. The man twisted and dodged the attacks that came at him.

The man's movements were blurs at best. The tendril's movements were happening without Elric saying a word or lifting a finger. He didn't know whether to be frightened or happy.

Boy, a voice rumbled from within his belly. *You should be grateful for my power. Otherwise, you'd probably be dead by now.*

Elric swallowed hard, listening to the voice. His hands trembled, but he clenched them with resolve. *Yeah, whatever,* he replied to the thing inside.

A fifth tendril smashed into the tar and vanished beneath the ground. He didn't have a clue what was happening or how to brace himself for an attack. The man jumped and dodged, running to keep out of reach of the appendages.

"I'm going to take a guess and assume you're not Ermakian?" The man chuckled.

"Ermakian? What the hell is that?"

The fifth tendril tore from the ground wrapping around the man's leg, before he could tear it away with sharpening claws, his legs were pulled from beneath him.

Elric cringed from the smack of flesh and skull hitting the pavement made Elric cringe. The tendril raised the man high in the air and hurled him to the ground, cracking the tar. Elric jumped, expecting to see the man's body splatter.

This isn't me, Elric thought. This viciousness came with the darkness. A tingling moved through Elric's fingertips. He could feel the tendril's like a snake wrapping around its prey.

The tendril slung the man into a building. The weakened structure collapsed, crushing everything below. The shattering crash reverberated over Lexington. It wouldn't be long before the army showed up.

The fifth tendril withdrew from the toppled house and joined the others hovering above Elric, waiting. Digits formed from the sleek black streams, forming into grotesque scale covered claws.

A vehicle flew at Elric. Two of those strange claws grabbed it out of the sky before it reached him. "What the hell!"

The appendages guarded him with a mind of their own. Through his own fingers he felt the cold metal of the car, as if his own fingers wrapped around the crumbling vehicle.

An obnoxious cackle echoed from behind as Elric turned. There still wasn't a scratch on the man. His shirt was nothing but rags, revealing a slender, pale body. His pants shredded, but his body untouched.

The dark appendages threw the car back at the man, Elric stumble forward from the force. Like shooing a fly, the man batted the car away, clipping the roof of a house. If the soldiers hadn't heard them before, they knew something was going on now.

"Here I thought I found another human to play with for my own amusement, but I found something much more interesting."

Whatever this guy was, he was too strong. Elric contemplated making a run for it and letting the army handle it. In a blur the man raced over with a punch that shattered the dark aura around him.

Elric slammed through two houses, coming to a sliding halt on a kitchen floor next to a dishwasher. "My back," Elric groaned. "I can barely feel my arms and legs."

This one is quite the nuisance, the voice from within growled. *You might have to allow more power to seep in if you hope to survive.*

Elric looked down at his fingers as he tried to move them. Nothing, he was numb all over. *Am I paralyzed?*

The voice grumbled from the darkness, *your cervical spine has been fractured. Both arms and legs are useless to you.*

Sweat raced from his reddening face as fear came rushing back in waves. His fingers lay motionless by his side, and his legs slumped sideways.

I . . . how? He thought about all the injuries that healed before.

You ask such a question, but it was your fear that made you weak, the voice replied.

A burning sensation raced across every inch of Elric's body, delivering a strange warmth that brought life back to his arms and legs.

It was your fear that kept you from using my powers. It was fear that nearly got you killed by this insignificant creature; the rumbling voice spoke condescendingly. *You let this garbage harm my vessel!*

Elric stood up. The dark cloak around him intensified. He clenched his fist and cracked his neck from side to side as his rejuvenated body returned to action. He was ready for more.

"Cervical fracture," Elric replied. "That was my neck, right? I remember that from anatomy class. You're pretty smart, aren't you?"

The beast roared with anger. *Don't you dare take what I've done for you as kindness, boy. I refuse to die within you at the hands of this creature!*

Elric nodded, listening to the voice of the beast within. He coughed as he stepped out of the large hole left from his forceful entrance into the house. He could see the destruction from when he smashed through the first house that was in front of him.

He stumbled out of the house and dropped to his knees on the sidewalk. Elric looked between the houses on the other side of the street where the man was, but he couldn't see anything. The sound of heavy vehicles roaring down the street took away his focus.

"There you are," a voice yelled from above.

Elric looked up into the bright sky, shielding his eyes from the bright sun. The man glided down, powerful bird-like wings propelling him forward.

"I thought I killed you." Even in battle, the man was in a jovial mood. "I would have hated for the fun to end so soon!"

The large wings were covered with thick, golden-brown feathers and flapped with enough force to blow wood chunks and gravel through the streets. The edges of the feathers seemed to almost spike at the edges.

The darkness intensified around Elric. This guy was doing most of the attacking, yet he didn't drop a bead of sweat. Elric threw his hands forward as the dark appendages raced toward the man. One hand grabbed his wings binding them and preventing him from flying.

With claws covered in golden scales, the man slashed himself free, and raced between the tendrils, bolting for Elric. A tendril raced from the cloak, puncturing clean through his right wing. The man racked Elric's face with a left hook. The cloak vanished.

A sharp jab dug into Elric's stomach. He doubled over as a swift kick threw him back. The man snickered, pressing his ragged sneaker on Elric's throat, crushing his larynx.

"Mankind was given a little freedom, and now you think you run the place. You see, we're coming back. We want what belongs to us. No man, or whatever you are, is going to stop us." The man looked down with a cheshire grin. "You know what? I'm gonna bring you home to my leader. Blight would love to meet you. You might even see some of the pathetic humans from this town there if they aren't dead already."

Are you done yet, boy? an echoing voice spoke from within Elric. *Are you done being frightened of my power?*

Elric looked up, his vision fading from the lack of oxygen. The veins in his face filled with pressure. His eyes were going to pop from the sockets, and he was once again losing feeling in his body. This time it wasn't a fractured clavicle, but maybe death.

The voice was right; it was time to stop being afraid. The whole point of going to Boston was to find this man who could help him control this power. How could he learn to control something he was afraid to use?

Yes, Elric replied to the voice, accepting the darkness. *Help me.*

An explosion erupted throwing the man back. Elric's wounds healed as the dark aura roared around him with fury. The ground shook as surrounding structures collapsed from the quaking force.

This thing inside of him was getting stronger. Its grasp was tighter than ever. His blood boiled with excitement. The thrill of the kill became an appetite, like a high he couldn't shake.

"Well, we're just full of surprises, aren't we?" The man's voice became deep and raspy. "I'll admit, kid, you have real potential."

The man's head and face changed. Muscle and bone cracked and twisted. His nose and mouth stretched into a hooked, golden beak. His eyes enlarged becoming black and glossy. The clothing and shoes shredded away, revealing a broad muscular body covered in dark brown feathers. Sharp talons tore through his shoes and smashed into the tar.

"The name's Carnage. I am one of the four generals of Blight's army," The feathery chest expanded as it took a deep breath and exhaled. His voice was strong and proud. "It's been a while since I've been pushed to this point. Who would've thought it would happen in this world?"

"Blight's army?" Elric had heard the strange name too many times to count now. "Who's Blight? And what does he want?"

Carnage tilted its head in curiosity. "Blight is our sovereign leader, the one who will lead Ermak to true peace. He's our symbol of justice who continues to sacrifice all he is in order to bring our people back to superiority. He's absolute righteousness and all that is good!"

"Are you insane? How can someone who's good slaughter hundreds, even thousands, of people for peace!" Elric thought about the people of Lexington who didn't make it; he thought about Mrs. Lee. "Your Blight, is a monster and in my opinion, the biggest douchebag I've ever heard of."

"Douchebag?" Carnage cackled shaking his head. "I don't know what that means. What you humans consider to be good and righteous is meaningless and an impossibility. Trust me, I know. We've studied you for centuries. But here you are, speaking of slaughter and genocide, but your kind's very existence and society is built on this notion!"

Elric glared. "What?"

"Your country alone, this America, is responsible for the deaths of millions, possibly billions, including its own people." The creature looked around at the destruction of Lexington. "You're a child so you've never witnessed true war and destruction. But your kind has wiped out entire races: men, women, and children. Your species fight daily to destroy themselves. It's comical really, but we'll change all that. Believe me."

The darkness violently flowed around Elric. "I guess that means the portals aren't really gone then?" The flurry of blackness began to corrode the streets. Carnage's mocking tone cut deep.

"Our gateways to this world? No, not for long anyway. This was a test. What this world witnessed is nothing compared to what's really coming. We wanted to give mankind the benefit of a doubt, so we sent a few forces over at a time to see the reaction of your military force. Unfortunately, it was very unimpressive, but then again, what would you expect from a species of primates?"

The darkness seeped into Elric, feeding his anger and hatred. "You're not going to stop then? You'd rather listen to the twisted words of your leader and kill innocent people until there's nothing left?"

"Oh, no. Mankind will have its place as servants and food, nothing more. Just like the age of gold when we once ruled this world previously. We're gods amongst you, and nothing you say or do will change that."

"Your far from a god," Elric said in a low, crackling voice. Tears trickled down his cheek but burned away with the darkness that grew. "You've taken everything from me, so I'll do the same to you!"

Elric raced toward him, Carnage took one flap launching himself to the sky. He looked down, hovering over Elric.

"You think you can stop us." Carnage laughed. "If you oppose Blight, you'll die!" His voice was raspy and dry. "You should die right here, and let it be that!"

"No, I'm going to end this, and I'm going to start by killing you!" Elric's voice was cold and firm.

"You threaten me? You fools of this world will quiver under the feet of our great armies. We'll feed on your flesh and crush your bones to dust! You're all nothing but cattle!"

Carnage launched himself down at Elric, talons stretched for the kill. Elric dove out of the way, a tendril pierced through Carnage's right wing as he continued to fly.

Carnage let out a hoarse screech, fighting to rip free, but the tendril ripped him out of the sky. A plume of dirt and cement sprayed around them as he hit the ground.

Elric studied the humanoid bird struggling to rip free, another screech escaped Carnage's curved beak. Fear deserted Elric as he fixated on his struggling prey, he raised his hand to the sky.

One of the dark hands formed into a blade and pierced Carnage through the left shoulder. "Curse you!" He slashed away, trying to remove the tendril. "Curse you and your whole species!"

Through the tendrils Elric could feel Carnage's heart racing with fear. "You mentioned your leader, the one who's causing all this. What's his name again?" Elric's tone was cold and void of emotion.

Carnage paused for a moment and chuckled. "Blight."

"Blight," Elric said to himself. "Where can I find him?"

Carnage began laughing once again. His head lay on the chunks of broken tar as he cackled. A tendril pierced through his left hand. Four of the five talons scattered in the pit he lay in, the force nearly severing the hand clean off. Carnage screeched in anguish, flailing to break free.

"You really are something, but you're nothing compared to the others who will come searching for you once you're done with me. Unfortunately, I'm not as strong as my comrades."

"Who are the others?" Elric's jaw clenched.

"My comrades, the other generals. It has been deemed that if one of us is slain in battle, and if the slayer isn't killed, then it's up to one of the other generals to take pride in avenging the fallen."

Elric swallowed hard, listening to his words. Was he just talking to save his own skin, or was this some strange code shared amongst these monsters that considered themselves gods among man?

"Once they hear of my demise, your scent will be like blood in the water. Blight won't take the death of one of his chosen kindly. I would choose your next moves wisely. You humans have such tight networks with one another. Blight will crush whomever you hold dear, and if you go after him, you'll surely die."

Elric raised a fist above the creature. "No more laughing, huh? And here I thought you were this general of an army." A fiendish smile stretched across Elric's face. "Some commander you are, killed by a kid."

"You little worm! You wouldn't dare!"

With an impish grin, Elric opened his hands. Dozens of tendrils raced forward, impaling the beast. Carnage shrieked, coughing up black fluid.

He looked over at Elric. "I'll be revenged. There are eyes all around this town, watching my demise, and they will inform our leader," He sputtered. "And you will feel pain unlike you have ever felt before." The black fluid trickled from the corners of his beak.

A tendril smashed into Carnage's skull, it burst open like a melon. The wings gave one final flap and dropped. Elric fell to his knees, exhausted. The dark aura faded from around him, the rage right along with it. He looked down at Carnage's corpse. He killed for the second time . . . and enjoyed it.

I'm impressed, the voice said.

Horrified, Elric looked over the dried black blood that came from the beast he killed. "You made me do this. This wasn't me at all."

You've made your first step into darkness. It was a little rough around the edges, but not too shabby for a human child.

He shook his head in disbelief. "No, I'm not a killer. I'm not a monster!"

It runs in your blood. Eventually you'll realize that, just like the others before you.

Elric's body shook. What did it mean by the others before him?

"What are you?" Elric yelled into the silence of the ghost town. His voice echoed. It replied with a monstrous roar that faded with the rest of his anger. He had to find a way to control this or stop it, but he just stumbled onto something much worse. Something that put the entire world at risk.

Vehicles racing down the street snapped him out of deep thought. He darted through the buildings and found his bag next to an overturned SUV. He slung his bag over the sharpened wire that protected the town and crawled beneath it.

He left the ghost town, looking back on it one last time as the sun set. There wasn't a single seagull calling, no bellowing horn of incoming ships. Death swept everything away. those portals weren't freak accidents; they were a declaration of war, an invasion.

Chapter 17

>‹((O))›‹

Onward to the City
Beneath the City

Night fell as he reached the edge of the forest that separated Lexington from civilization. There were barriers and vehicle checkpoints set up across the highway by the army. Traffic was overwhelming, and the idea of hitchhike to Boston became an afterthought.

Cars beeped their horns as a man wearing a camouflage uniform and a bright orange jacket directed traffic.

Elric remained hidden in the woods, waiting for his chance to spring across the highway. He gripped the straps of his book bag and rushed across, dodging in front of vehicles that waited to go through the barriers.

Once on the other side, he hid behind some trees, sighing with relief. Sweat trickled down the sides of his face. He was close to Portland now.

The familiar rumbling of military trucks echoed in the distance. Down I-95 a convoy of trucks blew down the road to the city. There were at least fifteen vehicles of different sizes with a few having men on large gun turrets.

He hid in the growing darkness of night, concealed by his black hoodie and torn, jeans. A cool breeze rode up his leg, spreading goosebumps over his body. He made up his mind about trying to find a ride and pushed on down I-95 south, keeping the highway on his left.

A light jabber of voices in the darkness divided the insults of pissed off drivers that echoed from the highway. Bright flashlights flickered in the distance. Whoever it was, they were coming towards him.

He hid in a thicket, listening for the voices. Three men and two young women came walking through the brush. They were exhausted and white with fear as if they had seen something awful.

"We have to keep going. I got family up north, Clemson's safe and the rest of the northern counties are too. We can't stay around here, and Portland's a steaming pile," one of the men spoke.

One of the women collapsed from exhaustion, she hit the ground with a thud.

"Jamie!" The other woman knelt, trying to wake her. "She's hungry and thirsty. She needs something! We've been doing this for almost a full day without food."

"We're all hungry," one of the men replied without empathy. "If we don't want to end up dead and eaten by one of those things, we have to keep going!"

Elric tightened his fist, thinking about the extra food and water he had in his bag. If he shared it with them, he wouldn't have any left for himself. He bit his bottom lip. *screw it.* He rose from the bushes and made his way over.

"Who's there?" one of the men asked, raising his flashlight up at him. "What the heck are you doing out here, kid?"

"You guys need food, right?" Elric tossed his bag to the feet of the men who looked up confused. Elric looked down at the woman who was lethargic. "She needs food, right? That's all I have left. Take it."

"Why? Why are you helping us for?" The women asked, trying to keep the other girl conscious.

Elric focused on the path they traveled up from. "I'm almost to Portland. I can find food there anyway. Besides, you guys need it more than I do."

"Portland? Are you nuts? I don't know if you've been watching the news, but it's been evacuated, kid. After that portal tore through, Portland's crumbling piece by piece."

"Well, I'm from Lexington. I was right under the portal that opened up there, and it destroyed everything."

They were all silent. Only their eyes gave the gesture of condolence.

"Clemson's good, I was there for a bit. They have a refuge station set up too. If you go north and head to the road, you should see vehicles from the military going by Clemson. I bet they'll bring you the rest of the way." He swallowed hard, thinking of Jen and her parents.

"Thanks, but if you know what's good for you, don't go to Portland. It's nothing but death down there. You have to believe us," the woman said, digging in the bag.

He thought about what the woman said.

"Is there any transportation going to Boston?" he asked.

"No, there's nothing. Everything's been blocked off by the army. This is the real did kid, it's the end of the world!"

"Yeah and Boston is worse than Portland. Just come with us to Clemson," the woman replied.

Warmth spilled over him, thinking about Jennifer and her family. They were waiting for his return. He had to keep going no matter how bad it got. If transportation to Boston had ceased, there was no way he could get their now. He leaned against a tree, hitting the back of his head against it. Everything was pointing to go back to Clemson.

"Just come with us. I mean, I'm sure you could use help too," a younger man replied before drinking some of the water.

"No, I'll be fine." Elric flipped his hood over his head. "Whenever you get a chance, tell the army that more portals are coming,"

"What are you talking about? They're all gone, right?" the woman asked. She looked back at the men.

Elric shook his head. "I know it's hard to believe, but all of this is an invasion. Let them know."

They nodded. Whether they believed him or not was another story. Elric disappeared into the woods, leaving the remainder of his food and clothing behind. He was angered by what he was told. There was no way to get to Boston now.

He looked up at the star-filled sky and fell against a tree. He wondered if everything he had done to this point was worth all the trouble.

"You second guess yourself too much, you know that?" a voice said from the darkness of the woods. "Maybe this was where you were supposed to end up?"

Elric jumped to his feet, looking around, but he knew who it was. That soft voice. He searched the darkness and found what he was looking for, the shimmering eyes of the strange young woman.

"I'm glad you made it this far, Elric. I'm proud of you." She held out her hand. "Let me get you the rest of the way, okay?"

He took a step back. "After everything I've been through, I'm supposed to know you aren't one of those things?"

"If I were one of them, I would have killed you that night. You must trust me. It's the only way if you want to control that thing inside you and stop all this from happening."

He hesitated. Life and warmth radiated from her fingertips like a welcoming flame of hope. The influence of the thing within was having a stronger hold with each use. Sooner or later, it would take control. Sooner or later, he would become a monster like Carnage.

The thought of Jen and the sadness in her eyes when he left sunk in. He had to make it count, all of it. The world was in danger. He had to stop being a coward; he had to take the risk. "Fine, but how can you get me to Boston without a vehicle? That's got to be over a hundred miles easy."

"Trust me. It'll only take second." Her hand stretched toward his.

He grasped it, looking into her eyes. Darkness rushed over him everything around them; trees, starlit sky, even the head lights from the line of vehicles on I-95 vanished. The rustling leaves, the chilled air blowing, and the traffic horns blaring in the distance died out. An eerie vibration replaced the subtle tones. Only the two of them remained.

"What's going on?" He couldn't see anything, but he could still feel her clenched hands. "Where did everything go?"

"Elric, don't be a baby. It's not that bad." Her voice echoed in the darkness. "And don't you dare let go of my hand!"

He felt himself free falling. It reminded him of the small rollercoaster ride at palace playland in Old Orchard Beach, except a hundred times worse. He feared being cast into the endless abyss forever. He did as she demanded, tightening his grip around her hands. The sensation dwindled as his sweaty hands were released. The ground hardened but was uneven.

Thin and vibrant lights replaced the high beams, and a pungent odor of old urine and metal, fouled the remaining scent of pinecones. He stepped back as gravel crunched beneath his feet.

"Wh-where are we?"

He looked over to see the young women's frown of disappointment. It was mortifying to Elric.

In a condescending tone, she said, "We're in a Boston subway station."

His eyes widened. "Boston? That's impossible. We were about ten miles from Portland, in the woods. How can we be in Boston?" He looked down at the garbage and debris that surrounded them.

She sighed as if exhausted from his shock. "Umbraportation—or in a way that you can understand—moving from one place to another using darkness."

"How's that possible?"

She ignored him, going on a rant of her own. "It's pretty embarrassing for someone with power like yours to be so easily frightened and shocked." She looked down the deep black subway tunnels where the tracks traced down endlessly. "But, in due time, I'm sure you'll grow into them." She began to walk down the tracks.

He cleared his throat. "Hey! Wait!" He followed alongside her.

Her eyes fluctuated from blue to green to yellow to purple; it was amazing. She was about his height, wearing skintight jeans that revealed the curves of her body. She had on a black leather jacket, but you could see her pierced bellybutton if she moved a certain way.

"Do you want a picture? It'll last longer."

He looked away focusing on the tunnel, face reddening. "Who are you?"

"A friend. Someone who wants to see you succeed." She focused forward.

Rats scurried all around. The sound of pipes dripping added to the symphony of rat squeals that echoed down the strange path. The tunnel widened and forked into three separate paths. The middle and far-right tunnel were modern and very well kept, while the far left tunnel looked old and decrepit as if it were leading to the gates of hell. A train hadn't passed through in centuries from the looks of the rust and mistreatment of the rails.

She took the far-left tunnel, which was more like the Hilton for rats as dozens of them scurried along, filling the tracks. They weren't even frightened by the presence of the giants that stepped over them.

The lights that once guided them faded as they traveled into absolute blackness. He couldn't see his hands anymore. The soft, cold hands of the young women grabbed his and continued to lead him through the darkness. He wasn't surprised that she could see in the darkness. He half-expected it with those eyes of hers.

A dim lit area with a huge obstruction blocked the rails. Elric followed as the light grew brighter. The strange object began to take shape, an old train that looked as if it hadn't been used in centuries.

A thick, rusted door was just behind the train. The ominous light shone over a sign that read: "Do not enter! All those will be persecuted with the utmost violence!" The woman placed her hand on the sign and smiled.

"Well, this is it. Behind this door, you'll find the person you've been looking for."

"Wait. Are you serious?" He looked at the door suspiciously. "Behind this old door is Zarale or Zure whatever his name is?"

"Zaroule, yes."

He gritted his teeth. "Look, I don't know what you are, but you're telling me that in this old subway tunnel, I'm going to find a guy with a crazy, ridiculous name who's going to tell me how to control whatever it is inside me?" He looked at her as if she were joking. "Behind a door with a sign that says I will be physically harmed if I enter?"

She took another look at the sign and nodded. "Yes."

Elric sighed, "What the hell have I gotten myself into?"

He took the crumbling old steps to the door and looked back at the young woman who watched, gawking, like a mom sending her kid off to their first day at pre-k.

"Well, aren't you coming?"

She shook her head. "Unfortunately, this is as far as I can go. We'll see each other soon though."

"I'm sure." He looked up at the door.

"Oh, and Elric,"

He turned, sighing in frustration.

"Through those doors, I don't exist. Tell no one about me or how I helped you. Do you understand?"

His eyebrows bunched with concern, and he nodded. He turned his focus back on the strange door, studying it with uneasiness. "Should I knock or . . . " He turned, but she was gone. Using the ability that got them down there in the first place. She didn't make a sound. It made sense now. She would come out of nowhere and just like that be gone.

He tried to turn the old knob, but because of the rust it didn't jiggle, let alone turn. He banged on the door. He sighed after waiting for a couple of minutes. "This was a waste of time. I knew it. I'm just going crazy."

He turned, ready to leave, as a jingle behind the door caught his attention. Dust and sand hissed from beneath the cracks of the door as if it hadn't been moved since the tunnel was built. The door squeaked open. The hinges struggled to support the weight of the steel door.

Elric's fingertips tapped his side as he waited. He wondered if he'd be met with violence like the old sign said. He half expected it. Violence was becoming a part of his daily ritual.

A man opened the door and squinted his eyes. He poked his head out, looking around with large bulging eyes. A few dainty strands clanged to his shinning scalp for dear life. He studied Elric, lips quivering. *Eyes like a Chihuahua,* Elric thought. The man was thin and pale, built like a coat rack with clothes barely able to hang on.

"Nobody's used this entrance since the 1930s. What's your business here, boy?" he asked in a low voice.

"I'm searching for somebody. His name is Zaroule," he said, scrunching his face as he tried to remember the odd name.

"Yeah, I know of him, but that doesn't mean I can let you in.

We don't just let anyone walk in here like they own the place."

"Look, I've been having a really bad couple of days." Some of the dark energy began to seep from Elric's pours. "I don't want to take it out on you, so please, just let me in."

The man's eyes widened, beads of sweat forming across his wrinkled forehead. The rusty doorknob that the man gripped with his boney fingers jiggled from his shaking hands. He nodded. The dark essence seeping from Elric's body rose from his clothing like black smoke.

Elric walked into the dark room. The old man closed the door as all light vanished. Nothing could be seen. The sound of water dripping in the background and their heavy footsteps were all that could be heard.

The ground shook with tremors like an earthquake. Elric threw his hands out for stability, but the darkness gave way to nothing solid to keep a steady balance. Golden light pierced the darkness like a sharpened blade, shining through the outlines of a large door. A dust cloud kicked up as the door opened.

Elric shielded his eyes from the bright light and dust. He looked back at the man who watched, keeping a safe distance from Elric. He didn't regret the glare he gave the old man. Maybe if he had known Elric's story, it would have created a different situation, but it was too late for that now.

The door opened out into a large dirt tunnel. The smell was earthy but had a hint of metal and oil like the subway station, minus the putrid smell of garbage and urine. The light that illuminated the tunnel came from strange, carved openings that lined the tunnel on the right side. Every ten feet, there was an opening high above in the crease where the ceiling met the wall.

"It's just an old tunnel?" Elric asked, lowering his hands. He didn't know whether to be shocked or disappointed.

"Just an old tunnel? You kids these days have no respect for architecture," the man muttered under his breath as they walked on.

The man wobbled from the door he guarded, taking his time down the dirt path. The tunnel was blinding compared to the subway tunnels, the light seemed artificial, like a light dangling in the basement of a home.

Pipes lined the left side of the tunnel, giving off heat. They were old and rusted, hissing as pressure built. Then with a furious scream, they released hot steam into the warm, damp air of the tunnel. They reminded Elric of the boiler room down in Lexington High where he usually hid during lunch to read his comics. The old man was short enough to walk right underneath the hot steam. Elric ducked, hoping not to get scalded from the condensation. The old man looked back with the tiny hint of a smirk at the corner of his wrinkled mouth.

Bells rung, and light music echoed from the tunnel as they treaded deeper. They came down a long set of metal stairs, which shook from their weight. Up ahead, the brightness of light radiated through a larger opening.

"Not too far now," the old man muttered. His wobble became an exhausted limp.

The music was more pronounced now and the sound of people talking and laughing echoed below as they looked over a rusted banister.

"Welcome to Zenith!"

Below was a vast shanty city made of stone, scrap metal, and other strange metals that glowed a vibrant blue hue. There were hundreds of people below; he couldn't make out their outlines or details. Hundreds of small huts stretched across the earthly cave. Some were structured into the walls of stone and clay; others were welded by metal beams.

Elric's eyes widened. It was true that everything he had ever known was no longer a factor. The air was humid and sweet as the smell of good cooking floated to him. Conversation, music, and laughter echoed below. It was as if he had entered another world; a brighter version of what had befallen the world above. Elric kept his composure despite how shocked he was.

"So just a tunnel still, huh? Welcome to Zenith! It the fourth largest out of fifty underground cities in the world!"

Elric swallowed hard, looking down at the large opening. Though it wasn't the size of Boston, or even a city like Portland, the fact that something of this size could exist just beneath the surface seemed impossible.

Elric looked back, shocked from the statement that missed his ears. "There's fifty?"

"Yes, fifty." The man pointed above the city with a long skeletal finger, the nail looked like it hadn't been cut since birth, curving downward in a grotesque manner. "The lights above Zenith help keep everything moving during the day, and at night, they dim to conserve energy."

"How's it possible that nobody knows about this? What about electricity? Wouldn't it draw attention?"

"We schedule our electrical use around the surface world. If it is night above, the lights come on down here. Day above, lights go out here. You are correct. If we ran the lights the same time exactly as they did, it would be too much to sustain both Boston and Zenith. There would be speculations from above. Besides using electrical power, we have our own source of energy and electricity."

They walked down the metal stairs that rattled. The bolts in the stone wall struggled to stay attached. With each step, Elric prayed that it wouldn't be his last. A drop from this height would hurt, even with powers.

They came down to a dirt path that broke into a fork in the road. The old man pointed down to the right side of the fork.

"This route takes you to Zenith, and the other takes you to our natural source of energy. We use an underground water supply like a mill to keep our power going. That's so we don't just rely on the power of the above-worlders. We have our own system of hydropower."

"I see." Elric scratched his head, trying to understand the technology. "Why do you guys live down here instead of up there?"

"What? Are you stupid?" He looked at Elric. "That would be breaking the code we Ermakians have. Living amongst humans . . . disgusting."

Elric swallowed hard, thinking of the man's words. It sounded as if he didn't regard himself as a human being. Was he insane? And what was this Ermakian code?

"You must be one of those above-worlders, aren't ya? What? Your father's a human, and your mother's an Ermakian? Or is it the other way around?" He shook his head annoyed by the confused look Elric gave him. "Forget it. Just get out of here. Follow the right side of the road, and you'll go straight to Zenith."

Elric nodded and took the path that led to the populated shanty city. The man made his way back up the tunnel that led back to the doorway.

153

"Go on. And don't tell anyone I let you in. I don't know what you are." He turned and looked over his shoulder with a shiver. "But I hope to never see you again . . ."

Elric followed the path until it opened to the city. The path was made of smooth stone that must have taken proficient masonry skill to make. Someone took great pride in laying in all this stone. The underground city was unlike anything he had seen before. The structures were small; they were made up of remnants of old scrap metal and pipes from old subway stations and other material he couldn't recognize. They were based off stone and another glowing metal he never saw before.

The sound of laughter echoed a couple of yards away. He crawled behind a pile of old rubble and pipes. A group of kids who looked as if they belonged in elementary school were chasing each other around in a game of tag. They wore tattered clothing and played barefoot through the scrap metal. Their faces were covered in dirt.

One of the children, a young boy, struggled to get the others and became frustrated. The other children teased and laughed, reminding Elric of his own personal struggles as a child. The boy stopped and released a monstrous roar that rattled the sheets of metal next to Elric and even his insides.

"What was that?" Elric lay low behind the crevice, gripping his chest. He peeked back over.

The boy's tan skin became covered in a thick, orange fur with black stripes. A long, striped tail ripped his pants, and strong legs covered in striped fur shredded the remaining bits of jeans. The boy's head changed to that of a tiger as his feet and hands became claws. His body mass doubled, towering over Elric by at least a foot.

"He . . . he just transformed into a monster . . . just like the others?"

His heart thrashed against his chest. These kids were in danger. He tightened his fist and knew what he had to do. If he didn't, they wouldn't stand a chance. They'd be slaughtered—killed like those in Lexington. He took a deep breath and came out from behind the pile. His determination faded to fear and confusion as they began to laugh!

The children laughed and ran from the creature as it chased after them. It lunged and tagged a little girl, who pouted in anger. She folded her arms in frustration before stomping away.

"You cheated! No changing allowed!" she yelled.

The others took off into the urban town with the beast behind them. She cried, trying to catch them. Elric fell back, wondering what he just witnessed. They weren't frightened. In fact, they were happy, playing as if that thing were one of them.

"They must all be monsters!" He sunk deeper behind the pile of debris, hoping to avoid being seen or grabbed by any of the creatures. All he could think about was the general.

"What is this place?" he asked.

Chapter 18

—⟫«(◉)»⟪—

The Inhabitants of Zenith

Fear kept him from moving. He was surrounded by beasts—the very beings that he tried to avoid at all cost. Maybe this is what Carnage was talking about. Maybe this was all a set up right from the get-go. The girl was in on it too. He tightened his fist.

He took a deep breath. It would be easy to avoid any confrontation with any of the creatures out there if he blended in, but that was easier said than done. He stepped onto the dirt road which still had the heavy footprints of the beast and small children.

He entered Zenith and was consumed by strange tunes and the chatter of people talking and laughing. The different types of structures varied from small huts and stores to tall medium structures which hung overpopulated roads.

Monsters walked amongst people. Hulking, bear-like creatures laughed as their exaggerated bellowing overpowered the combined chatter. There were all kinds of them: bears, tigers, and panthers. There were too many to count. This wasn't just an underground city; it was an entire underground civilization!

Elric kept his eyes hidden and head low, hoping that his fear wouldn't overwhelm him. He sidestepped into a narrow alleyway between two structures. Elric's heart pounded against his chest as regret took over. He tried to control his breathing to keep from hyperventilating.

"I have to keep going." He closed his eyes and whispered to himself, "I can't stop now. I have to." He tightened his fists.

Beads of sweat glistened from Elric's forehead. The humidity and heat were heavy in Zenith; it was nothing like the cold, brisk New England air above. He looked up at the stone ceiling, which was a good fifteen stories above the city. He looked outside the narrow alleyway, which opened into the monster-infested walkways. The silhouette of a small, shadowy figure came into view.

Elric's eyes squinted, making out the figure of a boy. He was maybe eleven years old, and his were locked on Elric. *That's not good.* Elric wiped the sweat from his face and began backing deeper into the alleyway. He turned to go behind one of the tattered structures when he was decked on the chin.

He stumbled back, hitting the stone ground with a thud, cupping his mouth with a groan.

"You see? That's how you hit somebody!" A tall kid about Elric's age celebrated over him.

He was slim with dark brown skin and a cocky smile. His hair was trimmed, long enough to reveal the tiny curls that glistened from sweat. His nose was thick and rounded.

Behind him stood a girl with smooth caramel skin. Her hair was braided into a thick ponytail. She was much shorter than the guy parading around like a jerk and examined Elric with piercing green eyes.

The young boy he saw first took his place next to the girl. they looked alike; even down to the long dark brown hair, but his wasn't in a ponytail. Through his long eyelashes, the sharp, green eyes focused on Elric.

"Here. Let me help you up." The dark-skinned boy picked Elric up, tearing his shirt, and pinned him against the stone wall of one of the small shanty homes. "I smelled you as soon as you entered Zenith. You're not from around here and you're not Ermakian. Who are you?"

Elric looked down, amazed by the boy's strength. He wasn't muscular; he was nothing like the boys on the Lexington football team. Yet he had Elric pinned against the wall with one arm.

"I don't know what you're talking about. Get off me!" Elric tried pushing him away, but he didn't budge.

The boy clenched his jaw, digging his fist into Elric's stomach. "We trailed you as soon as the gatekeeper brought you through the tunnel." The boy threw Elric to the ground and picked up a cement block from behind a door.

The girl shook her head. "We know everyone in Zenith, and with everything going on now, we don't accept new blood." She stepped from behind the boy.

The dark-skinned boy raised the cinder block over his head, preparing to drop it on Elric.

"I don't have to tell you anything!" Elric kicked him in the ankles, dropping the boy to the ground. He jumped to his feet and took off between the other two into the cluttered streets.

Elric forgot about the creatures that overran the streets. His fear was diluted by the long-forgotten will to survive. He bumped into a large tiger who turned with a ferocious roar. He fell back. It shook its head and kept walking, ignoring the contact. Elric scrambled to his feet again, bolting into another alleyway. The three pursuers were right behind him.

Why don't we show them what you're capable of, Elric? The voice rumbled through his frantic thoughts, echoing louder than his beating heart.

He dipped and dodged around corners. He threw garbage cans down, hoping to slow them down. Their laughter echoed just behind. They were toying with him.

"Fine!" Elric yelled, fed up with the chase. He gave into what the voice implied. He stopped and turned to catch the dark-skinned boy lunging toward him.

The tall lanky figure shredded away his clothes transforming into a wolf. His claws reached for Elric, and large golden eyes brimmed with excitement. Elric nailed him on the snout and sent the beast howling into the side of one of the metal-framed structures.

The girl jumped from wall to wall with incredible acrobatic skill and kicked Elric in the face, sending him stumbling back.

Shaken by the kick, Elric wobbled to his feet. The younger boy looked on, not making a move. His green eyes wide with disbelief.

"Alfred, get up and stop playing around!" the girl demanded.

"I know." The wolf growled, rising from the ground, and shaking the dirt out of its shaggy fur like a wet dog. "I want first dibs," He said baring his canines. He leaped over the girl toward Elric.

Before anyone could react, a purple aura covered Elric in a glowing sphere, knocking the wolf away. He recovered, ready to make another attempt.

"That's enough!" a stern voice came from the opposite side of the alleyway. A girl stepped from the shadows, making her way toward them.

"C'mon, V!" the wolf growled.

The girl had long, dark red hair that fell just over her shoulders. Her eyes glistened, glowing purple as she stepped closer. She wore a torn, black gown with leather boots that clunked across the paved road. She studied Elric. "He's not some ordinary kid, trust me. I'm sure you figured that out when he knocked you into that wall." She glared, never taking her eyes off Elric.

The four of them gathered around him as if studying an animal in a zoo. The large wolf-like creature hovered over the three of them. Its long claws and large monstrous hands were draped in messy, grayish-brown fur. The girl with the glowing eyes was different than the other three; she had powers like Elric's.

"You're obviously not from around here. What do you want?" she demanded, pushing a few strands of hair behind her ear.

"I don't know who you guys think you are, but I'm not in the mood. I'm looking for someone." Elric tightened his fist, trying to suppress his anger. "And I was told they could be found here."

Let's kill them, Elric. The voice from his stomach began to cloud his mind, becoming much more persuasive.

Shut up! I can get out of this myself without your help! he snapped back.

"Whatever voice that's talking to you isn't going to help you get out of this," she replied.

He looked at her in amazement. "You . . . how did you hear that? I didn't say anything."

"You're way out of your league. Just tell us what you want and who you're looking for," she said raising her voice.

He thought about the last words that were given from the young women who helped him. *Through those doors, I don't exist* "I'm here to find Zaroule. I was told he could help me."

The girl's glowing eyes widened. The large beast behind them began laughing.

"Fat chance we'll let you see Z," the wolf growled.

The darkness forced itself through Elric's body as the black aura formed around him. No matter how hard he tried to fight, the beast's strength was greater than his will.

"Honestly, I don't care if you believe me or not." Elric looked up with piercing crimson eyes. His body was shaking, sweat pouring down his face. "You have no idea what league I'm in!"

"I believe that's enough." A dark-skinned man—who must have been in his fifties—limps out of the shadows with a cane snapping against the pavement, eyes hidden behind black shades. "Unfortunately, this boy's right. You have no idea what league he's in."

Unable to hold the darkness back Elric released a wave of fury that shattered the purple sphere he was trapped in. They all covered their eyes from the wave and roaring wind that blew dust and debris through the walkways. The darkness roared around him, tearing through the metal frames of the huts, creating a whirlwind of destruction.

"What's happening to him?" The red-haired girl stepped back in awe.

"Stand back." The old man pushed them away. "I'm the one you're looking for, correct? I'm Zaroule!"

Elric raced toward the old man, no longer in control of his own body and mind. He wanted to kill; his fingernails curving into black claws. Adrenaline flushing his veins, and the pleasure rising from this new desire turned him into something inhuman.

Before he could get to the man, he was thrown back by a wave of white light that glowed as bright as the sun. It blew forth from the old man, consuming everything in the alley, including the darkness around him.

The white light of the wave covered everything. Even the shapes of people vanished as he felt his body go numb. The darkness that coursed through Elric's body crumbled within as he closed his eyes.

Damn you, runt! How dare you let this petty freak of human nature stop us! That old fool is still strong!

Still? Elric whispered to himself as he blacked out.

Chapter 19

———— ⫷((◉))⫸ ————

The Old Man with a History, Zaroule

Elric opened his eyes, coughing as the thick dust cloud filled his lungs. He crawled on all fours, trying to focus, but something was missing. The darkness was gone. He had full control of his body again. His arms and legs shook as his strength came back.

"An ancient power I haven't seen in quite some time has finally caught up with me." The old man chuckled. "As old as it is sinister, that darkness will consume you before you realize you're even under its control. I assume you've come for me?" The man's voice penetrated through the thick smoke.

Elric's legs wobbled from his weight. Everything began to clear. He could see the shadows of the monstrous crowd standing around him. That power was amazing, unlike anything he'd ever felt before. Elric glared at the wrinkled, dark-skinned man whose eyes remained hidden behind the black shades.

"If you're coming for revenge, then please leave these children out of it," He spoke with a calm acceptance. He stood over Elric with folded arms.

Elric saw his own eyes and dirt-covered face in the man's black shades. He was confused by the man's words. "Revenge?"

The man unfolded his arms as they fell to his side. Elric could see the strange white aura surrounding him like a glowing beacon. The very presence of this man's energy was incredible and strong. No way he was human.

The group of teens and the large wolf took their position just behind the old man. Elric could tell they would die for him in an instant.

"Violet." His dark shades remained fixed on Elric. "Get yourself and the others out of here now!"

The redhead looked up. "What? Are you crazy? We're not leaving you by yourself, Z!"

"This boy is no normal human being. He's come for me. This has nothing to do with you, Alfred, Sasha, or Manie. Leave this place now and get as far away as you can."

Elric was confused by the man's words. The old man spoke as if they had history.

"Z, we're not leaving you." The wolf growled.

"I don't know what the hell is going on. I'm here to find Zaroule." Elric rubbed the dust from his eyes. "It sounds like you're him?"

"I am." The old man's fist began to glow with a strange light. "But not many people up there know me by that name, so for you to have found me down here . . . you did a lot of digging."

The old man's face wrinkled, trying to see if he remembered Elric from somewhere. The man's arms and face were riddled with scars and old injuries from a life long ago. Elric was sure the eyes behind those black shades hid the same story. He stood up, dusting himself off.

"I'm here to find you because I was told you could help me."
Elric's strength was starting to come back. "I don't want to fight. I
need help."

The old man's forehead furrowed, confused by Elric's words.

"Please, I—"

"It's alright." His hands relaxed as the strange white aura that
covered his fist faded. "You're telling the truth," the old man said as
if shocked by the very thought.

Elric wiped the sweat from his face as a strange weight lifted
from the air. He hadn't noticed the atmospheric pressure. The weight
of power he thought came from the darkness, was coming from the
old man. *Who is this guy?*

"It's been a very long time since I've seen the dark Titan." He
laughed, scratching a gray-goatee.

Elric looked up, confused by the word he used. "Titan?"

The man smiled and turned away, walking down the alley that
filled with people and monsters alike. Elric caught up with him,
walking past the others who wanted to finish the fight they started.

"Wait, what's a Titan? And do you know me, or know something
about me?"

The man stopped and looked Elric over, scratching his goatee.
"I don't know. Do you know something about me?"

"All I know is that you can help me with these powers and this
thing inside me." Elric looked away, hiding his own secrets.

"Hmm." He groaned. "Nope, can't help you. And since you
don't know anything about me, I'm nothing but an old coot with a
crazy name."

Elric looked up with eyes that scrutinized. "What?"

"Whoever told you to come find me played a horrible trick on you, kid. I don't know nothing about helping you control anything."

"No, no," Elric replied with disappointment. He jumped in Zaroule's path. "I came down here to find you because I was told you could help me. You know something. A lot. Especially if you think I was after you for revenge!"

The old man's eyebrows pinched together. He maneuvered around Elric and continued through the city of monsters. Elric became nervous when he saw the hulking beasts with large claws and teeth that could tear through flesh.

"Please," Elric pleaded. "If you can't help me, then I don't know how I'm going to keep the people close to me safe!"

The old man stopped. For a moment, it seemed as if time froze between the two of them. Elric couldn't move. Even his fingers cramped. He wondered what was happening. The people and creatures faded around him, and all Elric focused on was his plea.

The old man nodded. "Fine. I'll shed some light on a few things. I don't know how much it'll help you or if it'll make your situation better or worse. But, yeah, if it'll make you feel better and get you off my back, follow me."

A shaky breath rolled from Elric's lungs as he relaxed. After everything he had been through, he worried it would have all been for nothing. The red-haired girl brushed by him, ignoring his existence.

"Z, are you serious?" She walked beside the old man.

"Violet, I don't want to hear it. Let's go."

She mumbled, lowering her voice so Elric couldn't hear. She would look back every so often with a scowl. Her fiery red eyebrows bunched, giving her an intimidating appearance.

"Violet, enough," the old man said with a stern voice. "I already gave my word. I'm not going back on it. Elric is coming with us."

She turned making her way toward Elric. His hands trembled as she grew closer. The smell of her sweet perfume didn't go with her animosity and bullish ways, she grabbed Elric by the shirt and brought her nose down to his.

"If you lay a finger on him." She pointed to Zaroule and added, "Or the others, I'll bury you so deep beneath this city that not even the worms will find you. Get me?" A purple spark flickered from her eyes.

Elric nodded with raised hands. She released him and met up with the others who followed just behind him. He turned to see them laughing about the situation. He swallowed hard and raced to the front to catch up with Zaroule. He'd been stunned by her eyes— how purple they were and how much pain rested behind them.

Though he wanted to keep his composure, Elric couldn't help but be fearful of the creatures that surrounded him. Their human characteristics were small five digits, and they walked upright, using tools as if they were normal people. They even draped themselves with clothing that was made for their large bodies. There were wolves like the beast that stalked behind him. The wolf mocked Elric in a deep growling voice, still upset about the punch that laid him flat, calling it a cheap shot.

Through the crumbling roads that struggled to hold the group and other creatures that went about their business, they made their way through the shanty town of crumbling history. Some of the debris that littered the streets and made up the structures of Zenith were from Earth, while some stone and metals were from a different world all together. They came to a structure that was dug out of the walls overlooking Zenith. A metal staircase stretched from the building entrance.

"I'm going to head up and get dressed. I'll meet you guys up there," the large beast of a wolf half-said and half-growled.

"Make it quick, Alfred. It's your fault you tore up your clothes anyways!" Zaroule replied.

His large, perked ears fell flat like a dog being punished. Alfred leaped up the banisters, making his way to a large window, claws digging into the stone that made up the structure. He disappeared into a gap near the top.

Though from the outside the building looked like a mansion made for the mole people, the inside was decorated like a 1960's apartment building. Doorways spaced throughout the hallway, Elric raced his fingers along the rippling glowing metal. A strange vibration prickled his fingertips. "What is this?"

"Scintium, a metal not found in our world." Zaroule stopped in front of the sixth door, placing an old key inside.

"Our world?" Elric looked down, taking his hands off the wall.

"By your expression, I'm going to assume you have no idea of the world you stumbled into." Zaroule smiled. "I would've never thought you'd come to seek me out."

Zaroule opened the door to a room that smelled of earth. The room rotted from the inside out with walls green and flaking from age, revealing a red undertone. There were huge holes in the walls, and the wooden floors were scraped and gashed as if claws dug through them.

"Violet, can you and the others give me and Elric some privacy? We have some matters to discuss." He said to the red-haired girl.

She nodded, giving Elric one last scowl as they left the room, closing the door behind her.

Elric cleared his throat. "Yeah, she's not too fond of me."

"They're a little overprotective of me, but it's understandable. I'm all they have." He shrugged.

Elric nodded, gulping from the glare Violet gave. He stared at the man who he had gone through so much trouble to find. He wasn't what he expected, but then again, what was he expecting?

The cane he walked with was slick and white with the head of an eagle. It clicked against the old wooden flooring. Zaroule cleared his throat as he searched through the apartment.

"You can't outrun the demons of your past." He walked toward a bookshelf and pulled out a couple of thick journals with wrinkled pages. He nodded as he sat down on a raggedy couch. "I thought burning and tossing out all my old research notes would keep me away from my past. Take a seat."

Elric plopped down on an old sunken couch. The cushions had long since worn out, and the couch itself looked like something found in a garbage heap—it didn't smell as bad as it looked. He rested his arm on the exposed wood, watching Zaroule flip through pages of an old journal.

"You called me a Titan earlier, right? What's that?"

Zaroule lay back on the couch. "You really don't know what's inside you, huh?"

Elric leaned in, shaking his head.

Zaroule exhaled. "You have quite the heritage, kid. A bloodline that goes way back to the beginning of civilization itself."

"What?" Elric swallowed. "You expect me to believe that?"

Chapter 20

What's a Titan?

"We had no idea what they were. We gave them the name Titan because it was only fitting. I'm sure history had many names for these people who had power to control the elements, masters of their dominions. These beings looked human, but within them rested something else."

"There . . . there are others?" Elric swallowed. "Others like me?"

"Yup, five more actually. Look, I'm old, and I'm trying my best to give you your damn answers. Let me finish where I'm going with this!"

Elric nodded his heart racing. A deep feeling of belonging wrapped around him that he had never felt before. He wasn't alone.

Zaroule sighed, fixing his shades. "In time and with research, we came to find out that Titans shared their physical bodies with what we called Devas. In the metaphysics realm, a Deva is any of the spiritual forces or beings behind nature. But Devas are much more then spiritual forces and are frightening as all hell. They were immense-sized behemoths, highly intelligent, and powerful enough to do some serious damage."

A chill raced down Elric's neck as he thought about the monster that spoke to him from within.

"We weren't sure if they were gods, demigods, angels, or demons.

All we knew was that you were living weapons of mass destruction."

Elric took a deep breath. "So, I'm some kind of monster?"

"Elric, what's inside you doesn't make you who you are," Zaroule replied with a stern voice. "You came to find me in order to get help and find answers. When I sensed you, I felt the desperation in your heart to help those you care about. You have a benevolent spirit."

"But this thing inside me could care less about saving and protecting anyone. I can feel it." Sweat dripped from beneath his arms. The beads of sweat rising on his forehead were a harbinger of his fear.

"You're right." Zaroule scratched his chin. "But with your powers awakening now at a time like this, being a Titan is a gift. It's a sign. This is destiny!"

Elric wiped the sweat from his face. "Destiny, huh?"

"We're under attack, but I think you and the other Titans may play a key role with preventing the genocide of humanity."

The thought of others like him settled Elric's discomfort. It was bad enough he was a monster, but at least he wasn't the only one who suffered. Whether it was a good way of thinking about it or not, it gave him some peace from belonging.

"There are other Titans?" He thought about the Devas within them. "Where are they?"

"I don't know where they all are. I know some are in America, last I checked anyway."

Elric listened to the words that came out of Zaroule's mouth. He was patient, but it was starting to overwhelm him. Zaroule knew a lot more than some hermit that lived underground with monsters.

"The last time you checked?" Elric dug deeper. "Old man, there's something you're not telling me. I can feel it." Elric was on edge.

"Good. That's good because in the world you're in now, kid, you're going to need that vigilance." Zaroule cleared his throat. "Now, do you want me to finish or not?"

Elric thought about how discreet Zaroule was. He had the face of a poker champion and the shades to go along with it. Not only that, he had his own abilities that could suppress the darkness within Elric. He nodded, keeping his thoughts to himself.

"Fire, earth, wind, water, light, and darkness," Zaroule continued. "These are the powers of the Devas. One Deva for each element."

Elric looked away from him. "Darkness . . . that's the one inside me, isn't it?"

Zaroule looked up from the book. His shades gleamed in the dim light. "Yeah, the Deva of darkness, the being opposite of light. The one I fear the most. Its very nature is sinister."

Elric's entire body shivered. This thing inside him made multiple attempts to take over his body, forcing him to do awful things. It made sense now. The beast's embodiment was based off chaos and malice; its very nature was to destroy. "Explains why it made me feel like some kind of psychopath then." Elric lay back in his chair feeling a strange assurance that he was sane. "I get it now."

"Elric, I'm not gonna sugarcoat it. That Deva isn't something you want to wake up to first thing in the morning. I do know that as a Titan, you have the power to control what's inside you and use it for your own goals. That can only happen with resolve and faith."

Elric bristled. "Sometimes when I'm losing control, I can hear it. Then there are times where I end up in this cave of blackness."

"Your inner world," Zaroule said.

"My what?"

Zaroule sat back in his chair. "Your inner world. The place where you and your Deva's bond is strongest. I was there right before you attacked us. It's the most terrifying place I've ever been in my life. Not going back anytime soon. But every Titan has an inner world."

"That's insane. How were you able to go there?"

"I'm one of the few anomalies that can, due to my telepathic abilities. And, yeah, it is wild. Technically, in your inner world, you're a god. You can do whatever you want in that world as long as your faith and resolve are strong enough."

"What if they're not?" Elric swallowed hard.

"Then your inner world will look like what I walked into: the home of a monster. Your Deva will take root and take over. It's kind of what they do if they realize they have a weak host. I think it's a defense mechanism they have."

"You make it sound like they're living things!"

He laughed. "They are. And through you, their vessel, they can become flesh and bone. If that happens, that means you're most likely dead."

Elric thought about the meetings with the beast inside. His fears were true. This thing *was* trying to take over his body.

"Each Deva has its own body and presence, which I'm sure you've felt. They have their own physical characteristics, size, and personality. The more you use their power, the more you'll take on those characteristics and traits."

"Just like earlier today . . . " Elric stared into one of the large holes in the wall that opened to Zenith. "That feeling of rage and anger. I wanted to kill you guys." Zaroule nodded.

"I-I don't get it. You're fine with that? That's okay with you?"

"Kid, you're not the first person who's tried to kill me. You certainly won't be the last, and those kids out there will take whatever you throw at them too. Don't underestimate them!"

Elric's foot tapped against the wooden floor, he couldn't stop. He knew Zaroule meant well, but what Elric had been feeling since the Deva made its presence known has been nothing short of manic and frightening. Most of what Zaroule was saying made sense, and deep down it felt true.

"Elric, I know this is hard to understand, but I personally believe that what you are is a gift from someone higher. I don't believe the Titans were meant to be used as weapons, but right now I don't think we have a choice."

Elric was silent. He thought about his journey for answers, leaving Jennifer behind, and everyone who lost their lives in Lexington. He wanted Zaroule's answers to be lies. He wished he had never come here to find Zaroule. He left the comforts of the only family he had left, and it was all to listen to this? He could hear Zaroule still talking, but he blocked him out.

"Do you need a break?"

Elric looked up. He wondered what his face might have looked to Zaroule. He imagined it was exhausted, beaten, sad, and pathetic. What the hell was he doing here? Why did he leave? He cursed himself for feeling sad all those years in school after Mr. Lee's death. He hated himself for thinking about how bad he had it. After listening to Zaroule and looking at the world now, he was a fool. Everything he had back then he took for granted.

"No." His hands relaxed. "No, I'm sorry. I'm okay." Elric whispered as to not awaken the thing inside him. His thoughts of saving the world fell apart piece by piece. If this awful thing inside him was destructive, what was the point? "How am I supposed to use these powers without losing it and causing more harm than good?

If what you're saying is true, it won't matter what I do. This thing makes me enjoy doing horrible things. I'll eventually be consumed. How do I use something that's pure evil for good?"

Zaroule stood up. His left hand began to shake. Elric focused on the hand, but Zaroule stuffed it in his pocket. "Kid, how old are you?"

"Fifteen." Elric swallowed, watching his movements.

"Fifteen. For centuries, man has grown and prospered way before you were born. Whichever parent passed the powers down to you found a way to do good things. Or at least control them enough to not destroy the world." He shrugged.

"Yeah." Elric thought about his biological parents and what they must have been like. *Which one of them controlled the thing inside me?* he wondered.

Zaroule closed the journal and tossed it to the ground. He took a deep breath and exhaled before scratching the back of his scalp. He pushed his shades up close to his face as if they were reading glasses.

"So, any other questions?"

Elric thought about the man and his powers. "What are you?"

Zaroule raised a single brow. "I'm human, with a little extra flavor. I'm what the world calls an anomaly: a human with telepathic and telekinetic powers. Violet's an anomaly too."

"Telepathic and telekinetic powers?" He thought about some of the heroes in his comics. "You can move things with your mind, and communicate to others with your thoughts?"

Zaroule leaned forward. "You're not as dumb as you look kid. Yes, telepathy is the ability to share and receive information through the mind, which is why I can hear your thoughts when I want to. If I wanted to, I could send you my thoughts too." Elric leaned forward biting his bottom lip. "And telekinesis; the ability to influence the physical realm without lifting a finger."

Zaroule smiled as dozens of books rose from the bookshelf and began floating around him. The books circled him as if they had their own orbit and Zaroule was their center. It made sense now. That's why Violet was able to hear his thoughts even in his inner world. Elric couldn't believe people like them existed. Things just got weirder and weirder.

Elric was still trying to process it all. This wasn't like some class where everything was spoon fed. There was nothing fun about this. Elric made sure he hung on to every word. Inside him was a Deva, a being of incredible destructive power.

"Your knowledge of the Titans is not just miscellaneous information you picked up through life, is it? Who are you really?"

"You're a very observant kid. Attention to detail will save your life in battle, I always say." He chuckled. "I'll tell you a little bit more about myself, including how I know so much about the Titans, too. I think we both have some secrets that may need to be brought to light, but not right now."

Elric stared into the black shades that covered Zaroule's eyes. He wanted to see his pupils and then maybe he could get a sense of whether Zaroule was lying or if he had anything to hide. Zaroule was a smart guy. Elric felt like there was a lot that the man had left out. Elric would have to wait to find out why Zaroule wasn't being forthcoming with all he knew.

He rose from the couch, grabbing his cane, and strutted toward an area that was set up like a kitchen. "I'll tell you some more after we get some food. How does that sound?"

"Yeah, that sounds good." Elric nodded. His stomach growled at the sound of food.

Zaroule pulled out a basket of eggs from an old refrigerator and began to scramble them. He added some bacon to the mix, along with chopped onions and potatoes. Elric looked on with excitement; he was pleased to be eating normal food. He must have gotten this food from the above world. Finding fresh meats and food items didn't seem sanitary in an underground city.

"So, you're not going to tell me about the one who told you to find me, huh?" He looked at Elric with raised eyebrows.

Elric swallowed hard, knowing Zaroule could pull the information from his thoughts if he wanted to. "I gave my word I wouldn't." Zaroule sat a plate of food in front of Elric, who inspected the bacon and searched through the eggs for something unpleasant. "Like you said, we both have secrets."

He laughed, placing a fork beside Elric's plate. "I tell you what, kid. You're not as dumb as I thought you were."

"What's that supposed to mean?"

Zaroule continued to laugh as he ate his food. Elric finished off the small meal, forgetting just for a moment he was in an underground cavern. The bacon was sweet and crispy, and the eggs were scrambled with peppers and seasoning. He hadn't had cooking like that since Mrs. Lee cooked for him.

"Where did you get this?"

Zaroule looked up with his eyebrows raised above the dark shades. "Just because we live underground doesn't mean our food comes from down here." He took Elric's plate. "Merchants go above and trade their fresh goods with others. Well, until the portals hit anyway. I'm sure there's going to be a shortage soon."

Elric nodded, thinking about the creatures that could shapeshift whenever they wanted. They could move amongst the crowd in the above world. He wondered how many he saw and thought were normal people.

"You're welcome to stay here as long as you want till, I'm able to figure out a couple of things." Zaroule walked to the living room.

"How about you go outside and tell the gang to show you around. They'd love to have a new addition to the group."

Elric shook his head. "I don't know if you noticed or not, but we all had a pretty bad first impression of each other. I don't think they're interested in showing me anything."

Elric walked over to the sink to wash his hands, thinking about the boy that transformed into the wolf. The faucet shook and struggled to release clean and clear water. He was surprised about how they lived down here. The apartment was something that should have been condemned, but the food and drinking water was just as good, if not better, then that above.

"I know, but once they know you're alright, they'll take you in pretty easily." Zaroule opened the door to the corridor and called their names out. "Violet, Alfred, Manie, Sasha!"

The multiple doors that lined the hallway opened. The tall, dark-skinned boy who became the giant wolf was human again and was wearing new clothing. Violet's face was cold and indifferent.

"What's up?" she asked.

"Our new friend here will be staying with us for a while. Treat him with the same respect you want to be treated with and show him around."

She looked down at Elric in pity, then rolled her eyes. "You have to be kidding me, Z. This kid?"

"Violet, he's a guest with us, and a special one at that. Treat him as if he were part of the group, okay?"

The facial expressions of the three of them changed to frustration and disappointment, except for the younger one who smiled.

"Alright. Come on, Fresh Meat," Alfred said.

Zaroule turned. "And take him to see Eden."

Alfred looked back, confused. "Why him? He's nothing but a cocky piece of work."

"I think Elric will get a kick out of the entertainment around here, and that new fighter, Eden, may shake things up a bit."

Elric walked out, watching Zaroule close the door. Once the lock clicked, he was fair game. He kept a small gap between them. It was going to be a long day—night—whatever it was right now.

Chapter 21

—⟫⟪◉⟫⟪—

The World of Misfits

"So . . . what are you?" Violet asked. Her voice was callous and uninterested. Elric wondered why she even asked.

"I'm . . . I'm just human."

Everyone except Violet burst out laughing as they made their way down the metal staircase.

"Are you kidding me?" Alfred asked. "Alright, I know we don't like you, but you don't have to be scared to tell us what you are. Obviously, you're not human. No way a human could hit me that hard when I'm in beast mode." They all started laughing again. "I doubt you would have the guts to do anything like that if you were human. Now I'm sure Pops probably told you everything about us. I'm Alfred; I'm not a human as you saw from the fight earlier."

He pointed over to the light-skinned girl and the young boy who was by her side.

"That's Sasha and her younger brother, Manie. He doesn't talk much, but they're both like me, Ermakians." He nodded up front at the redhead. "And that's our wannabe leader, Violet."

"What is she?" Elric asked.

"She's an anomaly like Zaroule," Sasha said.

"So how old are you anyways, Fresh Meat? Thirteen?" Alfred laughed, mocking him.

"No, I'm fifteen. What about you guys?" He ignored the title he was stamped with.

"Well, I'm fifteen. Alfred and Violet are sixteen, and Manie is eleven." Sasha worked her way back into the conversation.

The three of them walked around barefoot while Violet wore old leather boots. Their clothes, ragged and loose were like hand-me-downs from a generation ago. Everyone down here seemed to sport that same look.

The Zenith society was a melting pot of different creatures that seemed like the animals in the above-ground world. The only separation was the fact that they had humanoid characteristics, mainly the ability to walk upright and talk. Some of them spoke English while others spoke in an entirely different language.

"What are they saying? What language is that?" Elric asked, listening to a giant bear talk to a small girl.

"Masa, the native language of Masalisk," Sasha said.

"I still don't know what that is."

She sighed. "You haven't heard of Masalisk? Next you'll tell me you haven't been to Ermak."

"But I haven't. What's Ermak?"

They all looked at each other, then back at Elric as if he were crazy. He was still lost and confused. After that statement, they didn't say anything else to him. He liked it that way. It seemed like all they wanted to do was make fun of him and boast about themselves.

He shivered at the sight of the different creatures that lived down below. Elric was still traumatized by the beast that attacked Lexington only days ago. Though they didn't seem as sinister, some of them still had a fearsome presence. What were they?

"They're Ermakians," Violet replied from the front.

Elric looked up, surprised by her response. "What are Ermakians?"

Sasha giggled. "Obviously, you know we're not humans. We have another side to us. We can change the way we look like Alfred did earlier."

"So, you guys are like werewolves or something?"

The three of them laughed except for Violet. She shook her head in the front and mumbled something.

"Nah, Fresh Meat, but I'm sure the whole werewolf aspect spawns from some of my ancestors." Alfred laughed. "I can change into a wolf because that's my species. Sasha and Manie are foxes. The moon and magic garbage have nothing to do with it. We can do it when we want."

"I still don't understand."

Violet stopped and turned around. "Look, just like the above world has different races, the Ermakians have the same thing, but instead of races, they have different species."

Elric swallowed hard. Violet was angry, but he had no idea why. Ever since they first made contact, there was always this negative feeling he got from her. She didn't like him at all. The others' eyes widened in disbelief. They smirked as she turned around and continued walking.

He shook it off. "So, where are we going?"

The narrow pathways were cluttered with garbage. It wasn't as busy as it was a couple of hours ago. Being down here could make anyone claustrophobic. Buildings were crumbling to pieces with minor work done to patch them up here and there, but they weren't livable by human standards. Not that anyone down here was human to begin with. Ermakians lived like a third-world civilization. With their abilities to look like normal people, it was strange that they chose to live like this.

"We—as in Alfred, Sasha, Manie, and I—are going to the brawling ring to see some fights. You, on the other hand, can do whatever you want. We're not responsible for you," Violet replied in a belittling tone.

"But Zaroule said—"

"Zaroule said we could show you around. I don't think you need us to do that. You're old enough to find things out for yourself, aren't you?" Violet asked.

"Nah, he's too much of a punk. Maybe we should bring him to the brawling ring. It might toughen him up." Alfred sighed. "Besides, Violet, Z did say to bring Fresh Meat to see pretty boy." She flicked a stare of frustration Alfred's way; he flung his hands up. "Just saying."

"Whatever. Come on, and don't straggle behind. If you get lost, we're not going to come looking for you."

They walked to the edge of town to a small crowd of people that waited in line. Loud music bumped from inside the building, like a night club. Everyone in line was in their human form so it wasn't all that bad.

"This is the place. Act cool. Don't act . . . human." Violet gave Elric a death stare.

They walked toward the crowd and past the line of waiting individuals. A large man who towered over everyone allowed a few people through the doorway.

Violet looked over at Sasha. "Connections, right?"

"Yeah, no biggie." She trotted over to the large man, gave him a weird handshake, and then waved for them to come over. The giant man moved to the side, allowing them to pass. He had a large, jagged scar that ran down the right side of his face. He stared at Elric with a face as if he smelled something rancid. His large hands began changing into claws.

"You might want to keep it moving if you want to keep your eyes in your head. He'll kill you in a heartbeat." Sasha grabbed Elric by his sleeve and pulled him into the building.

Inside the lights flashed in time with the music blasting as people danced. The entrance opened out into a large space that was once part of the old Boston subway that had been forgotten centuries ago. They walked through the dance hall, which swam with people. The music was the same that they listened to on the surface world. The song was one of Jennifer's favorite artists; she loved mainstream music.

A girl smiled as she danced close, looking at Elric. Before he could look away, another young woman pulled him close. Their bodies pressed against one another and he could feel her beating chest. He began to sweat, not knowing how to react.

She looked up with dark brown eyes that could be seen in the flashing of the club lights, exhaling as her lips curved, showing a row of sharp teeth that lengthened. Elric's eyes widened as Manie pulled him away from the situation.

"You should've let him have some fun, Manie. Then we wouldn't have to babysit." Sasha laughed.

"What is this place?" Elric looked around gasping for air.

The music blasted, shaking the walls, and making the floor vibrate. He couldn't hear himself think. There were dozens of people, all of them shapeshifting monsters.

They walked into a side door, following a group of people. The tunnels reminded him of when he first entered the underground city.

The music faded behind them and was replaced by another echoing sound, something more pronounced. Loud chanting and stomping echoed down the hall. A steel door opened ahead, unleashing the excitement of a growing crowd. The stomping of feet and clapping of hands blended in with the crowd's screams of excitement.

Once they passed through the narrow opening, the place shook with excitement from the crowd. It was a huge underground battle ring. Almost every row was filled with creatures and people alike. The construction of the arena was accomplished by using the leftover rails from the ancient subway stations and concrete columns that were left untouched. It gave the impression of the old Roman Colosseum.

"Hey, down there." Alfred ran down the cement steps toward an empty row of seats. They followed him to five empty seats and sat down.

A short, stubby man came out and made his way to the center of the dirt-filled arena below. The crowd went nuts as he waved his hands. This was a hundred times louder than any high school football game Elric ever went to. He could feel the energy; the roars and shrieks of excitement forced their way through his body. His fear was replaced by excitement.

"Eden, the winner of last week's fight against Rocklin, will be fighting Zenith's very own homegrown champion, Axe!" he yelled through a microphone.

A large, dark-skinned man walked out. He was covered in scars; he was a brute of a man who looked to have seen his fair share of war. *This must be Eden!*

Alfred's voice deepened with a growl. "Axe, he's going to take this kid down with ease, I know it!"

"Wait. That's not Eden?" Elric's eyes widened.

Alfred turned with disgust and anger. "No, are you serious? That's Eden!" He pointed toward the entrance of the ring.

A young boy around their age stepped into the arena from the side. He had an athletic build. His messy, dirty-blond hair stuck to his forehead from sweat and dirt. Raising his hand to the crowd, pounding his chest. The hair on Alfred's neck stood on end as his fingernails lengthened to claws. He hated this kid.

"Folks don't let his size and looks fool ya! Eden's fought in underground brawling arenas all over the country!" the stocky announcer replied.

The two competitors stayed on their respective sides as the announcer got the crowd riled up. "The match goes as follow. If any fighter dies, gets knocked out, or quits, the opponent wins." The announcer looked at both fighters. "But with these two fighters, I doubt anyone will quit, and Axe won't show mercy!"

The crowd was filled with excitement. Monsters were coming out of their seats. They whistled and cheered with no regard to the people around them. It reminded Elric of the pro football stadiums. He studied the crowd. As fierce as it looked, it wasn't that different from a crowd on Earth.

"This kid is nuts. What's he thinking?" Elric shook his head, feeling sorry for him.

The boy jumped from side to side, shadowboxing. He was quick and had moves, but would it matter with an opponent who was double his weight? Elric wondered why Zaroule wanted him to see this kid. Maybe it was a joke.

"You've probably never seen anything like this before, Fresh Meat. Back in Ermak, only the strongest were selected to take part. This is nothing compared to the real deal back at home. The king selected the cream of the crop of warriors to take part and gathered beasts from all over Ermak. It was way better than what humans call entertainment." Sasha laughed.

Elric ignored her comment, disliking the fact that his new nickname was becoming more popular by the minute.

"Let the round commence!" the announcer yelled as the crowd roared.

Chapter 22

Something in the Air

The two fighters watched each other, circling and sizing each other up. Eden's lips angled in a cocky smirk. They were exchanging words that Elric wished he could hear. Axe swung with a punch that had all his body momentum in it. Eden ducked. Axe charged and went to grab him, but all he got was air as the thin boy maneuvered around him with incredible quickness, slipping right through his grasps and attacks.

"Whoa, that's fast . . . really fast." Sasha stood up.

Eden turned to the crowd, raising his hands and taunting Axe further.

"Who does this kid think he is?" Alfred yelled in anger.

The man ran at him once again. This time Eden wasn't paying attention; he was too focused on the crowd. Sharpened claws were outstretched; they slashed down from behind. Those claws would shred him to ribbons. Elric wanted to look away, but the excitement had him hooked.

"Yes, and this should end the match!" Alfred stood up with excitement.

Eden dodged the attack, crouching to the ground, and kicked the man in the ribs. The force sent Axe into the fence with a crash. The force was felt by everyone in the stands. Eden raised his hands in triumph, yelling with excitement. There was no fear, just pure confidence. As cocky as he was, he had the actions to back it up.

"Who is this kid?" Violet asked, looking down. "Someone needs to put him in his place. If this guy can't do it, I'll gladly jump in."

Axe got up, holding his side, and looking over at a celebrating Eden. Even from the stands, you could tell that the large man's face was filled with utter humiliation and anger. Elric wondered what hurt more: his sides or his pride.

Axe gave out a monstrous roar that drowned out the screaming crowd. His clawed hands became draped in gray fur. The snapping and popping of muscles and bones made Elric shake.

He was much larger, more muscular, and heavier than Alfred was. This wasn't good. Now a full-on beast, Axe dropped to all fours and galloped toward the young man who was still facing the crowd.

Eden dodged the attack as six-hundred pounds of muscle and animosity slammed face first into the fence. The crowd roared with excitement, chanting for both opponents. This was bigger than any athletic event Elric saw on the above world. This kid was making a monster look like an idiot. He had to be an Ermakian, but what would he turn into?

"Come on, Axe. Break his legs. This kid's nothing but a walking, talking toothpick!" Alfred ranted.

Axe got up and stood his ground. Eden ran toward him, going on the offensive. His movements were so fast they couldn't be seen; no living thing could move that fast. Elric couldn't believe Ermakians could have this ability.

"Whoa! That's fast, even for an Ermakian." Violet stood up.

Elric rose from his seat. If this caught her attention, he must have been seeing something never seen before.

Axe tried to grab him, but Eden maneuvered around his body with such agility and finesse that nobody in the stands could keep up. He smashed into the belly of the beast. The force knocked the wind out of Axe, forcing the monstrous creature to his knees. Eden grabbed him by the tail and slung him into the steel cage. The crash was devastating with the sound of metal bending and giving way. The crowd remained silent as the steel cage fell, creating a pile on top of the beast. All that could be heard was the metal falling and whispers of people in shock.

"Wow, the guy you're rooting for isn't looking too hot," Elric said, looking over at Alfred.

He turned with wild eyes like a wolf. "C'mon, Axe. Kill this guy!" he roared, getting out of his seat.

Everyone was on their feet, waiting for movement from the pile of rubble. Sasha was talking with Manie and laughing. Violet watched with folded arms and a stare of disappointment. Elric was starting to relax around them.

Alfred nudged him with his elbow. "Look, I told you."

He pointed to the arena. Axe rose from the metal heap, shaking the dust and dirt out of his thick, matted fur. He stalked Eden from behind. With two strides on all fours, he slammed into him, sending Eden flying into a fence. Eden never saw it coming.

"Never doubted him one bit. He's too strong; no one can beat him. He's the city champion. No one can beat Axe!" Alfred said nodding with pride.

Axe walked over and picked the small boy up by the throat. The large clawed hands wrapped around Eden's throat.

Nervousness swept Elric as he contemplated whether to jump in and stop the fight. These people were barbarians. They were going to watch this kid get ripped apart. Why didn't he transform like the other guy?

Elric's stomach was queasy as if he were free falling. The air was electrifying as goosebumps rose down Elric's arms.

A powerful wind burst forth from the ring like an aftershock of a bomb exploding. All five of them looked at each other confused. They tried to cover their eyes to protect them from the dust and debris. Elric looked out into the arena as a small tornado formed and engulfed the two fighters. The force of the wind blew the cage onto the spectators.

"What's going on?" Sasha yelled through the howling wind.

Violet's eyes begin to glow. "Something's not right. You guys feel that?"

A terrible feeling hit Elric in the pit of his stomach. It was ten times worse than the last. Something awful was happening. He felt chills down his spine. It was worse than when he fought that man in Lexington. What was happening down there with those two?

The spinning vortex began sucking everything in as the wind howled through the arena. The sounds of cheers changed to screams of horror and pain as people were ripped from their seats and sucked into the tornado. Chairs were stripped from the aisles as garbage and debris were sucked in.

"Manie!" Sasha screamed as she grabbed his hand to keep him from being taken away into the vortex.

Everyone gripped onto their chairs and struggled to pull themselves out of the aisles. Elric followed them but stopped. His heart thudded with terror as he looked down into the arena. Bright golden eyes and large teeth were beginning to protrude from the center of the tornado.

"What are you doing just standing there? We got to get out of here now!" Violet screamed, trying to get Elric's attention.

The huge crowd poured into the thin hallway. Anyone that fell was trampled by heavy feet and claws. A pop echoed as the door behind them ripped from its hinges. A powerful squall pushed through, forcing everyone through the tunnels.

Screams wailed behind, but no one turned to see why. The sheer strength of the wind increased with every terrifying moment. It roared like a freight train through barren land. Elric frantically fought through the crowd as the humid air smacked against his face. The pressure made it hard to breathe, increasing his exhaustion.

"This doesn't make sense! How can a tornado form in the basement of a building?" Violet shouted in confusion.

Elric couldn't understand what was happening either. This power he felt reminded him of when the darkness would take over.

"We're almost to the club. C'mon!" Violet yelled.

Alfred pushed open the doors as the crowd emptied out onto the dance floor. People were knocked down or pushed to the side. The powerful wind roared, sending speakers flying into the wall. Fear and chaos swept through as everyone emptied out of the structure.

Elric tried to stay focused on the others, but the panic of everyone around him made it hard to concentrate. He kept his eyes fixed on the long, puffy hair of Manie, who was being dragged by Sasha. Alfred was right next to him.

A girl fell, tripping over a table that had been crushed by the stampede. She changed. Shimmering, tawny fur covered the parts of her body that tore through her clothing. She took on the appearance of a feline creature. She looked like a leopard. As she rose to her feet, Manie tripped. She hissed and took off into the crowd, knocking anyone in her path out of the way. Elric went to help, but Alfred grabbed Manie and threw him on his back before changing into his wolf form. His shirt shredded away, but remnants of his pants managed to stay on his waist.

"Good idea. I'm all for that," Sasha yelled as Alfred finished changing. Her smooth, caramel skin was replaced by silky, orange fur, and a long, bushy tail ripped through her pants. The shirt she wore was torn away by the change in her size, revealing a white, furry chest that got thick and fluffy near her throat. Her feet transformed into slick paws.

Her ears were pointed and perked in an alert position. Maneuvering through the crowd, she used her dark brown claws to smash through the stone wall like a sledgehammer, creating another exit for others to escape through.

Elric stood frozen, shocked by her appearance. "She's a fox!" She wasn't as frightening as the other creatures of this world. She was beautiful, in a humanoid fox kind of way.

"Hurry up or you'll die down here!" Sasha yelled in a deepened voice.

Elric pushed forward through the crowd as the others rushed by. His body was starting to give out from exhaustion; even the adrenaline wasn't enough. A strong forced crashed just behind as the powerful wind rushed up through the tunnel that lead to the arena, releasing a strange ripple. Elric was overwhelmed by its strength and was knocked to the ground.

The wind roared in his ears as panic set in. The dust and debris kept him from seeing anything as he lost track of Violet and the others. Something grabbed his leg. Elric froze with fright; his eyes teared with fear as he looked down. A clawed hand gripped his ankle; the wind was taking on a physical form. Its white, creamy texture dug into Elric's leg as he looked toward the doorway. A monstrous mouth with sharp teeth was making its way toward him. A face formed from the vortex. The details of its mane and fangs were visible, including its glowing eyes.

"This isn't happening!" Elric looked up desperate for help, but everyone was gone.

Only darkness remained.

"They left me." He was losing oxygen; the wind was taking his breath away. Elric crawled across the dance floor with all his might, but the wind pulled with enough strength to lift his legs off the ground. His fingertips were slipping. Soon the beast would have him. With fangs like that, it would devour him; he could already see it tearing away at his flesh. Blood seeped from his fingernails as they tore away from the bed of his fingers.

"Whatever you are inside me, where are you?" he screamed out loud, begging for the darkness to protect him. There was no answer. There was no monstrous growl or sinister coaxing to do evil. This was it. He could see nothing but blackness. Back behind him, the shapes of two glowing, yellow eyes grew larger as they made their way closer. Elric's face was red from the pressure of the wind and the force that slashed away at his hands and face.

"Somebody help me!" he yelled.

He thought of Mrs. Lee and Jennifer. He regretted leaving; it had been nothing but trouble since he left.

Two claws grabbed his arms as he was pulled forward to the exit. *This is it. This is as far as I'll go. I'm sorry, Jen. I guess I couldn't help you keep your promise,* he thought to himself as he closed his eyes.

He felt himself being yanked forward as he lost consciousness.

Chapter 23

─────◀((◖))▶─────

An Unknown Guest

"Hey, wake up," a voice said. Someone began shaking him. "You okay?"

Elric looked up to see Violet standing over him. "Yeah, I'm fine. What happened?"

He sat up and looked around. Everyone was outside now. The building they entered was nothing but a pile of rubble and bricks.

"Nobody knows. Alfred found you like this." Violet's hair fell just below her chin, framing her face. She had small lacerations across her face, but they were nothing serious. He looked up at her.

He looked over her shoulder to see a bunch of monsters pulling people out of the debris. Screams and yells of pain filled the air. Sasha and Manie were a couple yards from them, helping others get to safety. Sasha in her fox form must have been six to seven feet tall. Manie looked like a stump in comparison.

"Where's the ambulance? These people need help," he mumbled in exhaustion.

"You really don't get it, do you?" Violet shook her head in disappointment. "This is the help, us, all of us. The aboveground world doesn't care about us. They don't even know we exist. The only hope we have for survival is each other!"

Violet walked away, shaking her head, eyes shimmering with purple light. The pile levitated above the ground, allowing those trapped beneath to pull and claw themselves out. She wasn't like the others who could transform into beasts, but her abilities alone were astonishing.

He closed his eyes and sighed, feeling like an idiot after what he said. People and creatures poured from all around to help. All this time, he feared them, thinking they would kill him if they found out he was a human. They didn't have a clue about his existence. They cared for one another like a family even if they were strangers to one another.

"They aren't like us, Elric." A voice came from behind him.

He looked up to see Zaroule scanning the area. "Zaroule?"

"Ermakians, as an entire civilization, have overcome horrific factors in their own world, but they were only able to do it by uniting as one. Mankind has a long way to go before we reach that point." He chuckled. "We still separate ourselves by our beliefs, geography, and even the color of our skins." He looked down at his brown hands gripping his cane. Elric looked over at them all working hard to dig injured people out of the rubble. Zaroule looked up, shaking his head. "What happened?"

The environment was intense as people ran and tried to help one another. Violet was right; it was only them. No police and no sirens from emergency vehicles. This was a hidden civilization beneath the twisted metal; it was hidden from the eyes of everyone above. Looking at the damage, memories awakened of what happened that night in Lexington. The images flooded his thoughts. Though it was minor compared to the damage done in his small town, the panic and the fear was the same.

"We were watching a fight in the arena when—"

Zaroule immediately cut him off. "Damn it," He wiped the sweat that glistened from his scalp. "Did he lose control down there?"

Zaroule shook his head. By his expression, Elric could tell he knew something. His hands remained fixed, but his cane trembled.

"Come on, Elric. These people need our help." Zaroule took off his shades and made his way to a group of Ermakians.

Elric's eyes widened as he tried to get in front of him to get a closer look at what he hid behind the black shades. A powerful quake shook the ground, putting everyone on guard again. It kicked up a large dust cloud where the building once stood. The pile of debris sunk into the ground.

"Everyone get out of here now!" someone screamed.

They all jumped out of the pile as it swirled into a vortex. An ear-piercing howl bellowed from below as a powerful wind burst from the ground, spewing stone, and metal.

Elric ducked behind a pile of scrap metal, blinded by dust. He used his shirt to cover his face, keeping the dust from seeping into his lungs. The blowing wind threw people into buildings and slung them into the air. Most of its power poured from the large hole that appeared.

"It's him! The boy from the fight. How could he have survived?" someone shouted.

Elric removed the shirt, looking up with squinting eyes as Eden floated from the hole. He rose with the wind as it carried him through the air. Then, without warning, he dropped from the sky and hit the ground, unconscious. The awful power of the wind vanished as quick as it came.

"Is everyone alright?" Zaroule yelled out. "Violet?"

"I'm good. Sasha and Manie are alright too. I don't know where Alfred is though."

A giant purple sphere of energy carried the three of them toward Zaroule. Elric followed the bright sphere like a beacon of hope. He could see the outlines of Violet, Manie, and Sasha inside. Elric pressed his finger against the glowing object; it pulsed like a heartbeat.

"Elric," Sasha yelled. "You're alright. Then where's Alfred?" She looked around like a mother hen who just lost one of her chicks. "Violet, can you find him?"

"I'm already on it." The purple sphere glowed as it protected them from the outside world.

"Elric, you alright?" Zaroule asked.

"Yeah, I'm fine. Wish I could say better for this place." His eyes searched the damage. How could one person do this? It was hard to see; everything was still blanketed by the thick dust cloud. The purple aura of energy that surrounded Violet was all that was illuminated.

"Found him. He's under a pile over here," The bright ball of energy lowered the three of them to the ground and vanished. "Elric, I'm going to need your help; he's hurt."

Elric ran over toward where Violet was levitating a giant pile of rock and brick away from the area. He was amazed by her powers.

"Don't just stand there. Help!" she demanded.

"Right. Sorry." He snapped out of his astonishment and dug up large chunks of metal and stone.

"Good job, Violet! You get Alfred out of there. I have to check on something." Zaroule went past the large group of people and vanished amongst the crowd.

The smothered sounds of yelling came from the pile as they unearthed Alfred. He had returned to his human form. He was holding his head, which was dripping with blood.

"Damn it!" he yelled.

Sasha pulled him out of the pile. The only remaining fabric on him was his torn pants, which were now shorts.

"Quick! Put this on your head." Violet ripped off a large piece of her gown and placed it on his head to stop the bleeding. "Hold it tight, alright?"

"Yeah, no problem. Thanks." Alfred winced as he applied pressure to his scalp. "What the hell happened anyway? I was helping this guy get his friend out from the dirt, and the next thing I know, I'm being thrown into the side of a building. And on top of that, a ton of bricks fall on me!"

Sasha looked up with a smile. "He'll be alright."

Violet looked around. "Where did Z go?"

"He said he had to go take care of something; he kind of just vanished," Elric said, trying to sound confident.

"Of course. Let's get out of here and head back to the house. Looks like everything's under control here anyway," Violet said, wiping the sweat and dirt off her face.

They helped Alfred up and began making their way to the opposite side of Zenith, back to the apartment. Elric trailed up the twirling stairs as everyone dragged themselves forward. The mettle staircase rattled from the weight of Sasha's beast form.

Elric's legs felt like he was wearing boots made of lead. Even the hallway to the rooms felt longer as exhaustion set in. "So, where's my bed?" Elric asked. All the room doors slammed shut. He turned to find himself alone in the hallway. "Does anyone even care?" he murmured to himself.

He walked toward the room Zaroule had brought him to. He tried turning the knob, but it was locked from the inside. His back smacked against the wall as he slid to the ground. He was covered in filth and starving, but nothing could compare to the exhaustion. He was also pissed because that monster inside him was ignoring his pleas for help; something didn't feel right.

He closed his eyes and found himself back in his inner world, but it was different. Instead of an eerie, damp, black cave, it was now a bright, white room with a single jet-black door. The door had a note nailed to it:

Elric, this may be hard to understand, but only open this door during emergencies. I will explain things later. I promise!

-Zaroule

Elric opened his eyes, remembering what Zaroule said. Right before Elric lost control, the old man was in his inner world.

Elric started to doze off, but the sound of footsteps coming up the stairs kept him awake. The shadows of two figures came into the light. It was Zaroule helping someone up the stairs. Whoever it was, he or she was in bad shape. Elric tried squinting to get a better look but couldn't. The head was tilted down, motionless.

"Elric, Elric, wake up." Zaroule struggled to put the key in the door. "I need you to help me get him in here; he's hurt pretty bad."

He helped Zaroule unlock the door and pushed it open. Zaroule stumbled in, laying the person on the couch on his back. That's when Elric got a good look at him. "No! Eden. He's the one that caused what happened down at the arena. Zaroule, if he wakes up, he could do the same thing here!"

Elric went to get help, but before he could get to the doorway, something grabbed his shoulder.

"No, Elric!" Zaroule said from the other side of the room.

Elric looked around the room, trying to find out what was keeping him from moving. It felt like these huge hands had him in their grasp; he was too weak and exhausted to try and fight them off.

"I-I can't move." No matter how much he fought this force, the grip only tightened.

"Sorry, Elric, but I had to bring him here. They'd probably try to kill him. You and Eden have more in common than you know. I won't be able to tell you and the others what's going on till morning." Zaroule fell back on the chair that was next to the couch.

Elric searched Eden, wondering what Zaroule meant. Eden had dirt smeared across his face. Elric wouldn't forget the fear of the power that came from the boy who he thought was Ermakian.

"Hey, you got to trust me on this one. I'll tell you everything I know. I won't waste your time any longer." The old man smiled, fixing his shades.

Elric's eyes focused as he saw Zaroule's eyes without the dark shades. Sweat raced down the sides of his wrinkled face; even his short sleeve button-up was soaked and dirty from the dust. His pupils were milky white, like a blind man's, but Elric knew he could see clearer than anyone else. His eyes became dark brown, and the grip around Elric's shoulders loosened.

"What did you just do to me?" Elric rubbed his shoulders.

"Telekinesis. Anomaly, remember?" Zaroule took a deep breath and placed his shades back on. He rose to his feet and limped to the back room. He brought out some covers for the boy and then fixed Elric a sleeping spot on the floor.

"I know you want answers, so just work with me for now, okay?" Zaroule turned out the lights, and the clomp of his cane faded into the darkness.

What's going on? Elric thought to himself. At least he would get some more answers. The sooner he could get answers, the sooner he could understand this thing inside him. The thoughts ran through his head, making it difficult to fall asleep. It didn't help that he had this lunatic lying on the couch beside him. *What the hell is Eden?*

Chapter 24

The Wind Titan

The next morning, Elric awoke, stretching on the floor. The thoughts of last night lingered like a fading dream. As hazy as they were, he remembered one distinct fact. He looked up on the couch, searching for the boy who toppled an entire structure like a kid knocking over blocks.

Elric's eyes widened. *Where is he?* He searched through the apartment and even knocked on Zaroule's door. There was no answer. He opened the apartment door and ran down the halls and banged on everyone's door in fear. "Hey, wake up! We have an emergency!"

All four doors swung open. Everyone's eyes were red with sleep and exhaustion. Confusion fed their anger. With pajamas as their attire, they were ready for a fight. Elric forgotten how much they hated him, but that didn't matter, they could kill him later.

"What's the problem, Fresh Meat?" Alfred asked, rubbing his eyes.

"Seriously?" He thought about the awful nickname. "Look, Zaroule brought that guy Eden home, he was the reason . . . "

"He was the reason for the destruction that happened last night." A voice came from the stairwell.

They all looked over as Zaroule strolled down the hall. Eden was behind him with his hanging his head low. He looked up with a defiant stare that connected with Elric's.

"You all remember Eden?" Zaroule nodded to Elric. "Don't worry. What happened yesterday was an accident; he lost control. He's what you call a Titan."

Elric pulled himself away from Eden's glare and looked up at Zaroule; he was astonished by the revelation. Just a couple of feet away was someone just like him.

"A Titan?" the group asked.

Elric looked him over, still surprised that he wasn't alone. "I get it now. That's why you wanted me to meet him, right?"

Eden looked away, ignoring Elric's searching eyes, and focused on Violet. Dirty blond hair covered his eyebrows and piercing blue eyes. His thin lips and strong chin made up a face that looked to be sculpted by god himself. He was athletic and toned with a body built like a fighter. Life would've been given to him on a silver platter back on the surface. The world was kind to people like Eden, Elric saw it all the time in school. He hated it.

Eden looked Violet over and smiled.

Violet rolled her eyes and turned to Elric. "You woke us up early in the morning for this?" Her eyes turned purple as an invisible force grabbed Elric's arms and torso.

His arms squeezed against his ribs, his body like putty in the hands of a large, invisible force. It was unimaginable to think Violet's powers could be this strong, let alone know she could control them so well.

"Violet, enough. He was just trying to help. Release him because what I have to tell you will change the way you see Elric," Zaroule demanded.

The powerful force released Elric as he fell to the ground. He held his ribs and coughed, trying to force air back into his lungs. Zaroule helped Elric up and walked them all into his apartment before sitting them down on the couch. Eden sat across from Violet, lying back with his face cocked to the side to get a better look at her.

"I'm sure most of you, like Elric, may have put it all together already, but, yes, Eden did destroy the night club last night, but it wasn't a deliberate attack." Zaroule stood up with his hands in his pockets. His cane rested on the side of the couch. "Like you Elric, he's still getting used to his abilities."

"Makes sense." Alfred smirked. "Figured you'd use some freak abilities to beat Axe, loser."

With incredible speed, Eden grabbed Alfred by the throat and lifted him off the couch. "That's not how I remember it!"

Alfred began to transform, and Eden's grip loosened. Alfred raised a large, hairy, clawed hand and smacked Eden across the room. The wall cracked and the old green paint chipped away from an already deteriorating surface.

"Enough, Alfred. Shut up! I don't want to hear another word out of you, Eden. You need to calm down and listen!" Zaroule mustered up enough strength to head to the other room and grab the old journal he read through yesterday.

Elric studied Zaroule and his veiny wrinkled hands moving through the pages

"Before I begin, I have to let you all know about my past. A past that I thought I could run away from." He smiled, looking at Elric. "But apparently you can't run fast enough. Prior to meeting any of you kids, I was part of a specialized group created by the U.S government. We were selected, educated, and trained daily on subjects that nobody in their right mind would believe or be able to fathom. Our top subject, our priority above all else, were the Devas and the vessels they inhabited. This was called Project Titan."

The room grew silent. Everyone looked on as if Zaroule was crazy, Violet's face scrunched in confusion as her eyebrows bunched together. Her eyes watered, and her lips quivered. "Zaroule, please don't do this."

"Violet." He shook his head. "I know you think I'm crazy, and I'm sorry for not letting you see me and my past. But I'm not crazy!"

She bit her bottom lip and focused on the floor. Elric was surprised to see her tears.

Zaroule talked about the Devas. They were living, breathing, behemoths of inconceivable power that were the incarnation of the elements: fire, water, earth, wind, light, and darkness. They roamed the world, changing the landscape and causing destruction on a massive scale. They were natural disasters that could think and feel. He told the story of an ancient civilization of people called the Cimmerians and how their greed for power led to the creation of the vessels, the Titans.

"We believed the Cimmerians used an anomaly, probably the most powerful anomaly that ever lived, to not only capture the Devas but harness their powers as well."

Violet wiped away a few tears from her reddening cheeks, shaking her head. "If these things were considered gods, how could mankind harness that kind of power?"

Zaroule sighed. "Exactly. Not like they could throw a leash around something the size of the Sears Tower, right?" He closed the journal. "It was human sacrifice."

Sasha looked confused. "Sacrifice? What kind of sacrifice?"

Zaroule stood and grabbed his cane. "In order to truly control the Devas, they had to raise them. The logic behind it all made perfect sense, but the risk factors bordered on insanity." He let out a deep breath. "They used children. Only the strongest and most confident were chosen. It was considered a sacrifice because most of the children didn't survive."

Elric's eyes widened. Was this real? Could it be true? \
history this frightening? He looked down at his hands, thin.
about the monster inside him. Why would they do such a thing
Why would these people sacrifice their own children?

"Why?" he whispered.

"When the Devas were captured, they were torn from their
physical bodies and only their energy remained. The process to
make a Titan required the child to have the energy of the Deva
embedded within them. The spiritual walls of the host had to be
powerful enough to hold the Deva, but the key to it all was to have
an unshakable resolve—an absolute will to fight the Deva's power
and hone it as their own."

Tears ran down Elric's face. "They killed their own children just
for control. Just to have power?"

"It's hard to understand. Like other civilizations starting out,
their means were barbaric. It was just the way man was."

Elric fought to control disgust and anger, taking deep breaths,
but he couldn't accept it. He thought about what he learned in history
and social studies class. Mankind's existence was built on blood and
the destruction of one another, even to this day. It was a cycle of
blood and self-destruction. "Okay, so what exactly is a Titan?"

"The best way to put it is that they were human containers,
housing the power of monsters that most likely shouldn't have been
messed with." His voice became low and frail. "From what we were
able to understand, these children were treated as objects, weapons,
and even outcasts by the ones who bore them into this world."

Elric thought about his own life. "Bull! They turned them into
monsters and then treated them that way!" His knuckles cracked as
he slammed his fist against the wooden arm of the couch, cracking it
in half. Pieces of plank splintered onto the floor from his anger. He
thought about high school and his life at Lexington.

"Elric, what's inside you doesn't make you who you are," Zaroule replied with a stern voice.

"But it does. I'm a freak, just like them!" Elric shook his head.

Violet rose from the chair, shaking her head, unable to listen anymore. "I can't sit here and listen to you spout this garbage, Z." She looked at Elric. "You won't suck me into this fantasy realm. I don't believe it. I never did. I never will."

She left the apartment, slamming the door. Eden stood up, about to go after her.

"No." Zaroule stopped him. "No, let her go. She needs some space anyways."

Alfred sighed. "Well, I'm with Violet. C'mon, Z. We aren't kids anymore. Fairytales are left in la-la land. Besides, where's the proof?" Alfred asked, laughing. "I'm sorry, but you gotta do better than that. Monsters and gods?"

"Proof?" Zaroule looked at Alfred with one eyebrow higher than the other. "These two are your proof." He pointed at Eden and Elric. Elric looked at him as if he were crazy.

"Listen, Elric. Remember I was going to tell you more?"

Elric looked on. "Well, yeah."

"Right, well, I'll start with Zenith. You see, Violet, you, Eden, and I are all from this world, Earth. Alfred, Sasha, and Manie are from another world entirely."

Elric remembered the conversation he had with Alfred and the others yesterday and nodded.

"Just like everyone has a shadow, every planet has one too. These shadows are an entirely different version of the world they mimic. Imagine it as a multiverse. Their world is called Ermak."

"Wait. Wait. Wait, if that's the case then Ermak is earth, meaning you're talking about the existence of a multiverse," Elric thought of the concept in his comic books.

Zaroule snapped back. "That's the smartest thing I heard you say since we've met." Zaroule nodded. "Though it hasn't been proven, I do think Ermak is another version of earth, but that can't be proven because no one has studied the existence of Ermak.

"Everything that's been happening in this world isn't a coincidence. This is something that's been in the making before you kids were even born." Elric began thinking about the portals and those monsters. "Earth is under attack, and the destruction that's hit so far is nothing compared to what's coming. These portals and minor attacks are tests for something bigger, something much worse," Zaroule exhaled.

"You mean someone's responsible for what's happening up there?" Eden asked.

"Yes, there is." Zaroule's eyes narrowed and eyebrows furrowed. "This force is also the reason why the Ermakians fled to Earth centuries ago to find refuge."

"Blight!" Alfred smashed a hole in the wall with a clawed fist.

Zaroule nodded. "Exactly. He is the one orchestrating these attacks on not just Ermak, but this world as well."

"That name." Elric thought about the creature he fought in Lexington; he said the same thing. "Who is that?"

"You've heard this name before?" Zaroule stepped toward

Elric.

"On my way here, I traveled back to my hometown. It was hit by a portal. When I got there, I met up with some strange guy. Well, I thought he was a guy. He called himself Carnage." Elric watched Alfred's eyes widen in disbelief. "We fought, and he turned into this monster. The darkness it just took over. I didn't know what happened, but . . . I killed him."

Zaroule looked on with what Elric thought was fear.

"I don't believe you. There's just no way you took down one of the four generals," Alfred growled. His deep, monstrous voice faded to a teen's voice as he became a human once more. "An above world like you? You're lying." His clothes stretched, tearing in some areas.

Elric's heart sunk as he asked, "Four of them?"

"Yeah, each worse than the next. Carnage is the weakest one. Then it's between Eminence and Allure for second and third. Then you have . . . " Alfred looked at Sasha. "Nevermind, there's no way."

"Yeah, no way. I don't care if you're a Titan or whatever you guys are. There's no way you took on a general and, in the process, killed one." Sasha laughed. "I've seen a general destroy an entire village with ease. It's just not possible. I mean, look at you, no offense, but you're not the warrior type, Elric."

Elric ignored their comments of disbelief; his anger and sorrow were overwhelming. "I don't care what you think. Everyone I knew died at the hands of those monsters." He looked up at Alfred and Sasha. "I know you guys aren't like them, and I know the people of Zenith are different too." He looked over at Eden. "But I'm going to kill this Blight guy and anyone else who's responsible for what happened to Lexington."

Elric was shocked to see rage in Alfred and Sasha's eyes. Alfred's hands trembled by his side as Sasha's nails lengthened to claws. Her eyes became large and orange; they were wild like they were in her fox form.

"You have no idea what I've lost!" Sasha growled. Her eyes burned into Alfred's.

Elric wondered what she had been through; her glare alone sent a cold chill down his spine.

"So, who's Blight then?" Eden asked.

"He's a murderer, and one day I'll join my people to bring his empire down," Alfred spoke enraged. His teeth sharpened as a tear caressed his cheek.

Zaroule looked down on Alfred. "You're not even close to being ready to face the force and power Blight has control over. You wouldn't even be a minor nuisance."

"Well, what are we supposed to do then? If you're right about this, he'll be planning more attacks up there." Sasha was doing her best not to get upset. "No one has a clue what they're in for. We have to at least warn them."

"Trust me, they're aware." Zaroule swallowed. "But the force they'll bring through those portals will overwhelm even our own power. These attacks are going to increase in scale."

"What're we going to do then?" Elric asked. "If this guy is planning something big, a lot of people are going to die."

"Isn't it obvious?" Zaroule turned to them. "I think it's up to you guys to stop him."

"What? You just said that we don't stand a chance to take him on," Violet said.

"Not in the state you guys are in now, but if I can teach these two to control their powers, you all might be the only ones capable of stopping what's coming."

Worry spread across their faces. Elric's expression was no different. There was no way they were going to take down some monster tyrant. Blight's army would tear them limb from limb. If Carnage was the weakest, how strong were the others? Some may be even stronger.

"We're just kids. I think you got it all wrong, Z," Alfred spoke up. "I've seen the things Blight's done. My people are as tough as they come, and when his army came through . . . " Alfred fought back tears. "We didn't stand a chance. What are six kids going to do?"

As tough as Alfred presented himself to be, Elric could tell that Blight frightened him. Even Sasha kept to herself and out of the conversation—and she was a talker—her gaze focused on the floor.

"With the help of these two, I promise, you'll accomplish more together than you know." Zaroule's voice was filled with hope and belief.

Elric thought about the monsters he had faced, the destruction the portals caused, and the people he had lost. This was all because of Blight. If stopping him meant keeping who he had left safe, then it was worth the risk.

Everyone sat frozen. The hiss of the steam and hot water flowing through the large pipes broke the silence. They knew nothing about each other, but Zaroule had enough faith to believe they could accomplish anything together. How could he know?

Chapter 25

———— ◖◖◉◗◗ ————

Birth of Heroes

Elric couldn't stop thinking about Violet; and how she left the conversation. "Hey, I'm going to get some air. Is that okay?"

Zaroule looked up and tilted his head. "Come right back." Elric nodded.

"Oh, and Eric?"

"Yeah?"

"Be careful with Violet. If you go to talk to her, be sure not to push any buttons when she's like this."

Zaroule knew he was going to check on her. The others didn't pay him any mind; they were still upset and lost in Zaroule's words, but he wanted to know why Violet didn't listen. He found her staring out of a large broken window that overlooked Zenith. He hesitated before stepping closer.

She sighed loud enough for him to hear. "What do you want?"

"I just wanted to make sure everything was okay."

"Yup, peachy!"

"Cool." He walked away; he knew coming was a bad idea.

"Do you really believe him?" she replied. "Or are you just feeding his sickness?"

Elric turned around, confused. "What do you mean? Why do you think he's sick?"

"I've known Zaroule since I was three; he raised me. He used to tell me these stories about the world hidden within the world, the Titans, different universes, blah blah blah. I believed him when we came to Zenith, but as my powers matured, I sensed there was something off about Z."

"What do you mean by off?"

"He's sick, and he's been sick for a very long time. In fact, dying."

Elric walked back toward her. "Dying from what?"

"Something with his brain." Violet turned with watering eyes. "For a while now, his memory has been off. Even his powers have been on the fritz. I've been hiding it from the others. There were times I've found him in his apartment just shaking and unable to move. He was just out of it."

"Parkinson's." Elric sighed, thinking about the disease they thought Mr. Lee had before his cancer diagnosis.

"What's that?"

"A disease that slowly destroys the brain. Over time, he'll die." Elric shook his head. "But are you sure what he was saying in there wasn't the truth?"

"How could it be the truth?" Violet looked Elric up and down.

"You don't look like the type to have that kind of power."

"But I do." Elric raised a brow. "So, which is it then?"

"Excuse me?" she asked with raised eyebrows.

"Do you think he's crazy, or do you just not believe him?"

"Well, all things considering, if you had a monster inside you, I think I'd pick up on that by now. There's nothing in that head of yours but a scared little boy who wants to wet himself every time he walks by an Ermakian."

"What the hell is your issue? Since I got here, you've been treating me like garbage?"

Violet turned from the window and stepped up to Elric, trying to intimidate him; it worked. Violet was taller than he was, and it wasn't because of her leather boots. Even her scowl was beautiful. Her short fiery red hair bounced with each step as a few strands fell over olive eyes. A light band of freckles crossed the bridge of her nose, which scrunched in anger. "Surface-world garbage like you are my issue!"

He refused to back down. "Oh yeah?" *Smooth comeback, idiot,* Elric thought.

"Yeah, you really are an idiot." Violet fixed the strands over her face. "You probably had everything given to you up there. Nice home. A family. Spoiled like every other runaway!"

Elric stopped for a moment, gathering his thoughts. For someone who had the power to read minds, Violet had no idea how wrong she was. "Yeah, you're right. I did have everything. I'm here right now because I need to learn how to protect what I have left! Whether you believe Zaroule or not, I don't care, but before you start judging him, you should check the facts."

He turned, leaving Violet to wallow in her bitterness. He wasn't sure if he won the argument. It didn't matter. She wasn't worth the effort if she saw her father figure as a nut case.

Elric walked into the apartment. They all looked up, before Elric could get a word out, Violet came in, bumping him into the door. Zaroule smiled, nodding to Elric in assurance.

Elric shrugged and took his seat back on the decaying, green couch.

"Well, what do you think, Elric?" Zaroule leaned forward in his chair. "What do you think about everything I just told you?"

Elric gave Violet a quick glance; her expression was frightening. "Do you really think you can help me control whatever it is inside me?" Elric asked.

"I know you've visited your inner world, Elric. You saw the note I left you, right?"

Elric nodded with tight lips.

"I put four doors in your inner world. Used a good chunk of my life to do that, too." He smiled. "But I believe this will help you learn not only to depend on your own strength, but slowly give you the chance to understand and control the powers of your Deva."

"Wait, so what did you do? Is it gone?"

"No, but it's locked away behind the power of your own resolve and some of my power as well. It'll give you a chance to use a little of its energy at a time without losing your mind to it, but there's a catch . . ."

Elric swallowed. "And what's that?"

"You can still use some of the dark energy, but if a situation arises where you have to open one of those doors, it'll be like opening the gates of hell." Elric's arms became rough with goosebumps. "From the day your Deva awakened, your body was used to the darkness and its overwhelming power, but the more you relied on it, the stronger its hold on you became. That's why you lost control yesterday; you have no idea how far gone you were."

"So, these doors are like choke collars for this thing. That's why I can't hear him or feel him right now, right?

Zaroule scratched his scalp. "When you open a door, it'll take your body some time to get use to that kind of energy pouring out all at once again. I hate to say it, but I don't know how your mind and body will react to it. It could be devastating, but I had to shut off the immediate access your Deva had to you!" Elric could hear the desperation in Zaroule's voice, but that filled him with even more concern. "Just remember what I told you about the Devas. You must keep your resolve strong. You won't even realize it's taking over. Before you know it, your minds will be like one. I pray you never ever have to open that fourth door." Zaroule took off his shades, revealing stern, dark brown eyes. "I will do everything I can to help you both control your powers, but the work is on you."

Elric thought about the doors. It was amazing how free he felt; he was no longer enslaved by the darkness that wrapped itself around him. He was afraid, but maybe it was good that Zaroule did this.

Elric stood up. "I'm in." They all looked up at him as if he were crazy. "A portal took away the only family I ever knew, I won't let it take away anyone else," Elric said, looking down at Violet.

She looked away.

"I'm in, too." Eden stood up, giving Elric a nod.

"Fine." Sasha rose to her feet. "And if Z believes us, we might as well try."

"Well, without me, there's no muscle on the squad. I'm pretty much forced to come along for the ride." Alfred gave a cocky smile, keeping his arms folded across his chest.

"You're joking? None of you are serious?" Violet stood up, and she scanned the room. "This is not real. These two don't have that kind of power. Blight's a monster, and he'll kill us. Don't feed into this!"

"Violet, it's okay." Zaroule stood up on trembling legs. "I know why your worried, and it's okay. Really."

"Violet, what's going on with you?" Sasha asked.

"Are you going to tell them, or am I?" She shrugged. The sadness that Elric saw when she stared from the window returned.

"What's going on?" Sasha looked at Violet, then at Zaroule. "Z?"

He nodded. "Violet's concerns are legitimate." He gripped his cane as his hand trembled uncontrollably; he didn't try to hide it. "I'm sick. In fact, I'm only going to get worse."

"What?" Manie asked.

"Z, why didn't you tell us?" Alfred swallowed hard.

Zaroule shrugged. "I didn't know how to tell you. The only reason Violet found out was because she found me at my worst."

Sasha turned to Violet. "You knew and you didn't tell us?"

"He promised me not to tell." Tears rolled over her freckles. "You have no idea how much I wanted to tell you guys, but Z's not thinking clearly. Tell them, Elric."

Elric swallowed hard, wishing he could stay out of it all together. Violet was right, and wrong at the same time. Zaroule was sick, and though his cognitive level was deteriorating, everything he said about the Deva was true.

"This is not Violet's fault, and my well-being isn't important right now."

"But Z—" Alfred began to tear up.

"But nothing!" Zaroule slammed his cane against the wooden floor. "My time has been over for a long time now, and I've accepted it just as you all should. Blight's forces have declared war on this world, and soon he'll come to destroy Zenith and every other underground city. Every single one of you have to focus on that, not me."

Sasha fell on the couch as Manie joined her. The excitement that once filled the room faded; it was taken away by dread, confusion, and pain. Elric looked at them all. As much as it hurt them, Zaroule was right.

"He's right," Elric said. He wondered how the words escaped his lips. How did he have the courage to even talk at a time like this? "If we don't find a way to stop Blight, he'll destroy everything."

Violet rose to her feet. The olive green in her eyes became a bright purple. She was going to kill Elric.

"Elric's right," Eden said, swallowing hard. Violet's glare focused on him. "It sucks, and it's hard to hear, but Elric's right. We must do something. We must fight."

"You're damn right it's hard to hear," Alfred growled as he struggled to fight back tears. "Zaroule raised us when our parents were killed or when they left us." He looked at Violet. "He took us in when nobody else would!"

"He fed us, clothed us, adopted us." Sasha's voice was soft. She wiped her face, shaking her head in disbelief.

"He loved us like a father." Violet wiped her eyes and took a deep breath.

"You're all talking like I kicked the bucket already. Give me some credit!" He smacked the cane against the wooden floor. "Look, I need all of you. Whether you've been with me for thirteen years or just two days, trust me. I'm begging you." Elric agreed.

"Everyone here was brought together for a reason. None of this is a coincidence. Elric and Eden have power within them that goes beyond understanding. I know you're going to change everything." Tears raced down Zaroule's face. "So please, please believe me."

"You're beating a dead horse, old man." Alfred smiled, wiping his face. "I think you already sold the situation to everyone, right, Violet?"

She wiped her face.

Zaroule nodded, wiping his own tears away with a shaking hand. "So, it's agreed then. Everyone here is willing to risk it all, even their lives, to keep both worlds safe, no matter what?" They all agreed, no one wavering or second-guessing his request. There was only hope. "I'm going to create a training regimen for all of you. It won't be easy." He cleared his throat. "And it's going to be a lot harder for you two." He looked at Eden and Elric. "Especially for you, Elric."

"Right." Elric gritted his teeth. He was the unlucky soul with the dark Deva inside of him.

"This means you'll be staying here for a little while longer. No contact with anyone from the outside world for the time being."

Elric's head snapped back in surprise. "Are you crazy? That wasn't the deal; you can't keep me here!"

"If anyone found out about the existence of this place or the Ermakians, Zenith could be put at risk. I'm sorry, Elric. It's just until the training is finished."

"You're telling me to forget about the last bit of family I have left?"

"I'm sorry, but if you want to save their lives, you have to make sacrifices."

Elric looked up at him in disbelief, thinking about Jen and her family. If this was the only way to protect them, then he didn't have a choice. "Fine. I won't."

"By putting your lives on the line, you'll be put to the test. You'll become a family." Zaroule smiled.

They nodded, looking at one another. Elric thought about everything he had been through in the last week. This was just the beginning; maybe this was his destiny.

"You'll start your training in three days. I'll have to make some immediate contacts today to find the best help. For now, get to know each other. I don't care what you do as long as it doesn't consist of buildings being blown away or fights to the death." Zaroule glared at the four next to Elric and Eden. He stood up and began to leave the apartment.

"Zaroule, how do you know so much? There's no way it's just random information you picked up." Eden snickered.

Zaroule turned. "I spent thirty years of my life in the army, ten years as a ranger, twelve years in special forces, and eight years in a special division that as far as anyone above knew never existed."

Violet's eyes widen with confusion and concern. The man she knew most of her life had a secret. Elric wondered if she thought Zaroule was still crazy.

Zaroule chuckled. "I know it's hard to believe, but in my prime, I was a pretty cool guy. But that part of my life is dead and gone. That's why I'm down here. I wanted to start over."

Eden laughed. "That's pretty badass."

"It was an experience."

They all looked at each other, shocked by what Zaroule just told them. Elric knew there was more. "What did you spend the other eight years doing? And don't beat around the bush."

Everyone was silent. Even Violet looked over at Zaroule, hoping for an answer. Elric was tired of the secrets. If he had to stay down here and train with them, he needed to know what he was in for.

"I spent eight years in a division of the military, a task force of a hundred soldiers with the mission to hunt," he faced Elric, "you!"

"Me?" Elric said, taken back by Zaroule's statement. A chill rolled down his neck.

"I know so much about the Titans and the Ermakians because the American government has known for decades of their existence. On countless occasions, they have tried to capture the Titans." He began to walk toward the door of the apartment to leave. "Elric Blake, if it weren't for your parents, I don't think you'd be alive."

"My parents?" The chair splintered and cracked as he propelled himself forward. "What do you know about my parents?"

Zaroule turned taking his shades off. Elric—for a moment—thought he saw Zaroule's eyes watering. He placed the thick shades back on. "I know they loved you very much and that they sacrificed everything for you, till the end." He left the apartment and closed the door behind him.

Elric stood, stunned by Zaroule's words. This was as close as he had ever gotten of knowing anything about his real parents and this man. He knew them.

Eden walked over to Elric. "You think he was serious?" He nodded to the door. "About hunting us?"

"I don't know." Elric shook his head. "But I have a bad feeling about all of this."

"Forget about all that. You know we're all in way over our heads, right?" Alfred stood up, scratching his head.

"What do you mean?" Violet searched his worried expression.

"You above-worlders don't get it." He shook his head, thinking hard. "Listen up!" Elric watched Alfred as he glared out one of the large holes in the wall that showed a gleam of light from Zenith. "Blight's someone my people talked about like a demon. He's a living nightmare. He's slaughtered millions!"

Elric couldn't focus on Alfred's warning about Blight. His thoughts were taken over by what Zaroule said. He had never come so close to knowing about his parents until he met that strange young women; now he met someone who had been in contact with them.

It was a lot to take in and everything Zaroule said still left him with questions. Elric's mind raced about his parents. It was hard for him to picture having real parents. He always saw them as silhouettes. He used to daydream about what they were like. Now he knew they loved him. The thought filled an empty gap that was missing for a long time.

Chapter 26

——————⟫《◉》⟪——————

A Time to Unwind

Elric stood, gasping for air. The humidity and dampness of the air mixed in with his own downpour of sweat. His body was sore; it was riddled with cuts and bruises. Not even the regenerative abilities of the Deva's power could keep up with the training that Zaroule put Eden and him through. Between the running, the intense exercises, meditation sessions, and hand-to-hand combat training, Elric couldn't remember what life was like before he came to Zenith.

He stood in front of an exhausted Eden; his fist and knuckles were red from throwing blow after blow. Elric smirked, realizing he was getting better, stronger, and faster on his feet.

The sweat dripped off him and ran down his back. The training changed him; he was more confident in his abilities and more confident in himself. The grueling exercises changed his body; he was stronger and faster. Eden raced at him with the speed of the wind Deva; his arm bent back to throw a punch.

Elric lunged forward, grabbing Eden's bent elbow. He stuck his leg behind Eden, grabbed his throat and slammed him to the ground. Eden looked up with worry and confusion, but Elric's face softened holding his hand out.

"Good match, Elric!" Zaroule said from the side as he clapped. "A little rough around the edges but not bad!"

Elric smiled, helping Eden up, who looked disappointed.

"About time I finally got you."

Eden sneered. "Every dog has its day, right?"

"C'mon. Give me some credit. You've made me eat dirt every time we've fought. Now when I finally win one, you're pissed?" Elric grabbed his shoulder to get his attention.

Eden turned in anger, his eyes wild from the power of his Deva. His canines protruded down from his upper gums as a growl escaped his lips. His nails lengthened as his dark blue pupils faded to a pale blue. He was angry. Elric let him go.

He walked off, grabbing his shirt, and began making the three-mile hike back to Zenith. Elric shook his head, brushing it off. He knew Eden hated to lose. His pride and confidence were what drove him this entire time. Though Eden didn't know it, it was what drove Elric as well. As they trained together side by side, their own rivalry became the building blocks of their strength.

"Don't worry about Eden. Let him sulk." Zaroule came over and handed Elric his shirt.

Elric looked up, watching him fade into the distance towards the city. Eden's shadow faded in the distance; his worn shoes slapped against the clay floor.

"You really *are* getting better."

Elric looked up at Zaroule. "Yeah, you think so?"

"You two have come a long way. Eden already had an instinct for fighting. He was an arena champion, beating out anyone who challenged him in the other underground cities and so his talent is not surprising in the least."

Elric thought about the last arena fight that Eden took part in. It was the day he lost control and his Deva came out of him, almost destroying a good portion of Zenith. To think that was only two months ago.

"Unfortunately, you weren't gifted like Eden. Back then, you couldn't fight your way out of a paper bag." He sighed.

Elric didn't say a word. Zaroule was right after all. Growing up, he was bullied. On the rare occasions he tried fighting back, he'd walk home with a bloody nose and a bruised ego, lying to Mrs. Lee about his injuries. He always told her it was from playing with the guys. As if he had friends. It wasn't until the power of the Deva awakened that he stood up to Simon and made a difference.

"The reason you beat Eden, someone with raw fighting ability, isn't because of your training or the power of your Deva. It's because you have something or someone driving you."

Elric looked up, trying to read the old man's expression through his thick shades. Elric's drive was simple: All he wanted to do was keep the people close to him safe. Jennifer and her parents were all he had left of his past life, but now with Eden and the others, he had to be strong for them as well.

They began walking back toward Zenith. Elric was no longer shocked by the immense size of the cave. His time in Zenith made him immune to the heat and the dampness that almost felt like he was breathing in steam. Maybe it was the six mile runs each day that did it.

"Z, when did you find out Eden was a Titan?" Elric asked.

"I guess it was the second arena fight I saw him win." He chuckled, scratching his shaved head. "Yeah, that was it. Not once did he transform like the other fighters. He had a strange presence about him too. I tried going into his mind. Let's just say I got a nasty surprise."

Elric nodded. "I see."

"Well, you go on ahead. I'll take care of some things here and catch up." Elric gave him a quick wave before he jogged up the path of the cave.

Elric looked above at the large stalactites that hung over the cave in thick patches, leaving just enough room for the lamps to be set in place. Thick electrical wires and cords were anchored into the ceiling of the cave. He wondered how long it took them to do such work.

After the rigorous training, he often thought about what the world above was like now with everything that had happened. The thoughts of Jen and her parents were drowned out by the constant combat that Zaroule pushed on them. Through his painful experiences, he matured. With the monster inside locked away, there was no voice to keep him off the path he was on.

Unable to find anyone else with the proper strategy for training Eden and Elric, Zaroule took it upon himself to do so.

Zaroule forced them through emotional, physical, and mental training that brought Eden and Elric to the brink of losing their humanity. In the end, it was all worth it for the feeling of control. Two months ago, they were frightened by the very thought of Blight, but now they were ready. Elric was confident that his powers could be used to save lives rather than destroy and create pain.

The six of them grew for the most part. Each one of them found a way to control their powers and abilities. Working together to overcome the atrocious training they went through helped them understand one another's strengths and weaknesses. Zaroule himself was amazed by how close they became.

He walked the crumbling streets of Zenith by himself.

"Elric, what's going on?" A large, bear-like creature waved to him from the other side of the road. Elric returned the gesture with a smile.

A little way down the road, he noticed Violet walking with a woman. She was older with gray hair flowing down her back. She walked with a straight posture and a snobbish expression as she raised her face high to the lamps above Zenith. If Elric walked close enough, he could see her nose hairs.

Violet waved her hand high. "Elric, where are you going?"

He swallowed hard trying to avoid the sharpened glare of the elder. "Just, umm, hanging out and getting some fresh air."

"I see." She looked to the woman next to her. "You remember Sage, right?"

Of course, who could forget Sage? Like Violet and Zaroule, Sage was a powerful anomaly from the above world. She was the one that helped mentor Z and was now taking Violet under her wing as well. Her cold, stern demeanor could ruin a great day. She was impossible to please, and her criticism was harsh. She was perfect for Violet.

"Yeah. Hey, Sage." She responded with a cold glare that sent shivers down his spine. It swallowed whatever positive energy he tried to send her way.

"Well, everyone is meeting down at the training site."

"Really?" Elric was puzzled; he was just with Zaroule not too long ago. He wondered what the deal was.

"Instead of asking questions, how about you make your way down there so we can speed up the process, boy!" the elder woman scolded with a strict British accent.

Boy was her title for the four of them. Alfred, Eden, Manie and Elric never had names. They were just boy, never plural. He always thought she had something against males, but she talked to Zaroule, like a mother talking to her eldest son.

"Well, I'll walk back with you guys then?" He hated to ask.

"Sage and I have some things to work on. We'll catch up with you there, okay?"

"Sounds good, see you in a bit". He dodged a bullet. What was he thinking asking to walk back with them? His hair would have stood on end the entire time, not to mention the stutter he got talking to Sage.

He laughed thinking about how close he and Violet became over the past few weeks. Violet wasn't so bad. In fact, she did everything she could to keep order; she a true leader, and a loyal friend.

The training site was located on the outskirts of Zenith, an empty subway tunnel that was always dark, but they made it work.

"Where are Violet and Sage?" Sasha asked, looking up as he came running down.

"She said they'd catch up. They were going to handle something."

They were all puzzled. Sage and Violet met up with them early after every training session.

"Just be patient. I'm sure they'll be here at any minute." Zaroule smiled.

Dust started to pick up. The air became warm, and Elric's skin prickled. A large purple sphere formed out of the dust cloud, and everyone watched as it took form. Two silhouettes came into view from within it.

Chapter 27

Power of an Anomaly

"What was that?" Alfred asked with wide eyes.

Zaroule started laughing as Sage and Violet stepped forward.

"Sage, you finally found a pupil that could grasp the power to teleport, huh? Violet must be quite the student!" He continued to laugh.

Violet shot them a glance, and at one point, it looked like she might have been blushing.

"I must say, the young lady is quite talented, indeed. Her powers surpass ours at her age." Sage smiled. "She's a prodigy alright."

"I'm sure," Zaroule said with a smile.

"Teleporting? How's that possible? How can she do that?" Elric looked at them in disbelief.

"Psionic energy," Zaroule replied. "It's rare and extremely risky for some anomalies to try, but with the proper focus and enough energy, a highly-trained individual can gather limitless amounts of energy. They can create a fold in space. All it takes is the picture or a memory of the place."

Sage nodded. "But even with enough power, it takes a certain class and a distinct bloodline for someone to accomplish such a feat without destroying themselves." Sage laid a hand on Violet's shoulder. "The individual's molecules are broken down and are realigned at the destination. If, for any reason, focus is lost or disturbed, it can cost you your life and those around you!"

Elric shivered at the thought.

"Whatever," Alfred murmured under his breath.

Sage's face softened with joy as she spoke to Violet. "I expect great things from you, Violet. You're an excellent strategist and tactician. That, coupled with your powers, could possibly make you one of the strongest anomalies the worlds ever seen."

"Coming from my old mentor that's saying something. Is she the next Absolute?" Zaroule chuckled.

"Absolute?" Violet asked. "What's that?"

Sage shook her head. "A myth for fools. Legend has it there was an anomaly who lived eons ago with the powers of a god. Rumor has it, they created the Titans. But like I said, a myth for fools." She gave Zaroule a scowl.

Was Zaroule and Sage correct, was Violet that powerful? Elric watched Zaroule whose smile was like a parent watching his child walk across the stage on graduation day.

Sage walked over to Zaroule, and the two of them separated from the group to talk. While the six waited, they bragged about their accomplishments. Butterflies filled Elric's stomach as Sage and Z returned with frowns. Elric's hands became sweaty.

"Well, Sage and I talked it over, and we've realized that the past couple of weeks have been horrendous, but all of you pushed through together. I'm quite impressed!" Zaroule said.

"Indeed, you've all showed some promise. Well, most of you," Sage said, smiling at Violet. "Even though I've personally trained only one person in the group, I've watched all of you train. Your skills are banal at best, but it'll do.

A smile etched across Sage's hardened face. "So, this is what we agreed on. We made a bet that if Violet learned how to teleport, we would cut training down by a week and even let you go out into the city."

"Awesome, but what's so special about the city? We're here every day," Alfred asked.

"The above-world city, Al!" Zaroule laughed.

"What? Are you serious?" Sasha jumped up and down like a child.

"Yes, on one condition." there was hesitance in Zaroule's voice.

"What is it, Z?" Violet pushed a strand of hair behind her ear.

"You can't be seen doing anything out of the ordinary up there. No shape-shifting and no using powers of any kind. And you can't leave Boston. You must stay in the city. Things up there are much different after the portal appeared. It's a matter of life and death."

They nodded, disappointed. It was as if they had been punished for a horrible crime. They had trained all this time on how to control their powers. Now when they had the chance to have fun, the powers, and skills they trained so hard to master were taken from them.

Elric tightened his fist in anger. He wanted to go back to Clemson to see Jen. He understood the reasoning behind the decision made; the world was still in turmoil. Even though he hadn't been up there in a few months, he knew that if they slipped up, it could bring a lot of attention to them.

"Fine. It's better than nothing," Violet agreed.

"Good. It's about two in the morning eastern time. You have until the first sign of light to come back down here, no later. Sage and I have some important things to discuss and prepare for." Zaroule shot the silver-haired women a gaze.

Nobody moved, anticipating another statement from the two.

"Well, go!" Sage yelled.

They all took off back toward Zenith. They had been freed from a horrible training camp.

Elric rushed to an open bathroom and jumped into a standing shower. He was used to the slosh of water that came out. He dried off and wrapped himself in a towel as he ran by the other three boys who waited for him to finish.

"About time. What the hell were you doing in there? Happy hour?" Eden asked.

Elric smirked, rushed into the room that he shared with Eden, and got dressed. The clothes he wore weren't the best. Torn jeans and a ragged, long-sleeve thermal made up his attire, but it didn't matter; he was thankful for anything he could get his hands on.

He was the first one down at the bottom of the staircase.

"Well, is everyone ready or what?" Violet shouted, running down the spiral staircase.

"Let's kick rocks, ASAP!" Alfred yelled from just behind her.

Manie and Sasha leaped from the building down next where they all met. Elric used to fear they would break a leg when they jumped off roofs of buildings or high structures, but their bodies could handle a hundred times more punishment than a regular human could.

"Wait up!" Eden trotted down the stairs as fast as he could.

They were all excited though before entering Zenith they became calm and collected. They built a reputation in the underground city with their abilities and everyone loved them for it. Part of their training was community service, that's how Elric got to know so many of the people. Each day was filled with fear and heart throbbing anxiety, but he got over it.

They came to the stone path that brought Elric to the beginning of Zenith. He smirked, wondering if that old, strange man was still watching over the door that lead to the subway.

With a voice filled with sarcasm Eden asked, "Hey, prodigy, how about you just teleport us up there?"

Alfred fist-bumped him and laughed.

"Look. That's not as easy as you guys think. Besides, you heard what Sage said. We could be killed!"

"And we can be killed fighting Blight and his goons, too, yet we live with one foot in the grave. C'mon, Violet!" Alfred said with folded arms.

"All right." She rummaged around in her pockets, muttering under her breath in frustration. "I need a picture of the place to get us there. Otherwise, I could get us lost."

"I remember a little bit." Elric stepped forward, remembering the subway portion. "The subway?"

Everyone was silent.

"It's better than nothing if you guys really want to risk your lives with me." Violet walked over to Elric and placed her hand on his shoulder. He swallowed, staring into her dark brown eyes.

"Why don't you kiss him already?" Alfred shouted.

Her face became red. "Will you grow up, Alfred?"

Elric felt a strange pulse in the back of his mind. He could feel her searching through his memories. She took her time, trying not to tread too deep. He smiled, getting lost in her vibrant purple eyes.

Violet looked away. "There, I think I found a good spot." She turned and extended her arms. "All right everybody, grab on. If you guys are touching a part of me, everyone will get there safer."

"Does it matter what part?" Alfred giggled. A purple force of energy knocked Alfred to the ground. "I was . . . I was just joking." He coughed.

Manie giggled as Eden helped him to his feet. They grabbed onto her arm.

"Don't get too curious, Elric," Alfred whispered in his ear, hoping Violet wouldn't hear.

"I heard that!" she shouted.

A giant burst of energy came forth, throbbing like a heartbeat. A large purple sphere surrounded them. It was warm and comforting, and everything from the outside world was shut out.

"Hold on," she said on a deep exhale. "This is my first time teleporting this many people!"

A giant flash of purple light covered everything, followed by a fading crackle. Elric looked up, opening his eyes as the brightness began to fade. It felt like he was free falling; his stomach wasn't agreeing with the unknown movement. It felt like a roller coaster.

Everything outside the sphere was a blur.

Chapter 28

The Surface

It didn't take two seconds before they found themselves standing at the glimmering light of the subway station.

"That was still too slow," Violet whispered to herself.

Everyone was stunned by her comment and feat.

"Alright, Elric." Sasha looked around with a scrunched face. "Where are we? And what's that smell?"

He remembered the smell. The air was cool and damp, and it felt like freedom. "The subway station." He ran down the gravel path, keeping away from the rails. "Don't touch the third rail!" Alfred shouted from behind. "Why not?"

"I'm pretty sure it'll kill you," Elric replied as he raced forward. He was following the draft of cool air rushing from the tunnel. He knew he was getting close to the outside world. Up ahead, a bright light remained as he raced forward. "Just a little farther. I think it's an opening!"

Elric ran, gravel kicked up and clinked against the rails behind him as the others followed. They made it to the empty downtown crossing subway station. There wasn't a single person in sight. Elric pulled himself upon the subway platform, and the others followed.

"I'm pretty sure I killed over a dozen rats," Sasha replied with lowered eyebrows and a wrinkled nose.

"'Downtown Crossing,'" Alfred said, reading the sign. "So, is this the surface?"

Elric nodded. "Yeah, I haven't been this far, but I'm pretty sure it is." He smiled and raced toward the staircase. The air was bitter cold as snow danced in the darkness of the streets, glittered by the towering buildings that brightened the night sky. "I never really got a chance to see the city before." Elric's eyes widened in disbelief.

Small groups of people walked through the streets. Damaged traffic lights hung over intersections and most of the buildings were draped in plastic and caution tape; surrounded by construction vehicles. As dark and gloomy as the atmosphere was, the shimmering lights of the buildings gave Elric hope.

"C'mon, Manie. We don't have all day," Sasha said, pulling him along.

The cobblestone roads were marred with empty and burnt spaces where burning cars once rested. Pieces of steel and chunks of concrete littered the alleys, and deep fissure's riddled the streets.

The night air was freezing, sending shivers down Elric's spine. The temperature difference between Boston and Zenith took its toll. Down in Zenith, the temperature was always between seventy and eighty. It must have been in the thirties in Boston.

Alfred rubbed his hands together, trying to keep warm. "If I go beast mode right now, that'll be a bad thing, right?"

They glared at him. He raised his hands and eyebrows in an innocent manner.

"This weather is unbearable," Eden said shivering.

"I wish we could go somewhere tropical . . . like the Virgin Islands," Sasha said, looking over at Violet.

"No! Remember the rules! Besides, nobody here has a clue where or how to get to the Virgin Islands."

"Worth a shot," Sasha said, shrugging her shoulders.

They walked around for hours; destruction was the largest part of the scenery. Boston was still a sight to behold with the large buildings towering over everything, reaching for the skies. The darkened windows of closed stores fed the curiosity of Sasha and the others. It was easy to tell Sasha, Manie, and Alfred never came up here often, if at all. Eden laughed mocking their comical shock of the above world.

They walked deeper into the city. The salty scent of ocean air trailed with the brisk breeze; the memories of Elric's past life flourished with the scent. The life he had left behind to pursue his goals caught him off-guard as the memories eased back in.

"You okay?" Violet asked.

"Well, all of this is not right. An entire city empty because of what this maniac's doing." Elric tried to shake the thoughts of Jennifer and her parents.

"You're right." Violet stood next to him. "But that's not really it, is it?"

Elric dug down deep. "The smell of the ocean brought back some memories; that's all."

She gave a deep exhale; her breath escaped from her lips like smoke. "Is it your family?"

He nodded, looking up at the blackened sky, wondering what Jen and her parents were up to around this time.

"You miss her, don't you?" Violet asked.

Elric glared, knowing she searched his memories. "You had no right to do that."

"I'm sorry. You just had a lot of memories in there about her. Jennifer. She means a lot to you. I felt the bond you two have," she said, looking up to the sky.

"Yeah, we're close."

Violet grabbed his hand, pulling him into an alley while the others kept walking and talking up ahead. "I'll do this quick, and it can only be for a couple of minutes. If they find out I brought you somewhere, they're all going to want to go somewhere."

Elric swallowed, Violet's warm breath caressed his cheek, droplets of sweat begin dripping from beneath his arms. "What are you talking about?"

"Taking you to see Jen!" she whispered.

"Would you really do that?"

"Yes, now hold on to me."

He grabbed her hand. The purple sphere surrounded them as Elric looked up at Violet. She looked down at their clutched hands.

They both looked out of the alley to see Eden and the others watching them. By the time Violet had a chance to say anything, they were already standing in front of the same hotel that they brought the survivors of the Lexington attack.

They both looked down at their clutched hands. Violet quickly pulled her hand away. "They're never going to let us live this down when we get back," a breath of frustration escaped her in a white puff.

"Yeah, but it' worth it." Elric raced over to the hotel. He was stunned and mesmerized by the thought of seeing Jen again.

He made his way to the windows that lead to the room he stayed in. It was dark, but someone lay curled up on the bed. Elric looked around before opening the window. He tried to make as little noise as he possibly could.

Violet tagged along.

"What are you doing? If someone sees you, there's no telling what they'll do," she whispered, there was a hint of old Violet coming out.

"Trust me. I'll be quiet," he said smiling.

Before he could finish his sentence, he was dragged into the hotel room and slammed to the floor. Violet rushed over to the window speechless; her eyes rose to see someone standing over Elric. Tear drops fell on Elric's forehead as he looked up.

"I knew you'd come back." Jen stood over him with a clenched fist. "What took you so long?"

Her long, dark hair hung over her face. It was longer than what Elric remembered. Her body had changed a lot, too. She slimmed down; her round cheeks now thin. Jen kept herself in shape. *Once an athlete, always an athlete,* Elric thought.

Elric swallowed hard as he stood up. Violet was shocked and frantic; she must have felt like grabbing Elric and teleporting back to Boston. Knowing Jen, she would have grabbed on and came right along with them.

"H-how are you?"

Jen punched him in the face, knocking him back to the ground. The back of his head slammed against the wall. Violet stepped back from the window, confused by what was happening. Elric knew it would be risky to come back, but this was ridiculous. She was going to kill him.

"Where've you been? Why didn't you at least write or call?" Tears rushed from her eyes. "You don't even know what you put me through, not to mention my parents!"

Jen wrapped her arms around him. A nervous breath rattled from his lungs. It felt like years had passed since they had last seen each other; he wished things could have gone better.

"Jen, I can't stay long. I have to make this quick."

She wiped her tears and looked over at the window. "Who are you?" Her eyes homed in on Violet.

"That's Violet. She's one of my good friends; she's sacrificed a lot to bring me here to see you. That's why I have to get back soon." She smiled, holding her hand out to help Violet in.

"Oh, no need." With a flash of light, she appeared next to the window, kneeling next to Elric. "Was this a bad idea?" He shook his head.

"So?" Jennifer stepped back. "You have powers too then?"

"Yeah, but not like his." They both stood up as the three of them eyed one another. Silence took over the room as the cold draft blew around the rustling papers that lay on the desk. Nobody knew what to say.

"I kind of took over the room you stayed in once you left; it was roomier." Jen shrugged, fighting to keep her cheeks from rising with joy.

He nodded, insides bursting with butterflies. Hands trembling by his side. "Yeah, I bet."

"How have you been?" She sat on the bed and looked him over. "You look like you're doing well . . . and going to the gym."

His face reddened. "Things have been crazy to say the least. We've been training and preparing for what's coming."

"More portal attacks, right?" Her expression became cold and emotionless.

Violet and Elric nodded.

"I knew it." She sighed, closing her eyes. "I always had a feeling we didn't see the last of the portals. The world is trying so hard to understand what happened, but nobody knows. People are freaking out. We're in a state of emergency right now."

Elric scratched his head, thinking about the war that was coming. "Yeah, but we're going to take care of it, I promise."

"You promise?" Jen turned to look into his eyes. She saw a confidence and courage he had never shown before; Elric meant his promise. "Well, you definitely don't look like the same kid I grew up with."

"I won't stand by and just let things happen. I won't just let people die or fight my battles anymore. I'm not afraid. I'll keep you safe, okay?"

Jen crossed her arms standing up straight. "You went from being afraid of a jerk in high school to this brave person who wants to save the world." She shook her head in disbelief. "I feel like the weak one now."

Elric laughed, thinking about his past. "If it weren't for you, I don't think I would be the person I am today."

"Oh? How so?"

"Growing up with no friends and no real family, I felt alone, like an outcast. You saved me from that, so it's time for me to return the favor."

Jen nodded. Elric could tell she was fighting back tears. He was too. He meant every word of what he said.

"Elric, we got to go; the others are probably worried sick." Violet nudged him.

"But you just got here. What about my parents? They'll want to see you too."

"They can't know about this. No one can," Violet advised with glowing eyes.

Jen grabbed Elric's wrist. The heaviness of her breathing was followed by tears hitting the wooden floor. She wiped her face. "I'm glad you're doing well, Elric,"

She turned to Violet with an unforgiving stare. "You better take damn good care of him," she said, tightening her grip around his wrist. "Because I can't do it right now."

Violet's agreed. "Alright."

"That's not good enough. Promise me!"

Violet took a deep breath. "I promise. I'll do whatever it takes to keep him safe!"

Jen hugged and kissed him, melting his nervousness away. Her lips separating with a sweet warmness he wished he could keep forever.

"We'll be right here waiting," Jen said walking back to her bed.

"Elric, we got to go," Violet whispered, grabbing his hand.

He looked over at Jen, who had turned over in her bed. "Go and come back!"

The darkness of the room became bright as the purple energy took over; Jen didn't flinch. In an instant, they returned to the dark alley.

"Took you guys long enough. We would've given you space if you wanted to be alone," Alfred said, laughing from behind.

"Yeah, we would have given you space." Eden looked at Elric with anger-filled eyes.

"Alfred, shut up, or I'll dump you in the ocean," Violet said shooting Eden a glance. "What's your problem?"

He just shook his head and walked away. Alfred went after him while they stayed behind.

"We don't have time for this. We have to get back soon," Sasha had a jitter in her step that Elric wasn't used to seeing from her, but knew all too well.

"I know. I know," said Violet.

They walked around the block, calling out for Eden and Alfred. They were both standing on the corner. Eden was red in the face.

"Are we ready to go or what?" Sasha yelled.

"Yeah. We're good to go, right?" Alfred asked, nudging Eden.

Eden gave a terse nod walking over. They all rushed into the closest alleyway, and Violet threw her arms out. The dark space glowed florescent purple. Empty bottles and papers twirled in the breeze as they vanished into thin air.

They were back in Zenith, kicking up dust in the same spot they started from. Alfred, Sasha, and Manie talked about Boston the entire walk back. Eden was aloof and so was Violet. On the other hand, Elric was filled with excitement; Jen had waited for him! The group walked up the long staircase that led to the apartment above.

Zaroule yelled down to them. "Whoa, you actually came back! Didn't think you guys would actually listen to me."

"Yeah, we're exhausted. We figured if we turn in now, we would be well rested for tomorrow," Violet shouted.

"Oh, okay. Well, come on up then. Hope you kids didn't get into too much trouble up there."

They walked by him with large smiles on their faces. Elric was sure he and Violet looked suspicious. They all went straight to their rooms. Eden brushed past Elric, knocking him out of the doorway. Eden's bed was on the left side of the room while Elric's was on the right.

Elric ignored him, shaking his head, and leaped onto the bed. He stared up at the ceiling. The lingering butterflies in his belly was a feeling he wanted to keep forever. Eden lay on his bed with his back turned to him.

"Hey, what was up with you tonight?"

"What was up with me?" Eden jerked around. "You!"

"What, me? What did I do?"

"Where did you and Violet go, huh?"

Elric never took into consideration that Eden had feelings for Violet. From the first day when Zaroule brought him back to the apartment, he couldn't stop leering over her. He thought it was a joke.

Elric shook his head. "Look, me and Violet are just friends. You guys blow things out of proportion. She doesn't like me like that."

"Oh really? Then tell me where you guys went then."

"I can't. I told her I wouldn't."

"If you guys weren't doing anything, why is it a secret?"

Elric jumped out of bed in frustration and walked to the bedroom door. He looked both ways down the corridor to make sure no one was coming. "Promise me you won't tell anyone I told you!" He knew if Violet or Zaroule found out, Violet would skin him alive. "Yeah, yeah. Just tell me, damn it!"

Elric told him the truth about everything; Jen, going back to Clemson, Eden calmed down, knowing it had nothing to do with Elric and Violet having a romantic relationship.

"So, was it good to see your family?" he asked.

"I only saw Jen, but it was good enough. The Reeves's aren't really my family, but I guess they're the closest things I have to one."

Eden nodded and rolled back over, he didn't have to apologize; Elric figured he meant well. Eden was the cool kid of the group. A lot of the females found him to be attractive, but he didn't pay them any mind. He wanted Violet.

Chapter 29

—◦(◉)◦—

Allure, the Second General

The next morning, Elric awakened feeling better than ever. It was amazing to get a full night's sleep. For the past couple of weeks, they were only given four to five hours before they went back to training. He turned on his side. Eden was gone; he must have been in the bathroom. Elric got out of bed and headed to Zaroule's room.

The hall was smothered with the smell of a home-cooked breakfast as it drifted from the cracks of Zaroule's apartment. More doors opened behind Elric as everyone came out of their rooms. Eden eased his way by as Elric opened the door.

"Whoa, it smells great in here," Eden said, standing next to Elric.

"Well, since everyone's up, I'm guessing you might as well come in here and take your seats at the kitchen table," Zaroule yelled from the kitchen. The table was covered with bacon, eggs, sausage, chopped potatoes, peppers, and fruits. Everything smelled incredible and looked just as good as it smelled.

At the table, everyone laughed about last night's events. No one said a word about Violet and Elric's side trip. If Z found out, it would destroy the chance of going back up to the above world.

It had been awhile since Elric felt like part of a family. The laughter and joy that filled the apartment was something he had missed for a long time. *If we beat this Blight guy, will we all still be friends?* Elric imagined bringing Jen down to Zenith to meet everyone. *She'd freak,* he thought.

"Where's Sage?" Violet asked, digging into a crispy strip of bacon. "She seems to disappear a lot."

Zaroule nodded. "She's always been that way. She is most likely on the surface world doing some research into what's happening with Ermak and possibly the next attack."

"My question is: Where did you find her?" Eden asked with a mouth full of food. "She doesn't seem like the type you'd find down here in Zenith."

"Yeah," Alfred said, shaking his head. "High-class grandma is a savage."

"I've known Sage almost all my life now. Our relationship is kind of like yours and mine, Violet." He leaned back into the chair. "If I were to have a mother figure, it would definitely be Sage."

Violet's cheeks rose turning pink. "Like ours, huh?"

Zaroule took off his shades, revealing dark brown eyes. Elric noticed that the right eye was cloudy. "Yes." He smiled. "I have a few friends left on the surface world; one I hope you meet soon. Her name's Samantha."

Sasha looked at him with bunched eyebrows. "Who's that?"

"She's currently someone who's working on introducing the Ermakians to the surface world." Violet and Sasha nearly jumped out of their seats. "If she's successful, there probably won't be a need for the underground cities anymore. Ermakians will be able to live on the surface world like they did centuries ago, side by side with man."

"Is that possible?" Manie asked.

"I think so." Zaroule nodded, putting his shades back on. "She and a few other government officials have been working on this for quite some time. The portals couldn't have come at a worse time. I assume she's losing her mind up there." He laughed.

"How do you know Samantha?" Violet asked. Elric wondered if she believed Zaroule or still thought it was his sickness.

"We served together in the military. Only difference is I fell under Project Titan and she was dedicated to a sector focused on Ermak." He laughed, deep in thought, and rubbed the scruffiness of his chin. "I really wish I could have introduced you all sooner; you would have loved her, and she would have loved you."

Alfred nudged Elric. "Sounds like Zaroule had a squeeze on the side. Weird."

An explosion shook the entire apartment. The breakfast plates rattled on the dining table. Paint and rotting ceiling pieces fell to the floor as the sounds of screams echoed from the city. They all rushed out of the apartment and into the hallway. Smoke bellowed from the entrance that led to Zenith from the old subway station.

People scattered through the narrow walkways that made up the streets of Zenith. Ermakians rushed into their homes made of sheet metal and stone. They picked up children and loved ones, transforming into their beast forms. In the distance, something hovered in the sky and darted toward the apartment.

"What the hell is that?" Eden asked, his eyes changing colors.

Violet's purple aura began to flow around her. "Whatever it is; it's not in a good mood."

The grotesque face of a white bat came into view. He knew it wasn't just an ordinary Ermakian. No, this was Blight.

"Run. Now!" Zaroule yelled in anger as he turned to them.

A horrifying shriek shattered the side of the building, throwing them into the walls of the hallway. The sound of heavy flapping above caught Elric's attention as he looked up. The entire roof and ceiling of the apartment were gone. A grotesque bat-like creature hovered above them. It was covered in white fur and had large, strong wings. The creature was like the one in Clemson. Even from a distance, the glare in its eyes had that same blood-thirsty look as the other's eyes did.

"Run now. Get out of the apartment! It's not safe here!" Zaroule yelled.

"But what about you?" Violet screamed, helping Sasha up.

"Violet, get everyone out of here now!"

They took off out of the apartment and down the stairs. No one had a clue about what was happening; they didn't even look back. The sound of Z's voice and the look on his face didn't make any of them think twice about getting out of there.

They ran down the street a couple of yards, looking up to the apartment where Z's room was. The monster hovered above, looking as if it were talking, but nothing could be heard over the screams of terror from people and monsters running through the streets.

A loud explosion, followed by a white flash, blew a hole in the upper level of the building, sending stone and pieces of the wall throughout the streets. The blinding, white flash forced everyone to cover their eyes. The wails of women and children added to the chaos. Smoke filled the air above Zenith, creating a darkness that had never been witnessed before. Not even the large lamps that hung over the city could shine through.

"Okay, what the hell was that?" Eden asked, looking up with squinting eyes.

"It couldn't be. It just couldn't." Sasha knelt, gasping for air.

"What? What is it?" Eden asked.

"It's Allure, one of the generals." Sasha's voice quivered. The smoke cleared as the creature spread its great white wings open, moving from the building and over the streets, searching. It glared in their direction.

"Damn. Damn. Damn." The pitch of Alfred's voice heightened. "I have a feeling she's looking for us."

Elric's body froze. Once again, fear gripped him. *Another general? They're after me, aren't they?*

"Damn it," Sasha yelled, shaking Elric. "Don't look at her. Even as far as she is, her glare can petrify you!"

She darted down toward them with incredible speed.

"It looks like she's spotted us!" Violet screamed.

They took off down the street as people ran through the city, clearing out of the way. An ear-piercing shriek brought them all to their knees; the sound waves shattered windows and crumbled buildings.

Elric covered his ears in pain. The pulsing felt as if his brain was going to explode. A warm fluid ran out of his ears. He looked down to see his bloodstained hands; his entire body became paralyzed and numb. He fell over, unable to keep a steady gaze or focus. His hearing became disoriented as if he were holding his breath underwater; he couldn't make out any words.

Something sharp dug into Elric's shoulders as weight pushed his body and face into the clay earth of Zenith. Large clawed feet grabbed his pants and shirt as they lifted him into the air. Elric looked up to see what was happening.

Snow white fur covered the creature's body. Its grotesque pink face and large pink ears remained perked. It shrieked, focusing orange eyes on Elric; all he could do was watch.

"Help . . . " he cried.

"Shut up," she hissed. "You'll beg for death after we're done with you. You thought you could kill one of us and get away with it?"

Elric looked down, watching the crowd of Ermakians and people running to get out of the way. In the distance, a figure scaled the buildings behind them, moving with grace over the huts with long strides. The orange fur and large bushy tail wasn't hard to miss. Sasha kicked the creature in the ribs.

Elric was tossed in the air as the large bat smashed into a steel beam. Sasha grabbed him out of the sky and landed with a softness that didn't make a sound.

A growing crowd begin whispering.

"It's Allure. What on earth is she doing here?" Sasha asked.

"You know I love you, right?" Elric said as he tried to gain his composure.

Sasha stood still as her ears flickered back and forth. "Yeah, I know. You owe me. Let's get out of here before she wakes up."

She slung Elric over her shoulders and dropped to all fours. She leaped over the crowd and dashed to where the others were.

Violet grabbed Elric. "You okay?"

"Yeah, I'm okay, but they're definitely after me." Elric looked over at the pile of debris and collapsed sheet metal. A shriek echoed from the area where the creature fell as more homes collapsed. Dust and smoke covered the area. Whispers echoed around Elric and the others as people began to back away.

The creature jumped out of the heap of debris, its wings spreading open, throwing anyone nearby out of the way. It strutted toward them with one foot in front of the other like a predator stalking its prey. Manie whimpered just behind them.

The wings began to slip away as the creature's form became more human. Long, white hair cascaded over her shoulders. The large, orange eyes faded to a pale blue. The sharpened teeth and pungent nostrils faded into a beautiful, sculpted face with delicate features.

The woman grabbed a large brown cloth from a window and draped it over herself as she fully took form. The beautiful woman batted people away, tossing them like rag dolls.

"So, a fellow Ermakian helps a human. A human who has killed one of our own," she said.

"You're a real piece of work Allure. How dare you compare yourself to an Ermakian? Real Ermakians don't kill or bring war! You're nothing but a murderous traitor like *him*," Sasha bared her canines, and the fur down her back spiked and ruffled.

"You still whine about your poor species being eradicated, poor child," Allure replied in a mocking tone. "I have no idea why he let you two live." She glanced over at Manie and Sasha. "Maybe it was on a whim. He is your uncle after all."

"You're nothing but a disgusting abomination!" Sasha roared.

"How dare you speak to a general in such a way? I could have you skinned for that, ugly vixen!"

"Oh, please. You're all looks!" Sasha balled her clawed fist. Her fur stood on end as her tail rose.

"Come and test me then. I hate you foxes. You're a proud and snobby species of fools. Your pride is the reason why you're an endangered species!" Allure shrieked.

The wings tore away the cloak, revealing a white, fur-covered body. Allure shrieked as her pale eyes darkened into a fiery orange, and sharp, dagger-like teeth protruded over her lower jaw. Her powerful wings propelled her toward Sasha as they collided. Everyone cleared out of the way as they stumbled into more homes.

Elric and the others watched from the side as they threw each other into buildings, going blow for blow. Allure grabbed Sasha by her thick, bushy tail and slammed her down onto the pavement. She went to pounce, Sasha kicked her in the chest.

"Sasha is throwing down against a general!" Alfred said, watching in amusement.

"This is bad!" Eden said, looking at Alfred.

Elric regained his strength and watched the battle. "What are we going to do? Shouldn't we jump in?"

"Well, it looks like a pretty even fight, and if I know Sasha, she's going to try to take Allure down herself especially if she feels she has the upper hand." Alfred smiled.

Dust picked up as the two of them battled it out. Screams and howls of anguish echoed as they shared blows. For someone that was so fearful, Sasha was holding her own against one of Blight's subordinates.

Violet watched; jaw clenched. "This isn't funny. We need to go check on Z. Alfred, you, Manie, and Eden, stay here just in case things get out of hand. Elric come with me."

They ran back to the apartment and rushed up the staircase. There was debris everywhere. They opened the door to Zaroule's apartment. He was lying on the couch unconscious. His dark shades lay shattered by the dining table. Violet placed a shimmering hand of purple energy over his forehead, and his eyes fluttered as he regained consciousness.

He moaned sitting up. "Where's the rest?"

"Sasha's fighting Allure while Alfred, Eden, and Manie are standing by to back her up."

"Are you insane? That isn't going to be enough. Come with me!" He rose as blood dripped from his forehead. He walked to the giant hole that showed his entire apartment and jumped out.

He stood in mid-air as if he landed on an invisible platform. A force grabbed Elric by the waist; he couldn't see the powers like he could see Violet's, but he knew it was Z's. They floated down, making their way to the fight.

Eden and Alfred rooted Sasha on as the fight continued. The crowd watched from a distance. Sasha slammed Allure into a wall and began kneeing her in the stomach. The two seemed matched.

Why did everyone make a big deal out of her? Elric wondered, looking on. Sasha, only a teen, was taking the woman on like it was nothing. Carnage was a lot more powerful. The fighting came to a halt as the dust cleared.

Sasha stepped out in her fox form, dusting the dirt off her fur. She stretched out and shook her body like a dog. "Way too easy. And here I thought generals were something to be feared. No wonder Elric took out Carnage so easily."

A dark energy came from the area where Allure laid. The darkness was like Elric's and Carnage's. He looked up at Sasha with eyes filled with worry. What was happening?

Chapter 30

―――――――=)(❪❪◉❫❫(=―――――――

The Death of Our Hope

"Aww, poor little pup. You think you've won." Allure's white wings stretched out as she released a shriek that threw everyone back. Anyone nearby dropped just from the powerful sound wave. She walked over to Sasha and grabbed her by the throat. "I'm going to show you the full force of a general."

Dark energy seeped through Allure as she began smacking Sasha with clawed hands. Allure's wings became demonic as the darkness corrupted her. Sasha screamed, each blow drew blood and tore clumps of fur away.

"Oh, now your whimpering and clawing like a pup too?" She laughed. "How amusing!"

A burst of energy blew forth from the side.

"Put her down. Now!" Zaroule demanded.

Allure looked over and laughed. "Big talk coming from a human. She was getting boring anyway." Allure threw Sasha to Zaroule's feet. She was unconscious but alive. Violet grabbed her and dragged her to the side where they all stood and watched. "All of this could've been avoided if you would have just given me the boy!" She glided toward Zaroule with a force that sent them both flying into a row of metal-framed huts.

Allure's powers were growing stronger by the second, already surpassing Carnage, and climbing. *We don't have that kind of power.* The thought made him shiver.

"She was hiding her powers all along. That's why we didn't feel her enter the city." Violet's voice crackled with sadness as she held Sasha.

The darkness made Allure's fur stand on end as she became fiercer. Zenith became a battleground for two warriors of incredible power. Nobody was safe. People cleared buildings and dashed out of the area of destruction.

Elric looked on. "This . . . This is my fault."

"There's no way I'm gonna sit here and watch this. Z needs our help. I'm going in," Eden said.

A powerful wind built up, roaring out of Eden and spilling into to the streets. A loud explosion from one of the buildings stopped everything, including Eden's outburst of power. Allure flew out of the building, holding Zaroule by the shoulders. She bolted toward the ceiling of Zenith.

"Oh, man. She's going to drop him. What are we going to do?" Alfred yelled. His eyes were fixed on the two in the sky.

An awful shriek echoed from above the city, creating a miniature black hole in which they both entered. It collapsed, disappearing into thin air. The five of them looked on, stunned by what just happened.

"What . . . what just happened?" Alfred asked, looking into the sky in disbelief.

Violet knelt over Sasha and healed her injuries. Sasha winced and moaned as her wounds mended. Manie sat by her side, holding

Sasha's hand. Tears rolled down the sides of his face as he tried to comfort his sister.

"Where did they go?" Eden asked, looking up at the ceiling.

Violet stumbled widening her stance. The exhaustion of healing Sasha took a lot out of her. "I can feel Zaroule's energy." The purple glow of her hands faded as she tightened them into a fist. "Alfred, can you stay here with Sasha and Manie?"

"That was my plan anyway," he said, kneeling next to them.

"Good. Let's finish this," she said, looking at Eden and Elric and throwing her arms out.

They grabbed on as the purple sphere covered them. With a flash of light, they found themselves in the alley from last night. The sounds of police sirens and people screaming flooded the streets.

They came out of the alley, looking at the destruction that only took Allure minutes to produce. The city was already in shambles from the influence of the portals; now she was just having fun. Buildings were battered with their windows shattered on the first five floors. Emergency medical technicians and police officers swarmed the city, helping the injured.

The awful shrieking could be heard in the distance; the echoes had enough force to shatter windows as glass rained all around them. People ducked and covered their heads and necks as they ran out of the way.

They followed the horrible sound down the main street of downtown crossing. There was the large Paramount Theater sign dangling from a building; half of it was smashed on the sidewalk. Across the street, a park was swarming with police officers who were setting up blockades around it. The flashing lights were like a beacon.

"This isn't good. It's not good at all," Elric said.

The shrieking pierced through the streets. Everyone that was running collapsed to the floor in the fetal position. As the sound faded, the three of them snuck through the blockade. The power radiating from Allure and Zaroule was incredible; Elric couldn't believe that the wrinkled old man had that kind of power.

Allure hovered over a battered Zaroule while he stood in a weakened state in the middle of a clearing. Zaroule held his ground, but he was bloody and battered, exhausted, and the deep lacerations showed the pain he carried. To Allure this was a game of cat and mouse.

With all his might, Zaroule launched a blast of energy that scattered into multiple orbs. Elric watched as she a few orbs away, two blew up in her face.

She glided higher and screamed in frustration. Zaroule's breathing was heavy; they could hear it as they ran over. Large claw marks in his shoulders seeped with globs of blood. He nodded with a smile and gave a weak wave.

A helicopter hovered overhead: the four of them covered their eyes from the wind.

"I must say, for a human, you did put up a good fight," she hissed.

"What do you mean did? I'm still in it!"

"Let me take care of that!" She screamed, nosediving with great speed toward Zaroule.

He shot a blast of energy from his hands, but she dodged it. Elric exhaled as everything slowed around him. Violet's eyes widened as she screamed. Eden tried to race forward, but it was too late.

Allure thrust her clawed hand into Zaroule's chest. He looked over with a smile that dripped with blood and winked. She pulled her clawed arm away, letting him fall forward.

"No!" Tears rolled down Violet's face as she screamed. She raced to where he lay lifeless.

Allure jumped away; wings folded to her back. She looked over, cheeks high, eyes thirsty for more. Elric tightened his fist and prepared himself as she walked toward him. Eden stepped next to him.

"Now come with me. We can make this easy, or I can just have more fun." Allure scanned the city. "I don't understand how a little brat like you was able to kill Carnage. Humans are weak. Tell me: How did you do it?" She tilted her head to the side.

"I'll kill you for this," Elric whispered, balling his fist. Violet sobbed over Zaroule's body.

"Are you going to cry now?" she asked, folding her arms. "The pain you've felt today will be nothing like the pain Blight will inflict on you!"

Elric's emotions began to overwhelm him as the darkness crept in and consumed his thoughts. He closed his eyes. He pictured Zaroule's lifeless body. He had flashbacks of Mrs. Lee on the stretcher, dead. How could he be a hero? He couldn't save the people he cared for most, let alone the whole world. He found himself in his inner world, standing in front of a black door. The room was bright with white light. A key dangled from the doorknob by black thread. Elric reached for it with a trembling hand.

"Wait." Elric looked up with tear-filled eyes. Zaroule stood next to him arms folded. "I don't have much time, kid."

Elric's eyes widened. "Z! You're dead!"

"Almost." He smiled. "Before I leave, I wanted to give you one last bit of advice." He looked at the door and placed his hand on Elric's shoulder. "Elric, do your best to make the right choices. It's up to you guys now, and I wanted to apologize."

"This isn't your fault. This is Allure's . . . and Blight's!"

"No, not about this fight and the generals coming after you." His breaths were a guttering wheeze. "Your parents died because of me, Elric. There's nothing I can say or do to take that back."

Elric took his hand from the key and turned to face him. Deep down, he knew Zaroule was keeping something from him. "I figured it was something like that. After that day when you told me about them. I saw the tears."

"You're very observant like your mom. And when it counts, you're brave like your dad."

Elric nodded. "Thanks for helping me get this far." He couldn't look Zaroule in the eyes. He didn't ask Zaroule anything else about his parents' death. "Thanks for telling me about my parents."

"I know I don't have the right to ask, but can you do one thing for me?"

Elric raised his head.

"Don't open this door right now. I beg you!"

Elric looked up, but Zaroule was gone. Elric searched the bright room of his inner world, hoping to see Zaroule, but hope had died. He remembered the last words Zaroule gave him and put all his fear aside. Elric faced the black door, the dark presence growing as he snatched the key in anger and placed it in the keyhole.

No, he's right. Not yet. The darkness covered his body, caressing his face. It submerged him in its power. *I'll use what I already have!* Elric opened his eyes.

Eden stood a couple of yards away from Elric.

"That's how you did it then. Interesting." Allure smiled; her eyes were filled with excitement.

The thoughts of people suffering from what she had done filled the hunger of the black energy within Elric. Long tendrils sprouted from the black aura that draped around his body; the more he concentrated, the longer and larger the tendrils grew. They flailed, multiplying with his rage.

"Very interesting. I never knew humans had this kind of power." Allure laughed. The tendrils launched toward her. She dodged them; her wings jetted out as she took off to the sky.

She twisted away from the long tendrils, enjoying the chase. Elric's anger and frustration increased as the tendrils turned into clawed hands. One grabbed her wing while the others wrapped around her body. She struggled to break away as they lowered her to the ground.

"So, you have the same powers as us," Allure said, trying to break free. "You are very fascinating." Her eyes glistened with joy even in the face of death. An explosion of energy blew the arms and hands apart. Her wings spread as she ascended to the sky once again. Not even the dozens of tendrils were strong enough to reach her.

He looked up in anger. "Come back. Aren't you here for me!"

She hovered over them, looking down laughing. They couldn't reach her. Her ears flickered as she turned to the side with a surprised look. A large blast of purple energy hit her in the back. Violet stepped out of the darkness. She was surrounded in a purple aura. It was brighter than ever; her eyes were filled with tears and rage as she continued to launch blasts of energy from her hand.

Allure did her best to protect herself, but the blasts overwhelmed her. "You'll all die. I'll make sure of it personally!" She screamed. She shrieked, tearing a black hole into the sky, and glided in as it vanished without a trace. She was gone.

Violet fell to her knees, sobbing. The fury of the energy that surrounded Elric calmed, disappearing deep within him.

They ran to Zaroule who lay on the ground. Elric was afraid to approach him. It was just like watching Mrs. Lee.

Zaroule looked up at the three of them with glazed eyes, smiling. "You kids . . . did good . . . " He coughed spewing blood.

"Please, don't talk. Let me heal you!" Violet placed her hand over the large, gaping wound.

He grabbed her hand with the last bit of his strength. "If you try to heal me, you'll die. You don't have that kind of power yet. My wound would take too much of your life force away."

She nodded, knowing the truth. Violet watched with tears of despair; the only father figure that supported her since she was a child was fading away. She slammed a fist into the ground, creating a small crater.

Zaroule looked up at Elric with exhausted eyes. "I knew you could do it without opening the door. How do you feel?" He exhaled.

"I'm sorry that it wasn't enough."

"The three of you did great. I just wish . . . " He started coughing again.

"Z, you got to relax. You're losing a lot of blood," Eden said.

He grabbed Violet's hand. A bright light surrounded them both as her eyes filled with tears. Her hair flowed as their eyes searched one another. Her eyes widened with shock as if she had seen something frightening.

"Never give up on one another . . . always trust in . . . each other. No matter what. Promise me . . . "

The three of them nodded, listening to his lungs fill with blood.

He nodded with relief. The hand that lay on Violet's arm fell to the cold ground, and that's where Zaroule departed. Violet laid her head on his blood-soaked stomach tears soak his shirt.

Chapter 31

Tears Filled with Blackness

Zaroule's body was battered and broken. They stared at the fatal wound. Allure's claws ripped through him. There was no way any of them could save him. The helicopter hovered overhead.

Heavy boots stomped all around them, but they didn't belong to the police. There were attached to men dressed in camouflage who were holding rifles pointed at the group. Red dots covered their bodies as the soldiers took aim. One of the men talked on a radio. "We have them surrounded, sir. I doubt they have any chance of escaping."

Elric looked over at Violet; she hadn't even noticed. She was wrapped in sorrow; she was still embracing Zaroule's body. Eden placed his hand on her shoulder. "We have to go."

"I'm not leaving him here. Not like this." A purple orb surrounded them in a bright bubble; Metal chimes echoed as the soldier's weapons locked and loaded.

Elric laid a gentle hand on Violet's back, Eden did the same as she cupped Zaroule. A bright flash brought them back to the apartment.

She stood up with tear-filled eyes. "Eden, please go down and check on the others. Tell them what's happened," She said with a trembling voice.

Eden nodded and rushed down the stairs.

She wiped her face and grabbed Elric's hand. "This is what he wanted me to show you."

Memories raced through Elric's mind. It was like a movie. Zaroule's life was flashing right before him.

He could see Sage teaching Zaroule how to control his powers when he was younger. Everything was clear. Zaroule's parents, his childhood, a girl he knew for a long time . . . Samantha. Elric saw Zaroule saving Violet from some special school; she was young. He raised and loved her like a daughter.

Then Elric saw a couple. A man with a woman. The woman's stomach was swollen. He felt Zaroule's happiness and excitement. Then Elric saw the image of a man lying face down, his body broken and bruised from torture. Elric felt Zaroule's grief and disappointment; he hated himself for whatever happened.

Violet let go of his hand as Elric fell to the ground, gasping for air. She squeezed his hand, hoping to get a reaction.

"He loved you like a daughter," Elric said, taking deep breaths.

"Yeah. He did. Because my own parents threw me away like garbage. Abandoned me in a place that made my life hell." Violet's eyes glowed with tears; her breathing was ragged. She looked to the ceiling. "The people up there only care about themselves. They'll destroy anyone who doesn't belong even if it's their own flesh and blood."

Elric swallowed, listening to her words. He and Violet were more alike than he realized. She felt like an outcast just like he did before he came to Zenith. There was no bullying, nobody trying to ruin his life. There was just unity. Violet was right about the above world.

He wanted to comfort her, tell her she wasn't alone in how she felt. He never knew his real parents or what happened to them either. He thought about the couple in Zaroule's memory. Were they his parents?

"Violet, I—" The door burst open as the others rushed in.

Sasha pushed everyone out the way. "No, no, no. He can't be. Violet help him!" She screamed. "Use your powers to help him. You can bring him back. Please!"

She shook Violet and Violet wrapped her arms around Sasha as she cried in anger.

"No, this isn't real. Z's not dead. He can't be!" Alfred smashed a hole through the wall and ran out into the hall.

Eden's head hung low as he walked over to Violet and Sasha to comfort them. Manie stood there, eyes watering. Elric fell on the couch, head hanging down to his chest. Even with the power he had, he couldn't save Zaroule. He couldn't prevent the sadness that struck Violet and the others. In the end, he'd still failed. He ripped himself away from the sadness and guilt.

"We don't have time for this," Elric said. "There's a war coming. I know we're all sad about Z, but if I knew anything about him, he'd want us to be ready."

"What can we do? Can't you see? We can't do this. They've already won," Sasha said as she sat on the floor crying. "Elric, just make it easier for us. Turn yourself in. Please?"

His eyes bunched. He tried to talk. He wanted to. But the sadness of the room descended on him. Maybe Sasha was right; they were fine until he came. Now Zaroule was dead. Violet glared at Sasha.

Elric looked out the hole in the wall and jumped out. It must have been the dark energy that protected his legs from shattering from the impact as he landed. He ran as hard as he could, ignoring the voices and whispers all around him.

"Elric, stop! Come back!" Violet screamed from the apartment.

He ignored her and kept running. The streets were filled with people trying to clean up the debris from the battle. They cried as they tried to rebuild what was left. He couldn't believe one general could cause this much damage.

The hundreds of eyes he passed in the city were filled with anger and revenge. Maybe it was just Elric feeling guilty, but the people of Zenith's eyes were filled with blame.

There was a place where Zaroule use to take him and Eden to hone their powers in silence. Elric needed to get his thoughts together and figure it all out. At least there he could hide himself from the pain that Allure left in Zenith.

It was dark and damp as his sneakers smacked against the wet, stone pathway. He slowed down, fighting back tears. Droplets trickled into a distant puddle, echoing throughout the space. A sense of serenity put his mind at ease.

The sounds of everyone screaming in fear and pain wouldn't go away; the thought of the world coming to an end became real. He could see the eyes of the lifeless people that would lie alone, even Jen's face and her parents appeared in the blackness.

"I failed before I even got a chance to try," he said to himself. "I can't take this anymore."

The sound of a woman humming in the darkness made him look over to the darkest part of the cave; someone was coming.

"Who's there? What do you want?"

The woman who started this crusade and helped him get to Zenith stepped forward. This was her fault. She was the reason why Elric was here to begin with. His anger was uncontrollable as it poured out. The darkness wrapped itself around the woman, bringing her close to him.

His eyes widened. "It's you?"

"Oh, I didn't know you missed me so much?"

"You wanted me to come down here and have all of this happen. How do I know you're not general?"

"Oh, please, Elric. If I were one of them, I would have killed you by now. I've had ample opportunity to do so. Besides, why would I go through the trouble of helping you get stronger? I'd be a foolish enemy, wouldn't I? You wanted control over the beast and knowledge and so I provided it to you. Now you're mad?"

Elric tightened his fist. "Why is all this happening? I know you have answers."

"I told you all would be revealed in good time. But it seems you're a very impatient boy." She smiled as the darkness released her. "Your destiny is calling, Elric. Are you going to answer?"

"What are you talking about? If I fight Blight, I'll be killed. I don't have the power to fight the generals. I don't even have the power to protect my friends!" Tears raced down Elric's cheeks.

"How far are you willing to go for power?" she asked, turning her back to him. "What are you willing to do to protect those you care about?"

Elric thought hard about her question. He remembered the countless comic books he read about superheroes, but that was out the window. At this point, he was willing to do whatever it took to save his friends and the world. It wasn't about him anymore.

He looked down at the darkness that began to envelope him. "I'll do anything."

"Are you willing to give up your humanity and become the enemy of those you swore to protect?"

His eyebrows bunched. "I don't understand. What are you getting at?"

"You have to make a sacrifice, Elric Blake. It could mean going down a road in which no one else can follow. It'll be lonely and cold. Yet you would have saved this world and humans from being destroyed by a tyrant's reign."

"How do I get that kind of power?"

"You already have it. Give into the darkness within you. Only then will you become powerful enough to oppose Blight and his army."

Elric's eyes widened from her words. Zaroule said his powers would only bring destruction and pain if he gave into them. Either way, Elric knew he was in a losing battle. "No, I won't."

She turned with a frightening glare that glowed a raging, fiery red.

He looked on with unwavering courage. "I'll do everything I can to save my friends, but I won't become a monster to do it."

The intensity of her eyes calmed changing colors again. "Your choice, Elric. Let's hope it doesn't cost your friends their lives then." She shrugged. "I'll be watching."

She sunk into the blackness of the cave floor. As she vanished, it felt like a deep fear had been lifted off Elric's chest. That woman – or at least what looked like a woman – had begun to give him the creeps, but could she be right? Was giving into the darkness the only way to defeat Blight?

"I'm too young to be making these decisions!" He shook his head, looking up at the many wires that brought electricity to the crumbling city a hundred yards away.

"Turn yourself in, kid," a deep voice said from behind Elric.

He turned to see three men making their way over. They were burly men, intimidating as all hell. They were Ermakians from the city. Why did they follow him here?

"What do you want?" Elric turned with concern.

"I'm not going to let my friends and family die because of some human. We'll turn you in with force if we have to," one of the men said with a shaking voice. Two of the men transformed into wolves while the one who spoke changed into a tiger-like beast. His fur covered in black and white stripes

"But I helped you guys. You know me. I didn't mean for this to happen?"

"You brought this on yourself, Elric. We won't pay the price for what you did! Killing a general is blasphemy. We can't stop Blight, nobody can. All you've done is inherit his wrath. We can't do the same. We won't. Even Zaroule's dead."

Sweat rolled down Elric's face, a drop creased his lips as he thought of their desperation. They were right. All of this was his fault.

"Take him now!" the monstrous tiger roared.

I must be willing to sacrifice everything to save them, he thought to himself. This world was collapsing, but he had the power to stop it; he just needed to sacrifice himself. *Even if it means they learn to hate me. Even if it means giving into the darkness.*

The two wolves rushed toward him. Dark energy flowed through his body, changing Elric's skin, spirit, and conscious.

The two wolves stopped and looked back at their leader as the darkness enveloped Elric. Elric hunched over as it took over.

"What does it mean to be a hero?" he asked in agony as the darkness forced its way through the pores of his skin.

"What are you idiots doing? Get him!" the tiger roared again.

"I'll learn to control this power even if it kills me," he said to himself accepting the pain. They ran at him howling and growling in rage.

"He's talking to himself," the beast yelled. "Take him down. He's gone mad!"

A dark hand grabbed the first wolf by the throat and threw him into the wall of the cave. The other jumped into the air. His claws extended as he came down toward Elric's face. A dark hand grabbed him out of the sky.

Elric could feel the wolf's body; he felt the blood coursing through his veins and the racing heartbeat in his chest. The dark energy was becoming more a part of him as it rooted itself deep within. Why was his power growing? He hadn't even opened a door. The wolf struggled, gasping for air. Elric could see the desperation and fear in their eyes. All these Ermakians wanted to do was protect their families.

A slithery, dark voice whispered from his inner world. It was low and weak, but sweet. *Kill them all.*

The other wolf recovered and jumped, slashing at Elric. Another dark hand sprouted from the aura and snatched him out of the air. Elric looked up at the fearsome creatures that wanted to cause him harm.

"I'm not letting you turn me in." Elric's eyes watered with sorrow. He tightened his fist; the dark hands that held the Ermakians began to do the same.

The crack and snapping of their bones breaking rattled their leader. He ran at Elric with a monstrous roar. A wave of blackness threw him to the floor. He looked up, searching Elric's eyes for mercy.

"What are you?" The two wolves howled in pain as the life squeezed out of them.

"Leave me alone and tell that to anyone else who tries anything like this again!" Elric released them both.

The two creatures fell with a heavy thud. They were paralyzed with pain, but they managed to transform back into their human forms. Their leader grabbed the two men and tossed them over his shoulders and took off back to Zenith.

Out of breath and weakened from fatigue from overusing his powers, Elric fell to his knees. The aura of blackness shimmered around him. The crimson glow of his eyes was wild with chaos and destruction. He took deep breaths, remembering what Zaroule taught him. He had to gain control; he couldn't weaken now!

He knew he had to help the people of Zenith, but he wouldn't sacrifice his humanity. He wasn't a monster like Blight's minions; he just had one inside him.

Chapter 32

―――⫸《⬤》⫷―――

Sacrifice of a Titan

The next day was Zaroule's funeral. The city was silent, and the streets were empty. In Zenith, when someone of great respect and importance died, no one said a word for an entire day. Only those who were related to the individual gave their final farewells.

The silence was the same after Elric returned to the apartment. Nobody said a word. Sasha and Violet cleaned the blood from the floor and went on to clean Zaroule's body after. Elric was hardened by the sight of Zaroule's body. Even the wrinkles around Zaroule's eyes and mouth had deepened. He tried his best to fight the memory of yesterday out of his head.

People stared out windows and stood on rooftops as the casket was carried down the street. Alfred's head hung low; Eden kept his head up, trying to hide the true sadness he felt. Sasha was behind Eden. Heavy, dark rings lived around her eyes because she'd been crying all last night. In his fox form, Manie walked behind Elric. His large, olive-colored eyes were filled with sorrow.

Violet's eyes glowed from her hardened expression. Ever since last night, she'd refused to show sadness over Zaroule's death. Nobody

272

said a word about it. Elric knew she was holding it in. In a white dress, Sage walked behind the six of them. Even with everything that happened, her cold, stern face remained unchanged.

So much devastation was brought on the people of Zenith. Everything Elric said about protecting the people of Zenith and the people he cared about meant nothing now. There was no point in him coming to the underground city; only death followed him.

They dimmed the lights above the darkened the streets, allowing just enough light to guide them to the grave site.

"Zaroule was respected by all. His kindness and wisdom didn't go unnoticed. His spirit will live on through everyone he met," Sage said. "Let it be known on this day that a man sacrificed himself for the many. May he rest easy, and may his path to the afterlife be as bright as he was."

The casket shimmered in the artificial light; it was made of wood only found in Ermak that was given to them by people close to Zaroule. Two large, oxen-like creatures grabbed the casket. "We'll take it from here."

Using rope, they lowered the casket in the hole. Then they transformed into their human forms.

Sage dropped a large ball of white energy in. "I raised this boy into the man he came to be. Zaroule was a friend to all, a father to some, and a teacher to many. He will be missed by everyone."

Thousands of little lights blossomed from the hole and filled the air of the underground city. They darted in different directions, lighting up the dark gloominess of Zenith. Sage smiled as a tear fell from her cheek.

Elric and the others watched the casket for what seemed to be eternity. The last time he was at a funeral was when they buried Mr. Lee. He didn't know how to respond back then, and he still didn't now. Staring down at Zaroule's coffin was painful. It was just as painful as watching Mrs. Lee pass away.

Violet kept her hands close to her side, eyes borrowing into Zaroule's casket. Elric was familiar with that cold lifeless gaze, he had the same gaze after Mrs. Lee died. He knew what she was thinking, revenge.

Sage walked over and rubbed Violet's back, but Violet ignored the gesture, never taking her eyes off the hole.

"You guys ready to leave?" Violet asked, as if she were already over the death.

"What's your problem? We just put him down there. Don't you care?" Alfred snapped.

She looked up at Alfred with unblinking, focused eyes. "I don't know if you guys forgot, but we're at war now. If we don't start figuring things out, more of us could die. I won't let Zaroule's death be in vain, and I refuse to bury anyone else!"

"What can we do, Violet? What do we have to fight Blight with now? All we had . . . " Alfred argued, looking down at the casket. "We can't do this."

"That's not entirely true." Sage stepped forward. "Zaroule made many powerful allies here and up there. I'm sure if we use these connections, we can at least warn the people in the underground cities and the surface world as well. Maybe that could help out some."

"Sounds like a good start," Violet said.

"If you need me, don't hesitate to give me a shout." Sage walked over and kissed Violet on the forehead. "I'm going to reach out to some of the connections Zaroule and I made on the above world. We're going to need all the help we can get." Sage vanished with a flash of bright light.

"Let's go." Violet turned not batting an eye at Zaroule's final resting place.

They returned to the torn city. The decrepit apartment building waited in the distance as they trudged through the depression-stricken Zenith A woman ran up to them; a small group followed behind her. She glared at Elric as she stopped in front of them, keeping them from moving forward.

"That fiend. How can you all protect him? This can all end if we just bring him to Blight. He's all he wants!" she screamed.

The sound of apartment doors opening and the voices of people and creatures speaking started to build.

"That's right. Why should we all have to pay for something one boy did. I say we all take him and bring him to Blight," a bear-like creature roared. "He'll show mercy!"

The crowd grew larger and became more eager. More of them transformed into their animalistic counterparts. Their eyes were filled with determination as they surrounded them. A huge wave of energy blew everyone back.

Elric hit the ground, looking up surprised. Violet was illuminated with power. The purple aura of her energy was pulsating around her. "If any of you lay a finger on Elric, I promise it'll be the last!"

Her red hair hung over her eyes. The crowd stepped back. Some of them trembled from her words.

"I understand you're scared, but this is a time to come together and protect one another, not turn on each other. Can't you see this is what Blight wants?" Eden asked.

"But this monster nearly killed two of our own. Before he went to Ermak yesterday, Omis told us that two of the men may never be able to walk again!"

Elric swallowed, thinking about the fight yesterday between the three Ermakians. He knew he battered them badly, but he didn't think he destroyed their lives like that.

Violet turned to Elric. "Lies! And who's Omis? Why has he gone back to Ermak?"

"Allure promised we would be spared if we cooperated with Blight!" the angry woman screamed.

"Are you all that stupid? He's going to tear this place apart, even if he finds Elric," Alfred yelled. "We're all dead!"

"Maybe. But with the death of Zaroule, we understand that Blight's wrath has no limits. For the sake of our next generation and the generation after, we will sacrifice one being for such a cause." A woman held her children tight to her hip.

"You won't take him. None of you will," Violet said, standing next to Elric.

He swallowed, thinking of Zaroule's sacrifice.

"It's okay, Violet. It makes sense now," Elric said, standing up. "Everyone has always stood up for me. I never faced my own battles. This is something I can finally do. I have to."

Violet's lips quivered as she tried to understand. "Elric, what are you talking about?"

"I'll go to Ermak," he said.

"That's insane. He'll kill you!" Eden yelled.

"It's out of the question, Elric. I won't allow that," Violet demanded.

"You don't own me, Violet! This is something that must be done. Besides, it could stall him long enough for you guys to figure something out."

"I promised to protect you, Elric. How would Jen feel if she lost you?"

"Not as bad as I would feel if I lost her. It's not about me anymore; it's about the people above and the people down here. It's about Jen. It's about you guys, my friends." For once he was sure of himself. "I'll sacrifice myself for all of you."

He looked over at Eden and the others. Even Sasha's eyes teared with regret.

Violet grabbed his arm, and before Elric realized what she was doing, it was too late. Her eyes began to glow, and a blinding flash of purple surrounded them.

Chapter 33

Home Sweet Home

Elric opened his eyes, finding himself in a foot of snow. The cold, brisk air sent chills through his bones because his short sleeved shirt gave him no protection.

The heavy snowflakes continued to come down in a flurry around them. Violet backed away as Elric shook his head in anger; she brought him out of Zenith. "I won't let them have you, Elric. And if I can't stop you, I know someone who will."

Elric slammed his fist into his hand. "Violet, don't be stupid. You need me. If I'm not there, they'll destroy Zenith. You and I know Zaroule wouldn't have wanted this. Please, let me do this!"

Streams of tears raced down the band of freckles that arced over her nose.

Elric words blew clouds into the cold. "We're a family, Violet. Please, let's go back and get this situated together."

She walked through the snow and kissed him on the cheek.

"Please forgive me, Elric."

An enormous force threw him back, melting the snow around him, he hit the ground with a thud and looked up. Ice cold streams trickled down his back, soaking his shirt. The energy enveloped her, and with a flash, she was gone.

"No!" He yelled.

His fingernails grew into claws that dug into the icy snow. Without him, Blight would tear Zenith apart. Elric wouldn't be able to do anything about it. He rose to his feet, realizing he was in Clemson and not too far from the hotel.

His body shook from the blistering cold as he trudged through the thick snow. It seeped into his sneakers, freezing his feet as they began to throb in pain. He came to the opening of the main road, and in the distance, he could see the hotel. Shivering and wet, he ran in with sneakers soaked and squishy. He made his way past the warm fireplace to the front desk.

"M-my name's Elric Blake. I'm looking for the Reeveses." His words were broken up by chattering teeth.

"Elric!" a voice yelled from behind.

He turned to see Jen's wide eyes. Everyone in the hotel looked at her, startled by her surprise. She looked around, noticed the stares, and calmed down.

"Hey, where have you been?" she asked in a calm voice as she pulled him from the front desk and into an empty staircase used for emergencies.

"What are you doing here? Shouldn't you be getting ready to save the world?" she whispered.

"Yeah, but something happened." He lowered his eyes, thinking about the destruction and Zaroule's death.

She saw the sorrow in his eyes. "Are you staying for good?

"I don't know what's going to happen." He looked up at Jen.

She grabbed him, holding him close. Elric returned the gesture. His thoughts were with the others. How could he not be happy to see Jennifer? How could he feel distraught, even frightened?

Jen caressed his face. "Is everything alright?"

Violet and the others needed him. What else could he do but think of them? They were his family, too, and they needed him now more than ever. Elric shook his head. "There's a lot going on that I need to tell you. I'm confused myself, but I think I'm staying for a while."

Jen nodded.

"C'mon, it's been a while since I've seen your parents. I would really like to see them." He smiled.

Elric and Jen rushed pass the different unfamiliar faces to the rooms where they stayed, and she opened the door. Her mother's back was turned as she was making up the bed.

"Jen, is that you?" Her mother paused and looked up. Tears began to roll down her face, and she cupped her mouth. "Welcome back."

Elric agreed trying to stay composed. Seeing them was like reliving a time in his life where everything made sense. Times where they would go to sporting events to watch Jen play. The awful charity events. Tears began swelling in his eyes.

She walked over and wrapped her arms around him. "Elric, we were so worried about you. We thought you'd never come back." She started crying. "It's felt like you've been gone for years."

With sweaty palms and still shivering from the cold, he tried to remain calm. Mr. Reeves came out of the side room with a shocked expression. Elric nodded looking up at him. Jen smiled. "Well, let's get you into some warm clothes. You're freezing, and your clothes are wet. Where have you been?" Her mother pulled Elric along.

They sat Elric down in what was once his room, but Jen had taken over. Her parents weren't reacting like he thought they would. Elric expected them to be angry and filled with disappointment, but it was the exact opposite. Mr. Reeves was just as excited as Mrs. Reeves to see him return.

"I'm going to get you some dry clothes." An excited Mrs. Reeves rushed down the hall.

Jen and her father stared at him while they waited. "So, everything went well in Boston?" Mr. Reeves asked. Elric's eyes widened. How could he possibly have known about where he went? "Jen told us everything about what happened and what you had to do."

"She did what?" Elric yelled.

This was it. They knew his secret. They knew he was a monster . . . a freak. They would find out about the fight in Boston and realize he was there; they would turn him in. His mind raced with the worst possible outcomes.

"You don't have to worry about it, Elric. They're fine with it. I know you're mad, and freaking out, but I had to. It was the only way to keep them calm. Things haven't been all hunky-dory since you left."

"Well, why didn't you tell me the other morning that they knew everything?"

"You were here the other morning?" Mr. Reeves asked.

"I didn't tell them that though," Jen slipped deeper into her seat swallowing hard.

"I'm sorry I didn't tell you guys everything, but it was all new to me too. I mean, you guys could have thought I was nuts."

"Monsters are coming through portals, kid. The world's already gone nuts!" Mr. Reeves said, shaking his head.

"Your secret is safe with us, honey." Mrs. Reeves smiled, coming from down the hallway. "You saved our daughter's life, Elric. Why would we treat you any different?" Mr. Reeves agreed.

"Elric, you're part of this family. Our love for you will never change, no matter what." Mrs. Reeves put his hand on Elric's shoulder. "You're a hero in my book!"

Elric listened to their words. He looked into Jen's eyes; she never gave up on him, and she never turned her back on him. He found everything he needed in those sparkling hazel eyes. He would never leave her side.

"Elric you don't have to run. We'll be here for you no matter what, okay?" Jen whispered.

Mrs. Reeves handed him a pile of dry clothes. Elric nodded. The kindness he had received from Jen and her parents filled him with hope, but what he'd left back in Zenith was still tearing him apart.

"Hope you can still fit them. Looks like you've gained some muscles while you've been gone." Mrs. Reeves giggled like a schoolgirl. "Welcome home, Elric!"

It didn't seem real. He knew better than to let his guard down. Blight was still coming, and no one on the above world had a clue of the threat coming.

"I know you're happy to see me, and I'm happy, too, but where I was . . . something awful happened there. You're all in danger. The whole world is."

"W-what do you mean?" Mrs. Reeves asked.

"The portals that appeared aren't just random freak anomalies; they're doorways for an army to come through. Their leader is some guy named Blight who's already ripped one world apart and is trying to do the same with this one."

"What? You can't be serious. What are you saying?" Mr. Reeves said, trying to understand.

"Our world's in danger, and only a handful of people know what's happening, and that's not the worst part."

"What's worse than the world ending?" Mr. Reeves asked.

"The fact that he's after my friends and me . . . "

Mr. and Mrs. Reeve's stared in disbelief. Jen gripped the edge of the bed and shivered.

"I won't let anything happen to you guys. I promise!" He rose from his chair and his hands shook as he tightened his fist.

"I know you won't." Jen put on a fake smile, placing her hand on his shoulder.

He had the power to protect them, and he'd use the darkness in whatever way was possible. If the Reeveses considered him family, then there was nothing else to say on the matter. Looking into Jen's eyes, Elric found what he wanted most.

He ran away to find himself and to keep them out of harm's way; he even went through life-threatening experiences to control his powers. Jen and her parents were all he had left.

Elric carried in his heart the loss of Mrs. Lee and how she spoiled him with comic books. He wouldn't have made it this far without her. He remembered Zaroule, someone who had limitless hope in Elric. He had to keep everything that they taught him close to his heart; there was too much on the line now.

After the excitement of Elric's return, the Reeveses ordered a big meal. They laughed and talked about what went on while Elric was gone, and he shared the secrets of the underground world and its citizens. They were fascinated. Mr. Reeves was a little skeptical, but he believed.

After dinner, Elric and Jen hung out in her room. Elric sat on the floor, focusing a small, black mass of energy in the palm of his hand. She hung off the edge of the bed upside down as she watched him control the mass.

"Where does the darkness come from?"

"From inside me, but it comes out through my skin and pores. It can come out like energy too. I guess it all depends on the situation."

"Your powers are still hard to control, huh?"

"Yeah, it can be a handful." Elric smiled.

"You told me that there was something inside you . . . like a monster, right?"

He was quiet, looking down at his hands. "Yeah, but he hasn't said anything to me in a while."

"Whoa, it talks?" Jen sat up leaning closer to him.

He closed his hands, feeling the energy. "Yeah, when I was away, I learned about what it is and what I am." He laughed.

"What is it?"

"Just an annoying thing that talks whenever it feels like it."

She wasn't ready for the truth yet. When Zaroule told Elric, he wasn't ready either, but he had to accept it.

"Oh." She watched the energy form in his palm. "It's hard picturing you with powers, and not being the shy quiet type, you were back in school."

Elric focused on the black mass in his hand. "What am I, Jen?"

"You're like one of the characters in your comic books." Her eyes widened.

He stared into the palms of his hands. "It's weird, but there are more people like me." He smirked, thinking about his counterpart in Zenith. "There was a guy named Eden where I was. He controls air; Sasha can change into a giant fox, and Alfred, you would think the dudes a werewolf."

"Sounds like you found yourself . . . wherever you were."

"I always thought I would amount to nothing like Simon said that day. I hated myself for being alone. It felt like this pain was only happening to me. But then I met you."

"Really?" She smiled.

Elric shook his head with a grin. "Don't get a big head over it."

"Now why would I do that?"

He shook his head. "When I met you and we became friends, I felt like I found someone to relate to. Someone who believed in me. You saved me from myself."

She was silent. She slid down from the bed laying her head on his shoulder.

"Sorry. I know it sounds weird."

"Not at all. It's funny really. Something inside made me want to be your friend . . . like I was meant to get to know you. Then when we started talking and becoming closer. It felt like we had known each other for years, even as young as we were."

Elric sat back. Their heads were side by side.

"Well, I'm off to bed. Hopefully, I won't catch you trying to sneak out again?" She rose to her feet.

"Let it go," he said, shaking his head.

She closed the door.

Elric turned out the light and crawled into bed. The sound of the wind blowing the powdery white snow around whistled from outside the window. He stared at the ceiling, wondering about Violet and the others, hoping they were alright. He was happy to be home, but the others in Zenith were in danger. What could he do?

Chapter 34

Darkness

The morning was bright and warm, something he forgotten from living in the underground city for so long. The sun hitting his skin was a reminder that he was no longer with the others.

Jennifer burst into the room. "Hey, get dressed. We're going out to eat!"

Elric jumped up in fear. "How did you get in?"

She flicked the key card on his bed. "Forgot to give it to you. Hurry up. We're going out for breakfast."

Elric sighed as she closed the door and began getting dressed. He threw on the shirt he wore yesterday, realizing he didn't have any other clothes besides the ones Mrs. Reeves provided him with. He smiled thinking about going out to eat like a family.

He met them all outside. Mr. Reeves nodded. "While you were gone, we found a nice, family-run restaurant. The food's great. Maybe it'll help you relax after everything."

"That sounds great." He followed them down the road. The town was busy, unlike before. People were filling their vehicles up at the gas pumps, shopping, and strolling through town. Life had returned to Clemson.

They came to a restaurant called Market Square; it was filled with people. The atmosphere was relaxing; the laughter and warmth gave him peace after what he had experienced in the last few days.

The waitress was jovial, and the food smelled amazing. He talked about Zenith and the civilization of shapeshifters that inhabited it. Everything he had been through sounded like a movie.

They laughed and talked for hours about how much things had changed since Elric had left. The Reeves family was on the verge of getting a house and hoped to have one in a couple of weeks once the insurance on the house in Lexington paid out.

"Elric, you lost a lot in Lexington, if not everything," Mr. Reeves said, looking at Elric. "It would mean a great deal if you lived with us."

Jen's eyes widened with excitement. "Are you guys serious?"

Mrs. Reeves eyes focused on Elric. "Your father and I have given it a lot of thought, and we think it would be a good idea. We'll have plenty of room. But, it's up to you, Elric?"

Elric was lost for words. He looked down at his breakfast, fighting back tears. Through it all, there was still hope. It overwhelmed the darkness that began to retake his life.

"Elric, say something!" Jen nudged him.

"Ugh, yes. Really? You want me to?" He couldn't believe it.

Jen's parent's eyes were filled with joy.

"You both will go to Clemson High. It'll be a new beginning for the both of you," Jen's father said.

Elric chuckled to himself. Even the thoughts of Violet and the others disappeared for a moment. He was given peace and a glimpse of a dream that he had wanted for so long.

"Wow, it sure did get dark out there," one of the waitresses said. "I thought today was supposed to be a cloudless day."

Elric looked down at his glass of water, which was once glistening from the sunlight that poured through the window next to them. Mr. Reeves stared out the window. "I've never seen thunderclouds come that fast before . . . "

Elric eyes widened with worry as he leaped out of his chair and ran outside, never taking his eyes off the clouds.

"Elric, where you are going?" Mr. Reeves called out.

The sky was taken over by black clouds. This wasn't a freak thunderstorm. Elric thought about the night in Lexington; they didn't see it coming before because it was night, but this feeling was the same. Elric rushed back inside, knocking someone over.

"Elric, what's wrong?" Jen asked.

Elric's heart pounded against his chest. An ice-cold chill ran down his back. He clenched his fist, fighting the fear that brought him to his knees. He promised to protect them, no matter what, even with his own life. "We have to go. Now!"

"What? What's wrong?" Mrs. Reeves asked.

"Those aren't thunderclouds."

Everyone in the restaurant began to panic, and chaos erupted.

"We have to go. Now!" Elric grabbed Jen's hand.

They followed him out of the restaurant and rushed back to the hotel. People began stepping out of stores and apartments, staring in awe at the sky that darkened with heavy clouds. The realization of what was happening didn't hit the bystanders yet; it wouldn't until it was too late.

They ran into the hotel, but Jen paused for a moment, looking up into the darkness. The clouds had become thick and heavy. The sun ceased to exist. The air became dry and hot, like a summer's day, only this was winter in Maine.

"Pack what you can, let's go!" Mr. Reeves said, bent over wheezing.

They rushed inside. Elric grabbed whatever article of clothing that was near and helped everyone else pack.

"Where're we going to go, John? We were so close to having a home again," Mrs. Reeves said in tears. Mrs. Reeves shook her head, trying her best to accept it.

"I don't know, but we don't have a choice, if things are going to be like what Elric said, Clemson is gonna be a warzone."

An awful throbbing in Elric's stomach made him queasy. *What's happening to me?*

Sirens in the distance grew louder as they drove down the main streets, fussing became scream as word got around about the incoming portal. The blackness was heavy now and it looked like night had fallen.

The air was still. Silence settled the chaos that erupted in the small town. A chill and a strange vibration in the air made Elric's hair stand on end. Jen's eyes filled with horror; she felt the same sensation. Strands of her hair began to rise.

"Does anybody else feel that?" Mrs. Reeves asked.

A crackle shook the hotel, throwing everyone to the ground. Jen grabbed a hold of the table in front of her. Elric wrapped his arms around her, keeping her balanced.

"What was that?" Jen looked confused.

The wind howled outside. Elric took another peek out the window and watched roofs being ripped from buildings and trees being uprooted. He hoped it was just the worst tornado in Maine's history, but that would be too good to be true.

Elric didn't bother to pack anymore; he ran out into the hallway. Jen and her parents knew what it was that kept them in such fear; the sound of people next door screaming was enough to freeze everyone.

No place is safe. Elric thought about Violet and the others. He hoped they were okay. "These portals are probably everywhere."

Mrs. Reeves looked frightened. "What do you mean by everywhere? You mean all over town?"

Elric shook his head. "No, the entire world."

Wood shattering and twisting from above made them duck. The windows blew in with a roaring force as a black aura consumed them all.

"We have to go now!" Elric screamed, focusing on the aura to keep them safe.

They looked around, astonished by the blackness that protected them. Mr. Reeves nodded and helped his wife and daughter stand up. Elric led them outside. He looked around, watching debris bounce off the black mass that shielded them from chaos.

Elric kept his eyes forward. He focused on protecting the Reeveses. Just like Zaroule taught him, he bottled his fear and focused on the task at hand. People were whisked away by the strength of the wind; vehicles were lifted and flipped by its incredible force. Elric remained calm; the destruction was worse than Lexington's.

They made their way to the center of town. Cars and trucks were embedded in buildings; homes were shattered and dismantled. It didn't matter what the structures were made from. Even brick was toppled and crushed.

Elric saw a building that wasn't in that bad of shape on the strip that lined Main Street. "I think I found a safe place where we can wait this out," he said.

Black tendrils reached from the black sphere and began tossing debris out of the way, making a path for them. Once they were inside where the heavy wind couldn't touch them, he lowered the shield. Tables and chairs were battered and scattered all over the place, and broken glass covered the floor.

"Let's find the cellar. In an old building like this, there must be a cellar, right?" Mrs. Reeves shouted, looking around and knocking things over in fear.

They agreed, searching the floor for any sign of a cellar trapdoor. Glass crunched beneath their feet as they looked. A large grill still burned in the kitchen; the fumes of overcooked sausage made the air bitter. Elric turned it off to prevent a fire, hoping everyone who'd been here got to a safe place in time.

"I found it!" Jen shouted from the back.

It was a large, black room where they stored canned goods and sauces. Between the shelves was a hatch. Mr. Reeves knelt and opened it. "There's already a light on down there." He made his way down helping Mrs. Reeves, then Jen crawl down. Elric gripped the latter stepping down. It was a tight room filled with crates, canned goods, and preservatives. Mr. Reeves inspected every inch of the perimeter. "This looks as safe a place as anywhere else."

Waiting for the raging wind to stop was as close to death row Elric hoped to get, because once the howling of the portal eased down, Blight's soldiers would push through and destroy everything in Clemson.

An hour had past when the whistling faded. Elric stood up and went up the ladder. It was still dark, but the howling ceased.

Mr. Reeves asked, "How's it looking up there?"

"It's better than it was. We should go."

They made their way outside, taking advantage of the break. The air was thick with smoke. Behind Elric, Jen and her parents choked and coughed. He focused his powers as the darkness surrounded them again.

Without the heavy wind, it was much easier to see as they walked amongst the crumbling remains of what use to be the town of Clemson. In an hour, the entire town was reduced to rubble. Elric lowered the protective sphere as they got out of the smoke and searched for a way out, but the sound of a woman screaming caught their attention.

They ran, taking refuge behind a mail truck lying on its side, and peeked around the corner. A woman sprinted down East Main Street, begging for someone to help. Her clothes were torn and filthy from smoke and dirt. She rolled her ankle and fell, smacking against the pavement. She groaned as she struggled to stand.

"What are we going to do?" Jen looked up at her parents.

"I'm going to go help her. You guys stay right here," Mr. Reeves said.

Mrs. Reeves grabbed his hand. "No, are you crazy? We don't even know what she's running from."

A loud shriek echoed from the darkened sky above. Wings flapped overhead, but it was too dark to see anything. Everyone hid; they were bunched together behind the mail truck. The woman screamed in fear and begged for help. Elric scanned the back of the truck; two bat-like creatures descended upon her. They were just like the ones that attacked him and Jen back in Lexington. They were just like Allure.

Clawed feet dragged across the tar as they landed, hunched over. Decorated with armor, they circled the woman, stalking her before the kill.

"Do you think Eminence will allow us to have a pre-war meal?" one of them said, looking down on the woman with excitement, drool oozing from its jaws.

Elric turned to Jen. The memories of Lexington hardened his heart and strengthened his resolve. Elric rose to his feet, swallowing his fear.

Jen grabbed his hand and squeezed. "Elric, be careful!"

Chapter 35

The Fall

The creatures toyed with the woman, shoving her to the ground and mocking her.

"Humans, so weak and feeble. I still don't understand why the ancients allowed them to have this world."

The other creature sat back, watching the other.

"The ancients were fools! Now we have Blight! He will change everything; this world will be ours!" the other replied, hunched over the women, ready to attack.

Elric stepped forward from behind the truck. "No, it won't."

The creature stopped talking and turned its head in Elric's direction. "Oh, and another. Looks like we'll both have a satisfying pre-war meal!" It raised its wings with excitement.

The other creature searched Elric with its large eyes. "Something is different about this one, Ascar."

"Yes, yes. I know it looks to be a male maybe. No matter. The blood and the meat will be just as sweet!"

Elric tightened his fist as a wave of dark energy blew through the street. He'd have to make this quick. Any more attention could bring more of them.

"Ascar, it is him. He's the one with the power of a general!" the creature shrieked. "Eminence! We must get Eminence!"

"Relnoch, inform the commander that we found him, the one they call Elric."

Elric's eyes widened in disbelief. *They know who I am?*

"As you wish, but be wary of him. He slaughtered Carnage in cold blood. Remember the report, Ascar!"

"Yes." He eyed Elric greedily. "I know. Now go!"

The large creature took off. The remaining bat watched Elric, swaying from left to right, contemplating its next move. Tendrils sprouted from the darkness that draped over Elric.

"Get out of here! Run!" Elric shouted to the woman who looked over in fear and shock at the darkness around him. She nodded, crawled to her feet, and limped down one of the alleys.

"You've killed a general, human. You have no idea what you've brought upon yourself."

"You came here to kill us. What did you expect?" Elric glared.

"Our ancestors shared this world with mankind and then left it in man's hands like fools. You destroy this world daily and wasting it's potential!" It stood tall making itself bigger as it looked on. "Blight has come to wipe the earth clean of human growth and rule. We'll make it our own!"

"You came here and killed hundreds, maybe thousands, of people because it's your destiny?" Elric asked with a rising voice. The tendrils became clawed hands. "You killed men, women, families, because you think you have some right to do it?!"

296

Elric closed his eyes and released a sharp wave that threw the creature into a building across from him.

It screeched in agony as it crawled out, dripping with a black fluid. The force ripped its right wing off. The left was riddled with shards of glass. A mournful cry bellowed from its chest.

"All that armor was useless." Elric walked over. The darkness surrounding him intensified. "I'm going to kill every single one of you, you hear me?" His voice was cold and firm.

The creature struggled to stand as its fur became clumped together by the black blood that trickled from its back and sides. Its cackle echoed around them.

"You think you have pride now because you have victory over a grunt." The armor clanked over its shoulders. "My kin and my general will ruin this world and make you suffer endlessly. All you love will d—"

One of the clawed hands had formed into a sharpened blade and smashed through the armor that protected the creature's chest. Its eyes rolled back into its skull as they closed. The tendril let the lifeless corps fall to the ground as its armor scraped the sidewalk.

Elric walked back toward the truck where Jen and her parents were hiding. Jen stepped out from behind the building, watching the darkness and clawed tendrils sway around him.

"Is it done?" Jen asked.

"No. There's something much worse coming," Elric said, thinking about Eminence. He remembered what Alfred said about the generals. He gazed into Jen's hope-filled eyes, and the darkness began to calm. "We have to go."

"What are we going to do now? There must be more of those things," Jen's mother covered her lips with trembling fingers.

"We have to find a safe place for now. The best thing to do is stick to the sidewalks. That way we can duck into a building if any of those things approach," her father said.

They traveled along the sidewalk, following the sirens around town, but it was no use. Emergency vehicles were getting ripped apart by large groups of beasts.

Elric was shocked by the lack of a military presence. In Lexington, they had everything wrapped tight and secured in minutes. Now there was nothing, not even a helicopter. Maybe all of Maine, no, the world, had met its fate.

Was Zaroule wrong about us? Did we fail? Elric shook the thought out of his head.

They travelled to a part of town they hadn't been to, passing a McDonalds that was on the right. The yellow arches dangled from the pole that supported them, and smoke bellowed from the windows.

A group of people make their way to the south side of town and felt a sense of relief to see other humans. The sirens faded, disappearing amongst the pops and crackles in the distance; it was hard to tell if they were gunfire or just the sound of burning vehicles exploding. The hope of getting help withered to nothing.

"I assume you're the ones I've been searching for all this time," a voice shouted from above. The four of them turned to see a large, tan man with a shaved head standing at the top of a three-story building. He looked down at them with folded arms.

"What's he doing up there?" Mr. Reeves asked.

The man jumped off the roof, plummeting to the ground. Jen and her mother hid their eyes. Everyone anticipated the smack of a human body slapping pavement, but it was the opposite. A large crack split the ground in front of them from the impact of his landing.

He smiled as he rose and stood strong. No normal person could survive a drop like that, let alone land like he was an Olympic gymnast. The closer the man walked toward Elric and the Reeveses, the more sinister the man's presence became.

He wasn't like the others that were covered in armor. He wore torn jeans, was shirtless and ripped, and his hands looked like they could rip Elric in half.

"This is bad. There's something not right with him," Mr. Reeves said.

Elric turned to Jen and her parents. "You guys need to get out of here. Now!"

Jen's eyes widened. "No! Are you kidding me? We're not going to leave you here by yourself."

The man shook his head in disappointment. "So, you're Elric, huh? Man, you're a hard kid to find, but following that darkness leaking out of you is like following a trail of rotting breadcrumbs."

Elric shivered. "Who are you? What do you want?"

"C'mon. Don't play dumb. Since Allure couldn't do the job, the boss sent me to bring you in, dead or alive." He cracked his knuckles. "Most likely dead, I'm sure. They call me Eminence, the next in command after Malevolence."

A foul wave of darkness blew from him, crushing, and frightening. He was on a different level than any of the Generals . . . this was more then Allure and Carnage put together. Eminence sneered, folding his arms.

Elric knew not to jump into a fight without knowing the enemy's tactics. That was the first thing Zaroule taught them. "Sounds like you guys know a lot about me," Elric said, trying to stay calm.

"You become a popular guy when you kill one of the four generals. In Ermak, we're kings of our domains, so I'm sure you'll understand that what you did is not only an act of war, but an event that can only be answered with death."

Elric's stomach dropped, but he kept it together. *Don't forget what the old man taught you,* he thought. *Protect Jen and her parents and wipe that sick grin off this A-hole's face.*

Jen grabbed his arm. "Elric, we have to go. This guy isn't like those monsters. We have to go now!"

"Jen." Elric turned with a smile. "I'll be fine. I'm a hero, remember? Good guys always win. Go with your parents. I'll catch up, okay?"

Jen tightened her grip. "And if I lose you, what do you expect me to do?"

"Ahh, so you have a girlfriend." Eminence ran over and grabbed them both by the throat. "Maybe if I get rid of her, I might get your attention."

Elric watched as Jen struggled for air as Eminence's fingers cracked around her throat. Tears rolled down the sides of her face.

"Elric," Jen choked.

Elric's heart pounded through his chest; even louder as the darkness flushed his veins. A wave burst forth strong enough to blow everything and everyone back, forcing Eminence's grip to loosen. A dark tendril grabbed Jen as she fell, gasping for air.

Jen looked up as the tendril brought her close to Elric.

"You alright?" she asked as a tear trickled down toward her ear.

He shook his head, lost for words. "You're asking me when you're the one that's hurt?"

"Hey," Jen said looking into his eyes. "You can do it. I trust you. Crush him."

Elric nodded, taking a deep breath, and helping her stand. Not only was this guy a douchebag, but he was a confident one.

"You think this is a joke?" More tendrils slipped out of the dark mass that covered Elric and Jen. "I'm going to kill you just like I did Carnage!"

"Confident, aren't we?" Eminence shook his head. "Carnage was weak, and he was more of a basket case than a leader anyway, but I can see how killing him would give you self-confidence. Many people drop to their knees in fear when they face a general." He cracked his knuckles. "The fact that you're not running is honorable to say the least, but I'm still going to kill you,"

Elric raced toward him. "No, you won't!"

Eminence cocked his head to the side, waiting for the attack. Elric threw the first punch, a large fist caught it. The darkness covering Eminence intensified, overpowering Elric's own aura. The tendrils trying to assist dissolved, consumed by Eminence's overwhelming power.

He twisted Elric's wrist as a pop sent stabbing pain through his arm. A blood-curdling scream left Elric's lungs, blood splattered on the pavement from his left hand. The bone came clean through the skin of his wrist.

"Elric!" Mrs. Reeves screamed in terror.

Eminence kicked him in the ribs, sending him skimming across the pavement like a rock on water. Elric wailed gripping his disfigured arm. Even as his body regenerated, the pain was overwhelming and frightening.

Eminence made his way over to Jen, cracking his knuckles. She stumbled back, eyes searching for help.

Chapter 36

Corruption

"No!" Elric screamed as the muscle tissue and bone began to connect itself together. "Stay away from her!"

"A true warrior indeed, Elric." Eminence nodded as if to show respect. "But . . . " He grabbed Jen by the shirt and slammed her to the ground. "You have to be more than a warrior to come close to being what I am." He stepped on her back and applied pressure.

Jen screamed and Eminence laughed as she swung and kicked. Elric tried to release more darkness, it wasn't enough. This man, this monster, toyed with him as if he were nothing.

You promised to protect her. You promised her. Do something, he thought. Massive dep breaths escaped his lungs and his face reddened with suppressed rage. *Do something even if it means dying!*

Elric's fingernails lengthened; his eyes burned with hatred and anger. Large, black, sharp spikes cut through the skin of his forearms.

"Well, you're adamant." An expression of victory etched across his face. "I wouldn't expect anything less. I mean, you did take out Carnage," he joked.

Elric ran at Eminence with blinding speed, speed he didn't even know he had, and punched him in the face. Eminence glided across the tar streets, slamming into a telephone pole.

Elric raced over to Jen. Her neck was red and beginning to bruise. *How could you let this happen to her?* he thought.

Jen wrapped her arms around his neck and came to her feet, wobbling. Elric helped her over to Mrs. Reeves who hesitated to reach for him. She was frightened by the spines that split his skin, running down his forearms.

"Elric, please, let's just run. We can make it," Mrs. Reeves begged.

"He's not going to stop, no matter how fast we run, no matter how far we can go. He'll keep coming until I'm dead."

"Look at what's happening to you . . . your eyes, your hands, even your arms . . . It's turning you into a monster!" Jen screamed.

"Jen, he wants me. He doesn't care about you. It's me."

The darkness had taken over even without the Deva's influence on him, but he still had a handle on his actions, which was good enough.

"Please, go." He looked up at Mr. Reeves.

Mr. Reeves nodded. "I don't agree with your decision Elric, but I trust you." He grabbed his wife and daughter and rushed them up the street.

Jen struggled to break free, screaming Elric's name every step of the way. "Please, don't do this! Come with us!"

"No audience. We can't have that." Eminence took both of his fists and smashed them into the ground, creating a large trench in front of them. "There we go." He rose with a smile.

Elric ran at him lunging with a blow to the belly, it was like hitting a steel wall. He slapped Elric into a car windshield.

"Your powers are just like mine. Mine are better as you can see. And I haven't scratched the surface yet." Eminence took a deep breath and exhaled. "I'm going to enjoy this."

"I won't let you touch them! You hear me?" Elric said, wiping blood from the corner of his mouth. "You generals are proud and have so much confidence in your power. You think this Blight idiot is going to make all your dreams come true. My friends are gonna stop him!"

"Your world is doomed." Eminence said as Jen and her parents ran, ignoring Elric's words. "They're doomed!"

Eminence ran toward Elric. The ground quaked like a herd of elephants thrashing about, he smacked Elric out of the way and looked back with a smile. He was headed for Jen and her parents.

Mr. Reeves jumped in front of Jen and her mom. Still rattled by the blunt force of Eminence's attack, Elric crawled to his feet. In desperation, he concentrated all the energy that could be mustered and took off towards them.

I have to get there. I have too! he yelled.

Eminence grabbed Mr. Reeves by the throat, raising him high to the sky and turned to Elric. "A little pay back for Carnage even though I hated the guy."

He forced his fist through Mr. Reeves's stomach, his fist came out of his back. Mr. Reeves's eyes widened, and his head slumped to the side. Eminence threw Mr. Reeves's body across the street like garbage.

"Daddy!" Jen screamed.

Mrs. Reeves screamed too, holding Jen and watching with tear-filled eyes. Blackness massed around Elric's right hand, and he swung, desperate to protect them.

Eminence grabbed Elric's hand, looking at the black energy that covered his hand in awe. "You're definitely not like the rest of them, huh?"

Eminence punched Elric into another car, embedding him in the metal, and begin throwing a barrage of blows. Elric's regeneration couldn't keep up.

He lost a few teeth; a few broken ribs made it hard to breath, and he could make out bits and pieces of the world through his swollen eyes.

Elric felt a sense of relief from the pressure of his face, as he spat out a large blood clot. Eminence had already made his way over to Jen and her mom, forcing them apart. "No, no!" Elric groaned paralyzed from his entrapment.

They both screamed, reaching for each other. Eminence tightened his grip around Mrs. Reeves's throat, and Elric heard the snap.

"No," Elric muttered, watching Eminence cast her body to the side.

Eminence focused on Jen.

The car that entrapped Elric began to rot away the potent essence of the darkness. He ripped free, stumbling forward and dropped to his knees, his legs had no strength left.

"Please, don't do this! I won't fight. I'll just give myself up," Elric screamed. "Just don't hurt her!"

The true reality of it set in. Superheroes weren't real; these powers he had weren't enough. Jen's parents were dead, and once again Elric failed the people that counted on him most.

Eminence smiled, not a shred of mercy in his eyes as he raised Jen high to the sky. Tears caressed her chin as she cried, reaching for Elric.

"No, I won't kill her," Eminence replied in a casual tone. "She's not going to get off as easily as the other two. I bet your wondering how all these portals seem to spawn out of nowhere, huh?"

Jen did her best to fight his grip. Elric didn't want to make a sudden move in fear of him killing. He had to think.

"Just let her go." He lowered his head, accepting defeat. "I won't fight anymore."

He ignored Elric's plea. "You see, Blight found a way to create wormholes from our world to this one using our powers. The weaker species who call themselves Ermakians use ancient doorways which have been around for centuries, allowing them to safely come and go as they please. Blight found a more interesting way of coming here, by ripping holes into the fabric of the universe and forcing our way through both worlds. Obviously, Blight, being the strongest of us all, can make multiple portals, hundreds even. But if you put our powers together, we can make thousands." Eminence focused his hands toward the center of a building. With a thundering crash, a portal tore through the building.

"Elric, run!" Jen yelled, her hair flowing from the force of energy.

"This portal allows me to send things to the other," Eminence said.

Elric balled his fist. He had no idea what was going to happen, but he had to react.

The general continued, "On the other side of this portal is a world filled with pain, suffering, and death."

Elric focused his powers into his right hand once more before lunging forward. Eminence dodged the attack with ease, halting Elric from freeing Jen. He grabbed Elric by the throat and tightened his grip.

"Elric, no!" Jen cried.

"Elric, I'm disappointed in your powers. Blight was so concerned, but he'll see now that you were nothing to worry about." He raised Jen to the sky. "This is your end, Elric, and I want you to see the deaths of all you cherished before the light goes out."

"Please, I'll go with you. Just don't hurt her!"

Elric looked over at Jen. All he could think about was how helpless he was; he unable to protect the girl he had been in love with since the beginning. How could he bring so much pain and suffering to the people he loved more than anything? Her parents were gone because of him, and now she was next.

"Elric, sorry I didn't listen. I couldn't let you do this alone," She choked.

Eminence let her go as the force of the portal pulled her in. Elric tried to reach out for her with his opposite hand, "No!" The tips of her fingers grazed across his palm; she screamed as the dark hole devoured her. Her screams echoed through the streets, fading into the darkness of the portal as it collapsed, vanishing.

Eminence threw Elric to the ground.

This isn't real. It's not possible. I didn't save her? He closed his eyes as the warmth of tears built up behind his eyes.

When he opened them, he found himself in his inner world in front of a door surrounded by blackness. Elric fell to his knees, wishing this were a nightmare, but it wasn't. Jen was gone.

They were all gone. Loud whispers surrounded him in the darkness, echoing from all directions.

Let me out. I promise you I'll take away the pain and the sadness, the voice of the Deva echoed.

You let him get us, Elric. He killed my parents and me too, Jen cried.

A group of voices whispered through the darkness; *you're letting the world down. You're going to fail and die. Thanks to you, Zaroule is dead!*

"Leave me alone!" Elric screamed, covering his ears.

He ran toward the door in tears and turned the key. A large mass of blackness in the shape of a monstrous hand grabbed him and pulled him in. The memory of Elric Blake disappeared as he drowned in the sea of blackness. He stopped fighting the Deva's influence, there was no one else to fight for. What was the point? *I have nothing to lose.*

Elric opened his eyes as an explosion collapsed the surrounding buildings. The ground rattled with heavy tremors. Black scales covered his hands, as his claws curved. Three rows of black spikes raced down his forearm.

"Sounds like someone finally wants to play," Eminence yelled, rushing with blurring speed.

A swift jab smacked Eminence head on, his nostrils sprayed a crimson mist into the air as he stumbled back, stunned by the blow.

Elric grabbed Eminence's arm, breaking it in three places with a loud pop. The massive man roared in pain, dropping to the ground. "You killed them . . . without a care in the world."

Eminence took another swing, but Elric jumped back, dodging the attack. A blood stained grin etched across the man's face. "Now let's see what you're capable of with that hatred!"

His muscles twisted, popped, and stretched; black fur glided over his body in waves. His pants shredded away, revealing muscular legs draped with long black fur. Eminence snarled shaking his massive horned head, snot falling in globs. He looked like the minotaur on steroids, there was nothing human left.

"That isn't going to help you . . . " Elric's voice cracked over the monstrous beasts laugh.

The Deva's influence was stronger than before after opening that door. Zaroule was right, but he didn't have a choice? Why fight to keep his sanity, he didn't need it anymore, everyone he loved was dead.

Chapter 37

———)((O))(———

Wrath of the Dark Titan

"It's been a while since I've gone this far." Eminence stretched with a deep groan. "Usually I can tear an Ermakian limb from limb without changing. I tell you what, if you can force me back into my human form, I'll open a portal that'll bring you to Blight!" He ran toward Elric once more. The dark energy formed a protective aura around Elric. By leaning in with his head, Eminence shattered it with raw strength. The horns grazed his ribs, tearing through Elric's shirt.

Pinned between the massive horns Elric was slammed into a brick building. Eminence struggled to lift his head and break free, but he was trapped. Too bad.

Elric clenched his hands together and smashed down on Eminence's skull, shattering the horns in half, and leaving the rest still stuck in the wall.

A dark tendril wrapped around Eminence's waist, the dark essence rotted his fur and flesh as he bellowed. The black streams sent him crashing into a diner.

Eminence stumbled out of the rubble. "My horns, my precious horns!" He rubbed a furry finger across the broken stubs.

Even from across the street, Elric could see the madness taken over is glossy brown eyes.

"I'll stomp you into a jelly!" The general yelled.

"Enough!" Elric appeared in front of him.

"Fast," Eminence replied, eyes widening as he stumbled back.

Eminence cross his arms to shield the coming blow, Elric leaned low piercing clean through Eminence's abdomen. "That was for Mr. Reeves" Elric pulled back.

"H-how did you move like that?" The large beast stumbled back, trying to keep his intestines from spilling out.

"Those look important." Elric glared with the glowing crimson eyes. "I'd hold onto them if I were you." Elric threw his hand forward, releasing a black blast that threw the large beast back.

A sharp pain pierced Elric's right shoulder, "Argh!" He cringed, trying to control the throbbing. A pulsating stub on his shoulder brought Elric to his knees. "What, the hell is that . . . "

Eminence wobbled to his hooves, reverting to his human form. His body was battered, but the hole in his stomach was nothing more but a disfigured scar.

"Never have I ever been pushed to a limit where I felt I would be fighting for my life." Elric crouched over in pain. "What are you?"

Elric's shirt stretched tightening across his chest as another stub from his left side grew. Elric wailed. It was like someone was driving red hot blades of metal through his shoulders and back. With tear-filled eyes a large, black, bat-like wing tore through the right side of his back.

"I don't know what's going on, but I'll end this now!" he roared, bulldozing his way toward Elric. Eminence lunged with a heavy fist.

Another wing ripped through the left side of Elric's back, shielding him from the blow and knocking Eminence back. Elric looked over his shoulders at the powerful new extremities. Jet-black, long, and armored with scales. Spikes lined the edges, and the tips had large black horns like the ones sprouting from Elric's forearms. They protruded just below his shoulders and ended at his shoulder blades.

Eminence roared. "This is impossible!" He struggled to stand. "You're nothing but a human child, scum . . . "

Elric was confused by the transformation himself. He moved the wings, as if he had a second pair of hands. "I told you, I'll kill you and the rest of the generals, and I'll kill Blight too."

"Amazing. A human like you shouldn't exist. Regardless, killing me won't do anything or prove your worth." Eminence laughed as blood ran down his nose.

"Maybe not, but my powers are growing every second," Elric said, standing up. The pain was numbing. He looked don tightening his scale covered claws.

"You're bluffing. That's impossible!"

"Inside me lives a monster, and through that monster, I can harness its power. There're more like me with powers too." Eminence spat black blood on the floor glaring. "Before I kill you, where did you send her?"

Eminence bloody cracked lips curved. "The question you should be asking, is where's Blight? The girl's gone; we're past that."

Elric fought back tears. "Where's Blight?"

"By now he's in Zenith, and whatever friends you have down there, they're probably already dead."

"Open a portal there and I'll make your job and mine easier," Elric said walking towards him.

Eminence smiled and raised his hand. A portal thundered open. "This will bring you right to Blight. You better believe I'm nothing compared to the father of our powers."

"How do I know that's where it'll bring me?"

Eminence's jovial expression faded. "I'm a warrior with absolute pride in my word. You forced me back to this form. I respect power when I see it."

Elric tightened his claws. "I'm going through that portal and killing everyone who caused all of this."

"You're a powerful adversary indeed, Elric, but," Eminence bolted towards Elric, roaring. "You have to get through me to get to him!"

Jen's last words echoed in the darkness of Elric's mind, *sorry I didn't listen. I couldn't let you do this alone.* Elric focused the dark energy into his right hand and released it, sending a blast that cracked the ground to pieces.

Eminence eyes gaped open and he threw his hands up. "A warrior's death is very fitting for a general of my caliber. I owe you one, Elric, my only hope is my essence rests with my father!"

The blast ripped Eminence apart down to the cellular level, and smashed clean through a building, leveling the surroundings.

Elric fell to the ground from exhaustion. The large wings sunk into his back, vanishing beneath the flesh of his shoulders. His body was tight and sore as the stubs smoothed into the muscles of his shoulders. Even the claws and spines on his arms vanished.

The memories of Jen and her parents dying were all that remained. His failure to keep the ones he loved safe turned him into a monster. The happiness that he felt and worked so hard to protect was gone forever. It didn't matter how much good he did or how strong he became, this hole in his heart would linger, and it would grow. Tears fell from his face.

The black hole Eminence created began to shrink. Elric wiped the tears from his face and took a deep breath before rising to his feet. Rage and hatred filled his heart; he didn't hesitate to step into the portal that would lead him back to Zenith.

The hole spat him out into a place that he didn't dare recognize, but he knew it was Zenith. From the outskirts smoke and darkness covered the city. Most of the large lamps that hung above Zenith had been destroyed. Screams, and monstrous roars reached his ears.

He ran down the crumbling roads heart racing with each foot fall. *I'll end all this, Blight will die!*

A jolt of purple light sparked on the outskirts of Zenith. *Violet!* He raced to the opposite side of the city, using that jolt of energy as a beacon.

Elric found himself running into a dense forest of strange vegetation covering one side of the city. A maze of thick, dark-green bushes covered in massive thorns—curved like sharpened teeth— waited patiently for the taste of flesh. This was new, and they weren't from Earth.

In the distance, large blasts of purple energy flickered. He raised both his hands toward the mass of vegetation, releasing blasts of darkness that disintegrated the thick vines. A thick vine burst from the ground, replacing the ones that were destroyed. Elric tore it to shreds with sharpening claws.

As his anger increased, the dark energy intensified around him. The plants withered to soggy, gray sludge, never growing back as the darkness devoured the life from them. Up ahead, the voices of a conversation seeped through the thorny brush. Elric crept closer coming to the scene that drew his attention.

Hanging upside down, constricted by dozens of vines, Violet gasped for air. Someone faced her, and they weren't human, they didn't look Ermakian either.

Squirming vines slithered around a head-like structure, and florescent green eyes peered through black sockets. Long thorny branches made up the creatures' fingers, stretching out of a worn trench coat.

The creature gave a gurgling exhale, studying Violet like a ripe piece of fruit ready to be plucked. One of its fingers slithered across her cheek as she winced.

"I've already won. This world is mine." It hissed. "All I want now is to know where your friend is. Maybe, just maybe, I'll make you my slave of entertainment. Once I crush humanity, letting a couple live for our enjoyment is fair enough."

"Screw you!" Violet snapped back, trying to pull away.

The vines unraveled, and she fell to the floor. "But my dear, your friends are nowhere in sight. They're probably already dead." The creature laughed with a gurgle. "Besides, they wouldn't stand a chance even if they came to rescue you."

"You don't have a clue," Violet choked. "They'll come, and we'll end this."

"I must say, you and your friends have become quite galling, especially this boy who seems to be capable of killing one of my generals. Let's make a deal. You tell me where he is, and I'll let you and your friends get an opportunity to kill me."

Violet lunged forward with a hand covered in purple light. "Screw you and your deals!"

A vine wrapped around her arms, tying them together. The vines raised her high above the field of brush. Elric gritted his teeth. The vines began wiggling with life.

The plant-like creature turned and looked in his direction. "Someone spying?" the creature asked, peeking over.

Elric relaxed, doing his best to control his emotions, but the creature's attention was taken away by the heavy flap of wings from above. Elric eased to the ground as he looked up to see the white bat. Allure.

She circled overhead, scanning the field before she made her descent. She transformed into her human form and wrapped herself in a cloak.

"What's the problem now? Aren't they all dead yet?" the plant creature asked.

"That's not the problem, my sovereign." Allure kept her face down. "Eminence is dead. A scout that watched the fight spread the word, and that's not the worst part."

"Well, what could possibly be worse than one of my top subordinates being killed by a bunch of humans?"

"It wasn't a bunch . . . " Allure's eyes darted over to Violet with a scowl. "It was her friend, the boy."

The creature's glowing eyes shrunk. The vines slithered around its head as it gave a guttering roar. "Where is he now?"

Allure trembled, eyes focusing away from the creature. "He's here somewhere . . . "

"Good. This way I can kill two birds with one stone." The creature laughed, its branch-like hands cupped Allure's chin with tenderness and care. "Has anyone spotted him yet?"

"No, but I bet she knows where he is. I know it!" Allure glared at Violet.

Violet didn't say a word.

"She can feel him out." Allure looked at the creature. "She has powers that can find anyone."

Violet steamed. "That's impossible that Elric's here. I sent him away. Sounds like your messenger can't get her facts straight, Blight!"

Elric's eyes widened once he heard the name. Rage brought back an appetite he thought Zaroule sealed deep behind those doors. Maybe that's why the old man begged him to only open a door in a dire situation. Eminence was dire, and so was the current situation.

No, Elric thought to himself as he fought the darkness. He looked down at the claws, still trying to fight the darkness from taking over. He looked up at Violet, who dangled by a thread; he had to save her first.

Blight looked up at Violet. "Allure, let the grunts know we have a situation and to keep their eyes open. I'll take care of our delicate flower here."

Allure smiled, looking over at Violet. "Looks like I did get away with killing that foolish old man." She took off to the sky and made her way toward the city.

Blight brought Violet closer to his face; her nose crinkled. "So, why is this boy so strong? You know something that I don't? Please, share with me." His voice was calm and misleading.

"You can all rot in hell for all I care." She spat in his face. The vines squirmed around Blight's head. A thorn cut deep into her wrist as she winced in pain.

"I could easily just slit both your wrists and watch you bleed out. My plants would drink your blood just as they've done to so many over the decades. There are dozens of bodies all around. What's one more?" The thorn dug deeper as she groaned. "I'm going to give you to the count of three because my patience is up. If you don't tell me where he is, my vines are going to fillet you, girl."

A large mound rose from the ground, bursting open with dark green vines encasing Violet in a giant peapod. Thorns protruded from inside the casing and opened like a large gaping mouth.

"You think I care what you do to me? You'll never get what you want!" Violet yelled.

"But I already have. Look around you." Blight raised the long, plant-like extensions. "Zenith is no more. The ones who lived here are among the dead, or they have joined me . . . or will soon." The thorn casing closed around her; the sharpened thorns protruded, waiting to taste her flesh.

She pulled and strained to break free. The leafy case began connecting. Violet gave a bloodcurdling scream.

A cyclone of power erupted, ripping away all the vines around Elric as they dissolved to mush, revealing himself to Blight. The vines that tried to crush Violet opened back up and began rotting. Besides blood trickling from a few slashes, she was fine.

"Elric!" Violet screamed.

"You're the one who's been giving me trouble all this time? The boy who seems to know exactly how to push my buttons?" Blight lowered his head glaring.

Elric returned the expression; eyes burning red.

"You think you can stop me?" Blight asked with a muffled hiss.

"You've taken everything from me and Violet." His pupils flared. "You've murdered and slaughtered families. I won't let you get away with the things you've done."

"Well, that's the cost of a revolution. I'm not just aimlessly killing people like some psychopath. I give everyone a choice. You go against me. You die. You refuse me. You die. You join me, and I promise you sanctuary and peace. To bring peace, people will die. War leads to death, but it's worth it if you win."

"You're sicker than I thought," Violet mumbled. "You think destroying their homes, lives, and families is going to make them respect you. It only breeds hate."

"Good. Then they can understand what my species went through." Blight threw out his branch-like fingers as vines came squirming toward Elric.

A black wave pushed them back with a wave of Elric's hand. Blight raced towards him; his branch like fingers twisted into a giant wooden cleaver, slashing away with quick, unpredictable movements. Blight went through the black aura that surrounded Elric, almost as if the darkness allowed him to walk in.

Elric maneuvered around the attacks, jumping, and dodging. Blight threw his body into each attack, the cleaver, stretching and twisting at angles Elric couldn't keep up with.

Blight spoke not missing a step, confident in his abilities. Not wasting a breath. "You and your friends aren't normal humans. But there's something different about you. Something that reminds me of myself," Blight spoke, slashing away. "I can sense your hate enveloping you, making you stronger. Did I create you?"

Chapter 38

—————————))(((—————————

Blight vs. the Dark Titan

A sadistic laugh escaped the vines that formed Blight's jaws. As Elric dodged, Blight was right there to counter and make up for the miss.

Blight laughed again. "I always wondered what kind of creature could be savage enough and strong enough to take down one of my generals, so I put a bounty on your head. I even halted my plans to move my soldiers into this world just to find you."

The back end of the wooden cleaver smashed across his chest. A vine wrapped around Elric's ankle, tripping him. *What the hell's going on, I'm getting slower . . . weaker?*

"Looks like my vines are starting to do their job. It took long enough." Blight stopped attacking, hanging the cleaver over his shoulder. "My plants suck the life out of all living things in seconds, until your nothing but a mummified corpse, but here you are still fighting. What power you must have."

He walked around Elric, examining him like some animal in a zoo. The vines constricting Elric's arms and spread them apart. Blight laughed as he drew the cleaver back.

"What a shame. I had expected more from you." Blight raised the weapon high. The cleaver came down.

A large purple veil covered Elric in a bubble. Violet shook with exhaustion as her eyes glowed, hands stretched towards.

You alright? she asked telepathically.

Yeah, I'm good. He looked up, trying to fight the exhaustion.

"You children are quite the team, I see. She must be using some of her life reserve just to protect you. Too bad it won't do any good," A branch-like finger pierced Violet's shoulder. "It'll just accelerate her death!"

She screamed dropping to the ground. Blood seeping from the wound.

"No, Violet!" Elric yelled, his eyes were getting heavy. The feeling in his arms and legs were gone.

Looks like that hatred of yours is letting me out of this cage that old bastard put me in, a voice rumbled from Elric's inner world. Sad to say, he was glad to hear it. *It's been a while, Elric. Maybe it's time to open these doors and let me out so it can be like old times?*

Everything went black. He was back in his inner world. Deep groans and heavy breathing were all around him, the heavy thud of the Deva's heart was right on him. *It's you? Right?*

The Deva chuckled. *Yes, and I'm pissed. We had such a good thing going. Now look at you. This creature has taken everything from you. Why let him breathe another second when we can make him suffer together? Let the hatred take over. Stop fighting me.* The voice echoed in the darkness.

Elric wondered why he kept fighting the darkness after what happened to Jen and her parents. Was it his humanity? This little bit of light that struggled in the vast ocean of blackness and hatred within him? Elric saw their faces: Mrs. Lee's, Zaroule, Jen, and her parent's.

Elric's rage bubbled within. The only reason he defeated Eminence was because of the dark influence and energy of the Deva. Holding back only got people killed. Maybe . . .

That's it. Take your revenge. Show him the power of true darkness, Elric! the Deva grumbled.

Elric's insides swelled with a burning pain. Hatred filled his heart. He opened his eyes, regaining consciousness, staring into the gaping eyes of Blight. Blight stepped back gazing over Elric's shoulder.

Hovering over Elric was a massive, black dragon with wings spread wide. Piercing crimson eyes sat within a skull with large protruding horns. Several rows of jet-black teeth filled its jaws. The lack of flesh covering its gums gave the beast a frightening grin. Its neck was long and thick, covered in horns that glowed with red markings.

The semitransparent being towered over everything including Zenith. Its horns scraped the ceiling of the cave, knocking debris to the ground and rattling the remaining lamps.

I made that. Elric thought. Smoke poured from the nostrils as it snarled.

Blight eyes fell on Elric. "These powers you have at such a young age can make you a god. Why would you waste your time protecting this worthless world?"

Large rocks began to fall from the ceiling smashing into homes in the distance. Rocks turned to smoldering ash as they hit the creature that hung above.

"Elric, please stop. Think about the people still in the city!" Violet screamed.

Elric's face hardened "Stop? Why would I stop when my goal is right here in front of me?" Violet's lips quivered as she looked up at him. "The only thing that matters to me right now is *him*."

"What about the people who care about you here? What about us, your friends?" Violet screamed.

Elric remembered the meditation he and Eden had to perform daily. Zaroule said that it was just as important to train the mind as the body. This was especially true for a Titan.

Blight forced his branch-like fingers into the ground. Elric looked over at Violet and nodded, taking a deep breath, controlling his emotions. He raised his hands to the ceiling. The dragon copied his exact movements and dissolved into a swirling black mass of energy.

Even as he got his emotions in check, Elric's gaze remained cold and focused on Blight. "This is where it ends." Elric took off toward Blight, dark energy sizzling around his hand as he lunged forward.

Blight turned into a pile of vines, dropping to the floor. The pile wiggled into the cracks of the ground, his laughter echoing throughout the cave, increasing Elric's rage.

"Where are you?" Elric yelled. "You use your soldiers to do your dirty work because you know you're not strong enough to do it yourself!"

Blight's laughter answered the statement. "Who of importance to you did I kill? family? Friends? Someone you loved?" He continued to laugh. "It's funny how the loss of the people close to you can change you so much. Remembering the loss of my loved ones is what drives me; it strengthens me."

"Drives you," Violet screamed. "What could drive someone to commit genocide?"

"My family and my entire species were wiped out because of those arrogant fools who call themselves Ermakians. This is what drives me."

Elric searched the cave, enraged by the game of cat and mouse Blight played. He didn't move, scanning every dark crevice, hoping he would slip up.

"Ermak was becoming overpopulated. The top species divided Ermak into provinces for each species to help control resources, but it failed. Many species starved. Mine had it the worst. We soon began to attack one another for food. I did my best to stop my species, but starvation drove them to a new evolution, a new way of adapting."

"Is this the part where we're supposed to feel sorry for you?" Elric yelled as he searched the cave. "Just because your species suffered, it doesn't give you the right to take your anger out on everyone else!"

Blight's hysterical laughter was a cackle in the dim light. "Children, my species didn't suffer. They evolved. They became cannibals, hunting and killing those of our own blood not strong enough to fight! My true love and our child were murdered, devoured by the people I trusted most because I wasn't there to protect them." He paused, exhaling deeply with a trembling hiss. "I was too busy trying to find an alternative food sources so Ermak could be united like we once were." The hissing sound became calm. "Like a coward, I escaped and hid underground. After a couple of years, the famine ended. Would you believe the species of Ermak celebrated because a new harvest had blossomed? They failed to see that it had nothing to do with resources replenishing themselves, but it all had to do with weaker species dying out. This was the perfect example of survival of the fittest. Every species that survived got on with their lives, burying the horrible secret of what happened."

The vines wiggled further across the plain. Elric pointed, and Violet looked over, her hands glowing ready to attack.

"It could be him." Her voice was shaky, and her stance weak. Elric wondered how long she could keep going.

"I stayed underground with my hatred and misery festering. I became something different. I evolved. My animosity toward the other species became love and pity. So, instead of vengeance, I began to understand the pain my fellow Ermakians felt. That's when she came."

"Love? You are twisted and sick! You can't love!" Violet yelled in anger.

Elric stopped. "Who came?"

"The goddess of Ermak, Sheba, blessed me with these powers, making me the hero I am today." He laughed. "With this blessing, I led a revolution against those who believed peace was permanent. Peace is impossible when you're in a world of scarce resources. So, I stayed in the shadows preaching of a new world. Our world."

"You're talking about earth," Violet said

"Yes, exactly. All we had to do is wipe out the filth there, and we could start over new. It was such a simple task, but then you had the people who believed it was murder. You know what I did?"

Elric waited for his reply. "What?"

"I eradicated those who had absolute faith in the old system of Ermak. I made sure those in top leadership roles were assassinated. I couldn't allow the ones who let children and entire families like mine die mercilessly to live. I sought others like me and shared my powers as they harnessed it. Soon, more people sought me out for this power, and once I had an army, I began to push the ones who believed in peace out of Ermak."

"So, that's how you did it then. You poisoned their minds to get them to join you. You used lost souls in order to make your army and twisted them into monsters." Violet was infuriated.

"Poisoned their minds? I set them free, and I put the power back in the hands of the voiceless, the ones who were too weak to stand up for what was right!"

She closed her eyes and began to concentrate. "I won't let him get away with this, Elric. He's done too much to us. It ends now!"

Blight's voice echoed close by. "You kids are nothing like what I would have ever imagined existing among humans. Your powers are exquisite especially yours, Elric." He began to take form right in front of them, the vines piling up on top of each other taking the shape of a body. Blight was starting to solidify. Elric ran at him and, without hesitation, struck Blight in the chest with a mass of energy.

Blight stopped talking as their eyes met. The vines were spongy as his body released a warm, green liquid that ran down Elric's arm. The green fluid slapped against the ground, reminding Elric of summer drizzles in Lexington. For an instant, an image of him and Jen grazed his memory. They were in the fourth grade, playing in the park, and a huge downpour hit. Instead of going inside, Jen wanted to play in the rain. Even then, she never took a second of her life for granted; through the rain, she found happiness.

"You not only remind me of myself, Elric."

He snapped out of the memory and looked up at Blight.

"But the dark energy within you is exactly like mine. Whether you believe it or not, you're me." Blight stepped forward.

Elric's arm flowed through him, and he pulled his hand away. "I'm nothing like you. I'll never hurt innocent people, and I'll never do the horrible things you've done.

"You'd be surprised. And no matter what world you're in, there is always going to be hatred!" Blight smacked Elric back with a branch arm that was covered in dark energy and thorns.

Elric hit the ground and dug his claws into the ground to get his balance. He felt the side of his face. Blood trickled down, revealing a large gash on the left side of his cheek. It began to heal.

"I figured that if our dark energies are the same, it means that two bads can make a right." Blight laughed. "My powers can hurt you as much as yours can hurt me. The thing is that my powers have pretty much made me immortal because I gave into them long ago."

Blight grabbed Elric by the throat. His grip tightened every time Elric exhaled.

Violet ran over, releasing blasts of energy into his back and knocking chunks of vegetation out of him. Thick green vines burst from his back, smacking her away.

"Sorry. That won't work on either of us," Blight said, focusing his attention on Elric. "I wonder what would happen if I fed on your life force?"

His branch-like fingers transformed into snake-like vines, opening with mouths filled with razor-sharp thorns that acted as teeth. They snapped toward Elric.

Large wings sprouted from Elric's back as he ripped free of Blight's grip. Elric propelled himself away with a single flap of the powerful wings. A thick vine raced forth, wrapping Elric's wings together, and yanked him to the ground.

Blight shuffled forward.

"The light can only take you so far, Elric Blake. Why do you think so many joined my army? Once you give into darkness and hatred, the things you can accomplish are limitless." The vines covering Blight's head spread to create a grin. "Too bad you won't live to find out what you could have accomplished."

Chapter 39

====)((()))(====

The Rise and Fall
of a Monster

The vines drew closer to Elric's neck. A chill raced down Elric's back as a howling wind of energy smashed into Blight's ribs and sent him flying into the vegetation.

"Violet, you alright?" the sound of a familiar voice called out. Eden cut his way through the dark vines. Alfred in his wolf form was right behind.

"Elric, is that you?" Alfred looked on in disbelief.

"I know it's hard to believe, but it really is him. His powers turned him into this," Violet replied looking, she hugged Eden, keeping him close.

"Seems you've been doing a lot of changing," Alfred said. "Is this what's going to happen to you sooner or later?" he whispered to Eden.

An earthquake halted the reunion as large, thick, black vines burst from the ground. Blight walked between the thick, thorny stems, caressing the wooden fingers over the slick vines.

Alfred took off after Blight with recklessness anger. The vines wrapped around his legs and arms and slammed Alfred to the ground, he slashed and tore into the vines with gnashing canines.

"He's stronger than I thought. Don't treat him lightly," Elric said not taking his eyes off Blight.

Eden swallowed hard. "What are we going to do then? Violet's weak, and Alfred's a little tied up now."

Elric stood up, ripping away the vines that entrapped him. "It's up to us. Like it was always meant to be."

Eden nodded. "You sure you're alright? You sound different."

"I'm fine, but I need to see him die!" Elric's eyes glowed with hatred.

"So, these must be the friends she spoke of. Interesting." Blight eyed Eden. "So, you seem to be special in your own right as well?"

Alfred grunted and growled as he tore himself loose from the tightening vines. Elric flapped his wings, feeling them out. If they could help him fly, then he had a plan.

Elric launched himself to the sky with the strength of his wings. Black vines burst from beneath the ground, pursuing him, but they couldn't match the height. The vines shifted to Eden.

Elric yelled, "Move, Eden!"

Eden jumped back. With a swipe of his hand, a roaring gust uprooted the vines, scattering them throughout the cave.

That was close. Elric said, "We're going to need more help. Where's Sasha and Manie?"

"They have a little problem of their own right now. Allure came by," Eden said, watching Elric descend.

"Well, that's great." Elric swallowed, remembering Zaroule's confidence in him and Eden. "Zaroule knew it would come down to this."

"Yeah, I guess you're right. But what about you?" Eden's eyes scrutinized Elric's new physique.

"It doesn't matter anymore; it's too late for that."

"It's changing you. Zaroule warned us. He told us about the drawbacks of our powers and losing control. He told *you* about your emotions. Now look at you."

"You don't understand. Besides, if I can harness this power, we can take him down!"

Blight stepped forward. "Your friend is right, Elric. I wonder how long it'll be before it starts to take over?"

Elric tightened his fist in anger. The dark energy ran down his arm, filling his hand.

Blight said, "It's only a matter of time before you give into the darkness. It'll eventually catch up to you, and what will your friends do?"

"What are you talking about?" Eden screamed.

Blight laughed. "Elric knows what I'm talking about. I bet they'll have no choice but to put you down like a diseased animal."

Elric looked over his shoulder where Eden was, but he was gone. Eden was already in the air, releasing an air blast on top of Blight. His attack was almost instantaneous. The blast a direct hit, smashing into Blight's chest and scattering vines all around them. The vines that had Alfred tied up went limp, and he broke free. Alfred jumped back toward Violet as they watched Blight struggle to stand.

"One hell of an attack." Blight's lower jaw dangled by the tiniest threads of vines; he pushed it up as they began to reconnect. "Elric, when your loved ones died at the hands of my forces, did they beg for their lives? Did you feel that hopelessness when they took their last breath?"

Elric clenched his jaws. "How dare you!"

Blight sighed. "I know that feeling all too well. That feeling was the old you dying."

Elric tightened his hand as black energy formed around his arm and fist. Black sparks of energy snapped around his shoulders; the dark energy sliced through falling rubble as its pure essence changed the atmosphere around them. The ground began to crack apart beneath Elric's feet as he focused. The darkness caressed Elric as it pulsed from him in black waves.

"Whoa, did you see that?" Alfred shouted.

"Yeah, I felt it too. We need to get out of here now, Eden!" Violet screamed.

"What about Elric?" Alfred asked.

"Go. I'll be fine!" Elric demanded.

"I think he's got this one," Violet replied, looking in his direction.

Elric's skin rotted away from the potency of the dark energy, revealing muscle tissue and bone. The regenerative powers prevented permanent damage to his extremity. Blight watched on as the black energy tore away at Elric's body.

"I wish you could see yourself right now, Elric. I wish you could see the monster I've created. Or better yet, look behind you. Look at your friends flee in fear of you!"

A greedy smile slipped from Elric's lips. "They're running because they know this is it. Your time is up, Blight, and there's nothing you can do to stop it."

"Elric." Eden nodded, looking at him. "Are you sure you can take him?"

Elric looked back at Eden with glowing eyes that intensified as his rage built. "You should get out of here, Eden. This is new ground for me."

Eden swallowed hard, glaring into the eyes of his friend. He took off toward Violet and the others.

Vines started to slither toward the darkness that surrounded Elric. They decayed, withering like plants from a scorching sun. Every step rotted the vines and vegetation around them.

"Maybe I was wrong about you. Maybe you're nothing like me." Blight started to step back as the vines that covered his own body began to drop and decay. "Maybe you're worse."

Blight choked and coughed the closer Elric stepped. Black vines coated in dark energy raced to restrain Elric. They withered away. Blight covered himself in his own darkness as the cleaver made of vegetation formed in his hand and began an assault on Elric. His attacks were just as aggressive and ruthless as before. Elric dodged with ease as a sadistic smile formed. He could sense the fear gripping Blight.

"Blight, you scared . . ."

"You have no idea what you're talking about." The large cleaver smashed down upon Elric's right shoulder, nearly tearing his arm off. Blood splattered on Elric's shirt and face. "You fool. When you have a destiny, fear is crushed by boldness and perseverance. I have no fear!"

Elric expected pain, but the more his rage and hatred took over, the more joy came from knowing he was close to his goal. With blood dripping from his face, Elric grabbed Blight's arm and tore the cleaver away.

"Destiny? If that's what it takes, fine," Elric whispered.

Elric remembered Jen's face when she was thrown into the blackness of the portal and the merciless way her parents were killed. He remembered Mrs. Lee's face after she gave her last breath. Elric thought about his comic book heroes and how he dreamed to save the world and the people he cared about, but in the end, all he knew of love and hope was gone.

"So, you're finally allowing the hatred to seep into your heart now." Blight stepped back, watching the energy spark from Elric like an electrical storm. "It's unlike anything I could've ever imagined. I thought I was a monster, but you, Elric, I have high hopes for you!"

"You won't get away from me, Blight," Elric whispered.

"Well, I guess you're right. You've defeated two of my generals, and I suppose you think you'll do the same to me. I'll just show you my true face just like you're showing me yours. I'll show you fear in its physical form!"

Blight's vine-covered face split open, producing a huge bulb that blossomed into a giant head of a Venus flytrap. Two large, black eyes rested atop of the large mouth. Large, syringe-like teeth dripped with saliva that scorched the ground. Blight's arms lengthened and bulged into large thick vines; monstrous mouths filled with razor-sharp teeth replaced the woodened fingers. Large, thick, thorn-covered vines burst from his torso.

Elric looked at the grotesque beast before him, but it didn't stop making his way forward. There was no more fear. He was an empty shell of what he had once hoped to be: a hero.

The slithering vines smashed into the ground pulling Blight away from Elric. "Fear me," Blight hissed. "You should be dying; how can you possibly breathe?"

The mouths at the ends of Blight's hands spat acid, splashing against the black aura that protected Elric. The venom evaporated like water on a hot surface.

Elric released a blast of black energy. Blight smacked it away with one of his grotesque hands, but at a terrible price. The extremity dissolved to dust. Blight backed into a corner, roaring as Elric drew closer. One of the mouths went to grab him, but it turned to brown mush before it reached the aura.

Dark energy covered Elric's hand as he prepared for the final blow. Blight's eyes glistened as Elric's wings launched him forward toward his large head.

Dozens of vines sprouted from the ground, stretching forth to stop Elric. They collapsed into a steaming brown pile. Elric's hand smashed through Blight's monstrous head. Green fluid gushed forth as Blight fell back. His body turned into black sludge.

Blight gasped for air, spitting up the green guck. "You say I'm evil and I've done horrible things." Blight's body twitched. "Yet I was just an avenger, like you, making those around me pay for what they had done. All I wanted was peace."

Blight choked on the liquids sputtering from him and exhaled one last time, reverting to his original form as the vines that covered the area decayed. The vines that had comprised his face became black and rotted away. His glowing, florescent, green eyes disappeared behind the blackening vegetation that made up his head.

Elric dropped to the ground, exhausted from the battle, his body pulsating with pain. Large rocks fell from the ceiling, smashing into the ground next to him. Dark claws sprouted from the black aura, smacking falling debris out of the way.

Zenith was deteriorating. Elric thought about the faith Zaroule had in them. Elric lost everything; there was nothing left for him.

Elric, wherever you are. Hurry! Violet's voice hit him like a slap in the face. He crawled to his feet and started limping as fast as he could, following the direction Eden and Alfred took.

A giant portal was opened next to Zenith. Creatures were running into it; they were fleeing from the destruction. A purple sphere of energy covered most of the small homes, including the apartment building that Zaroule and the others had stayed in. *Thanks for the beacon, Violet.*

Elric stumbled into the large purple sphere, searching for them. Everyone was huddled together as he made his way through the crowd. Eden and Alfred looked on surprised. Sasha and Manie's eyes were wide from disbelief as well.

"We thought you were dead," Alfred said with disbelief. "Does that mean—"

Elric nodded. "Blight's dead . . . "

There was no telling how long Violet would be able to hold her shield up from the bombardment of stone, boulders, and bending steel. She was too weakened to protect everyone. They'd have to flee, but if she dropped that shield, they would all be crushed.

Elric released a mass of dark energy, adding a layer to Violet's shield and taking the weight away from her.

"Don't worry about this one. I got it from here," Elric said, looking down at Violet.

She smiled before collapsing into Eden's arms.

"What are we going to do? This shield can only last so long!" someone from the crowd screamed.

"Grab on to each other now, we're going to Boston," Violet muttered, opening her eyes.

"Everyone! Hold on to each other. We still have a chance to get out of here!" Alfred screamed. "Take on your human form, where heading to the surface."

Elric couldn't believe it, was she really going to try teleporting this many people? A purple flash covered everything.

Within seconds, they were all standing in the shattered city of Boston. Dark clouds were just starting to clear as the sun came through. In fear of being discovered, the Ermakians had already transformed into their human forms.

The streets were ripped apart. Traffic lights dangled in the air with telephone pole cords coiled on the ground. Most of the larger buildings were in decent shape, but others were destroyed and torn.

Bodies of dead wolves and armored creatures littered the streets as empty bullet casings lay scattered around them. Vehicles burned with thick, black smoke as gunfire and war echoed in the distance. The haze of smoke and sulfur filled Elric's nose, reminding him of Lexington and the battle that ensued once the National Guard got involved.

Elric looked up at the tallest building in the city, the John Hancock Tower. Large trucks rumbled through the streets as soldiers jumped out helping everyone onto oncoming vehicles.

"Where the heck did all you civilians come from?" one of the soldiers asked. "We evacuated Boston hours ago. I don't understand." He looked around at the other soldiers.

Elric made his way to the others as they held on to Violet. The men helped them onto the truck with six others. Violet laid her head on Eden's shoulder; she was exhausted from the courageous effort she just gave.

"So, it's finally over now," Violet whispered.

"What are you talking about? Blight is still out there," Sasha whispered.

"No, he's not. Elric took care of him," Eden whispered, looking up.

They all became silent.

"We really did it? We really stopped Blight?" Sasha asked in disbelief.

Elric wondered where they were going. The truck jumped and rattled as they held on. A hand grabbed his arm. He looked down, greeted by Violet's warm smile.

Chapter 40

———➤((●))◄———

The Beginning of the End. The End is the Beginning

They laughed and talked in the living room of their new apartment. Instead of conversations of war and victory, they discussed being enrolled in high school. Elric hated the thought of going back.

Six months had passed since the events that shook the world and even as Elric sat on the love seat of the couch, listening to the others' excitement, he was still haunted by the memories of war and loss.

"School will be good for you guys. I know Zaroule would have wanted it this way!" Samantha said with a smile. "Besides, after all you've been through, hanging out with kids your age will be fun."

Sage had introduced them to Samantha Endicott, but Elric remembered Samantha from the last Vision Zaroule gave Violet before he died. She was kind, and if it weren't for her, they wouldn't have this huge apartment in the city of Boston. Her hair was kept in a tight bun; it was absolute perfection. She wore her camouflage uniform. Like Sage, Samantha had a commanding presence, minus the stiff British accent. She was like an older sister.

"Sam, any word on the Ermakians that made it out of Zenith?" Alfred asked, unable to keep still.

Sam sat back on the couch. "For the few that are remaining here, we were able to build them identities and set them up with places to stay in the U.S. I'm sure it'll take some time for them to get used to surface living, but they'll be fine."

Alfred nodded biting his bottom lip.

Sasha cleared her throat. "I have to admit, Sam, I had some angst about meeting you, but after what you've done for our friends, for us, I just want to say thanks."

Sam smiled. "The benefits of being deeply connected in all the right ways with the CIA and being a lieutenant colonel in the army doesn't hurt either."

They laughed, overjoyed by her words, but Elric remained silent. He was wary of Samantha, just like he'd been at first with Zaroule. Elric looked up to catch Violet staring at him in confusion.

You okay? she asked telepathically.

Elric shrugged, but he wasn't okay. He hadn't been okay for quite some time now.

"Look, this isn't the first time we talked about this," Sam replied. "But the city could really use your help."

"You want us to be crime fighters, Sam. Really?" Violet asked with sarcasm in her voice. "I mean, I think we just need some time to relax. We've done enough already."

Samantha poked Violet's arm with her finger. "Oh, come on, Violet. Think about it. With your powers and abilities, you can all help make this world the way it used to be."

For the last couple of weeks, Samantha had been trying to recruit them to help keep the peace around Boston. Organized crime was on the rise, and the lack of law enforcement on the streets made it difficult for life to prosper.

"I don't know." Violet looked over at him. "What do you think, Elric?"

Everyone's eyes shifted in his direction.

"Honestly, do whatever you guys want . . . " Elric walked out the kitchen and crawled out the window onto the fire escape, leaving them in the living room to decide their destiny. He leaped up the staircase and made his way to the top.

The roof was covered with gravel that crunched beneath his feet as he walked over the ledge. He exhaled, looking down at the city. Vehicles and people talking echoed below the streetlights that began to come on. The buildings that surrounded their apartment were darkened and dead; they wouldn't be filled with life until next summer.

The moon was large and bright as the summer air blew through his hair. From the apartment, someone called Elric's name. He stuffed his hands in his pockets, fiddling with pocket lint and thinking about everything he had lost.

The sound of the fire escape screeching caught his attention, but his eyes remained on the glimmering specks that speckled the sky.

"So, I guess we'll be helping to keep the city bad-guy-free for a while," Violet mumbled. "Maybe this'll be another chance to help make things right, like they used to be, you know?"

Elric snickered. "It'll never be like it used to be. No matter what we do." His nails dug into the palm of his hand as he clenched his fist in his pockets. "Trying to make the world what it used to be is impossible."

Only the wind broke the silence. "I know the pain you feel, Elric. You've lost a lot of people you loved and cared about. I know how you – "

"Please don't say you know how I feel. None of you know how I feel. My home, my family, everyone that has ever loved me, I watched die, and there was nothing I could do about it."

"What about us? Don't we mean anything to you?" Her voice cracked. "I thought we were your family. I thought we were the ones you loved, too."

He looked to the sky. "You have each other. You love Eden just as much as he loves you, and even Alfred and Sasha have one another with Manie. But me . . . I'll always be alone."

Violet walked over and wrapped her arms around him from behind, laying her head on his back. The darkness gave a jolt of power that forced her to let go.

Elric heard her gasp and her footsteps. He turned, wanting to apologize, but he was met with tear-filled eyes. "Violet, every time you're all together, I can't help but get angry. I see how happy you all are, and I realize that's something I can't have. I feel like it'll be taken from me like everything else."

Violet shook her head. "You don't have to feel that way. We'll always be here for you. You'll always be one of us."

Elric remained silent, wanting to hold on to her words and believe her welcoming eyes. Ever since Zaroule died, she had changed. She grew from the pain of losing him, but for Elric, this wasn't the case.

"All I can say is I'm sorry, Elric. We can't bring them back. I wish I could bring Z back; I wish I could bring Jen back. I wish we could bring everyone who lost their lives back, but we can't. Like you said, it's impossible." Tears rolled down Violet's face as the moonlight glistened off her tears; the wind blew her dark-red hair wildly as she pushed the strands behind her ear.

"Then why are we having this conversation?" Elric's voice was cold and indifferent. "Why are you talking to me right now?"

She stepped back with trembling lips, staring as if she had no idea who Elric was. "We've all grown and changed, Elric, and I guess that's due to everything that's happened. But . . . "

"But what?"

"You've changed the most. You were the innocent, shy, caring one of us all, but you lost yourself. You've become cold, bitter, and hopeless." Violet continued to sob. "And by the way, I *do* know how you feel. I feel your pain everyday cause of my powers. Not a day goes by that I don't wish I could make you happy."

In silence, Elric looked down at her tightening fists; his face was emotionless. She stomped through the gravel and down the rattling fire escape, the window slammed below.

Elric turned to the city and faced the moonlit sky. Violet was right about everyone growing up and changing; their lives were becoming different and separate from one another. He wasn't the same person that he used to be, and he had no intention of being that lost, confused, weak boy who was scared to make decisions. He shed the skin of comic book heroes, realizing the view of the real world—the cold dark world—that created monsters and made the good suffer.

Staring into the night sky, he wondered where his new views would take him. His old life was gone. There was nobody else left from that time; they were all swallowed up in darkness and death. With two generals left, he knew the remnants of Blight's army would try to attack again. When they did, there would be no mercy for what they've done to him. There would only be suffering.

Made in the USA
San Bernardino, CA
17 May 2020